ROUGAROU II

JUDITH ANN MCDOWELL

This is a work of fiction. Names, characters, places, and incidents are products of the author's imagination or are used fictitiously and are not to be construed as real. Any resemblance to actual events, locations, organizations, or persons, living or dead, is entirely coincidental.

World Castle Publishing, LLC
Pensacola, Florida
Copyright © Judith Ann McDowell 2021
Paperback ISBN: 9781955086226
eBook ISBN: 9781955086233
First Edition World Castle Publishing, LLC, May 10, 2021
http://www.worldcastlepublishing.com
Licensing Notes
Cover: Karen Fuller
Editor: Beth Price

PROLOGUE

Viewed from afar, the three-story white house surrounded by lush green lawn and secured by black, wrought-iron fencing gives the appearance of warm serenity. Up close dark energy uncurling from its shadows allows one to glimpse a far more sinister portrayal.

The house, known throughout the parish as the Hindel Mansion, harbors a dark secret: A secret reaching back centuries for its strength.

Townspeople say stories surrounding the mansion, of hauntings and monsters killing young children are but a ruse to draw in the young and simple-minded. The bayou people do not say anything. They know far better than most the far-reaches of the unknown are better left alone, and they remain steadfast in their silence of a night the mansion was forced to give up one of its strongest evils. Evil, as the good people of Saint Anthony Parish are about to learn, has little mercy on those who destroy one of its own.

When the soul is surrounded by darkness
It is easy to lead the weak
On a downward spiral
It is when the soul is touched by light
One can perceive the real face of evil

CHAPTER ONE

Donavan Hays looked up to see someone he had hoped never to see again. He laid his pen down on a stack of papers, pushed back his chair to get to his feet as a deputy tapped on his door.

"Lieutenant Hays," the man jabbed a thumb in the direction of the visitor, "there's someone here to see you."

"Thanks, Jamison, I see him." Donavan walked past him.

"Lieutenant Hays." The man did not hold out his hand. He stood watching Donavan as he moved towards him.

"Mr. Hindel. Someone in the department isn't doing their job. I'm supposed to get a heads-up when a convicted felon comes back into the country. And for sure about one who spent a year locked away in a mental institution for slaughtering an entire family; or, at least most of them." He didn't bother to disguise the contempt slipping into his voice. "Then, I guess money has a way of quieting normal police protocol." Donavan smiled into the face staring back at him. "Wouldn't you agree, Mr. Hindel?"

The young man standing before him looked very pale; with light green eyes and lashes so long, Donavan wondered if they could be false. His thick, dark hair curled about his white shirt collar, and the thin material of his black suit fit his small frame so well it had to have been tailor-made.

"I didn't come here to swap pleasantries, Lieutenant Hays." He drew a slender hand down the length of his blue silk tie. A fastidious gesture not missed by Donavan.

"All right, then suppose you tell me why you *are* here." Donavan seated himself on the edge of a desk, folded his arms across his thick chest to stare over at the man.

"I came here to let everyone in the sheriff's department know I have returned to my home. Hopefully, that will deter anyone from inventing a reason to come onto my property. If anyone should come onto my property, now that it is known I am back, I will not hesitate to file trespassing charges and, if needed, harassment charges." His full mouth curled into a sneer. "Do we understand each other, Lieutenant?"

"Well...well...well! Do my eyes deceive me, or is it my old friend Master Lawrence Hindel, returned to the county of the crime?"

Donavan turned to see his partner, Jack Olivier', dressed in a light blue, short-sleeved dress shirt, dark blue tie and black jeans. Jack swaggered towards them, carrying two cups of coffee in Styrofoam cups, along with a filled paper bag.

Jack set the cups and bag down on the desk then stepped back, a sardonic grin covering his boyish face. "You shoulda let us know about your return, Lawrence. That way, we coulda thrown a kickin'-your-ass-back-outta-the-parish party." Donavan pushed himself off the desk to move between his partner and the angry man clenching his fists. "Now, Jack, is that any way to greet Mr. Hindel after he came all the way from England to tell us he's back?"

Jack walked around Donavan to seat himself behind the desk. Pulling the sack closer, he withdrew a strawberry-filled Danish. "House's been empty for almost a year, Hindel. Why the return all of a sudden?"

"Mr. Olivier', may I remind you, I don't have to answer to you or anyone in this department about my movements?" He took a step closer to the desk.

"You may not remind me of anything. I'll take care of any remindin' that's needed. Remember, you're still a certified nut case! And, I might add, someone the department's duty-bound to keep an eye on." Jack wiped his mouth on a paper napkin, threw it back down in front of him. "You may, however, address me as *Detective* Olivier', though!" He tossed a bold-lettered nameplate across the desk.

Lawrence looked down at the etched insignia. "My, my," he raised steepled hands to his poised lips, "the department must be in dire need of new blood if they took you back, Jack. Last I heard-you got thrown off the force for losing your mind when a certain lady, who will remain nameless, tossed you aside." A gleam of pleasure lit up his light-colored eyes as flushes of anger crept up Jack's face. "People who live in glass houses...well, I'm sure you know the rest." He leaned his hands on the desk, peered into Jack's hostile face.

Too late, he realized his mistake as Jack grabbed his expensive silk tie to pull him the rest of the way across the desk. "You gender-flawed little bitch!" Jack shoved back his chair, pushed the wide knot higher up the tie making Hindel gasp for breath. "If you wanna stay half-ass healthy, you'll keep your disgustin' little dick the hell outta my way!" He flung the man backward away from him.

As Hindel got up off the floor, Jack balled his fists.

Donavan turned the panting man in the direction of the door. "I think it would be a good idea if you left! Now, Mr. Hindel."

"Leave?" He shook Donavan's hand from his shoulder. "I want him arrested for assault!" He pointed a finger at Jack, his pouty lips curving with righteous anger as he saw a look of caustic humor slipping into Jack's unwavering stare. "You saw what he did to me!" Lawrence smoothed out his rumpled suit-coat as best he could, righted his tie.

Jack picked up the fallen chair, hung his black denim suit-coat over the back to walk around the desk. "In all honesty, do you think anyone 'round here's gonna listen to you, Lawrence?" The name dripped from his lips. "After what you did to the Rawlins family?" Jack shook his head, a wry smile splitting the corners of his mouth. "Jonathan Hindel bought your way outta that hospital. Naw," Jack held up a hand as Lawrence drew in his breath, "don't bother to deny it. It's already a forgone-know. The important thing you need to keep in mind is your daddy can't come to your rescue anymore, Lawrence. Thanks to Lieutenant Hays and me." Jack tried to hold onto his anger as Hindel gazed up at the ceiling. "I see that little piece of info didn't cause you any undue pain. That tells me all you cared about's the ole man's money. Which you got, I'll give you that. But! One thing you don't have is his pull with the names in the county. And that," Jack poked a finger in Lawrence's chest, "is what you had goin' for ya!"

A sharp glimmer of fear leaped into Lawrence's eyes as he backed away out of Jack's reach.

"That's a good boy," Jack nodded his dark brown head, "now; just keep backin' right on out the door. And, Lawrence," Jack edged closer, "a piece of advice? I'd stay as close to home as I could." He cocked his head, smiled a slight smile. "Accidents have a way of happnin' in the bayous. Never know when a stray bullet or a hungry gator might come lookin' for ya."

As the door to the station closed behind the man already moving down the steps, Jack turned to find Donavan watching him. "What?"

"Jack, I know how you feel about Hindel." Donavan mopped agitated hands over his depleted hairline, drawing them all the way down the thick, brown hair on the sides and back of his head. "I feel the same. As do most of the people in this county. But you can't go around manhandling people just because you have a strong aversion to them. Myself, I don't care what you do to the little puke." The nostrils of his hawkish nose flared with distaste. "The heads of the department don't care. However, when you do it right under their noses, they have to, at least, act like they care."

"Sorry." With a sheepish grin, he walked back over to his desk, picked up the paper bag. "I brought you a Danish."

Donavan accepted the roll, his hooded, dark brown eyes lingering a moment longer on the man grinning at him, then picked up the cup filled with coffee. "Let's go into my office." He glanced around the room to see how many of the deputies had witnessed the scene and, glimpsing, but a few heads still turned in their direction, nodded across the room. "I'd feel better talking behind a closed door."

Jack pulled a chair over close to the desk, laid his roll and coffee down in front of him. "Is this gonna take long, Lieutenant Hays?" He pinched off a small portion of the roll, popped it into his mouth, then drew his fingers down the leg of his jeans. "I hate gettin' my ass chewed on an empty stomach."

"No one's planning on chewing your ass, Jack, so get serious." Donavan cut short the smile rising to his mouth as he stripped off his light brown suit-coat to hang it on the back of the chair. "We neither one of us have any great liking for Lawrence Hindel." He bit off a piece of the Danish, allowed the smile to slip back in. "There is one thing you need to keep in mind, though." He chewed for a moment then swallowed. "Now that Lawrence is heir to the Hindel fortune, the city bigwigs are going to be thinking of ways to get their greedy little hands in his pockets."

Jack licked his fingers, picked up the cup of coffee. "Sounds like the "dance and bob" is startin' all over again."

"What do you mean by that?" Donavan reached into the bag for a napkin.

"Don't play stupid, Donavan." He walked over to the small water cooler, stuck his hands beneath the tap and pushed the button. "I'm talkin' 'bout the same shit Jonathan Hindel used to pull. The ole "I'll put a little jingle in your pocket then drop my drawers while you kneel an' pucker routine." Jack turned the crank on the paper towel machine and, when no towel came forth, ran his damp hands down the seat of his pants.

"Lawrence will never have the clout with the county his father did." Donavan righted his dark brown tie then pulled a pack of cigarettes from the pocket of his short-sleeved white shirt. "You told him that much yourself."

"Yeah, I did. But I didn't mean it." Jack flicked his lighter held it beneath the cigarette Donavan had poised between his lips, leaned in close as smoke curled into the air.

"Then why did you say it?" Donavan inhaled then blew the smoke in the opposite direction.

With a sour look, Jack plopped back down in his chair, propped his booted feet up on the desk.

Donavan glanced at the plain, black cowboy boots, then down at his own brown dress shoes and shook his head.

"I said it because, even though I still don't have any likin' for Lawrence Hindel and never will have, I still have to wonder. After what we learned, 'bout his father, I'm not so sure he did kill the Rawlins family. Hindel's a whacked little prick, but Jonathan turned out to be the real piece of work." His gaze lingered on the cigarette Donavan held between his fingers.

The black leather chair squawked its displeasure as Donavan repositioned his weight, trying to ignore the obvious look of yearning on Jack's face. "At the time, it seemed pretty obvious we had the right man for the killings, but after everything came to light about Jonathan, I'm not sure he did it either." Cursing beneath his breath, he brushed away the fallen cigarette ash from his light-brown suit pants.

"If that's true, then we helped put an innocent man in a mental institution." Jack drummed his fingers on the desk. "That don't set well with me." He bent forward, inhaling the smoke Donavan expelled into the air.

"If you're going to *quit*, breathing other people's smoke isn't the way to go about it."

"Cut me a break here, Donavan!" Jack shot an angry scowl across the desk. "At least I'm tryin'."

"I don't want to quit."

"Well, goddamn it, neither do I!" His feet hit the floor, rolling the chair backward and slapping his head hard against the wall. "I don't know why I agreed to stop in the first damn place!" He rubbed the back of his head, then smoothed his hair back into place.

Taking pity on him, Donavan shook a cigarette out of the pack, tossed it across the desk. "If you don't tell, I won't."

A long sigh of relief drifted from his throat as Jack reached for the cigarette putting it between his lips. As he flicked the lighter, though, he flipped the top closed to throw it and the wanted cigarette down on the desk. "I made a promise. I'm not that fuckin' weak!"

Donavan tried to hold back the smile slipping onto his face, then gave up the struggle. "I could offer not to smoke in front of you, but we both know I *am* that weak."

"How come Barb didn't make you quit smokin' when she got pregnant with Jenny? Or more to the point, why didn't you do it on your own?" Jack went back to drumming his fingers on the desk.

Donavan laughed outright. "She knew it wouldn't do her any good to even-broach the subject. With the job I got," he jabbed a thumb against his chest, "smoking is the one thing keeping me sane, and she knows it! Try that one on her."

Jack rolled the theory around in his mind then dropped it. "That little ploy wouldn't get me to first base. Seelah would pick up on it in a heartbeat!"

"That's what comes of having a psychic for a wife, Jack. You can't get away with the things a normal husband can."

"Yeah, I know." His head bobbed with each movement Donavan made in stubbing out the finished cigarette.

"Tell me something." Donavan glanced over at him. "Would you rather have your old life back again?"

Jack propped his feet back upon the desk, leaned back in his chair and, lacing his fingers together, placed them behind his head. As an image of the tiny woman he now called his wife moved into his thoughts, he relaxed, allowing his mind a glimpse into the past.

The first time he had seen Seelah, he had mistaken her for a teenager. With her five-foot stature and tiny-boned frame, he thought her to be a friend of Donavan's young daughter, Jenny. But when she turned out to be a twenty-eight-year-old woman, he looked at her with a different eye. A different eye, but not much else. At the time, he was trying to rise above a failed relationship with a woman who had shattered his life and almost his mind.

Tall, slender and beautiful, with her light brown skin and dark green eyes, Chandra filled his every waking moment for almost two years. Until the night she told him goodbye.

Jack went from a happy man to one who gave up on life. His job with the sheriff's department, his self-esteem and everyone and everything flew out of his mind and into a bottle of both pills and alcohol. He woke later in a hospital to find everything gone. He resigned from the sheriff's department, knowing if he didn't, they would resign him. Broke, sick and all but out of his mind, he had turned to the one person he felt he could trust not to turn on him. Donavan had not disappointed him.

Jack turned now, looking at the man sitting across from him and with a growing lump beginning to form in his throat, he smiled. "Never in a million years would I ever want to return to that time in my life."

"That's what I thought. So, do you still want a cigarette, or are you going to tough it out?"

"What kinda question is that? I'm gonna be a father!" The stern look spreading across his face lost its severity as a look of pride took over. "My son's gonna have a father who's got his shit together!"

***

Jack pulled the Chevy Blazer into the driveway of his modest, three-bedroom house sitting on a large and impressive corner lot and switched off the engine. The moment his feet touched the ground, the weight of the day slipped from his shoulders.

Rich aromas wafted out to him, putting a bounce in his step as he made his way up the sidewalk. He stopped mid-way up the walk and, bending down, plucked a weed poking its head from the row of pansies edging the lawn to toss it across the yard before continuing on his way to the house.

Busy in the kitchen, Seelah heard the door slam outside, and she pulled off her apron, hanging it on the small peg beside the stove. Fluffing her short, dark brown hair, she hurried towards the door.

Jack caught her in the archway between the kitchen and living room to swing her up in his arms, grinning as she squealed her pleasure.

"How's the most beautiful mother in the whole wide world?" He captured her full mouth with his cutting off the happy answer forming on her lips.

Seelah beamed at him as he continued to hold her. "Just as delirious as yesterday and the day before that and every day since I met you!" she laughed, spreading kisses over his face.

With little effort, he lifted her forward to place a quick and loving kiss on her rounded stomach. "Daddy's home." His face lit up as it always did with this ongoing ritual.

Seelah felt the child leap as though acknowledging his father's love for him.

Jack placed her on her feet and, turning towards the stove, rubbed his own stomach in anticipation. "When's dinner gonna be ready, baby? I'm a hungry man!"

"You have just enough time to jump in the shower and get dressed before everyone gets here." She took the bib-apron off the hook, tied it back around her waist to position it over her short-sleeved red top and black slacks.

For a moment, he stared at her then slapped his forehead. "Oh yeah! Donavan, Barb and Jenny are comin' tonight!"

"That's right, detective." She took a package of dinner rolls from the freezer, laid them on the counter. "You've been with the man all day. How could you forget?"

The happy moments slid to a halt as the face of Lawrence Hindel jumped into his mind.

Seelah glanced at him, the small brush she had been using to butter the rolls, still poised in her hand. "Jack, what is it? Did something happen today at the station?"

"Yeah." His brows knotted for a brief moment. "We had a surprise visitor this afternoon."

"Lawrence Hindel," she murmured, then dropped the brush into the sink.

Even after all the time they had been together, he still found it unsettling when she nailed something so accurately without even thinking about it.

"Yep!" Jack walked past her to open the refrigerator. Leaning in, he withdrew a bottle of beer from the six-pack setting on the shelf. "Breezed into the station to let us know he had returned and to inform us he would not be tolerant of any visitors on his property." He twisted the top on the bottle, flicked the cap into the trash.

"I have a feeling you aren't telling me everything," she said without turning.

Jack drew in his breath; let it out to take a long pull off the bottle of beer. "It didn't amount to much. Not really." He could feel her waiting for him to finish. "Oh hell! The idiot pissed me off, and I jerked him across the desk. No real harm done."

"Not yet, anyway." The words popped into the air before she could stop them.

He lowered the bottle as she turned to walk to the stove. "What's that mean? I might have'ta watch my back?"

"You destroyed his father." Seelah pulled open the door to the oven and, bending over, placed the tin of rolls on the top rack. "He will always have it in for you."

"I didn't do it alone." Jack grinned, trying to shrug off the feeling of unease, pushing his hunger-pangs off to the side. "Donavan has some rewards comin' too."

"This isn't a laughing matter, Jack." She flipped the oven door closed with a bang.

"What's the matter?" The unease dug in a little deeper.

"Lawrence Hindel isn't the evil man his father turned out to be. By that, I mean he isn't a monster, but he is still a very disturbed man."

"Hell, I could have told you that!" He laughed, swigging the last of his beer. "A person can't grow up in a household with a father who's out slaughterin' people on every full moon and come out sane for Christ's sake!"

Sliding her arms around his lean waist, she laid her head

against his chest. "That's true. That's why I want you to be extra careful when you're around him."

"I'll do my best, baby." Jack kissed the top of her head, pulled her rounded hips tighter against him.

The ringing of the doorbell drew them apart. Seelah ran her fingers through her hair, then gave him a gentle shove.

"You better hurry if you want that shower." She tried putting a happy smile on her face. When she looked up, she knew she hadn't fooled him about the frightening feelings still running strong through her mind.

"I think we should try and make this a short evenin'." Jack turned, tossed the empty bottle into the trashcan. "I don't know 'bout you, but I need some T.L.C. tonight."

As Jack walked down the hall to the bathroom, Seelah went to the door to welcome their guests. At the sight of her best friends waiting on the small front porch, some of the frightening feelings seemed to lift.

"Barb," she cried, spying the cake pan and covered dish. "You didn't need to bring anything."

"I know, but I also know how much you and Jack love my white cake, so I whipped one up complete with strawberries," Barbara Hays laughed, moving through the open door.

Seelah eyed her slim figure clad in tight jeans and a dark green pullover top, then looked away. "If anyone wants a beer, you know where they are. Jenny," she turned to the dark-haired young girl who stood watching her dad pluck a strawberry from the bowl, "there's also some coke in there. Help yourself."

"Thanks, Aunt Seelah," she grinned, as her mom slapped his hand then pulled the plastic cover back in place over the bowl to take it to the refrigerator.

"Where's the man of the house?" Donavan took the beer Barb handed him.

"In the shower. He should be out any minute." Seelah slipped an oven-mitt onto her hand, pulled open the oven door.

"At least he got one," Donavan grumbled, glancing down at the short-sleeved shirt and slacks he had been wearing all day.

"Barb, pull out the cutting board for me, will you?" She turned a pan of golden-brown dinner rolls in her hand.

Donavan looked around the tidy kitchen, noting the gleaming stove and matching refrigerator with its trail of healthy green ivy falling over the top and down the sides. Barbara glanced at him as she turned towards the sink, her hands filled with the makings for a tossed green salad. He moved out of her way to stand beside a table covered with a dark green linen tablecloth. A vase of fresh-cut red roses and silver candlesticks, each holding a dark green taper, occupied the center of the table. He recalled Jack telling him about green being Seelah's favorite color and about it being the color of healing. Donavan recognized the Rose-Print China and silver as the same pattern his grandmother had been so fond of and always brought out on special occasions. The silver had been polished to a bright sheen.

He felt tempted to give one of the knives a light tap on a goblet, placed just so, to see if crystal did hum when you tapped it. Without being obvious, he hiked the tablecloth to look at the round oak-wood table, with its legs formed in the shape of a lion's paw. Jack said Seelah refused to give up the table when they sold the house she had been living in when they met. As he dropped the tablecloth back into place, he noticed how well the dark green of the linen complemented the light, green and white floor tiles.

"Hey! Here he is." Donavan gestured with his beer bottle as Jack walked into the kitchen, dressed in a dark blue sports shirt and jeans.

"Yep!" He dropped a quick kiss on Barb's head, then pulled Jenny into a bear-hug. "Now the festivities can begin."

Jenny squealed with pleasure, her dark eyes gazing up at the man holding her close then drew away. "Uncle Jack." Her voice took on a more serious tone.

"That's me!"

"I have something I want to talk to you and Aunt Seelah about. Something very important."

Jack took her arm, turned her in the direction of the table. "If it's important, then, by all means, let's hear it!"

He pulled out a chair for her and then plopped down in the chair next to her, motioning for Seelah to join them.

"Well…" she gulped, tried again. "Well, you know I'm eleven years old now. Might as well say I'm a teenager." Jenny tugged her red shorts into a more comfortable position, smoothed out her matching red top.

"That's true, you are." Seelah rested her hands on Jenny's shoulders, already knowing what she wanted to say. "A very mature eleven-year-old, too, I might add."

Jack glanced over at her as Seelah smiled.

"Okay." Jenny rubbed her hands together in a brisk manner. "Here goes! Maybe some night, or day, it doesn't matter…"

Donavan tipped her face upward. "Sweetheart, why don't you just come out and say what is on your mind."

"I'm trying, Daddy," she giggled, her cheeks flushed with embarrassment.

"I have an idea, Jenny," Seelah spoke up, "while you're trying to think what you want to say, your Uncle Jack and I have something we would like to talk with you about."

Jack gave her a "what-are-you-talking-about" look, pulled the bottle of beer Barbara sat before him over closer.

"We wondered if, after the baby is some months old, you might like to babysit some evening. We would pay you, of course, and…"

Jenny jumped to her feet, threw her arms around Seelah's waist. "Yes! Yes! Yes!" she squealed, hopping up and down in her excitement. "And you won't have to pay me anything! This is so weird!" Her dark eyes moved around the room. "I planned on asking you the same, exact thing!"

"Wow! Imagine that!" Jack murmured, tipping the bottle of beer to his mouth, then coughed, spewing beer across the table as Jenny threw her arms around his neck.

"Good lord, Jenny!" Barbara grabbed a napkin from the table to begin mopping Jack's face. "You could have choked him!"

Jack reached out, stilling Barbara's attempts to wipe away

the beer. "Thanks anyway, Barb." He grinned up at her.

"Sorry, Uncle Jack," Jenny said, then squealed as he reached out, pulling her onto his lap.

"You didn't do it on purpose, baby child! But if you ram a bottle down my throat, you might end up baby-sittin' me 'stead of the baby."

"I think everything is ready, so if everyone wants to take a seat, we can begin." Seelah set a bowl of tossed-green salad down on the table.

"Sure, don't have to ask us twice! Right, Donavan?" Jack straddled a chair at the end of the table.

"Nope!" Donavan pulled out a chair for Barbara then walked over to seat Seelah and Jenny.

"Thank you, Donavan." Seelah smiled up at him. "Jack is still working on getting the hang of being a gentleman."

"Uncle Jack's a gentleman," Jennie spoke up on Jack's behalf. "He just doesn't stop and think sometimes."

"Yeah, like earlier today when Lawrence Hindel came into the station," Donavan breathed, then realized what he said as he heard the sharp intakes of breath from around the table.

"Lawrence Hindle's back in the parish?" Barbara filled the small salad plate, sitting to the left of her plate, placed the salad server back in the bowl. "You didn't mention anything about it when you came home, Donavan."

Donavan felt his stomach tighten as he helped himself to a slice of roast beef from the platter Seelah handed to him. "You know how I feel about bringing my work home."

"So he's back in town." Jack looked around the table. "Who gives a rats..." he swallowed the rest of his sentence as Seelah glanced at him. "Just tryin' to lighten the mood's all." He picked up his fork to begin eating.

Donavan took a drink of his iced tea, giving himself time to think of the words he needed to calm everyone's fears. "Maybe now that his father's no longer here to coddle him, he'll settle down."

"I wouldn't go so far as to say Lawrence could ever be

a model citizen, although I do think he will try to keep a low profile. And, if no one tries to antagonize him," Seelah shot a meaningful look at Jack, "he might leave everyone alone."

"I think you make a very valid point, Seelah," Donavan told her. "And with that said, I suggest we change the subject and just enjoy this fine meal."

***

Later, after everyone had left, Jack gathered Seelah into his arms. "I'm glad you told Jenny she could babysit some evenin'."

"Jenny is a responsible girl. She'll take good care of the baby." She nestled herself into Jack's arms.

Through the sliding glass door, leading from their bedroom out onto the patio, they could see the full moon. Its silver glow bathed the many potted flowers situated around the edges of the well-manicured lawn.

Jack heard her deep sigh of contentment and, bending his head, placed a kiss on the side of her face. He knew how much she had loved the house she had been living in when they met. But too many memories filled the house for them to ever feel happy living there.

Seelah was still mourning the death of her first husband when she and Jack met, and Jack had been trying to get up from a failed relationship. When they decided they would get married, they went house hunting. The moment they walked into the little house, sitting on a corner lot and a mere block from Barbara and Donavan, they knew they had found the place for them.

Now in two months, they expected the birth of their first child, and they couldn't be happier.

***

All remained quiet as Seelah left the comforting arms of her husband to walk through the sliding glass door and out onto the patio. A slight breeze blew across her face, and she reached up, pushing her dark hair back behind each ear, her movements stilted as though everything moved in slow motion. She turned as someone called out to her.

"Chandra?" she whispered, reaching out to take the

woman's hands in hers. "Chandra!"

Chandra pulled back to look at her. "*I thought it best to come to you while you slept.*"

"You've come back from the other side to talk with me?"

"*No, Seelah, not from the other side. I have chosen to remain earthbound. I have too much to do yet to go home.*"

"But...I don't understand. Jack and Donavan told me you burned up in the fire, yet your spirit carries none of the scares of such a death".

"*I healed my spirit,*" she told her, smiling as she glimpsed the disbelieving look crossing Seelah's face.

"*Simply because my body is dead does not mean my soul has lost any of its psychic abilities. My mind, soul and psychic gifts of healing are as strong as ever.*"

"Where do you stay now that you are no longer in your body?" Seelah could feel herself beginning to shake, thinking her friend had no place to go except back to the place where she had died such a horrible and terrifying death.

"*My spirit does not linger in the bayous, Seelah, but in the place where I can do the most good.*" She pulled away. "*I am here to warn you about staying away from the Hindel Mansion. Do not allow Jack to go there. If he does, it could mean his death.*"

Seelah sat upright in the bed, her body chilled and damp. Reaching out, she ran her hands over Jack's chest, assuring herself of his safety and to make sure he remained lying beside her before easing her head back against the pillow.

Sleep did not come easy, for she knew that for Chandra to come to her, she had to be very worried about Jack's safety. "How sad," she told herself before closing her eyes once more, "even death cannot silence the love we still hold in our hearts for another."

CHAPTER TWO

Lawrence Hindel walked through the front entrance of the estate, slamming the heavy oak door behind him, his uncontrollable rage right at that moment, in close proximity to that of the man who had sired him.

"Arrogant son of a bitch!" The venomous words erupted into the silence as the smug face of Jack Olivier' continued to swirl in the red haze gaining power over his thoughts.

"How dare he put his filthy hands on me? Me! The son of Jonathan Hindel!" His hands latched onto the lapels of his suit-coat, wadding the expensive material in his fists and amidst popping buttons tore it from his body.

A tall, brown-skinned woman drew back, watching the anger spew forth as Lawrence paced the floor of the living room, ripping and tearing at his clothing until he, at last, stood naked and panting.

"Father!" Lawrence screamed into the silence, the nails of his long fingers raking a blood path down his chest. "I shed the blood of my body for you! For you, I bring forth the taste of sweet wine to satisfy your hunger! Hear me!"

His thin arms raised in supplication. He fell to his knees, the blood coursing down his chest mixed with the sweat bathing his body.

The woman stepped forward, reaching out her hand to console his pain, then drew back, knowing he could not feel her touch.

As the silence in the room deepened, Lawrence raised his head as if waiting for someone to acknowledge his need. At last, he stood, the anger still very much a part of him, although he could already feel it beginning to drain away.

No one came to answer his need except the woman standing by his side, her green eyes filled with helpless torment. She watched him struggle to come to grips with the knowledge that Jonathan Hindel could not protect him anymore.

Wrapped within his fear, he walked over to seat himself on the long, white leather couch, uncaring of the blood dripping down his chest. A slight chill touched him, and he pulled the blanket he had used to cover himself the night before down from the back of the couch to spread it over his nakedness.

Alone in the silence, his mind slipped back into the past to a time in his childhood.

The many candles flickering in the darkness bathed the room in a silver glow that seemed to push the gloom, stealing forth from the shadows, to somewhere beyond the beauty of the dancing lights. He had always loved the dancing lights. Their silver glow reminded him of the frozen chips of water he liked to place on his tongue on the hot, humid days of summer. He remembered the woman who would come. The beautiful, tall lady with the light brown skin, black hair that always smelled of flowers and the dark green eyes that spoke volumes of love for him.

Lawrence shook his head, dispelling the memory before it had a chance to turn his angry heart into one of childish hope. Hope he could always count on to come crashing down to leave him wallowing in trembling despair.

The woman felt his pain and her heart went out to him. She wanted nothing more, right at that moment, than to gather him into her arms and comfort him just as she had all those years ago when, as a small boy, he would crawl onto her lap and rest his small head against her breast. A sob crept upward in her throat, and knowing no one could hear her, she allowed the anguish to continue out into the silence.

A sound slicing through the stillness brought Lawrence to his feet. At the same time, its intrusion silenced the feelings of sorrow the woman had been feeling to turn her suffering into a gripping hand of terror. Dropping the blanket to the floor, Lawrence walked out of the room through the front door and out into the night.

Standing in the glow of the full moon, a burning hope flickered then grew with an almost searing, inner-knowing as he waited to hear the sound once more.

A deep-throated howl split the silence sending a shiver of excitement through Lawrence's already pounding heart as he stood naked in the glow of the full moon. He waited for the hulking shadows, moving amid moss-covered trees, their red eyes glittering like burning embers, to show themselves.

"Come." He motioned them forward. "You have nothing to fear from me!" The words rushed from his throat in a crazed, disjointed tone. "This is your home!"

The woman standing beside him screamed a warning. "No! Lawrence, don't call to them. If you invite them, they will never leave!"

But Lawrence could not hear her. And even if he could, she would not have changed his mind. They had come to save him. Just as Jonathan had always saved him.

The hulking shadows moved from the trees now to come closer.

"No!" The woman ran forward, trying to halt their advancement. "Go back! You are not welcome here!"

The shadowy figures did not heed her warnings. Instead, they walked through her vaporous spirit, loping towards the mansion and the young man who welcomed them.

Covered in thick black fur, four males and one female moved closer. Their grotesque, almost human faces wore a look of complete dominance as their hungry eyes stared out at the man, still urging them to come closer.

"This is your home, now," Lawrence told them once more.

"No one will look for you here."

The female drew closer, sniffing the wind. She pulled Lawrence into her arms to lick the blood covering his chest, then jumped back, startled, as Lawrence let out a yelp of fear.

A sharp growl filled the silence as she came towards him.

The largest of the males stepped forward, and drawing back his hand, sent the female crashing to the ground.

She lay on the cool grass, watching him, her eyes glowing with anger, yet she made no move to challenge the dark shape standing over her.

Chandra watched as the leader reached out to draw the fallen female to her feet then into his arms. He caressed the swollen breasts lowering his large head to suckle the pink nipples, all the while growling his need.

Chandra glanced at Lawrence in disgust, then turned away as the two fell to the ground. The sounds and smells of their rutting turned the pale night into a frenzy of lust coupled with the overpowering stench of musk.

Lawrence found himself fascinated and repelled at the same time but was unable to turn away as he watched the male slam into her without mercy. A long, feminine scream ended on a soft moan as the beast rolled from her body.

Lawrence remained still, unable to decide what he should do next as the hulking male extended his hand in open invitation for Lawrence to join in on the pleasures being offered him.

The female motioned him to come to her. Lawrence backed away, ashamed of his nakedness to walk into the house.

After he had bathed and dressed, he sat in the darkness of his room, trying to sort out in his mind what new turns his life was taking. At first, he told himself the ones he had invited to share his home posed no danger. Now, with the scene he had witnessed replaying in his mind, he started to rethink what he had done.

A slight cramping in his stomach reminded him he had not eaten. Coming downstairs, he heard sounds of laughter on the front porch. Without turning on any lights, he crept to the window to peer out. The beat of his heart quickened as he glimpsed a small crowd of teenagers walking up to the front door.

"Did anyone think to bring a key?" A young male voice snickered, his words slurred and shaky as he tried to turn the knob of the heavy oak door.

"Fuck ah key! Ain't nobody here got a key!" His buddy pushed him to the side. "Break the goddamn window!"

"Hey, man, keep it down! This ain't the place to be grab-assin'!" Another male voice warned.

"You tell him, Paul." A drunken voice giggled.

Paul pulled the giggling girl against his hip. "You guys need to think about where you are." He looked around as the rest of the crowd climbed the steps to the front porch to set a Styrofoam cooler filled with ice and beer down on a small, white, wrought iron table. "I don't think this is such a good idea." He yanked the damp T-shirt away from his back. "Why don't we just pile back in our boats and go somewhere else to party?"

Alex, the boy nearest the cooler, flipped off the top and, reaching in, grabbed a can of beer. "Yo, Paul, catch man!" He tossed the can across the porch.

Paul snagged the beer in mid-air and, releasing his hold on the girl, popped the top.

"You gonna pass me one or keep them all for yourself?" the boy standing before Paul called out.

"You gonna maintain, Shrimpton?" Paul asked as Alex tossed another beer their way.

"Hell yes, I'm gonna maintain," he laughed, as the flying can fell into his hands. "Hey man, come on." He ushered Paul off the porch. "I thought we came here to party. I mean, look at this place." He swung his arms wide. "We got nobody around for miles! We're with the best lookin' sluts in the whole damn school!" Shrimpton nodded his blond head as a wide grin spread across Paul's face. "And last, but sure as hell not least, the best weed to be found anywhere in the parish. And all you can talk about is gettin' the hell outta here. You need to lighten up, buddy."

He tipped the can of beer to his lips. "Ain't nobody gonna tell the good reverend you're out gettin' drunk and with any luck, laid!" He wiped a hand across his mouth.

Paul felt a hot flush creep up his throat. He took a long drink of his beer. "I got a bad feelin' about this place. All right?"

Thinking she had been left out of the conversation long enough, the girl sauntered back over. Wrapping both her arms around Paul's slim waist and ignoring Todd, she pulled his head within inches of her face to nibble on his lower lip. "Stead of *feelin'* bad about this place, why don't you do something more fun and start *feelin'* me?" she purred against his mouth.

Paul felt his dick throb beneath his jeans and tried to pull away.

Todd snickered, grazed a fist across Paul's jaw. "You pass that up; I'll know your daddy's got you cowed! Yieeee!" he howled into the night wind. "Somebody throw me another beer! I already got the weed! It's Saturday night, people, and we all know what that means! So here's to all the ghosts, monsters and whatever else the people of this county can come up with!" He gulped a swallow of beer, let out a long, loud burp. "I got a strong feelin' tonight's the night our man Paul's gonna get his cherry plucked from the stem!" Todd wiggled his brows, leered at the girl pressed tight against his friend. "So, Tina, Paul," he withdrew a rolled plastic bag from the pocket of his jeans, "this bud's for you!" With that, he tipped the can of beer to his lips to drink nonstop. A loud crunching noise sounded as he closed a fist on the empty can then lobbed it over his head and onto the roof of the mansion.

"Oh, Todd, why don't you grow up and stop bein' such an immature piece of piss!" She swung, clipping him on the shoulder.

"You better call off your woman, Paul, 'fore she scares off all the ghosts and goblins."

"Shut up, Todd! We already know all the haunts around here live in your drug-crazed little mind!"

"Yeah? Try tellin' that to the bayou people. It just so

happens my uncle is in Search and Rescue and was one of the men up here the day they lost two of their divers." Todd inched his way towards her, smiled when she pushed herself closer against Paul. "He told me about an underwater cave near here and how ole man Hindel himself used that cave to get in and outta his house. And explain this," he moved his face within inches of hers, "how come, to this day, they ain't never found the bodies of the dead divers?"

Knowing her safety to be intact, Tina replied, "Because, like my mama says, they ain't been lookin' in the right place." She jutted her chin at him.

"You got all the answers, don't you, Tina?"

"No, I don't. But my mama does." Tina yanked the sleeves of her short, green pullover lower on her arms, flipped her mane of dark, red hair back over her shoulder. "She even knows how all the rumors about this house got started in the first place."

"Oh yeah? Just what might that be?" His gaze traveled up her long slender legs to stop on the defined "v" beneath her tight denim cutoffs.

Tina watched his dark eyes gleam with interest and licked her full red lips, enjoying his discomfort. "The niggers started the rumors to scare away the whites so they can practice their voodoo without being bothered!"

Paul thought for a moment, then nodded his head in agreement. "You know what? I think your mama has solved the mystery of the Hindel Mansion! Of all the theories I've heard concernin' this house, this one makes sense! Do you know what else I think? I think Todd's right! It's time to party!" He threw a surprised Tina over his shoulder and, with a jaunty wave of his hand, walked away towards the back of the house.

Lawrence stood back, trying to think what he should do. He knew he had to get everyone away from the house before the ones he had invited to stay knew about them. He did not need another blood bath, and that is what would happen if he didn't get rid of them. He reached for the light switch then dropped his hand back to his side. He walked to the door and, being very quiet, turned the knob.

Todd grabbed himself a beer, then reached for the joint Alex held out to him. He turned away long enough to shove his own weed back into his pocket. The pungent smell of the marijuana filled the air as he brought the rolled cigarette to his lips, pulling the drug deep into his lungs. Nothing in the world soothed like a good toke, he told himself as he waited for the effects of the drug to spread its relaxing warmth throughout his body. He glanced around, eyeing each unattended girl and tried to decide which one he would choose to work off the pounding need making itself known between his thighs. His keen eyes fell upon a short, petite blonde sitting a ways down the porch nursing a beer.

"Get ready, honey. You're about to get lucky!" Todd sauntered to his feet, then stopped as someone yanked open the front door. "What the hell?"

"I am sure you are well aware it is against the law to trespass, young man. Therefore you can explain why you and your friends have taken it upon yourselves to be occupying my front porch without an invitation." Lawrence Hindel stood in the doorway; his feet spread wide, his arms crossed over his chest.

"We didn't even know anyone lived here anymore," Todd tried to explain, a slight quiver sounding in his voice.

"And now that you know someone *is* living here?"

"We'll be on our way, Sir." He swung his arm, motioning everyone to gather their belongings.

Lawrence turned to leave, then turned back. "Tell everyone you know to think long and hard about returning to this house, uninvited. Sometimes what we perceive as a rumor turns out to be the complete opposite."

The man's words and the way he delivered them had Todd backing away, unable to respond or look away. He didn't realize he had reached the last of the steps until he found himself sprawled in a heap on the cobble-stoned driveway with his right ankle taking the brunt of the fall. A sharp pain shot up his leg releasing him from his terror.

Lawrence glanced at him then walked into the house.

"Quick, somebody help me up! I think I broke my fuckin' ankle!" he cried out.

Alex ran back with some of the other boys to pick him up. When they saw he couldn't walk, they scooped him up to cart him away.

"Goddamn it, you don't need to carry me! Just let me lean on one of you."

"Shut up, Todd. We gotta get the hell outta here! Now! Don't you know who that is?" Alex panted as they ran.

"Yeah, I know who he is. He's Lawrence Hindel, for Christ's sake! What's the big deal?" His ankle throbbed with pain, and he tried to not show it.

"Yeah, Lawrence Hindel, asshole! The same Lawrence Hindel who got locked up in a mental institution for slaughterin' an entire family!"

"Aw shit! You're right!" Todd could feel sweat pop out on his forehead and knew it didn't all stem from the pain in his ankle. "We need to get the hell outta here! That man's a ravin' lunatic!"

"No shit! That's what I already told you!"

The girls huddled in the boat, crying and holding on to each other.

Alex reached out and, with a trembling hand, tried to console them as best he could. "Damn it, Todd, hurry up and get in!"

Todd eased himself into the boat, being careful not to bump his already aching foot when his heart jumped inside his chest. "Oh fuck! Where the hell's Paul and Tina? They don't know Hindel's in the house!"

"Anyone know Tina's cell phone number? We already know Paul don't have a cell phone. His cheap ole man don't believe in them." As everyone in the boat shook their head, Alex shoved the small boat away from the bank then jumped in. "They got their own boat! We need to get the hell outta here! Now!"

"Yeah, they'll be all right. Let's go! My goddamn ankle's

throbbin'. Soon as we get to the car, you're gonna have to drive me to the emergency room. I just hope they don't do a fuckin' piss test! My ole man's gonna shit if they do!"

As they rowed away from the mansion, no one would let themselves think about the two they left behind at the mercy of a man they held responsible for the worst murders the people of Saint Anthony Parish could ever remember.

***

Tina breathed a deep sigh of contentment. Stretching her body out straight, she handed the carved pipe to Paul, then frowned as he shook his head in refusal.

"Come on, Paul! You haven't even hit the damn thing. I thought we came out here to get loose and party."

"I don't want anymore!" he snapped, wishing he could relax and enjoy himself instead of wrestling with the guilty feelings always plaguing him when out with his friends.

"Nobody's going to tell your daddy you're enjoying yourself." Tina laid down the pipe, then reached up to pull the flimsy top over her head.

As her well-rounded breasts popped into view, Paul reached out his hand. With a low groan, he trailed his fingers over their softness.

"Still want to call off our party?" she purred as Paul lowered his head to draw first one, then the other of her erect nipples into his hot mouth.

He drew back as Tina pulled away. "What are you doing?" he whispered, his voice breathy and deep.

Without a word, she picked up the pipe. "First we do what I want, then..." she gave him an impish little grin, "we can do what you want."

Knowing he had no choice, Paul reached for the pipe.

"I want you to hit it this time. I want you so relaxed you'll do anything I ask you to do!"

Anxious to please, he drew the smoke deep into his lungs and, within moments, felt his body let go of all its tension.

"That's a good boy." Tina smiled over at him. "Now, place

it in my mouth so I can get loose, too."

"Don't get too loose," he laughed, caught up in the feeling, "I like my women hot and tight."

Paul undid the snap on her cutoffs. Tina helped him by lifting her slender hips into the air.

"Do you like what you see so far?" she breathed as he slid the brief shorts down her long legs.

"I feel like I'm about to dive into a helping of strawberry shortcake," he groaned, eyeing her creamy skin and the mound of dark red hair between her slim thighs.

"Then I hope strawberry shortcake is your favorite dessert." She drew in her breath as he lowered his head to rub his face against her thighs.

"I think I just found something to take its place," he growled, then pulled his shirt up and over his head to throw it aside. He pushed himself to his feet to begin yanking off his shoes and socks.

Tina stared up at him, watching with growing interest as his nipples hardened. When he dropped down beside her, she skimmed long red nails over his bared chest then pulled him closer.

He moaned deep in his throat as her warm lips closed over one hardened little bud offering itself up to her hungry mouth, then felt his breath explode from his throat as she scraped her teeth over the throbbing nipple.

"You're bein' a very naughty girl."

Tina squirmed against the hand rubbing her crotch, then giggled as she felt one teasing finger push itself into her wet tightness. Her dark eyes flamed as she watched him move the finger back and forth beneath his nose, breathing in its intoxicating fragrance, then pop it into his mouth to devour its tangy sweetness. "Now, who's being naughty?"

With the taste of her bathing his senses, he reached out, placing her long legs on each side of his hips to stare down at her.

"I want to feel all of you." She pushed him back. "Take off your jeans. If I didn't know better," she teased him, "I'd think this is your first time with a girl!" She laughed as he scrambled to his feet to pull off his jeans then drop back down beside her.

"That's better," she whispered. "I want some heat!

"Oh, I'll give you heat," Paul promised, rubbing the tip of his cock against the soft pink folds luring him onward. A long sigh broke the stillness ending on a cry of both pain and pleasure, and he felt himself surrounded by liquid fire as he pushed himself the rest of the way inside.

Tina wrapped her legs around his hips to draw him ever deeper, her little round bottom bouncing up and down as she raked her long nails down his bared back.

Out of control, Paul bucked and rammed into the satin vault stroking him like a soft velvet hand.

As chills racked her body, she tightened the magic muscle responsible for crowning her the sweetheart of Parish High. Without warning, she felt hot liquid slam against the slick walls of her petal-soft tunnel, and she strengthened her hold. Keeping him nestled inside until all the throbbing, like a patting hand for a job well done, had ceased.

Tina sat up, fumbling through their scattered clothes for her pipe. "There you are, my little friend." She picked up the pipe, happy to see it remained full enough to do its work.

"Thank you, Tina." Paul glanced over at her, his boyish face flushed with feeling. "That felt good."

With the pipe halfway to her mouth, she flicked the lighter closed to stare at him. "Are you telling me you've never been laid before? When he looked away, she grinned.

"I just fucked a virgin!" She laughed. "And all this time I thought, with your looks, all those stories about your being cherry, had to be just that! Stories!"

"You don't have to make a big deal of it." He looked away as hot shame crept over him, overshadowing the good feelings he had been enjoying.

"Poor Paul." She laid back, crossing one long leg over the other to swing her foot back and forth. "Eighteen years old and never been laid! Until now!" She corrected herself. Enjoying the hell she had to be putting him through.

"I suppose you're going to tell everybody." He watched her, trying to gauge how much he could trust what she told him.

"Now, Paul, do you think I would do something like that after what we just had together?"

"I don't know." He gathered up his clothes then froze as he heard a rustling in the nearby trees.

"I'm not going to tell…" she broke off her words as he held up a hand for silence.

"Get dressed!" he hissed at her.

Tina jumped to her feet. "Don't you take that tone with me!"

"Don't cop an attitude, Tina. I think we got company." He pulled his shirt over his head, zipped his jeans.

"All right, Todd, you asshole! We know you've been watchin'. I hope you got an eye-full! You pervert!"

"Tina! Be quiet! I don't think it's Todd. He might be a lotta things, but he's not the kind to spy on me when I'm with my girl."

"How would you know, Paul? I'm the first girl you've been with!" she shot back, but as he continued to scan the trees, she felt her stomach roll. "Then who do you think it is?"

"I don't know. I do know we need to get out of here and fast!" Paul shoved her clothes into her hand. "Hurry up!"

Tina shoved one leg in the pant leg of her cutoffs then stopped as she saw someone walking towards them. Without hesitation, she ran to Paul. "Someone's coming."

Lawrence Hindel continued walking, his own fear of who else might be watching the young couple making it hard for him to breathe.

"Who are you, and what do you want?" Paul tried to sound authoritative.

"Lawrence Hindel, the owner of this estate." His breathless tone washed over them as his green eyes skimmed over Tina's nakedness. "I want you both to get off my property. Now!" His breath escalated as he glimpsed glowing eyes peering at them from the stand of large oaks.

With her usual arrogance, Tina tossed her head, making her long mane of red hair cascade down her naked back. "I would think a man small as you would show more respect when you know you're out-powered." She smiled up at Paul. "Don't you agree, love?" She trailed her long nails down his chest.

Paul jerked away, his heart thudding as he watched anger boil up in Lawrence's eyes. "Get your clothes on, Tina," he growled, ignoring the sullen glare she shot his way. "Mr. Hindel has told us to leave, and that's what we're gonna do!"

"A very wise decision, young man." Anger at Tina's rebellious stance silencing his unease. "However, I fear the choice has come too late."

With real fear choking the very breath from his lungs, Paul turned to follow Lawrence's calm gaze.

Tina cried out as she saw figures emerging from the trees.

Smelling her fear, they loped towards her, their claw-like hands reaching out to encircle her.

"Paul! Help me!" she screamed her terror as one of the beasts grabbed her by her long red hair to slam her to the ground.

"I tried to warn you, but you wouldn't listen," Lawrence told them. "Now, I guess you will have to pay the price for your stupidity."

Paul stared in open-mouth horror as the female tried to pull him against her. "Get away from me! You ain't real!" He could hear himself saying the words, but they sounded as though they came from a long way off.

"Oh, I assure you they are quite real." Lawrence laughed, backing away to give his guests more room. "I doubt you will enjoy what they have planned for you. However, as their host, all I can do is allow them their fun." He turned and, without another word, left them to the horror already closing in on them.

Chandra watched the grueling sight unfolding before her and tried to turn away. But the horror refused to loosen its hold.

Nothing has changed. I thought that by destroying Jonathan, everything would be safe again but, it isn't. The evil is still here surrounding my son with its filthy touch, just like it did when Jonathan walked these grounds.

Tortured screams split the silence, and she looked over at Lawrence. Hoping to see the same sick aversion covering his face as she knew had to be covering hers. She didn't see it. She saw the same depravity glittering in his eyes as she had always seen in Jonathan's.

"*Jonathan!*" she screamed aloud into the blinding chaos. "*Your evil is finished here. Go back to the darkness where your soul belongs.*"

"*Evil does not die, Chandra. Remember? It only lies dormant. Waiting.*"

She turned to see who could be voicing the same words she herself had spoken long ago, and her heart froze at the sight of a tall, handsome man dressed all in black, standing beside her. "*Rafael,*" she whispered. "*What are you doing here?*"

"*Did you think I would not come? My grandson is all alone now that you have destroyed his father.*" His steel-gray eyes, looking so much like Jonathan's, she felt her heart cringe in terror, stared out at her.

"*You should not be here.*" She found herself backing away from him and cursed her weakness. "*Lawrence does not need you to protect him. He has me.*"

Deep laughter rumbled from his throat, silencing her. "*You are but a weak shadow of what my son made of you.*" Disgust strengthened the coldness glaring out at her as he stepped closer. "*Lawrence will come to loath the memory of the woman whose body gave him transport to this plane. Yes, Chandra,*" his soul leapt with vindication as he watched pain replace fear, "*I know you are his mother.*"

"*He promised he would never tell anyone!*" She fought to stay in control. "*He promised!*"

"*Jonathan would never keep a secret of such magnitude from me. I gave him life! I gave him immortality!*" His anger mounted, and he did nothing to stop it. "*Together, for over two centuries, we walked the dark side. Together, we ruled over the accursed.*" He lifted a trembling fist wanting so much right at that moment to destroy her. Realizing he could do nothing against her spirit, he chose to allow his anger to destroy her instead. *"You ruined our empire."* He delivered the words on a whisper, and yet the hatred in those quiet words spewed forth with all the devastation of a crushing blow.

"Yes, I did." She nodded, acknowledging his words and, in doing so, felt her control flow back in. *"The time had come for Jonathan's evil to end."* The strength in her voice snapped his head around, and his angry glare flowed over her. *"I am well aware of how much you wish to destroy me. However, you know, and I know, you are powerless against me."*

"There are many earth-bounds roaming this land that would be happy to do my bidding." He leashed his anger refusing her control over his emotions. *"You are right, I can't touch you, but others can. Remember, they too are made up of energy and able to interact with the spirit."*

"You are speaking of dark entities, Rafael. Do you think they could be a challenge to me?" She smiled, pushing him to respond in anger.

He sidestepped her baiting of him. *"Yes, Chandra, I do. The dark side is getting stronger with every breath we take."* Rafael chuckled, enjoying the look of surprise slipping across her face. *"If you do not believe me, then look to the Church of Rome and all the evangelists hawking their wares each and every night on the airways and in their temples and churches."*

"You are not making sense. Are you trying to make me believe priests and other men of the cloth are dark entities?"

The look of confusion covering her face transferred itself to his. *"Are you telling me this is all new to you?"* The anger he had been harboring earlier dissipated as a feeling of euphoric joy washed over him. *"I will try to explain the workings of the world in a way even you, in your blind ignorance, will be able to understand."*

She tried to remain calm as his eyes filled with hunger at the sounds and smells filling the air around them.

With great effort, he brought his attention back to Chandra.

As though speaking to a child, he translated his beliefs. "*The struggle between good and evil has been going on since the beginning of time.*" He waited as she nodded her acceptance of his words thus far. "*The Catholic Church, wanting to be sure they had unquestionable control over the spreading of the word, took a verse from the Bible and held it up as proof that God entrusted His priests with His holy word. They alone could speak on what God would and would not allow. As if they didn't hold enough power,*" he shook his head at the enormity of the situation, "*they also let it be known for any soul to pass through the gates of heaven they first had to confess to the priests each and every sin they had ever committed.*" He glanced over at her. "*Chandra, even you must see the humor here.*"

"*I already know all this.*"

"*You will afford me the respect I am entitled to by remaining silent until I have finished.*"

He waited to be sure he would be obeyed.

"*In turn for this soul searching,*" he continued, "*the priests, at their discretion, could absolve that sin or continue to hold that soul accountable, thus keeping that soul earthbound for eternity. They had to know that by taking such power unto themselves, their own downfall would be imminent.*" He gave up and allowed the laughter to spill forth.

"*You believe that all priests are evil, then?*"

"*Not all, no. However, you must admit, what is going on in the Catholic Church today doesn't hold most of them up for sainthood!*" he countered.

"*You're referring to all the pedophiles in the priesthood.*"

"*Not just in the priesthood, in all walks of the so-called chosen. Evil abounds everywhere. What better place to hide from the unsuspecting-ignorant than in God's own house?*"

Words she had said some time back spilled into her mind like a forgotten foe. 'Children trust with their very souls. It is this innocence that calls and tempts the evil to come for them.'

As though he could read her thoughts, he replied, "*Children are taught to trust those who are deemed second to God. As long as they do, we, on the dark side, will never want for what we covet most.*"

Chandra stood in the shadows as Rafael walked past her to join in on the rape and destruction of the two unfortunate teenagers and her heart cried out for their souls.

She thought that by destroying Jonathan Hindel, she could put an end to his evil. Too late, she realized, Jonathan owned but a small part of the legacy.

CHAPTER THREE

Donavan walked past the desk, just as Jeff, the station's dispatcher, handed him the phone.

"I think you're gonna want to handle this, Lieutenant."

Donavan set down his cup of coffee, an irate glare, directed at the man sitting behind the desk as he reached for the phone.

"This is Lieutenant Hays." He tried to keep the anger from sounding in his voice. "What can I do for you?"

"I need you to get out to the Statler house as soon as possible," the man on the other line said.

"All right. What is this concerning?"

"My son, Paul, went out with a few of his friends last evening and hasn't returned."

"Has he ever stayed out like this before?" Bracing the receiver with his chin, Donavan worked on removing the lid from the Styrofoam cup.

"No, but then he never had a date with Tina Crawford before."

Donavan rolled the name around in his mind trying to put a face with the name, and came up empty. "What does this Tina look like? You say the name like I should know her."

"With her reputation, I thought *everyone* would know her." The voice of the man on the phone took on a pious tone.

"By any chance, am I speaking with Reverend Statler?" Donavan rubbed his eyes, his patience with the man growing short.

An exasperated sigh greeted him before the man replied, "Of course you're speaking with Reverend Statler! Why else would I tell you to get out to the Statler house!"

"I'll get out there as soon as I can." He hung up the phone, not trusting himself to stay on the line any longer.

"What's up, partner?" Jack walked into the room, picked up Donavan's coffee.

Before Jack could take a sip, Donavan reached out, retrieving his cup. "I just talked to Reverend Statler." He dropped the name on a sour note. "Seems his son went out with the town's wild child and hasn't come home yet."

"Nothin' strange 'bout that." He walked over to the coffee dispenser and, placing a cup beneath the lever, pulled it forward. "Maybe she's teachin' him some new moves."

"Let's hope that's all it amounts to. In any case, I told him I'd come over there and check it out. You going?"

"Sure. Why not?" He turned the sugar-shaker upside-down over his cup, something he had been doing of late since quitting smoking. "Are you gonna check with the girl's parents to see if she's showed up?"

"I thought I'd talk to Statler before I involve her family. Since I didn't find out how old Jr. is, I'm not sure yet what direction I want to go."

"Ready when you are." Jack closed the cylinder on a 38 Smith and Wesson.

"We're going to talk with a preacher, not the James Gang." Donavan placed a new notepad inside his shirt pocket. "When are you going to invest in a shoulder-holster? Jamming a gun in your belt looks a little unprofessional."

"Shoulder-holster won't work for me." He followed Donavan to the door. "Too much chance of the gun gettin' hung up in the leather." Jack gave him a wicked grin. "'Sides, seein' I'm packin' might make Preacher Statler a little more respectful."

***

A short, squat woman dressed in a dark brown dress

buttoned to the throat and hanging just below her ankles answered their knock.

"Are you the officers my husband sent for?" She dabbed at her eyes with a small handkerchief.

"Yes, ma'am." Donavan showed her his badge, and she stepped aside to let them enter. "I'm Lieutenant Hays, and this is my partner, Detective Olivier'."

"I'll talk with the officers, Doris," Reverend Statler told her without rising from his chair. "You can be about your business."

"Yes, James." She bobbed her head in compliance. "I'll bring some coffee." She turned away then stopped. "How do you gentleman take your coffee?"

"This isn't a social call, Doris." He dismissed her with a flick of his pudgy hand.

Doris dropped her eyes. Her unquestioning submissiveness reminded Donavan of a cowering dog who has been kicked to the curb, and he took an instant dislike of the obese man, dressed in a navy-blue suit, who remained seated as they entered the room.

"Thank you anyway, Mrs. Statler," Jack spoke up. "Price of coffee bein' what it is we can understand your husband wantin' to conserve on it when he can."

"Yes…well…I'll just be about my business then and let you get on with helping us find our son."

Without waiting for an invitation, Donavan and Jack sat down on the couch to find out what they could on the missing boy.

"What's your son's name and age, Mr. Statler and about what time did you see him last?" Donavan withdrew the notepad from his shirt, flicked open his pen.

"My son's name is Paul. He just turned 18, and I guess he left around six o'clock last evening."

"Ever had any problems with him staying out all night before this?"

"My son is a good, God-fearin' boy!" His proud head came up, and his fat hands latched onto the lapels of his suit coat. "I've never had a moment's problem with him since the day his mother gave birth to him." His fleshy jowls shook with conviction.

"My dad would have had just the opposite to say 'bout me!" Jack snickered.

Statler edged forward in his chair. "Your pa must not have been a God-fearin' man."

"My ole man didn't have to fear God. He had all he could do to handle mom!"

"Mr. Statler, we're here to find out about your son, so let's try and stick to the subject." The tone of his voice left no room for argument.

Statler looked at him for a moment, then decided he had said enough.

"You said on the phone your son had a date with a girl named Tina Crawford. Is that correct?"

"Yes." He swallowed as though saying her name left a foul taste in his mouth.

"You also said he planned to be with some of his friends?"

"Todd Shrimpton and Alex Johnson. Both are strong Assembly of God Christens. They belong to my church. I would take an oath that neither of those boys drinks alcohol nor do any kind of drugs. They're both God-fearin' Christens."

"Oh, Christ!" Jack breathed.

Statler's head whipped around. "What did you just say, Detective?"

Before Jack could respond, Donavan spoke up, "He said, Go Christ! Detective Olivier's parents raised him Baptist. That was one of their school cheers." He glanced at Jack daring him to argue. "Now, if we could get back to the business at hand. Have you called the other boys or Tina to see if they know where Paul might be?"

"No, I haven't."

"May I ask why? Could be he spent the night with one of them, and you and your wife are worrying for nothing."

Statler looked around, then lowered his voice to just above a whisper. "I trust my son to be strong and not give in to temptations of the flesh, but he is a young man, and I've heard rumors about this Crawford girl. If what I've heard is true… well…you know…my boy might not have been able to resist Satin's lure," he whined, needing to know they understood and agreed with him.

"Yeah, them hormones can be a real bit…ter pill to swallow." Jack caught himself in time.

"I have their names, so as soon as we get back to the station house, I'll call and see what I can find out."

Statler left his chair, held out his hand. "I would appreciate that. And if you could, ask for me. I believe it's the man's place to handle such things."

"Sure thing, Reverend Statler." Jack leaned in close. "God forbid your wife should find out sometimes men have sex for reasons other than to procreate."

"I… think we've got all we need for now. As soon as I know anything, I'll give you a call." Donavan ushered Jack out the door.

"Thank you, Lieutenant." Statler gave Jack a lingering glance before closing the door.

Donavan turned the key bringing the Jeep Cherokee to life. "I'm glad to see you haven't lost your professional touch."

Jack glared at him. "Cut me some slack, Donavan. The pious prick pissed me off! So what if his kid's out gettin' him some pussy! He's eighteen years old, for Christ's sake!"

"I'm not getting on your ass, Jack." He grinned over at him. "Tell you the truth, the son of a bitch started to get to me, too."

"So where do you think he is?"

"I hope he *is* out getting some dew on his stinger. But with kids, you just never know. One thing I do know, I'm not as worried as I would have been a year ago if we'd gotten a call about a missing kid." He glanced over at Jack feeling a moment of apprehension.

"That's for damn sure. All I can say is, wherever he is, it's gotta be a step up from where he's been!"

CHAPTER FOUR

"I'm glad you're back, Lieutenant." Jeff looked up as Donavan walked into the station house. "She's been sitting in your office for over half an hour."

"Who is she?" Donavan glanced through his glass-partitioned office at a slender woman holding a tissue to her eyes.

"Mrs. Crawford." A flush of embarrassment crept up Jeff's face.

Donavan withdrew two messages from his cubicle. "Seems like every time I hear that name, the person saying it acts like they got a crotch full of vermin."

"Her daughter's Tina Crawford," he voiced the information in a whisper. "My brother says she's the hottest thing to ever hit Parish High!"

"Oh yeah!" Donavan nodded. "The town's wild child."

"From what I hear, that's putting it in a mild perspective." Jeff turned away to answer a call.

Donavan walked into his office, pulling the door to after him.

The woman jumped to her feet. "Are you Lieutenant Hays?"

"That's right, Mrs. Crawford." His dark gaze skimmed over her. Taking in her clinging, bright blue dress, low cut and falling well above the knees and he could feel an ache already beginning to throb in the arches of his feet as his eyes fell on her six-inch spiked heels. "What can I do for you?" He motioned her back to her chair.

She sat back down, crossing her long legs, ignoring the fact her movement hid little from the man standing in front of her. "My daughter Tina is missing, Lieutenant."

"All right." With effort, he brought his gaze back to her face.

"She went out on a date last night, and when I came in this morning, she still had not returned."

"Maybe she went out to breakfast with Mr. Crawford. Is that a possibility?" He sat down behind his desk, loosened his tie.

"There is no Mr. Crawford!" Her soft voice cracked as she tried to make him understand.

Donavan glanced up at her. "Do you make it a habit of staying out all night?"

In an instant, her demeanor changed. "I have a job that keeps me out at night!" Her green eyes snapped with anger. "And before you go passing judgment on me, you need to understand I don't have a choice in where I work!"

"Everyone has a choice, Mrs. Crawford." He flicked a pen to begin writing down her information. "Where do you work?"

"You judgmental son of a bitch!" She jumped to her feet. "I came in here to get help finding my daughter, and all you can do is look down your nose at me!"

Donavan's head drew back. "No one is passing judgment on you, Mrs. Crawford. You said your daughter is missing. Therefore, I need to know where you work. I need to know what time you leave your house. I need to know what time you return to your house." His voice warned her to calm down.

She flipped her long, dark, auburn hair over her shoulder, plopped back down in her chair. "I apologize for my outburst."

"That's better." Donavan tossed the pen down on the desk. "So, where do you work?"

"I work at The Gentlemen's Elite Club." Her full, red mouth settled into a defiant pout. "In case you haven't had the pleasure of being a guest, I'll enlighten you." She licked her already slick mouth, leaned in closer to his desk. "I take off my clothes for the gentlemen."

Donavan picked up the pen, scrawled on the notepad in big, bold letters. "GENTLEMEN'S Elite Club STRIPPER!" He watched her out of the corner of his eye to catch her reaction. "Now, let's get to the timelines." He looked up, the pen poised in his hand.

"I get to the club at 10:30p.m. I get off at 7:a.m., she whispered.

"All right, Mrs. Crawford, what time did you tell your daughter she had to be home?"

"I don't set a certain time for her to come and go. I just leave that up to her." Her voice rose as she saw his brows lift. "Tina is seventeen. It isn't as if she's a toddler who needs me with her every waking moment!"

Donavan thought of his eleven-year-old Jenny and felt his temper flare. "Children need guidance no matter what age they are, Mrs. Crawford." He tried to keep the anger from sounding in his deep voice.

"Could we drop the Mrs.? Please? You make me sound like I'm old enough to be your mother!" She fluffed her silky, thick mane. "My name is Christina."

"When you got home this morning, Christina, what did you find?"

The woman with all the answers changed, and in her place, he saw a worried mother desperate to find her child.

"I always go in and check to see if she's okay, and I could see she hadn't slept in her bed. Tina has a habit of laying out what outfit she's going to wear the next morning, and I didn't see an outfit."

Donavan pushed the box of tissue over further on the desk. "I know how upsetting this has to be for you, Mrs....Christina," he amended, "but if I'm going to have any chance of helping you find your daughter, you need to take a deep breath and clear your head."

She reached out, pulling several tissues from the box to

press them against her eyes.

"What did Tina have on when you saw her last?"

For a brief moment, she remained silent. "A pair of cutoffs and a short, green pullover top." Christina tapped a long, red nail against her white teeth. "Oh, and a pair of green sandals." She smiled. "I know she wore the sandals because they're mine, and she asked if she could borrow them."

"You said she had a date. Do you know the name of the boy she went out with?"

"Of course, I know the name of the boy!" Christina sat up straighter in her chair. "Paul Statler. His daddy's a preacher, and believe it or not, one of my biggest tippers!" She waited to see what this little tidbit might bring from the man writing down her information and found herself feeling disappointed when he continued as though she had not spoken. "Anyway, Tina said Paul told her he'd pick her up around seven, and that's all I know."

Donavan tossed the pen on the desk, then got to his feet. "Thank you for coming in and bringing this to my attention, Christina. You can rest assured we'll get on trying to find your daughter as soon as possible."

Christina turned toward the door then stopped. "I just thought of something."

"What?"

"I almost feel foolish telling you." She gave him an uneasy little laugh.

"Anything that might find your daughter is important. What is it?" he asked, anxious for her to leave so he could light up a cigarette.

"Tina said she and her friends planned on partying at the old Hindel Mansion. At first, when she told me about it, I got real scared." She ran a hand over her throat. "You know...because of all the dumb stories people spread about the place. Then I figured since no one lives there anymore, what could it hurt? Anyway, that's all I can think of." With a nervous smile, she walked out the door.

Donavan glanced up to see Jack seated behind his desk. He tapped on the window to motion him forward.

"What's up? He pulled the door closed behind him.

"Did you happen to see the woman who just walked out of here?"

"How the hell could I miss her?" Jack wiggled his brows. "A woman that stacked could make a saint forget he's married!"

"Her daughter is Tina Crawford. She hasn't seen her since she left to go out partying last night."

"If she looks anything like her mother, it's a good guess she's still at the party."

"Tina Crawford is the name of the girl Paul Statler went out with. Remember?" Donavan flicked his ashes into the ashtray.

A wide grin started at the corners of Jack's mouth to work its way upward. "There you go! Two kids out havin' fun'n forgot 'bout the time."

"I don't know." Donavan stamped out his half-finished cigarette. "She said something that has me a little uneasy."

"And that somethin' is?"

"She said, Tina told her the kids planned on partying out at the Hindel Mansion."

The grin left Jack's face. "She didn't try and talk her out of it? What the hell kinda mother is she for shit sake?"

"She said she thought about it, but since she thought no one lived there anymore, she didn't see any harm in it."

"Except someone does live there. Don't they?"

"She had no way of knowing that. Hell, we didn't know he was back until he made a point of telling us. And, to let us know what he'll do about any trespassers..." his voice slid to a stop.

"He did make a big production of that!"

"Yes, he did!" Donavan leaned forward, punched the intercom button. "Jeff, run through last night's calls and see if a complaint came in from Lawrence Hindel about any trespassers out at his place."

"Will do," Jeff said.

"If nothing shows up, then it's a pretty safe bet the kids went somewhere else to raise hell," Donavan said.

"Nothing," the dispatcher came back to him. "I even checked back until the shift change at seven a.m."

"Thanks, Jeff." Donavan flipped off the intercom. "I guess nothing happened at Hindel's, or we would have heard about it."

Jack's head snapped forward. "I think we should put out the word on Hindel. You know, like we would on a known pedophile." Jack got to his feet, caught up in his idea. "He spent a year locked away in an idiot-bin. People deserve a head's-up 'bout somethin' like that!"

"Everyone already knows about his stay in a psyche-ward."

"That's true!" Jack whirled. "But...how many people know the little turd's runnin' loose again?"

"I get your point!" Donavan drew in his breath let it out. "Listen, you're a trained detective," he spoke his words in a calm manner in hopes some of what he said would filter out Jack's enthusiasm, "so I know you are aware of little things like... slander...harassment."

"Goddamn it, Donavan! Don't patronize me! I'm not suggestin' we put out a sign sayin' "Beware of the Hindel psycho!" What I'm sayin' — is, we use word of mouth to let people know what they're up against, smart-ass!"

Donavan nodded. "That we can do. Yeah, that's a good idea."

Jack turned to the door. "Since we know the kids are goin' at it someplace else, I guess we can consider this case closed."

"Except," Donavan rubbed a hand over the back of his neck, "something still ain't right. What the hell am I missing here?"

Jack had already reached for the doorknob when he stopped. "Today's Sunday. Paul Statler's a preacher's kid." He turned, staring at Donavan. "Like it or not, there's no way in hell he's gonna miss a Sunday sermon!"

"Looks like we're going to church."

***

Statler stood in the doorway of the church, shaking hands with the departing members of his congregation when he spied Donavan and Jack coming across the lawn. Without thought, he shoved his way through the throng of people to get to the detectives. "What are you doing here?" he growled, motioning them to follow him. When they moved out of earshot of everyone, he turned on them. "I don't want the people of my church knowing about my private business."

"Calm down, Reverend," Jack warned him. "No one is here to tattle on you. Besides, how do you know we're not here with some news 'bout your son?"

"Is that what you're here about?" Statler whipped a handkerchief from the inside pocket of his suit-coat to mop his face. "If you are, I would have appreciated hearing about it on the phone."

"We're not here with good news, Reverend Statler." He delivered his statement in a deadpan voice in an attempt to get Statler's reaction.

"Get to the point, Detective. It's very humid out, and I don't deal well with it."

"We talked with Tina Crawford's mother earlier."

Jack winked at Donavan as Statler started to fidget.

Coming up alongside her husband, Mrs. Statler reached for Jack's hand. In a trembling voice, she asked, "Have you had any word on Paul yet, Detective Olivier'?"

"Don't you think if they had any information, we'd of already heard about it? Just let *me* handle this!"

Jack turned on him. "You may wanna cut your wife a little slack here, Reverend. He's her son, too. Remember?"

Mrs. Statler's pale eyes rounded as she looked from one to the other. "No, it's, it's all right," she stammered. "Reverend Statler knows best about these things."

"Follow me." He took a few steps towards the church then stopped as his wife fell in beside him. "You can wait out here with Detective Olivier'. This is man's business. We don't have time to answer a lot of your fool questions."

"Why don't we go wait in the jeep?" Jack took her arm to lead her away. "You'll be a lot more comfortable in an air-conditioned vehicle than out here in the heat."

Doris Statler hesitated to look at her husband.

"Don't stand there like a ninny!" Statler waved her away. "The man's offering you a comfortable place to wait!"

Donavan shook his head as Jack took a step forward.

"Are you coming with me or not?" Statler growled as Donavan remained standing.

"I'll be back in a few minutes, Jack." He turned away before Jack could comment. "You behaved a little rough back there. Your wife is going through the same worry about your son as you are."

Statler never broke stride. "She's a woman, and women need to learn when to stay out of matters that don't concern them. Now, you said you talked to Christina Crawford. Did she tell you where my son is?"

Donavan tried to hold onto his temper. "No, and *her* daughter is missing, too. She did say something that may be of importance, though."

"The woman's nothin' but trash. Anything she has to say would be a lie."

Donavan stopped walking. "Do you want to hear what she had to say or not? If you don't, then I got things to do."

"Of course, I want to hear what you have to say." Statler halted his steps, unwilling to be intimidated in his own domain.

"What would you say if you knew your son had planned on partying with some of his friends out at the old Hindel Mansion?"

"Whoever told you that doesn't know what they're talking about. It's a place of evil." An angry scowl dropped over his face. "Paul knows I'd whip him good if he went anywhere near that place."

"Kids don't always do what they're told."

"Paul ain't just any kid. He's got the fear of God in him.

I've seen to that." He continued walking through the church until he came to a small office. "No! If I don't approve of something, I can rest assured he ain't gonna do it!"

Donavan couldn't resist. "He's out with Tina Crawford. You can't approve of that. Can you?"

The icy glare he turned on Donavan had Donavan taking a few steps back. "Paul knows it ain't wrong to fornicate with an evil girl," he delivered his statement in a calm voice before a look of righteous anger dropped once more into place. "At the same time, he knows the fires of hell await the man who touches a good girl! No! I ain't worried about him bein' out with Tina Crawford. Devil's got her soul just like he's got her mama's!" He licked his lips, and his hooded eyes iced over. "I tried to help her mama, but she wouldn't listen. I ain't even gonna waste my time on her daughter." He glanced at Donavan. "Is that all you came to tell me? If it is, then I'll wish you a good day."

"That's all I have at the moment. I plan to talk with Paul's friends in hopes they will have some idea where we can start looking."

"If you hear anything, you have my number. Goodbye, Detective Hays."

Back in the jeep, Donavan turned to Jack. "When we helped destroy Jonathan Hindel, I thought I had seen the epitome of evil. But I'll tell you something. The man I just walked away from is running a close second."

"You gotta hand it to Hindel, though." Jack pulled the seatbelt across his chest. "At least with him, you knew where you stood. Preachers today? Could be anybody's guess."

Chapter Five

Donavan knocked on the Shrimpton's door, then waited. "They could still be out. Some families go out to breakfast after church."

"If you say so." Jack stepped forward as they heard someone come to the door.

The young man who answered wore a dark blue suit, white shirt and dark blue tie. "Naw, we don't wanna buy anything." He dismissed them. "'Side's this is Sunday. You don't peddle things in this town on the Lord's day."

Before he could slam the door shut, Jack reached out, grabbing hold of the knob. "I been called a lotta things, but never a travelin' salesman! We're lookin' for Todd Shrimpton. That you?"

The boy pushed a lock of blond hair back from his forehead. "Yeah, I'm Todd Shrimpton. Who are you?"

Donavan pulled the door open wider. "I'm Detective Donavan Hays, and this is Detective Jack Olivier'. Can we come in and talk to you?"

The young man spread his feet wide, barring their entrance. "Could I see some I.D.? You two don't look like detectives."

After checking their badges, Shrimpton stepped back out of their way. "Sorry 'bout that. Person can't be too careful these days." He motioned them to be seated at the kitchen table.

Donavan came right to the point. "Where did you go last

night, Todd?"

Todd felt a tingle of unease slide into his throat. "Why do you need to know that? I didn't do nothin'."

Jack's eyes collided with Donavan's. "No one said you did anything. We're tryin' to find out where you went."

"I went out with some friends. There ain't no law against bein' with friends. Is there?"

"No," both men said at once.

"Who did you go out *with*? That's what we're trying to find out," Donavan said.

Jack, sensing Todd's reluctance to answer their questions, tried to put him at ease. "All we wanna know is who you saw. We don't care what you did." His dark brows lifted. "That's none of our business."

Todd's bravado plummeted. "I went out with Paul Statler, his girl, Tina Crawford and Alex Hampton." He tried to bring forth who else had been there, but as pictures of drugs and alcohol being passed around drifted into his thoughts, his mind blanked. "I can't recall who else."

"Where did you party at, Todd? At the Hindel Mansion?" Donavan asked.

In an instant, his unease escalated. "Well…yeah…" he stammered, "but we didn't do anything wrong. We just wanted to be together."

Donavan nodded. "Uh huh."

"Listen, Todd," Jack said, giving the hand lying on the table a quick squeeze, "like I said, we don't care what you did out there. All we want to know is if you saw anyone in the house."

The face of Lawrence Hindel flashed into his mind. "Yeah, Lawrence Hindel. He came outside and told us to leave."

"Did you leave?" Donavan asked.

"We left right away!"

"I notice you're wearing a cast." Donavan glanced down at his foot. "What happened?"

His face reddened, and he squirmed in his chair. "When Lawrence Hindel came outside, I got so scared I backed off the porch and fell twistin' my ankle. I was hurtin' so bad I just wanted to go to the hospital and get something for the pain."

Donavan leaned forward. "Now think back to before you went to the emergency room. Did everyone leave with you?"

Todd shook his head. "Two people stayed behind. We just left. We figured since Paul and Tina had their own boat, they'd be okay. Why?"

"Todd, I know you and the others didn't mean to be... uncaring of your friends. And under the circumstances, I can see how you needed to leave in a hurry." Donavan tried to ease any guilt he might be feeling. "The thing is, Paul and Tina are missing. Both parents have talked with us, and I have to tell you, they're pretty worried." Donavan watched Todd trying to gauge how the news about his friends affected him. When he saw the boy's face go pale, he knew he was getting the truth.

"Ah...shit," Todd breathed the words on a long breath.

"You don't have any idea where they are, either. Do you?" Jack said.

"I don't know where they could be. I haven't heard from Paul or...'course I wouldn't hear from Tina. But no, I haven't heard anything. I thought it strange when I didn't see him in church this morning. I just figured he might be sick from..." his words died in his throat. "God, I hope they're all right."

"So do we." Donavan pushed back his chair.

"One more thing, Todd and I give you my word it'll be off the record," Jack said. "Any drinkin' or smokin' out last night?"

Todd nodded, then glanced away.

"Thanks for all your help," Jack told him. "I'm sure if you happen to hear anything, you'll let us know."

As they drove away, Donavan couldn't still the all-too-familiar dread beginning to creep over him.

"You don't need to tell me where we're goin'."

"That's the last place anyone saw them," Donavan said, then added. "Here we go again."

***

The voice on the intercom sounded as unfamiliar as the

man who answered the door.

Donavan looked at him. "Who are you?"

The man stared back, his face devoid of any expression.

Jack wasted no time. "We're here to see Lawrence Hindel. You need to get him."

"Lawrence hasn't come down yet. If you would like to come in, though, you can tell me what this is all about." He moved to the side as Donavan and Jack walked past him. In the living room, he motioned them to be seated, but they declined.

The man standing before them reminded Donavan of someone. Although try as he may, he couldn't place him. "As I told you on the intercom, I'm Lieutenant Detective Donavan Hays, and this is my partner, Detective Jack Olivier'."

The man did not extend his hand. "You may address me as Rafael Hindel."

A cold tingle inched its way up Donavan's spine. "Jesus Christ!" Donavan breathed. "Are you related to Jonathan Hindel?"

The brief smile disappeared as a spark of anger lit up the steel-gray eyes. "Yes, I am Jonathan's father."

Instinct pushed Jack to reach for the gun he had secreted against the small of his back. As his fingers brushed the cold steel, he felt a modicum of calm slide over him then dissipate as Donavan jerked his hand away from his back.

He felt anxious to have them both away from the house and on their way. "The sooner we can talk to Lawrence, the sooner we can get out of here. If you don't mind, could you bring him downstairs?"

Rafael remained standing, ignoring the man's request. Then, in a voice so quiet the two detectives had to lean forward to hear, he said, "The loss of Jonathan does not touch those of his blood alone. There are many who mourn his passing from this plane."

Jack retorted. "I can guarantee you one goddamn thing they don't live 'round here!"

Donavan sucked in his breath to apologize when he looked

up to see Lawrence making his way down the stairs.

"Lieutenant Hays, Jack," Lawrence addressed each of them in turn. "I don't recall inviting you to my home."

"They say they have come to ask you some questions," Rafael told him, moving to stand by Lawrence's side. He nodded a brief nod to Donavan and Jack. "You may ask your questions, now."

"Tell me about the teenagers you told to leave here last night." Donavan watched Lawrence.

"Yes." Lawrence rubbed his thin hands back and forth, then laced them together, bringing them upward to his lips. "Some young people came here last night. They partied on my front porch. I came outside and told them to leave."

"Then what happened?" Donavan asked.

"They left, and I went back inside."

"No...I don't think so." Donavan stepped forward. "You see, we talked with some of the other kids, and they said they all left except the one friend and his girl. Where the hell are they, Hindel?"

In a calm voice, Lawrence replied, "I have told you everything I know."

"Lawrence," Jack drew out the name on a silky breath, "have you been a naughty boy, again?"

At Jack's words, Rafael glared at him. "You will afford the master of this house the respect he is due."

"Master!" Jack laughed, ignoring Donavan's look of warning. "I didn't even know anyone used that term anymore. At least, not since Honest Abe did his good deed for the century. But then...you're not like other folks, are you?" The laughter disappeared from Jack's face.

Rafael and Lawrence remained silent.

"You spent a year locked away in a mental institution for slaughterin' an entire family." Jack jabbed an accusatory finger in Lawrence's direction. "And your pa...he liked runnin' 'round the countryside, eatin' people. Naw, it's a safe bet you don't run with the normal folks. So, I'll just skip the master and keep on callin' ya…Lawrence."

The anger Jack expected didn't show itself. "No young people remained on my property last night. I saw to their leaving myself. I don't know what else I can tell you." He turned to leave.

Donavan spoke up, halting him. "Lawrence, if you have harmed these kids," he spread his hands wide, "maybe in a fit of anger or…whatever, your best bet is to tell me about it."

Lawrence started to speak, but Rafael placed a restraining hand on his shoulder. "You have asked your questions. They have been answered. Now, I suggest you leave this house."

The direction had been delivered in such a cold and menacing tone Jack whirled on him.

"And if we don't?"

"Jack," Donavan stepped forward, "he's right. We've asked our questions. They've answered them. Let's go."

"Yeah, we'll go. But rest assured, we'll be back. Best thing you can do, Hindel, is produce those kids alive and unharmed." He turned on his heel, strode to the door.

Standing outside in the driveway, Donavan tried to slow down his breathing, but the unrelenting fear refused to loosen its hold. "I have a sick feeling those kids are never going to be found. Not alive anyway."

Jack looked back at the house they had just vacated, and in his heart, he agreed. "This might be a terrible thing to say, but if Hindel did get hold of them, I hope they are…at least…safe in the light of home."

"So do I. And…since we're on the subject of Hindel, the big question now is, which one are we talking about?"

***

As soon as the door closed behind the two detectives, Lawrence turned, his pale eyes filled with fear. "They know about the kids who stayed behind. Now, what are we going to do?"

For a brief moment, Rafael's eyes closed on the memory of fresh warm blood bathing his tongue. "You must leave everything in my hands, Lawrence. Trust me to take care of you."

The confidant tone in Rafael's voice worked its magic as a feeling of calm washed over him.

"The men who helped destroy your father and my son must be made to search elsewhere. Their involvement in his death will not go unpunished."

For the first time since Jonathan's death, Lawrence felt his strength flow back in, and he walked toward the man reaching out for him.

Rafael enclosed Lawrence in his arms and, in that moment, vowed the destruction of the men he held responsible for the death of his son.

CHAPTER SIX

As soon as they returned to the station, Donavan got busy getting a judge to sign a search warrant. Now that Lawrence and Rafael Hindel knew the police suspected them, they would be moving on, destroying any lingering evidence.

"Jack, get Blain on the phone and have him meet us out at the mansion with his dogs. Tell him to give us about an hour before he heads out there."

Jack reached for the phone then grinned. "Sure you don't wanna check with Captain Sinclair first? You know how he feels 'bout havin' his K-9s subjected to danger."

Donavan cocked his head, glanced out the window. "Naw, he'll be all right. He just whines when we need them after sundown."

After talking with Blain, Jack hung up the phone.

"What?" Donavan could feel his anger starting to rise. "He refused to bring the K-9s!"

Jack looked up. "No. He's fine with it."

"Then what's wrong?"

"I can't believe this shit's startin' all over again. I mean...I thought when we got rid of Jonathan...this would all be like a bad memory." He drew a shaky hand through his hair. "It's like...we've skipped back to square one."

Donavan came up beside him, laid a hand on his shoulder. "Put that thought out of your mind. Right now! This is nothing like what we went through with Jonathan Hindel. If it turns out these kids are dead, then what we're dealing with is a killer! Pure and simple."

"Are you sure? I mean…hell…we never thought we were dealin' with anything but a psychopath when we investigated the Rawlins and Stewart killin's. Look what we ended up fightin' on those two!"

"Goddamn it, Jack!" Donavan turned him around. "What we had with Jonathan Hindel is a once-in-a-lifetime nightmare! What we got now is someone who has slipped over the edge!"

"Lawrence Hindel!"

"Yes! Lawrence Hindel! Christ! It had to happen sooner or later! I just hoped when he snapped, it would be in England where we wouldn't have to deal with him."

"You could be right." Jack breathed a little easier.

"You're damn right I am." Donavan voiced a slight laugh. Except it fell short. "Look, Jack," he dropped his hand back to his side, "I have to level with you. I can't say for certain what we're dealing with here. But given all the shit Lawrence had to contend with, is it so far out of the realm for him to end up being a killer?"

"I guess when you put it like that, no."

"There. You see? Things aren't as bad as they seem." Donavan picked up the phone hit the memory dial. "How's it coming on that search warrant?" He shot a quick glance at Jack. "Good. We'll be right over to pick it up." He dropped the receiver back in the cradle. "Now we can get this show on the road in earnest!"

***

Within moments of pulling up to the locked, ornamental gate, a four-wheel-drive pickup rolled up alongside them.

"I guess Sinclair had no problem, this time, with the dogs being brought out," Donavan said as the driver of the truck walked over to them.

"Nope. Not even when I told him we had to come out here." Blain held out his hand.

"Hey, ain't that Shadow?" Jack walked over to the truck to

stand gazing at the proud head of a beautiful Doberman Pincher painted on the truck's canopy.

"Yeah," Blain replied, turning away.

Donavan stepped from his jeep. "They did a good job." He remembered the large Dobie who had been killed during their investigation into the disappearance of a young girl named Margaret Stewart. They found the girl's body on the Hindel Estate. "They got him down pat, that's for sure!" He ran his hand over the words K-9 Unit emblazoned above the proud head, then glanced over at Blain. "He had to be one of the best in the unit." Donavan gave Blain's shoulder a squeeze. "I think it's damn decent of Sinclair to let you have his picture put on your rig."

Blain swiped a hand across his eyes. "So, what are we looking for this time?"

Jack positioned himself, so his back covered the painting of the fallen K-9. "We got two missin' kids. The last time anyone saw them is last night."

Blain's head swung around. "Jesus Christ, are you tellin' me they came out here?"

"We're afraid so. Jack and I already talked with Lawrence Hindel and his grandfather earlier this morning. We didn't get anywhere. This time we're going in armed with a warrant and your dogs."

"Did you say Hindel's grandfather?" Blain asked.

"Yep," Jack spoke up. "You may wanna brace yourself. He's 'bout as out there as his son was."

"Aw...shit! You don't mean we're gonna be dealin' with another Jonathan Hindel?"

"Right now, we're not sure what we're up against. Like I told Jack, I think Lawrence Hindel has slipped over the edge. If that's the case, we're not going to find these kids alive."

"I hope you included the cave in the search warrant," Jack said as Donavan pushed the button on the intercom.

"I included the cave, and I also put down Quigley's place." He turned away as a voice broke into the silence.

"Yeah, this is Detective Hays. We need to come in."

"I'm afraid you've had all the time we are prepared to give you, Lieutenant Hays," Rafael Hindel informed him.

"I don't think you understand, Mr. Hindel." Donavan's deep voice rose in anger. "I'm not asking you to let us in. I'm telling you."

"Do you have a warrant to come on these premises?"

"I do!" Donavan shot back, his patience, at being kept waiting, already wearing thin.

For a moment, nothing happened then the iron gate swung open.

"I will allow you and your men to come onto the property, but I must insist that you not bring any dogs with you."

"Not much you can do about K-9s, Mr. Hindel. They're included in the warrant." Donavan pushed the off button.

"Let's go!" Jack swung his arm wide.

"Can you believe the balls of that prick!" Donavan put the jeep in low as they made their way up the wide driveway.

"I've noticed something. The Hindels like to be in control." Jack tried to close his mind to the images flashing into his mind of another time they had driven up this same driveway to investigate a missing child.

"They're about to find out just how out of control they are this time. If those kids are still here, dead or alive, we're going to find them!"

"It's times like this, I hate this job!"

"Yeah, I know what you mean. You can't let yourself dwell on the bad parts of the job. We've gotten a lot of assholes off the streets. Jonathan Hindel goes right to the top of that list! That has to count for something. Doesn't it?"

"The thing is when you get rid of one, ten more jumps in to take his place!"

"When that happens, you treat them like any other bug. You keep stomping their heads into the pavement until there ain't nothing left!" Donavan could feel his anger spinning out of control, but he didn't care. Everything felt all too familiar.

"You wanna know what scares me?" Jack checked the

cylinder on his 38

"What?"

"I'm gonna have a son."

"Why the hell are you scared about that? I thought you wanted to be a father."

"I did. Hindel startin' up again's got me rethinkin' everything. Like...what if the sick son of a bitch comes after Seelah or the baby? Or...Barbara and Jenny?" The gun slipped from his hand to land in his lap. "Hell, you're just as responsible for Jonathan goin' down as me. He ain't gonna let that slide."

"Jack," Donavan pulled up a short way from the mansion shut off the ignition, "Lawrence is one man. We don't know yet if he's on a rampage."

"Don't you feel it, Donavan?" He looked through the window. "We didn't get rid of the evil. It's here! How many times do you have to fight your way outta the darkness before you can step into the light?"

Donavan turned in his seat. "I want you to take a deep breath and calm yourself. Do you want to call Seelah and have her relax you before we get into all this?"

"No. I'll be okay. I guess comin' here to look for missin' kids again got to me for a moment."

"I'm not surprised. We've investigated seven murders on these grounds. Now, we might be investigating two more."

"You're scared, too. Ain't you?" Jack looked him square in the eyes and knew he had guessed right.

"Yeah, I'm scared. Like you said, we both got families to worry about."

Donavan jumped as Blain walked up to tap on the side of the jeep. "You ready?"

"I guess we might as well get it over with." He slid his feet to the cobble-stoned driveway.

"Ain't you a big handsome fellow?" Jack patted the head of the beautiful German shepherd Blain had leashed beside him, ran his hands over his sleek black and silver coat. "What's his name?"

"Magnum." Blain declared. "I got him about six months after Shadow got killed. I couldn't bring myself to get another Dobie."

"Shepherds have always been my favorite. Not that there's anything wrong with Dobermans." He hastened to add. "I been thinkin' 'bout gettin' me a dog. My wife and I are expectin' our first baby. I thought it might be kinda neat to let them grow up together."

"Here we go," Blain murmured as someone walked outside to stand looking at them.

As they and the other deputies made their way up the driveway, Blain leaned over and whispered to Jack, "I thought you said Lawrence Hindel's grandfather's here. That sure as hell can't be him."

Jack looked at the man standing on the steps, and his heart plunged. Ever since they had walked into the mansion that morning, something had been bothering him, but try as he may, he could not put his finger on it. Now he knew. The man, who had introduced himself as Rafael Hindel, appeared to be no older than Jonathan had. Something didn't add up. The thoughts flew through his mind at breakneck speed, and he could feel his breath catching in his throat. Either the man lied about his identity, or… his mind slammed shut, refusing to delve any further.

"We'll check out the house first. Top to bottom. Just like before. After that, we'll go through the cave. Sound right to you, Jack?"

Jack felt someone shaking his arm, and he looked up to find Donavan beside him. "What?"

"I don't know where you been, but you sure as hell ain't been here. Are you sure you're all right?"

"Yeah, I'm fine. I'll talk to you 'bout it later. So what's the plan? Are we gonna do it like before?"

"Yeah." Donavan walked up the front steps. "But this time, we got more places to look."

A deep growl, erupting from Magnum's throat as they walked up the steps of the mansion, had Blain tightening his hold on the dog's leash. "Simmer down," Blain whispered.

Instead of heeding the command, the dog lunged, snapping and snarling.

Raphael backed up out of reach. "Now you see why I said no dogs are allowed on this property!"

"Out! Magnum! Out!" Blain commanded.

The K-9 dropped to his haunches, his large body trembling in his need to be released.

Jack trailed a hand over the dog's head. "Good boy! See," he continued to stroke the animal, "he's gentle as a puppy! Guess he don't like what he smelled."

Rafael kept his voice controlled in his anger. "I would appreciate you conducting your investigation as soon as possible. Lawrence and I are not idle people. We do not relish waiting around while you entertain yourselves with ridiculous paranoia!"

"Two kids disappearin' on this estate is not ridiculous paranoia." Jack sauntered up to stand beside him. "I been noticin' somethin', Rafael." Jack leaned forward, eyeing the other man and ignoring the smoky glare looking back at him. "If you are grandpa Hindel like you claim to be, then I gotta hand it to your cosmetic surgeon." Jack reached out and, before Rafael could move, pushed his face to one side. "I don't see one damn scar, and he had to peel…what…thirty… forty years off you?" Jack whistled through his teeth. "He hadda be a regular Criss fuckin' Angel to do you up that good!"

"Jack!" Donavan stepped forward. "Regardless of what Mr. Hindel thinks, we're not here to play games. Let's go!"

"Stay outta the sun. I hear its hell on facelifts!" Jack gave his cheek a few gentle pats before walking away to join the rest of the team.

"What the hell is wrong with you? Are you trying to get him to come after you?" Donavan all but shoved him through the front door.

"There ain't a goddamn scare one on him, Donavan! How the hell can a man who has to be…at least…bangin' eighty look like he's no more'n fifty?"

"Maybe he's lived an exemplary life!" Donavan shot back. Anger at Jack's antics, when they still didn't know what they faced, pushing him to lose all patience. "How the fuck should I know how he looks like he does!"

"Bullshit!" Jack rounded on him. "Think back to when we had to deal with Jonathan Hindel! Remember? He looked young, too! We're right back to a goddamn year ago!"

"We don't know that!" Donavan pulled him into the entry hall away from the other men. "I'll say this, though. If we are dealing with another Jonathan, then the best thing you can do is not go out of your way to antagonize the son of a bitch!"

Raphael walked up to them.

"Lawrence is here, so I am assuming everyone is ready to begin the investigation." He nodded to the men standing down the hall waiting for them.

"Yeah, we're coming," Donavan said as Rafael raked his cold eyes over Jack.

"Walks like a goddamn panther," Jack murmured under his breath as they followed behind the man who could be leading them into another nightmare.

Chandra watched each man as he came through the door. When her eyes fell on Jack, she came forward. Although her heart cried out with unspeakable fear, she could not keep herself from cupping his face in one hand while her other hand slid over his hair.

"*You should not be here, my darling,*" she told him, unable to pull herself away. "*So much danger lies in wait for you.*" A sob erupted from her throat, and she drew closer to place a soft kiss on his parted lips. "*Although I am no longer in body, the feelings I hold for you are as strong as though I never left this plane.*"

At that moment, Jack ran a hand over his hair and down his face. Chandra drew in her breath. "*He felt my touch.*" She twined her arms around her body in euphoric glee. "*He felt my touch,*" she laughed into the air.

"*If you choose to ignore my words, he will soon feel mine.*"

"*You will not harm him, Rafael!*"

He stood, transferring his thoughts into her mind. *"Take heart, Chandra. If all goes well, as I am sure it will, in no time at all, you will have your lover on the same plane you are. Won't that be cozy?"* His deep laugh echoed inside her head.

"If you touch him, I promise you I will destroy this house and everyone in it!"

"We both know that is an idle threat. You have given your soul to the light side, Chandra. Once you have done that, you are restricted from destroying anything or anyone." He sauntered towards her.

"You underestimate the strength of the light side." She forced herself to remain standing before him. *"The forces of evil have no defense against the Legion of Light."*

"Are you willing to take that chance?" His smoky gaze challenged her. *"Before you or anyone you call on can move to save him, I can destroy him! Think about my words, Chandra!"*

Chandra stepped forward. *"I lived my life controlled by Jonathan to protect Jack. I refuse to do it again! Make your choice, Rafael. You can reside on this plane. Or, you can be taken to the plane set aside for dark entities. Hopefully, you will find your son, who, I am sure, misses you greatly!"*

Rafael's steps faltered. *"You dare to threaten me?"*

"You know I can do what I say! Spirits from the light will come when they are called. I will call them, Rafael!"

He stared at her, his cold eyes mere slits in a mask of hatred as he tried to leash his anger. Then, as though she posed no threat at all, he became calm, and his voice slid over her in a whisper. *"I will grant you this victory, Chandra. For now, the man you chose over my son will remain safe."*

She did not trust him. She knew from living her days with Jonathan how fast he could change. Chandra listened as Rafael spoke to Jack and Donavan then beckoned them to follow him.

She had to think of some way to get Jack out of this house. His very life depended on it.

Without warning, the words she had said to Rafael slammed into her mind. 'Spirits from the light will come when they are called.' Of course! He would wait until he had Jack alone.

When she could not call on the spirits for help!"

He felt her touch once. Maybe she could make him feel her touch again. Without stopping to think, she moved across the floor to where Jack walked through the house with Donavan. She reached out, running one hand over his face. He did not respond. She tried again but knew he no longer felt her presence.

"Jack," she screamed into the silence, "*you must leave here. Your life is in danger!*"

"*He cannot hear you, Chandra.*" Rafael's voice broke into her thoughts. "*He is too intent on finding the ones who fed our needs to hear you.*" His laughter swelled until she placed her hands over her ears, trying to shut out his intrusion into her mind.

"*You are powerless, Chandra. He will not always be where you can protect him. See? Even now, the darkness follows him, waiting to swallow him up.*"

A dark shadow entwined itself around Jack, covering him until she could no longer see him. "*No!*" she screamed, running forward.

Jack lay on the cold floor gasping for breath, his hands clawing at his throat as Donavan tried to help him.

"Jack!" Donavan tried to remove his hands from his throat. "What the hell's wrong? Call an ambulance!" he shouted to the men standing nearby. "He can't breathe!"

Then as Donavan knelt by his side, Jack dropped his hands from his throat and stood up. "What's goin' on?" His voice sounded strong as he looked around.

"What's going on?" Donavan stared at him in amazement. "Are you telling me you don't remember grabbing your throat and falling to the floor?"

"No," Jack answered on a nervous laugh that ended as he glanced over at the men huddled around him. "Is this some kinda joke?"

"No, Jack. You almost took a ride with the paramedics."

"All right, if you say so. I sure as hell don't remember any of it."

"Do you want to go home and rest, or can you finish with

what we came here to do?"

"I already told you. I'm okay. Let's get to it."

Seeing Jack walking and talking with no lasting effects of what he had been through, Chandra once again turned her attention to the white spirits she had called upon. She sent them a thank you as they bound the dark entity in bands of shimmering white to propel it over to the dark side.

"*Do you see how easy it can happen, Chandra?*" Rafael moved to stand beside her.

"*Yes, I do.*" She looked up at him. "*And now you know how easy you can be thwarted in your attempts to harm someone whose soul is protected by the light.*"

"*Bravo, Chandra. Bravo.*" He allowed her a slight nod. "*You won a small victory. However, I would not get too optimistic. There will be another time. I promise you. A time of my choosing.*" He left her to think on his words as he followed behind the two men whose very presence filled him with killing anger.

Chandra knew that for now, they had won. But if she wanted to keep Jack safe, she had to go to the one person he would listen to. Before she left, she surrounded Jack, Donavan and the other men in the house with the White Light of the Holy Spirit. Then she surrounded Lawrence and Rafael with the light to bind them from doing harm while the men searched in vain for the bodies of two souls already safe in the Holy Light of Home.

CHAPTER SEVEN

Standing in the kitchen after a thorough search of the upstairs, Donavan spoke with Blain. "Magnum get any hits?"

"Not even one. Those kids never made it to the inside. At least, not upstairs." He massaged the dog's ears, patted his head. "I about shit when he went after Hindel!"

"You and me both! I recall one of the other K-9s reacting the same way to Quigly when we searched for the missing Stewart girl." Donavan drew his thumb and forefinger over his dark brown mustache. A habit he employed when his nerves strayed to overload. "I've heard dogs can see things we can't. Almost makes you a believer. Don't it?"

Blain pulled the dog closer as his eyes darted around the well-furnished house. "After what we went through with Jonathan, there ain't much I don't believe anymore."

"No shit! I didn't expect to find anything here. If we're going to find any trace of them, I think our best bet will be down in the basement." He glanced over Blain's shoulder to see Lawrence and Rafael standing off to the side, and he motioned them forward. "I want you both to wait upstairs while we conduct our investigation." The tone of his voice warning against any argument. "The dog doesn't like you, Mr. Hindel. I feel your presence will hinder the search."

Lawrence spoke up, voicing his unwillingness to hand over control. "This is my home, Lieutenant Hays. Anything you do will be under our watchful eye."

"I don't think so," Donavan said. "You see," he held up the four-page warrant, "this gives me the right to search your house, your cave and your grounds without you being present." Donavan grinned into the faces of the two men glaring at him. "Oh! And lest I forget! This little document," he smacked the papers, "also includes Quigly's house. Or I should say, Quigly's former house since he isn't with us anymore."

Walking down the basement steps, Donavan tried to hold on to his reason for being there. He refused to allow the memories of another time to enter in as he waited for the rest of the men to get there. To busy his mind, he looked around the large room taking in the familiar, top-of-the-line washer and dryer. Then he read the name brands of wash-detergent, bleach and fabric softener. "No generic brands for Lawrence Hindel"

"Looks like Master Lawrence has been a busy little housekeeper." Jack rumpled through a stack of folded clothes atop the dryer. "Guess we interrupted him on laundry day. Otherwise, prissy as he is, all these clothes would be put away in their little drawers and these," he ran a hand down the creased slacks already placed on hangers, "would be hung in the closet by now."

"Do you believe this?" Blain took down an expensive silk shirt. "He hangs his shirts on satin-covered hangers!"

"Oh yeah, he's a fastidious little prick. Good Christ," Jack blew out a breath, "I think we just passed weird and jumped straight into sick!" Jack unfolded a stack of under-shorts. "He even makes sure his underwear are all facin' in the same direction."

"He's a creature of habit, Jack. Although I have to agree with you on the shorts. The way he has them all lined out like that borders on O.C.D.," Donavan said.

"O.C. what?"

"Obsessive-Compulsive Disorder. A person with O.C.D. does everything the same way every time. For example, take the laundry. It wouldn't matter whose laundry he did. Each piece would smell the same, be folded the same way — and they would all have the same creases in the pants. Some people wash their hands ten times after they use the bathroom. Not nine, not eleven, but ten. The list goes on and on. It's a ritual, and try as they may, they can't deviate from that ritual. At any rate," Donavan ran his thumb and forefinger over his mustache, then, noticing what he had done, slapped his hands together. "I guess we've had enough psychology for today. Jack, if you're through playing with Lawrence's under-shorts, I suggest we get started on what we came here for."

"Fuck you, Donavan!" Jack snickered then became serious as they each turned towards some large shelves. Knowing behind those shelves, placed in an innocent manner against one wall, they would find a passageway leading to an underwater cave.

"I see the smoke and mirrors have been repaired and are back in good standing order." Donavan stood looking at the floor-to-ceiling shelves. "Wonder why he put them back up? The secret is out."

"Maybe they hold the key to another secret." Jack leaned over to run a hand beneath and to the side of each shelf.

"What's the matter?" Donavan moved closer. "Can't you find the mechanism? If I remember right, we couldn't find it the last time we looked for it."

"Just because Jonathan knew we were onto him and removed it. If you think back, you'll recall soon after Seelah told us 'bout the secret passageway we came in here with the wrecking crew to tear down the wall. For all his faults, you gotta give him credit. He was very thorough."

Donavan laid down flat on the floor and shone a light beneath the shelves. "Maybe too thorough. I'll tell you one goddamn thing. If I find another long black hair, I'm sticking this one up my ass until I can place it in the hands of the forensic team myself!" Donavan grabbed hold of the side of the shelves to hoist himself to his feet. "If we'd been able to have that hair analyzed, we would have known about Jonathan Hindel bein' a werewolf months before it came to light. Not to mention all the danger to each and every one of our men throughout that goddamn fiasco!"

"Shit happens, Donavan, even in the best of crime labs." He straightened up, wiped his hands on the seat of his jeans. "I can't find it."

"All right," Donavan mopped a handkerchief across his face, "here's what we're going to do. We got a warrant to search the cave. Right?"

"Yeah. So?"

"If Lawrence removed the mechanism so no one can get into the cave, then he's in direct violation of a court order. Now, he has two choices. One, he can come up with a way we can get into the cave! Or, choice number two, we can call out the wrecking crew and take down this whole son of a bitch, again!"

"I opt for choice number two!" Jack had already keyed his radio when Donavan jerked it away.

"It's not that easy, Jack. We have to give him his options first! Otherwise, he can sue the department for undue force and destruction of private property."

"God!" Jack threw up his hands. "I hate it when you insist on fuckin' everything up with logic!"

"Goes with the position, partner." Donavan grinned, handed him back the radio.

"Can you do me one small favor, though?" Jack looked at him with all the innocence of a small boy asking for his favorite toy.

"If I can," Donavan indulged him.

"Let me be the one to give Lawrence his options."

"I can do that. If…and I stress the word "if," you can give him his options in a professional, make-the-department-proud way. Can you do that?"

"Hell yes, I can do that! Fuckin'-a!" He rubbed his hands together in glee. "This is gonna be good!"

"Jack and I won't be long." He turned to the other deputies as Jack scurried to the stairs. "You can guard the shelves while we're gone," he told them as he saw their look of disappointment.

Lawrence and Rafael looked up from where they sat at the kitchen table, enjoying a cup of coffee when Donavan and Jack walked through the basement door.

"Are we to assume the investigation of the cave is finished already?" Rafael spoke up.

"No," Jack told him. "We've run into a slight snag."

"Oh? And what might that be?" Rafael spooned sugar into his cup, stirred the creamed brew.

"It seems, and I'm not going to point the finger," Jack hastened to add, "someone has taken it upon himself to remove the mechanism that opens the barrier to the cave." In a dramatic gesture, Jack tapped an impatient finger against his forehead, "Who in the world would do such a mean-spirited thing?"

Donavan sat down at the table. "Lawrence, do you think I could have a cup of coffee?" He watched as Lawrence jumped to his feet to fetch a cup from the cupboard. "Better bring two. Jack's a coffee drinker, too."

"To answer your question, Jack, I have no idea who would remove a mechanism. That is if such a thing ever existed. Do you know what Jack is talking about, Lawrence?"

The fragile china cups rattled, and he placed them on the table. "No, unless my father removed it. In which case, I would assume, the entrance to the cave is forever closed."

"There you have it, detectives. Your mystery has been solved with no harm done." Rafael smiled up at Jack.

"Oh...shit." Donavan dropped his head onto his chest.

"You're right. No harm's been done." Jack plopped himself down in one of the chairs, leaned in close to gaze into Rafael's scowling face. "You're gonna wanna stay with me on this, pal, 'cause, here's the kicker! We have a warrant, sayin' we have a right to investigate the cave. Except now, we find we have no way to get into the cave. Because it seems someone has removed the little mechanism that opens the barrier." Jack wiped a hand across his forehead. "We can't ignore a search warrant. I mean... that...just...would...not...be...." He looked to Donavan. "Help me out here, Detective Hays."

"Under penal code RCL61625 anyone, who does not adhere to said direction of said signed search warrant, is in direct dereliction of said search warrant under the law." Donavan sipped at his coffee.

"That's right." Jack shot a quick glance across the table. "You can see our dilemma. If we ignore a court order, which the signed search warrant is, then we can end up getting in trouble ourselves for breaking the law. I'm sure you don't want that to happen. Now, I am going to give you two choices for what you, Lawrence, since this is your house, can do. One, you can tell me how we can get into the cave via a key, another mechanism that can be attached to the shelves, or...whatever way you have. If you refuse or cannot give us a way to gain entrance, then we will have to go with option two."

"What is option two?" Rafael spoke up, his demeanor on the subject no longer calm.

"With option two, we bring in a wrecking crew and take down the shelves! Again!" Jack didn't disguise the elation in his voice. "I say again, in case no one enlightened you about the last time we investigated a murder here. We had to take down the shelves then, too."

"If you need a few moments to confer, Jack and I will wait in the other room." Donavan pushed back his chair.

"Yes, thank you, Detective Hays. Lawrence and I would appreciate a few moments alone to talk about this."

"Jack." Donavan motioned him down the hall.

"What do you think they'll do?"

"Depends on what means they've been using to get in and out of the cave."

"You're pretty quick on your feet." Jack rapped him on the shoulder. "You rattled them penal codes off so quick you had me thinkin' we had all the bases covered!"

At Jack's words, Donavan keyed his radio. "This is Detective Hays. I need backup at the Hindel Mansion. I want four cars with four officers in each. Also, I want another K-9 unit with at least five dogs." Donavan glanced at Jack. "We don't have enough men to secure the grounds and, for damn sure, the underwater cave if they try moving anyone who is inside."

"Better call in Search and Rescue, too!"

"Add Search and Rescue to that request," Donavan told dispatch.

"I don't know how the hell we missed that." Jack craned his neck to peek around the corner. "They're still sittin' at the table."

"Everyone's on the way. Depending on the answer we get from the other room, we may be adding a wrecking crew to the list."

"One thing's for sure they can't move anyone in or out of this place now.

"I guess we better call home and let everyone know we're going to be late. In fact, I think since we don't know what we're dealing with here, you should have Seelah go over to my place until we know more."

"Good idea!" He reached for his cell phone. "I can't get the feelin' outta my head we're right back to a year ago."

"I hate to admit it, but I'm starting to feel the same way. I pray to God we aren't stepping into another nightmare."

"Detective Hays," Rafael stepped into the entry hall, "could we speak with you for a moment?"

"I guess the time has come to see which door we're gonna choose." Jack followed behind, shoving the cell phone back in his pocket.

"I don't mean to be rude, Jack," he said over his shoulder as he walked back to take a seat at the table," but Lawrence and I would prefer to speak with Detective Hays alone."

"No can do, Rafael. If you read the warrant, it states Detective Hays *and* Detective Olivier' will be conducting the search." Jack gave him a sorry-to-disappoint-you look. "Now, what's it gonna be, option one or option two?"

"Neither. You see, the problem isn't that we don't want you to have access to the cave. The problem is in the fact that we don't have the mechanism. I guess whoever removed it destroyed it." Rafael watched anger spread up Jack's face and tried to control his pleasure at causing that anger.

"Oops!" Jack lifted the kitchen curtain, looked outside as he heard the sound of vehicles coming up the driveway. "Yep, the gang's all here."

"As a precaution, I thought it best to have Search and Rescue on hand in case, maybe, the missing teens found their way to the underwater cave," Donavan told him. "Now, I guess we add a wrecking crew to that list." He reached for his radio."

"I forbid you to destroy anything on this estate!" An irate Rafael Hindel jumped to his feet. "If you do, I will bring suit for the destruction of property against your entire department! Do I make myself clear, Detective Hays?"

Donavan held up his hand as Jack reached behind him for his gun. "I *can* have the shelves removed, Mr. Hindel, and I will unless you produce something to gain us entrance to that cave. Just saying you don't have the mechanism isn't enough to stop an investigation." He stepped forward. "Do you have the mechanism, or don't you?"

"My grandfather has told you, we do not. What we can do is go into town and buy a mechanism, bring it back here and install it. As you can see, this will all take time. What we want to purpose is you delay your search until tomorrow morning. At that time, everything will be ready, and you can enter the cave. There is no need to destroy my property, Detective Hays."

"Nice try, Junior, except it won't work." Jack draped an arm around Lawrence's shoulders, grinned when Lawrence tried to pull away. "The search warrant's only good for the time specified. See, if they issued warrants at the assailant's request, a lotta valuable evidence would just go 'poof.'" Jack flipped open his hand.

Donavan wasted no time requesting a wrecking crew. "Jack, go out front and tell Blain, when the wrecking crew gets here, to bring them downstairs. In the meantime, have him get the K-9s started on the grounds." He turned, walked to the basement stairs.

***

When he heard the front door slam, Lawrence turned to

Rafael. "What are we going to do?"

"Leave everything to me, Lawrence. They won't find anything of importance."

"But…where will everyone go?" His thin arms flailed the air in his frenzy. "They have no place to go!"

"Everyone will be fine, Lawrence. I did not come all this way to have everything ruined." Rafael pulled him into his arms. "You are safe. All our people are safe. You must learn to trust me."

"Yes, Grandfather." Lawrence leaned into his arms.

For a few moments longer, Jack remained standing around the corner. When the voices in the kitchen remained silent, he let himself out the front door.

CHAPTER EIGHT

Chandra stood in the bright nursery watching as Seelah folded each tiny undershirt to place it in the small chest.

"*Seelah,*" Chandra spoke into the silence.

Startled, Seelah looked up. "*Chandra. How long have you been standing there?*"

"*Not long. I am sorry if I frightened you.*" She walked over and, seating herself in a small rocker, picked up one of the shirts to hold it to her nose. "*You must have sprinkled this shirt with powder already.*"

Seelah laughed. "*I couldn't wait. I love the smells of lotion and baby powder. Jack says I'll keep him so clean I'll wash away the good germs right along with the bad.*"

"*Jack's son,*" she whispered.

Seelah got to her feet and, bending over, took Chandra into her arms. "*I'm sorry if this upsets you. I know how much you loved Jack.*"

"No," Chandra shook her head, "*I am not upset because you are having Jack's son. I am just happy he is having the life I could never give him.*"

"*Is this why you're here to talk about the baby?*"

"*No, Seelah. I am here to talk with you about Jack.*"

Seelah felt her heart leap, and she sat down on the twin-size bed. "*What about him?*"

"*Jack is in danger. He and Donavan Hays are at the Hindel*

Mansion right now serving a search warrant. A young boy and girl partying at the mansion have disappeared. Jack and Donavan believe they are still on the estate."

"*Are they, Chandra?"* Seelah looked at her.

"*I cannot speak of that right now.*" Chandra turned away, unable to look at her. "*A lot of things are happening I am unable to talk about. I am asking you to trust me."*

"*Are we back to dealing with the same evil as Jonathan?"* Seelah picked up a small blue gown to hold it to her face. The smell from the tiny garment gave her a modicum of comfort. "*We are going to be bringing our son into this world soon."* Without warning, hot anger pushed its way into her thoughts, and she swiped hot tears from her face. "*Chandra, I know how much you love Jack. I want to be sure you won't put his son in needless danger by keeping silent on what is happening at the mansion!"*

"*The child you carry in your womb is not just Jack's son, Seelah. He is your son. You have always been a friend to me. I do not forget a kindness. I must leave, but before I go, I want you to talk with Jack about the danger he is placing himself in by going to the mansion. You must keep him away from there."*

"*Chandra, I need to know one thing before you go."*

"*If I can tell you, I will."*

"*Jack says Lawrence's grandfather is living at the mansion. Is this man dangerous?"*

Chandra closed her eyes for a brief moment on memories of the past. "*I know everyone thinks Lawrence is responsible for all the wrong doings at the mansion now, but they are wrong. Rafael Hindel is the man Jack and Donavan must be aware of. They are the reason he has returned to the mansion. He holds them responsible for the death of his son. Even though I am the one who saw to his destruction."* She recalled their earlier confrontation and shuttered. "*When a man is as evil as Rafael, he can be a very formidable enemy. Please heed my warning, Seelah. I want you to be safe in the life you and Jack have entered into. For your sake and for the sake of your child, don't stay alone."*

Seelah's mind flashed back to another time she had been

warned against evil. If Donavan and Jack had not insisted she stay the night with Donavan and his family, she would not be here now. *"Are you saying this Rafael will try to harm us?"*

"This is a vendetta against Jack, Donavan and everyone in their family." She watched as color vanished from Seelah's face, but she could not stop her words. *"Until this debt is paid, he will not stop."*

"Oh my god!" Seelah cried, clutching her stomach in an attempt to protect her unborn child. *"I have to tell Jack and Donavan about this."* She reached for the phone as Chandra placed a hand on her shoulder.

"Tell Jack the bodies of the teenagers will not be found. Tell the families of the children their souls are safe in the light of home."

When Seelah looked up, Chandra had already gone. Knowing she had no time to lose, she punched in Jack's cell number.

CHAPTER NINE

"Looks like someone has been living here." Donavan kicked his way through the rubble of dirty laundry and soiled plates. "In fact, I'd venture to guess four or five people have been living here."

"Sure don't look like it did when Jonathan lived here."

"This doesn't bode well, Jack. If Lawrence has people living in here, then they must be connected to him somehow." Donavan tried to slow down his breathing as tension mounted. "Touchy as he is about anyone setting foot on his property, these people would almost have to be related."

"First the grandfather and now what…aunts, uncles and cousins? Ah, Jesus Christ!" Jack ran both hands through his hair. "I just had a terrible thought! We know about Jonathan Hindel bein' a goddamn werewolf! What if the people livin' here are werewolves!"

"Shut up, Jack! I don't need those kinds of thoughts running through my mind right now!"

"No, listen, goddamn it!" Jack refused to back off. "None of the people Jonathan attacked, other than Paulson, turned into werewolves! So what the hell does that leave? I'll tell you what it leaves. The people he attacked did not have to become werewolves because he already has a whole goddamn family of the furry fuckers."

"Jack, you're not making any sense! Whole families of

werewolves? Where the hell do you come up with this shit?"

"Go ahead and laugh, Donavan. But when this town starts losin' loved ones, don't say I didn't warn you!"

"All right, consider me warned. Right now, I suggest we get busy doing what we came here to do." He looked at the men standing off to the side, their faces covered in disbelief at what they heard. "Anything you hear does not leave this cave," he warned them. "Blain, get Magnum over here." Donavan shone his flashlight on the floor, looking for any sign the two teenagers may have been there. "I'm not seeing any blood. That's got to be a good sign."

"He's not gettin' anything," Blain said, pulling the dog to his side. "I guess now we get started on Quigley's place. Right?"

"Yeah." Donavan attached the flashlight to his belt. "How are the other dogs doing on the grounds?"

"I didn't have much chance to observe their reaction. They just got started when the wreckin' crew showed up."

"Don't get me wrong. I'm glad we didn't find anything here. However, you can bet your ass Lawrence Hindel is going to hand the department a hefty bill for our destroying his wall. Again."

"Fuck Hindel!" Jack said as they walked up the stairs. "If he'd told us the shelves could be activated by remote control, there wouldn't have been a need for a wreckin' crew. The department's not liable for shit! 'Sides that, I'll let you in on a little secret. Lawrence and grandpa got some explainin' to do. I overheard a conversation before I went outside earlier."

"Whatever it is, it can wait until we're out of here," Donavan said as they walked into the kitchen to find an anxious Lawrence and Rafael waiting for them.

"I understand your search of the cave proved futile, Detective Hays," Rafael said. "I hope you realize the sheriff's department is liable for the cost of repairing the shelves your crew destroyed. I will be sure they are made aware of the fact I tried to tell you there wasn't anything of importance there."

"Nothing except a remote-controlled panel to activate

the shelves and…the fact a lot of people seem to have taken up residence in there," Donavan said.

"Oh! Did I forget to mention the remote-controlled panel?" Rafael scratched his head. "I guess my memory must be getting foggy. In that case, I will forget about sending your department a bill for the destruction of the shelves."

"You do that." Jack came up beside him. "See, you're not as slick as you think you are. 'Cause the day I listen to you, 'bout ignorin' potential evidence? Will be the day the Saint Anthony Parish Sheriff's Department writes me off for good."

"All in good time, Jack." Rafael gazed into Jack's face. "All in good time."

Tension, fear and an unrelenting feeling everything was about to erupt into a hellish nightmare met head-on in a burst of out-of-control rage! "Now you listen to me, you smug mother-fucker!" Jack grabbed Rafael up by his throat. "You don't threaten me! I know you're an evil son-of-a-bitch. Fact, I would almost bet you're the same evil piece of piss as your son!" Jack shook a finger inches from Rafael's face. "I'm givin' you fair warnin' right here right now! You stay the fuck away from me! You got that?" Jack shoved the older man away from him.

Donavan remained silent, wanting to see Rafael's reaction to Jack's outburst. What he saw made him turn to walk out of the house.

"I know!" Jack put up his hands as Donavan walked towards him. "I lost it. Bastard made me lose all control. I hope you're not waitin' for an apology 'cause it'll be a cold day in the depths of hell when you get it!"

"Let's get away from the house." Donavan kept walking. "I saw something I don't believe!"

"What?" Jack quickened his steps.

"When you turned away after shoving Rafael back in his chair, I saw his eyes glow like red hot coals!" Donavan inhaled, trying to slow down his racing pulse. "Jesus Christ and all that's holy! I think we got another Jonathan Hindel on our hands!"

"Then let's go back in right now and shoot the son of a

bitch!" Jack turned on his heel.

"We can't shoot him! If I thought we could get away with it, we would! But it's broad daylight, and we're surrounded by cops!" His words slid to a stop as he grabbed his radio to answer a call. "Yeah, go ahead," he spoke into the mike.

"We found something you need to see, Donavan," Blain came back to him. "We're at the lake."

"We're on our way!" Donavan shut off the radio.

"What the hell's goin' on now?"

"Let's go. I think we may have found the kids!"

"Or at least what's left of them."

"What is it?" Donavan called out as they neared the water.

"We got some clothes here," Blain told him as the two detectives walked up to them. "I gotta tell you, though, something ain't right."

Donavan and Jack looked to the ground to see two sets of clothing scattered amidst the reeds.

"No shit, somethin' ain't right!" Jack bent over to get a closer look. "Nobody yanked these clothes off in a fit of passion or to go skinny-dippin'. Somebody tossed them here to make it look that way!"

Donavan lifted the camera he had slung around his neck, clicked off pictures of the clothing at different angles. Aware of a sweet fragrance, he leaned inward towards the clothes. With care, he picked up a green pullover top by its outer edges, sniffed and then held the top upward. "Take a whiff of this and tell me where you've smelled it before."

"Lawrence Hindel's basement," Jack said as Donavan moved the top back and forth beneath his nose. "Stupid fuck even left the creases."

"Obsessive-Compulsive-Disorder, better known as OCD. Just like I said."

"We got the mother-fucker, Donavan!" Jack smacked a fist into his other hand. "Let's see how cocky he is when he's got the cuffs on!"

"We can't arrest him, Jack."

Jack's head swung upward. "What the hell do you mean we can't arrest him? We got him cold!"

"We got a theory. The best we can do right now is get a sample of the detergent and the fabric softener used on the clothes. Without positive ID, we can't even say these clothes belong to the missing teens."

"Bullshit! You know these clothes belong to the missin' kids!"

"Yeah, I do, but just because I know what the girl wore. Most of all, those." He nodded towards a pair of light green sandals lying half-hidden in the weeds.

Jack grabbed his phone, checked the caller ID. "Hey babe, listen, I don't mean to cut you short, but we're right in the middle of checkin' some evidence we just turned up, so let me call you a little later." About to shut off the phone, he heard an anxious Seelah scream his name. "All right, what is it?"

When Jack remained silent for a few moments, Donavan glanced at him, then straightened up. "What's going on?"

Jack put up a hand. When he ended the conversation, he stood for a moment, not saying anything."

"What's going on?" Donavan grabbed his arm. "She's not going into labor, is she?"

"No. Seems she had an unexpected visitor today who's got her upset 'bout my bein' here. Some of the things she said are pretty strange, but we'll go into all that later." He dropped the phone back in his pocket.

"If you want to go home, I can finish out the search."

Jack shook his head. "Thanks, but tell you the truth, I feel better bein' here. Least this way, I know Rafael Hindel's not stalkin' our families."

"Okay, if you're sure. Tom," he turned to one of the deputies standing nearby, "go up to my jeep and get some evidence bags. We'll get all this bagged, then finish up the grounds. After that, we can start on the cottage."

While they waited for the deputy to return with the bags, Jack motioned Donavan off to the side. "Chandra came to visit

Seelah earlier."

"That had to be interesting."

"To say the least." Jack glanced around to make sure no one could overhear them. "Seems Chandra filled her in on our good buddy, Rafael."

"Did she say if he's a werewolf?" The words flew out of his throat before he could stop them.

"She didn't come right out and say it, but the way she described him, even if he ain't a werewolf, he's got evil covered so good he can do as much destruction as Jonathan on his best day!"

"What else did she say?"

"That Rafael came here to destroy you, me and everyone in our families for our part in losin' him his son."

"That sick piece of puke!" Donavan whirled, unsure which to grab first his gun or his radio. In the end, he grabbed neither. "What the hell are we going to do about this? We can't shoot the prick! What reason am I going to give? The spirit of a voodoo priestess told your wife Rafael Hindel is out to get us? I can't even arrest him."

"I don't know what we're gonna do. I do know I want to finish up here. Let's get started on the cottage. Maybe the dogs'll pick up somethin' we can use against these assholes so we can run' em in."

When nothing turned up during the search of the cottage, Donavan knew they had done all they could for the time being. Anxious to be home with his loved ones, he called a halt to the search.

"Let's go get a sample of the detergent and fabric softener. I want everything bagged, sealed, signed, dated and kept within our sights until we get it into the evidence room. I intend to lock the goddamn door myself, so when the Hindels are arrested, their lawyer can't even hint at the chain-of-command being broken on this one!"

"Sounds like you got it handled. First thing tomorrow morning, we can get it sent off to the lab, then it will be outta our hands."

"After we get the paperwork out of the way, we can head home. I think you should pick up Seelah and stay with us until we get a handle on all this."

"Yeah, Chandra told Seelah she shouldn't be alone 'til this nightmare's over."

With the detergent and softener bagged and logged with the rest of the evidence collected from the estate, Jack unlocked the passenger's door. He bent over to slide into the jeep when a movement caught his eye. He straightened back up and, turning, looked straight into the face of the man watching them from the living room window. To Donavan's disbelief, Jack raised a lone finger to his brow to snap off a farewell salute.

***

As the detectives and their men drove away, Rafael let the curtain slip from his hand. "After its dark, we will send everyone back to the cave. I don't trust the police not to leave someone behind to watch our movements."

"They aren't safe here, Grandfather. Hays and Olivier' know they are here." Lawrence paced the floor. "What are we going to do? They know about the kids being here." His childish voice rose in fear. "We should have hidden the clothes."

"They already knew about the young people being on the estate." He tried to stay patient, but Lawrence's nonstop pacing and screeching grated on his already overtaxed nerves. "They had to be made to think they drown or that the alligators destroyed them. That is why I had you throw their clothing around in the reeds." Rafael kneaded the back of his neck, trying to relax the taut muscles and ease the dull pain gaining strength at the base of his skull.

"I made sure the dogs couldn't find anything on the clothing." Lawrence halted his pacing for a moment. "I knew you would want me to do that."

A gateway between agony and reason swung open, allowing Lawrence's words to slam into his mind. "What are you telling me, Lawrence?"

"I washed the children's clothing before scattering them in the reeds." A childish giggle bubbled out into the quiet. "I washed them twice and used a softener to be sure there would be no evidence left."

"Tell me you are making this up, Lawrence." Rafael turned, his hands reaching out for him. "Tell me you are not stupid enough to have washed the clothes."

"I...I...thought that is what you would want me to do," he stammered. "There...they...had blood...."

Pain and rage fused together in a shimmering red haze blocking everything from his mind except the need to silence the one standing before him.

"Rafael...Rafael..." his name echoed again and again through the long tunnel of his senses until, at last, it burst through the haze. Rafael dropped his hands, shook himself to dispel the coldness numbing his mind. "What are you doing here, Rolan? You should have remained in the cottage until Lawrence came for you."

"If I had not come in when I did, Lawrence would not have come for anyone!" The tall young man with thick red hair and blue eyes stood beside him. "You should see to him, Rafael."

Rafael turned. He could see Lawrence lying on the floor, and he bent down to shake him. "Get up, Lawrence. I have need of you." When Lawrence remained unmoving, Rafael yanked him to his feet. "You have been a complete and utter fool. However, you are still of my blood." He turned Lawrence's face to the side where a dark, blue and red bruise encircled his throat. "You will need to put ice on this bruise. Otherwise, it will be noticeable. I will not tolerate questions about how the bruise got there."

"Yes, Grandfather," Lawrence whispered before walking away.

"I hope everyone got out of sight when the police checked the cottage." Rafael's gaze lingered on the man making his way across the floor.

"Yes. We got a little worried when we heard the dogs sniffing at the walls, but since all the police saw is a wall filled with adornments, they ignored the dogs. How wise of Lawrence to install a secret panel."

Rafael whirled to face him. "Lawrence had nothing to do with the secret panels being set in place throughout the estate. Do you think he would know how to do something that complicated?" His arrogant gaze skimmed over the man. "Jonathan, himself, put that panel and other panels in the house and cottage during the slave era."

"He used it to hide runaway slaves?" His dark brows lifted. "That's a side of Jonathan I never knew.

The smile Rafael turned on him held little humor. "It had many purposes. However, saving runaways from their rightful masters is not one my son went out of his way to entertain." The smile left his face to be replaced with a look of deep concentration. "The love I hold in my heart for Jonathan has no equal. Although, the burden he has left me with is one I am not sure I can carry."

"Grandfather." Lawrence came forward. "What can I do to make up for displeasing you?"

"There is nothing you can do, Lawrence." He did not trust himself to turn around. "The damage has already been done."

"They obtained the evidence today, so they haven't had a chance to have it analyzed yet." His voice sounded stronger now. "Why can't we get the evidence back before anything can be done with it?

"How do you propose we do this, Lawrence? The evidence will be held in an evidence room in the sheriff's department." His voice filled with the same controlled anger as before. "We can't stroll through the front door and request they give up their evidence."

"No, I realize that, but we can walk through the back door." He found it hard to contain his excitement.

"The back door to a police station is secured with a code that no one except working officers are privy to. I realize you are trying to help, but please, leave me to figure this out in silence!" His voice rose with his anger, and he walked a short distance away to put some much needed space between himself and the man pushing him over the edge of his patience.

"Grandfather! Listen to me. Please!" He waited until Rafael turned to face him before continuing with what he believed to be the answer to their problem. "You said, the officers, entering the station through the back entrance, have to enter in a code. Am I right?"

Rafael simply nodded.

"All right! All you need to do is wait outside the back entrance until an officer comes up to the door and listens as he punches in the code. With your ability to hear high-pitched sounds, you will be able to detect each number as it is fed into the system. Each number will give off a certain pitch." His voice trailed off as he saw Rafael's brows lift, then relax with understanding.

"I can write down each number as I hear it," he whispered the words, then shook his head. "That will get us inside. However, we will still have the locked evidence door to contend with."

"The locked door should not present a problem, Rafael," Rolan spoke up. "A small pocket knife would take care of that problem."

Rafael and Lawrence turned to look at him at the same time — and a grin broke out over Lawrence's face.

"Of course!" His thin face showed his enthusiasm. "The narrow blade of a pocket knife can be worked in between the door and the jam to slide back the bolt."

"I've never tried it, but if you can show me how it works, then perhaps some of our problems will be behind us."

"That won't be necessary, Rafael. I will be the one to enter the back door. And the evidence room," Rolan told him. "Don't you agree that of the three of us, I am the most qualified?"

"Of the three of us?" Rafael cocked his head, looked at him. "Are you trying to say something, Rolan?"

"Just that of the three of us, Lawrence would be the first one they would suspect. After Lawrence, you would be the next one they would look to. If you both have an alibi that cannot, in any way, be broken, they would be left with no one from this

estate to suspect. Am I right?"
        "When do you want to go?"

CHAPTER TEN

Without being obvious, Seelah watched as Jack continued to sip from his bottle of beer.

"Jack, are you going to join us tonight or just sit there drinking beer?"

"What?" He turned, anxious to go back to the thoughts running through his mind.

"I asked if you are going to join us tonight."

He looked around to see Donavan and Barbara staring at him.

"Sorry."

"Yeah," Seelah said, with no hint of anger in her voice. "Since we all know what is bothering you, why don't we talk about it? Barbara and I know better than to discuss anything that's said outside the house."

"You already know, pretty much, everything that's going on." Donavan shook a cigarette from the pack on the end table. "First thing tomorrow morning, we'll get the evidence sent off to the lab. If the lab report comes back testing positive for the detergent and softener, as we already know it's going to, then we're well on our way to getting rid of the Hindels."

Jack grabbed the empty beer bottle off the coffee table, lunged to his feet. "You know that is never gonna happen, Donavan. And I'll tell you why. The plain simple truth is the Hindels can't be destroyed. They're like roaches! It don't matter how many times you step on them or shoot them, or burn them up until there ain't nothin' left, they just keep comin' back! So don't spin us a fantasy on bestin' the Hindels, 'cause, like I said, it ain't gonna happen." He stomped past Donavan's chair on his way to the kitchen.

"I'm sorry," Seelah said. "You know he doesn't behave like this."

Donavan waved away her apology. "He's a married man with a baby on the way. Rafael saying he's out to destroy everyone has him uptight. I think he's acting pretty normal."

"Do you think we should be worried, Donavan?" Seelah asked, then reached for the ringing telephone. "Hello. Yes, he's right here." She held out the phone to Donavan.

"Lieutenant Hays," he spoke into the receiver, his gruff voice softening as he heard the voice on the other line. "No, I haven't forgotten about you, Christina. I planned to give you a call in the morning. No, now's fine." He gave Barbara a sheepish grin. "We found some clothing on the estate I think belonged to your daughter and the boy she went out with." He paused to listen for a moment before continuing. "I can't say for sure if the clothes belong to Tina, but...." His voice trailed off as she interrupted him. "Yes, we can do that. What time do you want to meet us? Eight o'clock will be fine. Alright, Christina, I'll see you then." He hung up the phone. "Tina Crawford's mother wants to meet us at the station in the morning to identify the clothes."

Jack sat down on the couch beside Seelah and, after taking a long pull off his beer, reached out to take her hand. "Sorry 'bout spoutin' off like that. I guess havin' all this open up again has me a little spooked."

"It has us all spooked, Jack," Donavan told him. "I hadn't planned on talking to the kids' parents until all the results came back from the lab. I guess now we're going to have to."

"Are we gonna give the Statler's a call and have them come in too?" Jack asked.

"Might as well. That way, we can get it over with in one fell swoop." Donavan glanced at his watch then reached for the phone.

Barbara got to her feet. "I don't know about you, but all this talk about murder and threats is getting to me." She held out her hand to Seelah. "Let's go in the kitchen and whip up something to make us feel better."

"Your sure-fire-chocolate-pick-me-up?" Seelah laughed as Barbara nodded. "Sure, why not?" She let herself be pulled from the couch. "What's another few pounds?"

Donavan hung up the phone. "Statler isn't happy about having to meet with us at the station. When I informed him that Christina Crawford would be there, he got upset."

"Afraid he'll get a boner in front of the wife?" Jack finished his beer, set the empty bottle down on the coffee table.

Donavan grinned, easing some of his tension. "He feels we should have come right over as soon as we found the clothes. When I tried to explain the importance of chain-of-evidence, he said we needed to get our priorities straight."

"Speakin' of chain-of-evidence, how's that gonna work with the parents checkin' the clothes before they go to the lab?"

"All I'm going to do is pull out the clothes, let them look at what we have, then bag it back up. Done deal. Besides, I think their giving us a positive ID on the clothing is going to boost our case."

"At the same time, they can also tell, from the smell, if the clothes have been washed in the kind of detergent and softener they use. How much do you wanna bet they smell a different brand?"

"I just bet on a sure thing, Jack. Statler allowing his wife to use a top-brand detergent and softener isn't even probable."

"Statler allowin' his wife to do anything ain't probable. I'll bet she ain't even allowed to be at the station in the mornin'."

"I won't touch that bet either. Statler's a man who needs to be in command. Allowing his wife to be around a woman whose very presence sends him into a fit of arousal isn't even a possibility."

"I shouldn't say this, but I'm gonna."

"You can say anything you want."

"From the few times we've been 'round the parents, we can tell Paul's life had to be anything but joyful. If he's dead, and I think we can assume he is, at least he went out with a bang."

***

The next morning as Donavan and Jack pulled into the parking space at the station, they could see Statler and Christina waiting for them in their vehicles.

"Looks like our mornin's 'bout to get off to a great start," Jack said.

"Yeah, I thought we could at least get a cup of coffee and go back over the evidence before we got started." He slid out of the jeep, slammed the door.

"Good morning, detectives." Christina walked up to them. Dressed in a black suit, white blouse and black heels, she looked every bit the respectable mother of a missing child.

"Christina," Donavan said, holding out his hand to her. "You look very nice this morning."

"Yeah, real nice," Jack told her, his voice low and respectful.

"Thank you." She smiled then looked across the parking lot as she saw Statler step from his car. "I don't look forward to being in the presence of that man, but under the circumstances, I guess it can't be helped."

"Don't worry 'bout it," Jack assured her, "you're among friends."

"Reverend Statler." Donavan shook the older man's hand. "I guess we may as well get this over with."

Jack nodded in Statler's direction before taking Christina's arm to usher her into the station.

Donavan pushed open the door to his office. "I'll go get everything ready," he said as Jack directed Christina to a chair nearest the desk. "While I'm gone, you can get us all some coffee."

"I didn't come here to hob-nob, Detective Hays. Just get the clothes so I can get done and be on my way," Statler said, refusing the chair Jack pulled out for him.

Ignoring him, Jack walked over to the big coffee urn,

withdrew some coffee filters from a drawer and proceeded to make coffee.

"All right then, since you have everything under control, Jack, I'll go get what we need."

"Everything's fine." Jack pushed the button on the coffee urn, took down four cups from the small cupboard. "Do either of you take cream or sugar?"

Donavan flipped on the light in the evidence room and proceeded across the floor to the shelves lining the wall. When he came to the shelf where he had placed the sealed bag, he stopped.

"What the hell!" The words shot out of his mouth as he stooped to look through all the bags still lying on the shelf.

"Oh shit! Don't tell me it's not here!" He continued to search through all the bags, but the ones he needed could not be found.

"I don't believe this! I put them here myself!"

He looked through all the shelves, hoping against hope they had been moved elsewhere. After fifteen minutes of futile searching, he knew he had a right to be worried.

Grabbing his cell, he punched in the numbers to his office. When Jack answered, he tried to keep his voice low and calm.

"Jack, I need you to come down to the evidence room right away. Don't ask why. Just get down here! Now!" He turned off the phone and, even though he knew he would be wasting his time, went back to searching the shelves.

Within moments, Jack came through the door. "What the hell's so urgent?"

"The evidence is gone, Jack."

"What the hell you talkin' 'bout?" His heart bounced inside his chest. "We put it here ourselves. Somebody's just moved it."

"I've been over every inch of these shelves, and it's not here! Jesus Christ, I don't believe this!" He slammed a fist down hard on one of the shelves.

"Who manned the desk last night?"

"I don't know. We'll have to check the duty roster. Why the hell would someone move evidence? It doesn't make any sense!"

"I want to see the videotapes from last night. There's a clear shot of everyone who comes into the station. I don't think we need to worry 'bout the back entrance. Anyone comin' in that way has to have the code."

"I want everything checked! Front, back and the windows! I want to know the names of everyone on duty. I want to know who came down here! I want this place gone over with a goddamn magnifying glass if need be!"

"Donavan, no one could come in here and remove evidence without bein' seen. Somebody knows what happened. We're gonna find out who that somebody is!"

"In the meantime, what the hell do we tell the two people waiting upstairs to see their kid's clothes? Oops! We don't know how it happened, but sometime during the night, the clothes disappeared!"

"We don't know that yet! It could be that someone just…" He threw up his hands at a complete loss as to what could have happened.

"Two people I can think of that would not want those clothes checked is Lawrence or Rafael Hindel. But there is no goddamn way either of them could get into a locked evidence room in a sheriff's department!"

"All right!" Jack smacked his hands together. "Here's what we're gonna do. We'll tell Christina and Statler the clothes need to be checked out by a Medical Examiner before they can be shown to anyone." He held up a hand as Donavan drew in his breath. "I know it's lame, but it's the best I can come up with. 'Sides, they don't know anything 'bout police protocol."

"All right, that will work for now. But if the clothes don't turn up, what then?"

"Donavan, for Christ's sake! Let's deal with one problem at a time! All right?"

"I'll go give the parents the news. While I'm doing that, you can get started on checking out the videotape from last night."

"Don't you want to look at the tape?"

"Hell yes, I want to see the tape! I don't think we're going to learn anything from it. But right now, I'm willing to try anything."

"I'll go get everything set up."

"Give me ten minutes, and I'll join you."

When Donavan came back upstairs, he could hear the raised voices coming from inside his office. Without hesitating, he pushed open the door. "What the hell is going on in here?"

They both turned as Donavan came through the door.

"What is going on does not concern you, Detective Hays," Statler informed him, his voice haughty and impatient.

"The hell it doesn't, Statler." Donavan turned on him. "In case you don't know it, you're standing in my office!"

"I'm sorry for this, Detective Hays," Christina told him. "Reverend Statler seems to think all this is somehow my fault."

"All what is your fault?"

"My daughter and his son being missing. I tried to tell him that I am as much in the dark about what has happened as he is, but he won't listen." Christina's soft voice rose with her anger.

"Mr. Statler, I realize you are upset, but I am not going to allow you to take out your fear on someone who is every bit as afraid as you are."

"You're mistaken, Detective Hays. I'm not afraid. Yes, I am worried about my son. However, fear does not enter in here. I know the Lord will bring my son back safe. But, if He doesn't, then I know without a shadow of a doubt, I can hold this woman, with her loose morals and the loose morals of her daughter, responsible."

"Don't you dare talk about my daughter like that!" Christina shouted.

"I will talk about your daughter any way I see fit, madam." His voice slurred over the way he addressed her, leaving no doubt how he thought about her. "If my son had not been with your daughter, he would be home right now where he belongs!"

Christina lunged, her long red nails raking a blood path

down Statler's cheek. "You hypocrite son of a bitch!" she spat the words in his face. "You think you're so holy! But we both know you're not. Don't we? If you thought you could get away with it," she jabbed a finger into his chest, "you'd straddle me right here!"

With some effort, Donavan stepped between the two. "All right! That's enough! Mr. Statler, I think it would be a good idea if you left. I've been informed we can't let you see the clothes until they've been checked by a Medical Examiner, so there isn't any reason for you to stay. I'll let you know when you can come back in."

Grabbing a handful of tissue from a box on Donavan's desk, Statler held them against his bleeding face. "And what do you plan on doing about the way she attacked me?"

"You brought on that attack, Mr. Statler. When I came in, I heard what you said to her. However, if you are intent on pressing charges, then all I can do is take your statement, and we can go from there. I would just let it drop."

With a look of pure hatred, Statler yanked open the door to stomp out of the room.

Donavan eased Christina into a nearby chair. "I'm sorry about that. He should keep his feelings to himself."

"Do you think he'll press charges against me?" Her voice dropped to a mere whisper.

"I wouldn't worry about it. I heard what he said, and if need be, I can testify about the attack being justified."

"I heard you say we can't see the clothes. Is the reason you can't show us the clothes because they are covered with blood?"

"I give you my word, Christina, the clothes aren't covered with blood."

For a long moment, she gazed at him, then seeing the truth in his eyes, she got to her feet. "Then I'll be going. Please call me when I can come back in. And, if you will make it, so I don't have to be here at the same time Statler is."

"I can't promise you that, but one thing I can promise you is that when you are in the same room with him, you won't be left alone. If I hadn't needed Jack earlier, you would never have been left alone with him."

"Thank you, Detective Hays." To Donavan's surprise, she brushed a kiss across his cheek.

Donavan waited until he saw her walk out the door of the station house before leaving his office.

Jack had everything ready when Donavan walked into the room. "Did you find out who worked last night?"

"Yeah, Jamison pulled the night shift. He's got a little surprise for you. I told him I'd let him tell you himself, though."

"Right now, Jack, I'm not in the mood for surprises. If you know something that's going to piss me off, I suggest you tell me about it."

"All right," he slid the video into the machine, hit the play button, "I got a feelin' this is gonna give you a little hint."

Donavan leaned his bulk against the desk, folded his arms across his chest. "Why the hell are you fast-forwarding? We want to see everything."

"Jamison told me what time the party got started, so I thought we'd get to the good part without wasting time. There," he stood up straight, moved back away from the television, "that should be pretty close."

As they watched the screen, Donavan drew in his breath. "I don't believe this." He pushed himself away from the desk.

The images on the screen showed Lawrence and Rafael Hindel strolling through the front door of the station.

"Look at those pompous pricks!" Donavan said. "They want us to see them."

"Sure, sets up a great alibi. Don't you think?"

"Yeah, as long as they stay in plain view. If they get out of sight of the camera, then we got them! What I want to know is why the hell they came here in the first place."

"Oh, you're gonna love this!" Jack laughed. "Accordin' to Jamison, they came in to see how the search for the missin' teens is comin' along."

"In the middle of the night?"

Jack grinned. "I thought it a little outta character too.

'Course Jamison said he couldn't tell them anything. He let them know, right up front, you and I are the lead detectives on the case, so anything pertainin' to the search has to go through us. Which, I'm sure they already knew."

"You can bet your ass they did!"

"Jamison said, they went into great detail 'bout everything said while the kids partied on the property. Like, how Lawrence came outside and told the kids to leave. How the one boy got so scared he fell off the porch. I mean, they didn't miss a lick 'bout what they claim went on that night."

"Except to say what happened to the two who stayed behind. I bet they didn't mention a fuckin' word about that!"

"Not accordin' to Jamison. He said he kept tryin' to get rid of them, but every time he thought the conversation to be over, they'd come up with somethin' new."

"Their entire plan centered on buying time. The thing I don't understand is why."

As they continued to watch the screen, Donavan leaned forward. "Did you see that?"

"What?"

"Hit the rewind!" Donavan walked up close to the television as Jack rewound the tape. "Stop! Now hit play!"

Jack stepped back, gazed at the screen.

On the video, they could see Rafael look up, smile, then, in a very straight and forward manner, bring two fingers up to his forehead to snap off a jaunty salute into the camera.

"Look familiar, Jack?"

"Yeah," Jack breathed. "'Cept he used two fingers."

"Okay, let's check out the video on the back entrance."

Donavan felt anxious now; sure, he could catch the Hindels in something that proved their involvement in the missing evidence.

Jack hit the eject button. "What the hell's that gonna show? We've already agreed no one can get in the back without knowin' the code."

"That's right, and that's why I want to see everything we

got on tape last night."

"I'll have to go get it," he growled as he slipped the tape into its case. "I figured this tape would be enough. I didn't bother to grab the others." He turned at the door. "Guess you're gonna want the ones showin' the parkin' area, too. Right?"

"If we got a tape showing someone taking a piss in the men's room. I want it!"

Within moments of his leaving, Jack came back with the tapes. This time they didn't bother with fast-forwarding.

The camera's eye and what it showed left no doubt as to why Lawrence and Rafael Hindel came to the station in the wee hours of the morning.

"They had someone else with them," Donavon breathed; as he watched a man, dressed in black, open the back door to walk into the station.

"The hood, he's got pulled up over his head, makes him impossible to identify, though it's as plain as the reason the Hindels came into the station this mornin' where he came from."

"The view of the parking lot shows him walking in, so we can't even get a make on a vehicle. The Hindels had this pretty well thought out."

"Have you decided what we're gonna tell the parents 'bout the clothes? They know we have them...had them," he corrected himself.

"Yeah, had them!" Donavan kicked a chair out of his path on his way to the door. "I want to know how that fuck got in here this morning! Without the code, it's impossible!"

"What I wanna know is why Jamison didn't catch it on the monitor."

"That one I can answer!" Donavan pushed open the door to his office. "He didn't see it because the Hindels had him distracted with all their babbling about the kids!"

"I hate to say it, but they pulled off a damn-near impossible feat! We know everyone in this department, so we can rule out any of them bein' in on it. But, if someone didn't give them the code, then how the hell did they get in?"

"I don't know." Donavan sat down in his chair behind the desk, pulled out a cigarette. "I have a thought running through my head, I'm not comfortable with, Jack."

"What's that?" he leaned back in the chair, propped his feet up on the desk.

"Before Jonathan attacked Paulson, we considered Paulson a fine, upstanding part of this department, too."

"Don't even go there, Donavon," Jack warned him, his stomach tightening as little voices of guilt, right on cue, slipped into his mind. Uncomfortable, he shifted, trying to shut out the pictures flashing into his mind before they could become shrieking flame throwers. "Paulson turned out to be just another of Jonathan Hindel's victims. But, he chose death rather'n become a monster. I oughta know," he flinched as one of the flame throwers made a direct hit, "I'm the one who shot his brains out."

Donavan blew a stream of smoke into the air, berating himself for bringing up the subject. "You're right. I shouldn't have gone there. But goddamn! How else do you explain someone getting in here this morning and walking out with an entire bag of evidence?"

"I can't explain it! One thing I can tell you is a person can't be a goddamn werewolf and work rotatin' shifts!" His nerves continued to jump, and the alluring smell of Donavan's cigarette didn't help matters. "If we learned anything from Jonathan Hindel, it's you're gonna be one of two things! Either you're gonna be runnin' 'round on all fours barkin' at the fuckin' moon or walkin' upright with your shit together! We might not have the smartest men workin' this department, but most of them got their shit together." He ignored the brief look Donavan shot his way. "But, gettin' back to who could have made off with the evidence, maybe he waited in the shadows while the deputy punched in the code."

"I don't think so. If he got that close, the deputy would have spotted him."

Out of patience now, Jack looked at him. "Do you have a better idea?"

"I'm all out of guesses, Jack." He rose to his feet, stubbed out his cigarette. "Nope, the way we're going to figure this one out is with a crystal ball."

"Shit!" His feet hit the floor. "Why didn't I think of that!"

"Don't be a smart-ass, Jack. I'm not in the mood for it!" He yanked his suit-coat from the back of the chair, jammed his arms through the sleeves.

"For your information, I ain't bein' a smart-ass! You said we need a crystal ball! What I'm tryin' to tell you is, we got somethin' a lot better'n that; we got Seelah!"

Donavan whirled! "Would she be able to tell us who came in here last night?"

"Hell if I know!" He grabbed his jacket, felt the last of his tension slip away. "Let's go find out!"

CHAPTER ELEVEN

Seelah breathed in deep and tried to relax her mind. "I'm not getting anything. I very seldom can unless I have something to hold or touch that the person I'm trying to tune into has left their energy on."

"Would it help if we went to the station?" Jack asked. "He had to touch the door in order to get inside."

"Yes, that could work." She got to her feet, stood for a moment, with one hand pressed against her stomach before walking from her chair.

Jack reached out to her. "Are you all right?"

"Yeah." She chuckled at his concern. "I don't know, but I think your son did a flip in the night and is getting ready for his long-awaited arrival."

Barbara placed her hand on the top of Seelah's stomach, pushed her hand inward. "You're right. The baby has dropped."

"Seelah, if you'd rather not do this, it's okay," Donavan told her, placing an arm around her shoulders.

"Oh, Donavan, I'm fine," she assured him. "He's just a little heavier now, is all."

"Are you sure, baby?" Jack pulled her close to him. "I mean, if you don't feel comfortable doin' this, we can figure out somethin' else to try."

"Would you stop worrying?" She extracted herself from his tight grip. "I'm in excellent health. At my last checkup, my pediatrician said the baby would be dropping any day now, and she told me what to expect. Guess what? She didn't lie." She giggled outright. "He dropped, and I do feel like I'm carrying an elephant."

"All right, if you're sure it's gonna be safe." Jack placed a quick kiss on the side of her face. "The last thing I want is for the Hindels to put you and my son in danger."

The moment the words left his mouth, he felt icy chills skitter up the back of his neck. He turned away.

"Jack," Seelah touched his arm. "What is it?"

"Nothin'." He breathed a deep breath before turning to face her. "I just don't feel comfortable with you bein' involved in any of this."

"Don't worry, my darling," she brushed a loving hand down the side of his face, "I have faith that Chandra would warn me if I could be in any danger."

"Yeah." Is all he could say as feelings of unease continued to mount in his already churning stomach.

"Okay then, I guess we're ready to go find out who stole the evidence." Donavan reached out to pull Barbara close for a quick hug. "We won't be long, hon."

"Oh no, Mr. Detective, you're not leaving me out of this! I'm going with you!" She slipped her feet into her sandals.

"Don't you think you should be here when Jenny comes home from school?" He tried to make light of his unease at having her along.

"Oh, Donavan, Jenny's almost a teenager. She'll be fine on her own for a little while." She looked at him. "Although, if you'd rather I don't go, then I won't."

"No, it's fine." He picked up his keys as Seelah and Jack walked to the door. "I guess I'm like Jack. I don't like having my wife involved with anything having to do with the Hindels."

"I appreciate your concern, but like Seelah said, we'll be fine."

When they pulled into the parking space at the station, they all drew in their breath as they saw Lawrence and Rafael

Hindel waiting for them.

"Can you believe the arrogance of those two pricks?" Jack opened the car door, stepped to the pavement. "You two wait here while we see what's goin' on." He shut the door before either woman could argue.

Donavan got out of the car, and together they walked over to the Hindel's minivan.

"What a pleasant surprise," Jack said, stopping in front of the two men smiling at him. "I didn't think you'd have the nuts to show your face after what you did this mornin'," he directed the comment at Rafael.

"Why, Jack, whatever do you mean?" Rafael's smile deepened. "We thought, since we couldn't get any information about the missing kids from your dispatcher when we came in earlier, we would come back and talk with you and Detective Hays."

"Where's your buddy?" Donavan moved up to stand beside Jack.

A puzzled frown creased Rafael's brow, and he became serious. "I am afraid I don't understand what you are asking me, Detective Hays."

"Sure you do, Rafael," Jack told him. "He's referrin' to the *other* night owl you brought with you this mornin'."

"Maybe you can enlighten me about what Jack is talking about, Detective."

"I'll be glad to *enlighten* you, Rafael," Donavan said, glancing at Lawrence, before bringing his attention back to the older man waiting for him to explain. "Jack's talking about the tall man, dressed in black pants and sweatshirt, with a hood pulled over his face. We got him on video."

"I'm afraid I still don't know what you are talking about." He swung around, looked at Lawrence. "Do you know what Detective Hays is referring to, Lawrence?"

"No." Lawrence fidgeted from foot to foot. "I didn't see anyone dressed like that."

"There, you see detectives? We have no idea who you are

talking about."

"In a pig's ass, you don't, you lyin' puke!" Jack moved towards Rafael.

"Jack! If Mr. Hindel and Lawrence say they don't know who we are talking about, then we will have to leave it at that."

Without another word, Jack turned on his heel to walk towards the front door of the station.

"Have you ever thought of sending Detective Olivier' to an anger-management class, Detective?" Rafael watched Jack yank open the door. "It appears to me he could benefit from such a class."

"He's a little disturbed about some evidence that came up missing in the middle of the night."

"For goodness sake." Rafael gave Donavan his complete attention. "I thought all evidence had to be kept in a locked evidence room. At least, that is what is always portrayed on all the police shows."

"That's right it is, except our visitor this morning somehow got into our locked room and walked off with our evidence." Donavan continued to watch Lawrence, noting the nervous way he kept switching from foot to foot and wiping his forehead on the sleeve of his shirt.

"My god!" Rafael's gaze switched from Donavan to Lawrence. "He must be talking about the evidence taken from the estate yesterday! If that's so, then how in the world are they going to find out what happened to the children?"

"Oh, I'm not worried about it." Donavan kept his voice even and calm. "It seems that on the way out of the room, the person who stole the bag let some of the evidence slip out. I feel sure we still got enough to take to forensics."

"I thought all the bags had to be sealed in keeping with the chain-of-evidence."

Knowing he had been caught in a lie, Donavan tried to make light of his falsehood. "I have to hand it to you, Mr. Hindel. Your knowledge of police procedure is astounding. Guess I didn't realize how in-depth those police shows are anymore."

"Yes…well, being isolated, as Lawrence and I are, there isn't a lot we can do for recreation."

"What about the people staying on the estate? Aren't they good company?"

Lawrence's breath rushed into his lungs then trickled back out as Rafael clamped a hand on his shoulder. "I am sure you have had relatives visit. For the first few days, everything is fine, but as the days continue to pass and they make no plans to leave, they begin to wear on one's nerves. Besides, they have been gone for quite some time now."

"Just where is it your relatives come from?"

"They live in New Orleans. Why do you ask?"

"No reason. I know a few people in New Orleans. I thought maybe my friends might be acquainted with them. Do they also go by the Hindel name?"

"In case you aren't aware of this fact, Detective Hays, the Hindel name is very old. My ancestors have been in Louisiana for many years." He held the other man's gaze for a moment longer, then replied, "I rather doubt any of your friends would be acquainted with them."

"You never know. Like they say, it's a small world. Maybe, just for the hell of it, I'll run a check on the name and see what pops up." Donavan almost grinned as he saw a look of unease slip across Rafael's face.

"I hope you are not inferring anyone carrying the Hindel name would be caught doing anything illegal, Detective Hays." Rafael's steel-gray eyes glittered.

"I'm not inferring anything. If your relatives haven't been *caught* doing anything illegal, again, then they don't have anything to worry about. And neither do you." Donavan allowed the smile he had been holding back to slip into place.

"Detective Hays, may I remind you, Lawrence and I came here, of our own free will, to inquire about the children who disappeared on the estate. Your treatment of us tells me you think we may be responsible for their disappearance. This brings me to a proposal."

"And it is?"

"Grandfather…"

Rafael's grip strengthened on his shoulder. "I would like to offer a way to take the suspicion off Lawrence and myself and allow you to get on with finding out what happened to those unfortunate children. Therefore, I think we should both be given a polygraph test." At last, he glimpsed the emotion he had been looking for.

"I think that's a great idea!" Donavan tried to remain calm. "We can get started on it right away!"

"No, today wouldn't be good. We have a full day ahead of us. However, tomorrow would be all right. Don't you agree, Lawrence?"

"Whatever you say, Grandfather."

"Then I'll set it up and expect the both of you tomorrow. Would noon be all right?"

"Yes, that would be fine. Until then, Detective Hays." He turned Lawrence in the direction of their vehicle. "Oh," he turned back, "tell Jack we look forward to proving him wrong in thinking Lawrence and myself had anything to do with the missing evidence."

"Oh, trust me, I'll be sure to pass along your warning." He forced himself to walk back over to the jeep where Barbara and Seelah waited for him.

When the three walked into Donavan's office, Jack got to his feet.

"So, did you find a way to trick the parish lunatics into sayin' anything helpful?"

"Believe it or not, I just may have." A satisfied grin spread across Donavan's face.

"I can't wait to hear this! What'd they do, volunteer to take a poly?"

"That's right!" Donavan danced a foolish jig over to his desk, pulled the telephone forward to punch in some numbers. "I don't like to brag, but I think this time a little bragging is in order."

Jack reached out, pushed the hang-up button.

"What the hell did you do that for? I need to set up the polygraph for the Hindels. I told them to be here at noon tomorrow."

"Why waste the examiner's time and the taxpayers' money? They knew about all this when they volunteered to take a polygraph."

"Jack, I don't know what the hell you're talking about! A polygraph, given by a trained paleographer, is damn-near foolproof!"

"I think I know what Jack is talking about," Seelah spoke up as Jack seated her atop his lap.

"I hope somebody does because I'm about to lose it!" Donavan walked over to seat himself on the edge of the desk beside Barbara.

"I'd like to hear this myself," Barbara said. "I always thought a polygraph test to be pretty-well foolproof, too."

"Nine times out of ten it is," Seelah told them. "Except, they are proving now when a psychopath takes a polygraph, they can usually pass it."

"How the hell can a deranged idiot pass a poly?" Donavan shot back. His smugness, at getting over on the Hindels, already showing a decline.

"A psychopath has no emotion, and emotion is what the graph reads," Seelah told him.

"Son of a bitch! Are you sure about this?" Donavan looked at her.

"Call the examiner. Maybe they've come up with new ways to read psychopaths.

"Ain't she smart?" Jack beamed up at her. "She's where I heard about all this."

"That remains to be proven," Donavan said, then back-pedaled his words. "I'm talking about this incident, Seelah."

Seelah nodded as she got off Jack's lap. "While Donavan is checking out the theory on the polygraph, I'll see what I can find out about your late-night visitor."

"Good idea." Jack rose to his feet. "Barb, would you like to come with us?"

"Thanks, but I'll wait for Donavan. He may need some tender care if the news comes back you're right."

"Okay then. See you in a few." He placed an arm around Seelah's shoulders as they walked to the door.

"I don't believe this horseshit! Are you going to sit there and tell me that a goddamn mental case is smarter than a proven, scientific procedure?"

"Donavan, would you please calm down and remember your blood pressure?"

Donavan waved her to silence. "No, I am not going to accept that! All you are telling me is some crack-pot-doctor out to make a name for himself thinks he has all the answers! Theory! That's all you got! Goddamn, unproven theory! You're damn right. I want to go ahead with the tests! If I didn't, I wouldn't be calling to set up the appointment, you fuckin' moron!" With that said, he slammed down the phone.

"Donavan! He is just telling you what he's learned about administering polygraph tests to mentally challenged people."

"No! He's telling me what a lot of blowhards have told him, and I'm not going to accept it!" He looked around the office. "Where the hell did Jack and Seelah get off to?"

"Seelah thought, since you would be busy, she might as well find out what she could about who broke in here this morning."

"Good!" He held out a hand to her. "Let's go see what she's finding out."

***

Jack followed behind as Seelah walked through the parking lot, allowing the energy left behind by the intruder to surround her.

"Getting anything yet?" Jack raised his voice to be sure he could be heard.

Seelah ignored him to keep her mind focused on the task at hand.

"Did she get anything yet, Jack?" Donavan called out as he and Barbara walked towards them.

"I don't know she ain't sayin' nothin'."

Seelah whirled. "Do you want my help or not? If you do, then you're going to have to be still so I can concentrate!"

"Sorry, baby. I just wondered if you'd found out anything yet."

"I'm sorry too, Seelah." Donavan gave her a sheepish half-smile. "We'll stand over here and let you work."

A tall man dressed all in black drifted into her mind. She tried to get a better look at him — but the hood he had covering his head obscured his face. Seelah pulled in her guides, sending them out to find the man who kept his face in shadow. But they too came up empty-handed. Without warning, the Hindel Mansion loomed into her thoughts, telling her the man she sought still resided at that house.

"I can't see his face, even after calling on the help of my guides, but one thing I can tell you is the man who broke into the station and made off with the evidence lives at the Hindel Mansion."

Thank you, Seelah, you've been a big help," Donavan told her.

"Just as we thought, Donavan, the man who broke into the station is one of the people living in the cave." Jack pulled Seelah into his arms for a moment.

"Sure as hell looks like it."

"So, are you still gonna go ahead with the polygraph tomorrow?"

"No. I'm beginning to see it would be a waste of time. I talked with three different examiners, and they all agree it wouldn't work. Until we get a better method of reading psychos, we'd just be wasting time and money."

"Then we're at another dead end with the Hindels?

"Getting to be a habit. I'll call and tell them we will have to have a delay on the tests as our paleographer is out of town."

"Do you think they'll believe you?"

"I don't care if they do or not. That's what they're going to hear. If you have a better idea, I'm listening."

"The only idea I have is to call it a day and start again fresh in the morning."

CHAPTER TWELVE

Chandra watched as Rafael and Lawrence walked through the front door of the mansion, and she listened to their words.

"You have to trust that I know what I am doing, Lawrence."

"But, Grandfather, the polygraph will show that I am lying when I say I know nothing of the children's disappearance. They will lock me away again! I couldn't stand to be locked away again!" He felt himself spinning out of control.

"Lawrence!" Rafael jerked him forward. "I said you must trust me. No one is going to lock you away. We will pass the polygraph."

"How? We can't fool the machine!"

"You idiot!" Rafael flung him backward across the room. "You have caused me nothing but trouble since I have returned here. I cannot think when all you do is complain!"

"But..." he cut short what he wanted to say as Rafael glared at him.

"Lawrence, you have nothing to fear from taking this test." He breathed in deep in an attempt to halt the rage building inside him. "I will see to that. Do you think I would risk everything we have planned by allowing you to walk in cold and be administered a test that could lay bare our darkest secrets?"

Lawrence shook his head. Afraid to speak, lest he incites the insane anger boiling to the surface before his eyes.

"Good." Rafael put both his hands on Lawrence's

shoulders. "You are Jonathan's son. I am duty-bound to protect you. Moreover, I will. With my life, if need be. Therefore, you have nothing to fear."

"Without becoming angry, can you tell me how you plan to do this?"

"Yes." Rafael ignored the nervous tremor sounding in Lawrence's voice. "I intend to put you into a semi-trance. You will be able to respond to everything being said to you, but you will have no emotional reaction." He waited to see if Lawrence understood what he told him.

Lawrence remained silent and thought about what he heard. "And you, Grandfather?" The tremor had disappeared now. "Will you be strong enough to pass the test?"

"Without a doubt in my mind, Lawrence." His reassuring demeanor wiped away the last of Lawrence's unease. In a surprising move, he pulled Lawrence against his chest. "The children who came onto your property invaded your space and, therefore, had to be taught a lesson. I have no feelings of regret for anyone who will not listen."

"*Why don't you speak the truth for once, Rafael?*" Chandra walked forward. "*You used the children to feed your appetite for evil.*"

"*Ah, Chandra,*" he breathed, "*how nice to see you.*" Rafael gazed at her over Lawrence's shoulder. "*Your continued presence strengthens my belief that I am needed here. However, I must disagree with you about the children. It is not evil to protect what is ours. Granted,*" he bowed a slight bow in her direction, "*the children did feed my appetite.*"

Lawrence could see the anger building in Rafael's eyes again, and he tried to see the person Rafael spoke with. "Grandfather, who are you talking to?"

"No one but an earthbound, who seems to think she is needed here."

"What did you call her?" Lawrence felt excited about having a ghost in his house.

"Her name is Chandra." Rafael watched the emotions flitting across Chandra's face as he discussed her with Lawrence.

"She is the one who destroyed your father. And my son!" His voice rose as the fury—he tried to ignore—pushed its way forward.

Although he could not see the woman standing across the room, Lawrence called out to her. "Why did you destroy my father?" The tremor returned to his voice and held all the suffering that continued to eat away at him.

Chandra stood silent, witnessing his pain.

Rafael watched her and, at that moment, hoped he had at last found the key with which to gain his control of her.

"*Chandra, if you knew how much the very sight of you rips at me, you would not be here.*" His voice grew strong now with none of the fury he had been consumed with moments earlier.

"*You do not frighten me, Rafael. I am beyond your reach. As long as you remain on this plane, so will I.*"

"*As I am sure you know, it does not pleasure me to hear you say that. However, you are wrong about my not being able to touch you.*" He chuckled as he glimpsed the wary look on her face. "*I see, by your confused expression, you do not understand my meaning. Perhaps I can help you. Lawrence asked why you destroyed his father. Would you like me to tell him?*"

"*I destroyed Jonathan because he grew too evil to remain on this plane.*" She tried to rid herself of the uneasy feelings beginning to rise to the surface. "*What other reason could I have?*"

"*I think we both know, the destruction of my son is but one of the reasons you did what you did. Could it be you also destroyed my son to keep a secret from your own son, Chandra?*"

"*Are you threatening me, Rafael?*" She hoped her voice did not betray her fear. "*If you are, I will not hesitate to call on every white spirit I can to destroy you and send your evil soul straight into hell where it belongs!*"

For a long moment, he remained silent, weighing her words. Then, feeling sure he held the upper hand in their battle for control, he sent his thoughts from his mind to hers. "*Let us be sure we both know what the stakes are before we issue any threats. I am telling you that the son you tried to keep secreted from the outside world will no longer be a secret."*

He watched with glee as he saw tears slip unnoticed down her face. *"Are you willing to risk Lawrence finding out about you, Chandra?"*

"I lived with that same threat for many years, Rafael. And it all but destroyed me and those I love. If you feel you must share this nightmare with Lawrence, then tell him," she called his bluff and said a silent prayer she had made the right decision. *"I will not be controlled by threats anymore."*

Her refusal to bend snapped the last thread of his leashed anger. *"My son should have destroyed you years ago! If you knew how many times I tried to get him to do just that!"*

"By your own admission, it would seem you could not control Jonathan any more than you can control me."

"Jonathan allowed the women in his life to enjoy too much control." His eyes lifted to a portrait hanging over the massive fireplace of a beautiful young girl standing naked and smiling. In his rage, she smiled, knowingly, at him. In two quick strides, he moved across the room to heft a poker from its place beside the hearth. He swung the poker aiming at the face on the canvas. *"Angelia is to blame for the ruination of my son!"* He threw the poker to the floor with great force. *"She turned him into a weak, sniveling shell of a man."*

"I disagree, Rafael. Angelia could have been the one good thing about Jonathan. She made him feel."

"She made him crawl!" The anger spun out of control now, and he did nothing to stop it. *"If not for her, my son would have stayed with me and the rest of our people the way he should have! Instead of taking her and using her the way he used and defiled you, he gave her our name!"* Spittle flew unnoticed from his lips. *"The name Hindel is revered and respected in Louisiana! It should never have been soiled and spat upon, the way it continued to be when Jonathan married his nigger whore and allowed you to produce his bastard heir!"*

Lawrence backed away.

"Look at you!" Rafael growled as he saw Lawrence slinking away. *"Weak! You carry the blood of my son, but not*

his strength!"

"*Rafael!*" Chandra moved towards him. "*You do not need to take out your anger on Lawrence. He is not to blame for being Jonathan's son!*"

As though doused with a bucket of ice, the rage drained from him. Although, what emerged turned out to be far worse.

"It is time for you to step forward and become the man your father would want you to be, Lawrence. This very night I will begin to teach you what it means to be the son of Jonathan Hindel.

"*No!*" Chandra cried out. "*I will not allow you to turn my son into the evil monster you are!*"

"*How do you plan to stop me, Chandra? Are you going to shoot me then set fire to the house, like you did with Jonathan?*"

"*I am warning you, Rafael! Leave my son alone, or I swear I will destroy you!*"

Deep-throated, diabolical laughter filled the air.

"Come here, Lawrence. It is time to take your first step in becoming immortal."

"*Rafael, no!*" Chandra ran forward.

With real fear pounding within his heart, Lawrence walked towards his grandfather's outstretched arms.

As Rafael encircled his slim body, a great howling erupted into the silence. Followed by a long, drawn-out scream of agony.

Chandra dropped to her knees, unable to watch the horror spilling forth around her.

When Rafael released him, Lawrence stepped back to gaze at his grandfather in both horror and awe.

"Now you have the strength I have wanted for you, Lawrence."

CHAPTER THIRTEEN

"I guess tomorrow we'll be getting in touch with the parents of the missing kids," Donavan said, standing beside the bed. "It's obvious we're not going to find them, and I think their folks deserve to get on with their lives."

Barbara laid the book she had been reading aside to reach for him. "Come on," she told him, "get in bed and let me relax you."

"You can give it a shot, although I doubt you'll be able to get the job done. Not as kinked up as my muscles are tonight." He shot her a half-grin as she scooted over to make room for him.

"I could always work the kinks out before." She lifted a bottle of lotion from the nightstand to squirt a liberal amount into the palm of her hand. "Lie down on your stomach."

Donavan did as she directed and felt her long legs straddle his hips and her warm hands glide over his back. "I guess I been pretty lax in the lovemaking department." He kept his face turned away from her.

"Mmmm, maybe a little." She continued to knead the taut muscles working her way up his back to his neck. "Maybe if we talked about why we could get a grip on the problem."

"Identify the problem. Solve the problem. Right?"

"That's always been your motto." She continued with his workout.

"Then we're in trouble, 'cause this time I don't know

where to start looking." His words sounded garbled as Barbara began to chop her way up and down his back.

"Could it have anything to do with Lawrence Hindel's return?" She eased herself off his back to lie down beside him.

Donavan turned on his side to look at her. "I never even thought about that."

"If you think back, you'll recall around this time is when you started sleeping in your chair again and would leave for work before I woke up."

Donavan rolled over and reached for the pack of cigarettes lying on the nightstand. For a few moments, he remained silent as he inhaled the nicotine. "Like I did when Jonathan Hindel kept me awake at night."

Barbara dropped a kiss on his cheek, leaned her head against his chest. "Yes. Although there's a bright side to this picture, too."

"What's that?" He could feel his muscles begin to relax.

"I sure enjoyed playing catch up when the case ended!" she giggled, then turned over, plumped her pillow into a more comfortable position and settled down to go to sleep.

Donavan stubbed out his cigarette and switched off the lamp. He lay in the darkness with the sound of Barbara's even breathing, telling him she had already fallen asleep. He tried to clear his mind enough to join her but gave up. The feelings creeping over him would not allow his mind to relax. Throwing back the covers, he got to his feet.

In the kitchen, he poured himself a tall glass of milk, then lifted the cover off the cake platter. He reached into the silverware drawer for a knife but withdraw a fork instead. With the platter in one hand and the glass of milk in the other, he walked into the living room.

"Can't sleep, might as well eat."

He set the glass of milk down on the end table, clicked power on the TV remote to surf the channels and see if anything caught his interest.

He looked up from taking a sip of his milk to see a well-stacked blond wearing a white cowboy hat, bouncing across the screen astride a man on all fours, wearing a wide grin and nothing else. He winced as he caught sight of the sharp spurs attached to her boots and the whip she kept slapping across the man's hapless buttocks.

He glanced down the hall, brought his attention back to the screen for a moment longer, then clicked the remote.

"Sure glad Barb's not into that shit." He took a large bite of cake. "She looks good in the buff, but one good bounce, and I'd be lying on the floor like a beached whale!"

He set the plate of cake down on the end table. "How the hell did I get into this shape anyway?" He ran a hand over his protruding paunch. "My stomach used to be as flat as Barb's. Now it looks like Seelah's."

A broad grin broke across his face as he thought of Jack's excitement as he waited for the birth of his son. In a little over a year, Jack had gone from being the saddest person he had ever seen to one of the happiest.

Donavan picked up his milk to take a long drink. "Funny what having the right woman in your life can do." He set the glass back down on the end table, but when he went to pick up the plate of cake, he pulled his hand away. "I guess if I want to get back into shape, I might as well start now."

He pulled the lever on the recliner, stretched his legs out straight on the footrest. Within moments of leaning his head against the back of the chair, he fell into a deep sleep.

He walked along the boardwalk leading up to a shack in the bayous. He knew who the shack belonged to and tried to think why he would be there.

He saw Chandra swimming towards a ladder sticking out of the water. He watched as she pulled herself up the ladder then stepped onto the walkway. She ignored him as she strutted naked in his direction. Although he remained steadfast in his dislike for her because of all the pain and suffering she had fostered upon Jack, he couldn't help but notice how striking she looked. When she drew near, he reached out and pulled her into his arms.

Chandra did not pull away. Instead, she answered his need by pressing herself against him.

Donavan could feel his body responding, and he picked her up in his arms to carry her to the old shack setting atop the dark waters of the bayous.

As soon as they stepped inside, he released her to begin yanking off his clothes. He could smell her arousal, and it made him rush to be with her.

Chandra pulled him with her onto the bed.

He had never felt such wild abandonment as he did with the woman already wrapping her long legs around his waist to draw him deep into her velvet tunnel.

Chandra urged him to go deeper inside her body. Donavan did not disappoint her.

He could hear her loud moans, and the sound drove him to greater heights as he raised his hips to slam himself into her again and again.

When he felt the hot liquids spew from his body, he slumped forward to try to regain his breath. He could feel her long nails trailing over his bare back, and he drew back to look down at her.

Donavan drew in his breath to scream, but no sound could escape his lungs.

Chandra wrapped her legs tight and pulled his mouth within inches of her face. A face covered with a thin layer of charred skin that oozed and dripped onto her chest. The foul stench of burning flesh swirled around him, and he gagged and screamed his terror.

"Donavan, wake up! You're having a nightmare!"

Still locked into the hellish dream, he swung his arms. "No! Let me go! You're dead!"

Barbara continued to shake him until, at last, he opened his eyes.

"Oh my god!" He covered his face with his hands.

"Donavan, are you all right?" Barbara knelt down in front of him. "You woke me up screaming the name Chandra."

"Oh, Barb!" He reached out to pull her into his arms and, like a small child, bury his face in her chest.

"Tell me about the dream. If you can get it out, then it will leave you, and you'll feel better," she crooned as she brushed a hand over his hair.

"In my dream, I had sex with Chandra!"

Barbara drew back to stare at him. "Would you mind repeating what you just said?" Her voice had lost its gentle tone, now.

Donavan tried to pull her back against him, and when she remained stiff and unyielding, he looked at her. "What?"

"You tell me you're having sex with another woman, and all you can say is, 'what'?"

"I didn't plan the damn thing!"

"Do you expect me to feel sorry for you?"

"Barb," he tried to reason with her, "I had a nightmare. Do you think I could enjoy having sex with a woman who stank of charred flesh?"

"Oh, my poor baby!" Barbara gushed over him, now that she knew what happened in the dream. "That must have been terrible!" She drew him into her arms to begin rocking him back and forth.

"I felt horrible," he whispered, glad to be held and made over.

"I'm sorry I doubted you, darling. After all, we can't help what we dream."

"Thank you, hon." He untangled himself from her arms to get to his feet. "I think what I need now is a relaxing hot shower. After that, I should be able to go to bed."

"I think that sounds like a real nice idea," she purred, coming up behind him to slide her arms around his waist. "I think my big strong man is in need of a live woman's touch. So I'm going to join you in that shower and finish what she started."

All he could do is keep walking and hope for a miracle.

CHAPTER FOURTEEN

The next morning, Donavan called the Hindels to tell them the test had been called off due to the paleographer being called out of town. He told Lawrence the sheriff's office would be in touch when another appointment could be set up for them. With that obstacle out of the way, he and Jack braced themselves for the unpleasant task of telling Christina Crawford and Reverend Statler about their findings.

"After a thorough search of the mansion and the grounds, it's my opinion, your children are not going to be found. I hate to say this, but I believe they are no longer alive," Donavan told them.

Christina spoke up first. "Can you say what you think happened to them?"

"We found the clothes next to the water..." Jack stopped in mid-sentence as Statler jumped to his feet.

"Are you sayin', you think my son got eaten by gators?"

"We can't say for sure what happened..." Jack tried again, and again Statler interrupted him.

"Paul would never be stupid enough to go swimmin' in a swamp filled with gators!" He smacked a fist down hard on Donavan's desk. "I think what's goin' on here is you don't have the first clue what happened to my boy!"

"You need to calm down, Reverend Statler," Donavan told him. "We did a complete investigation. The one scent the

K-9 dogs picked up on the children is the one right next to the water." Donavan tried to keep a hold on his temper as he saw Statler shake his head.

"I ain't acceptin' any of this! I raised Paul in the bayous. And I'm tellin' you," he shook a fat finger in Donavan's face, "he didn't take it into his head to jump in a swamp swarmin' with snakes and gators!"

"Is that what you believe happened, Lieutenant Hays?" Christina whispered.

As much as he hated to lie to her, he felt, right at the moment, he had no choice. "I think it's a strong possibility, Christina."

"Then I guess I will have to accept they're gone." She stood up and, without another word, walked out of the room.

"You might have fooled her with all your talk of what happened, but you'll never make me believe it." Statler walked to the door, then stopped. "I just remembered somethin'." He turned to face them. "You said you would show me the clothes. Where are they?"

"They're still at the crime lab. All I can offer you is my assurance that time-wise, they are doing the best they can. As soon as I know something, though, I'll give you a call."

"Maybe that won't be necessary. Do you remember what the clothes looked like?"

Donavan looked over at Jack. "A pair of blue jeans, a white T-shirt and a pair of off-brand sneakers. Does that sound right to you, Jack?"

"Yeah."

"What about ID? Paul always carried his wallet with his ID inside."

"We didn't find anything other than the clothes."

"I don't need to see the clothes to know, what you found belonged to Paul."

"I thought so. Christina told me what Tina wore, and some of the pieces of clothing fit her description," Donavan said.

"Well, even though I still don't know what happened to

him, at least I can take some comfort in knowin' he's in the hands of the Lord, now."

Donavan could hear genuine pain in Statler's voice, and he reached out to him. "I know it has to be hard. I have a young daughter, and I can tell you, if anything happened to her, I would be devastated, too."

"I don't know why the Lord seen fit to place that harlot before my boy." He dragged a slow hand through his sparse hair. "I guess I'll just have to live with it."

"I know you're in pain, Mr. Statler," Jack tried to reason with the man, "but Christina Crawford lost just as much as you and I didn't hear her throwin' out slurs on your son."

Statler whirled, and his cold, dark eyes raked over the detective. "Christina Crawford is as much to blame for what happened to my boy as her daughter. She's a whore. Put on this earth by the devil to ruin as many souls as she can. Her daughter ain't any different. The one good thing to come out of all this is the fact that now, I have one less evil to cast out of God's presence."

Donavan looked at Jack, warning him not to interrupt, so the man would say what he had to say and leave.

Jack glanced at Statler, then turned his back on the man. "I guess now is as good a time as any to get back to work. We'll keep you posted on anything we hear, Mr. Statler."

"Thank you. Now, I'll let you get back to what you have to do, and I'll get back to what I have to do." He turned to the door.

Jack spoke up as Statler started to walk out. "If you don't mind my askin', just what is it you plan on doin', Mr. Statler?"

"I'd appreciate it if you'd address me as Reverend Statler. Since I've been called to speak for the Lord God Jehovah, I have earned the right to be treated with respect."

"Okay," Jack stated, continuing to go about his work, "just so we know what Jehovah needs done, why don't you share it with us?"

"Why, it's quite simple, Jack." He stared over at him. "I intend to enlighten as many people as I can, 'bout the evil that has befallen our parish."

"I don't think you need to concern yourself with that task, Reverend Statler." Donavan got up from his chair. "As part of law enforcement, it's our job to protect the people in this parish from the Hindel Mansion."

"I ain't talkin' `bout the Hindel Mansion, Lieutenant Hays. Evil I'm referrin' to's Christina Crawford.

Chapter Fifteen

Rafael appeared in rare form that morning as he walked down the wide staircase to find Lawrence brewing a pot of coffee.

"Good morning, Grandfather." He turned long enough to greet the older man. "I trust you slept well."

"I slept better than I have in days, Lawrence. And it is all thanks to you." Rafael turned a beaming smile on his grandson.

Not used to finding such favor in Rafael's treatment of him, Lawrence did not hesitate to come forward. "Sit down and let me get you an iced sweet roll and a cup of coffee."

"I will be glad to share such a feast with you, Lawrence. We have much to celebrate this morning."

Lawrence tried not to allow his sudden unease to show as he worked on serving the rolls and coffee. "I am glad you are in such good spirits. I know part of your change of mood has to do with the sheriff's department deciding to call off the polygraph test, but I don't know what part I have played in bringing such a joyous occasion about."

"You have everything to do with why I feel so giving towards you, my boy." He bit into the roll, relishing its sweet taste.

"Can you enlighten me on what it is I have done?" Lawrence tried to say the words with strong conviction, but a slight tremor slipped into his voice.

Raphael ignored the whine. Telling himself it would take

time for the younger man to gain the confidence he would need to make his way in a world so much different than the one he had been familiar with. "Tonight, you will stand beside me and receive the gift of immortality, a gift given by the dark side."

Lawrence felt his stomach begin to roll. "I hope I don't disappoint you, Grandfather."

Rafael wiped his mouth on a white, linen-napkin then placed it back across his lap. "How could you disappoint me, Lawrence?" Rafael watched him. "You are stepping forward to receive a gift, that as your father's son, you are entitled to."

"I will do my best to make you proud of me. It is what my father wanted for me, and now, I will fulfill his wishes."

"That you will, Lawrence. This night, with all of our people surrounding us, you will learn what it means to carry the name of Hindel."

In silence, Chandra stood beside her son, and her heart wept, for she knew she could do nothing to stop the evil about to be born. She could not even call on the help of white spirits to help her. Freedom of choice is a gift given to each of God's children. As a child of God, Lawrence had the right to choose between good and evil.

"*Chandra, so good of you to join us this morning,*" Rafael spoke to her in his mind. "*I trust you have been listening to Lawrence's and my conversation. Tonight is going to be a very important time in Lawrence's life. You are welcome to join in on the ceremony.*"

"*No, thank you, Rafael. I have had enough of the evil surrounding this estate. I would ask you to stop this before it is too late, but I already know what your answer would be.*"

A deep rumbling laugh interrupted the silence. "*Yes, Chandra, you are right. This night has been prepared for, for many, many years. My regret is, Jonathan is not here to share in the wonder.*"

"*That is sad, isn't it?*" She did not bother to hide the bitterness in her voice. "*I know how much he would enjoy dragging his son into the filth he so enjoyed while on this plane.*"

"A plane he would still be enjoying if not for you!"

The anger in Rafael's voice made Lawrence jump to his

feet. "Why are you angry, Grandfather? Have I done something?"

"No, Lawrence, you have done nothing." Rafael pulled him back to his chair. "Our friend, Chandra, is here. I invited her to the festivities this evening."

"But why did you get so angry?"

A cryptic smile slipped across his face. "Chandra has a way of bringing out the anger in me, although she knows there is nothing she can do to stop what is going to happen this evening."

"Someday, Rafael, you will be made to pay for your evil. Just as Jonathan paid for all the suffering he caused."

Rafael replied, *"That time is not now, Chandra. I feel I have many more years, if not centuries, to bring the ignorant to their senses. Tonight is but the beginning. Before I am finished, this parish will know the full depth and strength of the dark side."*

"All right, Rafael, what can I do to make you forgo this night and leave Lawrence alone?"

"There is nothing you can do, Chandra. Jonathan has wanted this night for his son almost from the moment of his conception." His tone lost its fake softness allowing the full hostility of his anger to spew forth. *"You have already destroyed the man most important amongst all dark souls walking this plane. Now, his son will step forth and fill the void you have created. Without you, Lawrence would have had many years in which to walk this earth free of the dark side. Now, his fate will be forever sealed this very night."*

Unable to listen to his accusations anymore, she ran from the house and all the evil reaching out to surround her.

"Why do you take pleasure in tormenting the earthbound, Grandfather?" Lawrence asked, even though he knew it might bring the anger down on him.

"Do not waste your pity on a woman who deserves, at the very least, your hatred. She is responsible for the death of your own father."

"I know this, and yet for some strange reason, I feel sorry for her."

"After this night, you will be free of needless human feelings." He tried to leash the rage building within him at

Lawrence's empathy for a woman he himself loathed.

"I am not sure I wish to be devoid of all feelings." He spoke his words aloud. Then, realizing what he had said, dropped his head in shame.

"You feel this way because you have not given yourself over to the dark side. Immortality is given to those worthy enough to appreciate such magnificence in their life. Once you have tasted such strength within your soul, Lawrence, you will never wish to be without it."

The smug face of Jack Olivier' flashed into his mind. Lawrence saw himself cowering in the wake of the other man's strength. Without warning, he felt again that same rage burning through his mind as when he had walked through the doors of his home screaming into the emptiness for a father who could no longer answer his needs. A strange coldness spread throughout his body.

Rafael watched him with an inner knowing. "After this night, no one will make you bend beneath their will. The power will be in your hands, Lawrence. The Jack Olivier's of this world will bow to you."

The thought of Jack being made to fear *his* anger filled him with elation. He turned to the man waiting for his answer. "I am ready to accept my father's legacy."

CHAPTER SIXTEEN

When Barbara answered the phone and heard the soft, sexy voice of a woman asking to speak with her husband, she couldn't keep a slight edge from creeping into her voice. "May I ask whose calling, please?"

The voice on the other line became apologetic. "I'm sorry, Mrs. Hays, I should have identified myself right away. This is Christina Crawford calling, and I need to speak with Detective Hays for a moment if I could."

"Of course," Barbara told her, more at ease now that the woman gave her name. "He's in the backyard, so I'll need to go call him."

Within moments, Donavan came on the line. "Hello, Christina, what can I do for you?" The tone of his voice gentle and caring as he spoke with her.

"I wanted to ask your advice on something, Detective Hays."

"All right. I'll be glad to help in any way I can."

"I want to have a memorial for Tina and Paul Statler. I'm not a church goer, so I don't know how to go about what I want to do."

Donavan could hear her breath catch, and he hastened to put her at ease. "If you want, I can handle the memorial for you. My family and I belong to the United Presbyterian."

"But, since I'm not a member, wouldn't they think it

strange I want to hold a memorial in a church I don't go to?"

"No, Christina. Don't judge all pastors by what you've seen of Statler. The pastor at United Presbyterian is a very caring man. And one I feel was called by God to preach the word."

"All right." Her voice had lost its anxious tone now. "I just want to do something to let Tina and Paul know that I care."

"If it's any comfort, Christina, I believe they already know how much you care," he told her, then added, "if you would like, I could give Pastor Donaldson a call and ask him to speak with you this evening."

"Yes, Detective Hays, I would like that. And thank you for taking the time to help me with this. I didn't know who else to turn to."

"It's my pleasure, Christina. If you need anything else, please don't hesitate to call on me."

"Thank you, Detective Hays. You don't know what a help you are to me right now."

Barbara had been listening to the conversation, and when Donavan hung up the phone, she reached out her arms to him. "I'm so proud of you."

Donavan pulled her against him. "I wish I could do more for her."

"I just had a sad thought run through my mind."

"What?" He drew back to look at her.

"With Christina's and Tina's reputations, do you think anyone will even come to the memorial?"

"I never gave that a thought. I guess it might be a good idea to put a notice in the paper. That way, maybe someone besides us will show up. I know Jack and Seelah will go. Even if people don't come for Christina, they might come for the kids."

"If you want, I can write up the notice and call it into the paper. I don't know all the ins and outs of the kids' lives, but at least a little notice in the paper to let everyone know about the memorial is better than not saying anything at all."

"Thank you, hon." He dropped a kiss on the side of her face. "In the meantime, I think I'll take a run over and let Jack and

Seelah know what we got planned."

"Go ahead and take my car if you want. I haven't put it away yet." She turned to lift the keys off the hook beside the fridge.

"No thanks. It's just a block away, and the walk will do me good. I've been thinking about getting back into shape." He gave her a sheepish grin.

***

Jack opened the door. When he saw Donavan standing on the front step, he pushed open the screen door. "Well, this is a pleasant surprise. Come on in." He stepped back out of the way.

"I thought I'd stop in for a few moments. I got something I want to run by you."

"All right. Seelah just went to the store, so we'll have plenty of privacy."

"Oh, it's nothing she can't hear."

"Okay, that case, I gotta couple beers in the fridge. Want one?"

"Naw. I'm trying to get rid of some of this weight." He smacked a hand against his stomach. "But don't let me stop you from having one."

"I won't." He reached into the fridge. "What's up?"

"I talked to Christina Crawford earlier." He sat down at the kitchen table. "She wants to have a memorial for the kids. I told her I'd talk to the pastor, where Barb and Jennie and I go to church and see if he would mind having the memorial there. I don't see him having a problem with it."

"Sounds like you're all set. Since she'll never have her daughter's body to lay to rest, havin' a memorial might bring her some closure." Jack joined him at the table.

"That's what I thought."

"I can already see a problem here, though." He raised the bottle to his mouth.

"What's that?"

"Statler ain't gonna like her havin' a memorial for his kid. If it ain't at the Assembly, where he can be in control of everything, it ain't gonna happen."

"He's going to know about it. Barb's writing up a notice to put in the paper. I thought if people read about it, some of them might show up."

"I see where you're comin' from. 'Cause of Christina's reputation, all the Christians will feel it their duty to stay home." He snorted a derisive laugh. "But maybe a few will show up outta curiosity. Right?"

"That's what I'm counting on. They'll all want to get a good look at the woman their husbands are talking about."

Jack raised his bottle in a toast. "Amen to that!"

"So, you think having a memorial at the church is a good idea, then?"

"Hell yes, I think it's a good idea! In fact, I think it's a great idea. You know you can count on Seelah and me to show up."

"I already knew that. This way, if Statler shows up to start any shit, you'll be there to help me handle it."

"He'll show up. It involves his kid. He'll wanna be there to call the shots."

"I'm still iffy about taking Jenny, though. This would be her first funeral. If things go the way I think they will, I don't want her first time to be a frightening experience."

"I'd just tell her to be prepared for somethin' that wouldn't happen anywhere but this one time. She's almost twelve years old, Donavan. You can't keep shieldin' her. Otherwise, she'll grow up thinkin' the world's a safe place. And we know that ain't so. Don't we?"

Donavan looked at him for a long moment. "If you said that to talk me into taking her, I think you just lost your fight."

"You know what I mean! I want her to know sometimes, the world can be a scary place. People like Statler do a lotta good, believe it or not." He twisted the cap off the last bottle of beer.

"I can't wait to hear this!"

"Hey, they do. I'll tell you why, smart ass! They teach people what to stay away from. If Jenny goes to the funeral and sees Statler foamin' at the mouth and spewin' out warnin's 'bout the world bein' the devil's playground? She's gonna know to run like hell!"

"You know, Jack," Donavan chuckled, "you never cease to amaze me. Every time I think you can't wind up a point with a valuable lesson, you pull it off!"

"Then you're gonna let Jenny go?"

"Yeah. I might have a hard time talking Barb into it. But yeah. I think, if it'll show her what not to follow, it'll be worth it."

"If she gives you any shit, tell her to give me a call. I'll straighten her out."

"I'll do that."

"In all seriousness, though, Statler has problems. I'm talkin' big problems." Jack drank the last of his beer.

"I know, and that's the last thing we need right now. I think the parish is in for another nightmare like the Jonathan Hindel fiasco. I hope I'm wrong, but the way things are shaping up, I don't think I am. Which brings me back to a point we're still not in agreement on."

"Seelah and me stayin' with you and Barb until this is all over. Right?"

Donavan nodded. "We both know it isn't safe for the two of you to be here alone. You should reconsider and move in with us."

"Seelah says she's confident Chandra would warn us if anything's comin' down. And, she likes being in our own house." He gave Donavan a sheepish grin. "I don't like arguin' with her right now."

"Or any other time." Donavan laughed outright. "Okay, if that's what you feel is best. Just know the offer is always there. I got a feeling that all hell is about to break loose in this town."

"I wish I could disagree with you, but I can't. If ever a town needed to be surrounded by angels, Saint Anthony Parish is that town!"

CHAPTER SEVENTEEN

A full moon enclosed the mansion in a silver glow, but deep in the bowels of the cave, there dwelled an unhealthy darkness.

Chanting voices rose to a fever pitch as one by one the torches, placed in the many holders along the walls, were lit to bath the faces of the assembly in an orange-yellow glow.

Dressed in a long, black, hooded robe, Rafael Hindel stepped forward to place his hands upon an altar. As he picked up a silver chalice, the chanting stopped.

With the chalice held upright with both hands, his deep voice rang out. "Hear me, oh father of darkness. This night, another son will take his place beside you to fulfill your desires upon this plane and ask to receive your sacred gift of immortality."

The faithful parted as a lone figure, dressed in a long, blood-red robe, made his way towards the altar. Lawrence Hindel reached out to grasp the hand being held out to him.

"Are you ready to meet the one master of this plane?" Rafael asked him.

"I am," Lawrence answered, stepping to the altar.

"What are you willing to offer to the master for the gift you covet?"

"To the master, I pledge to embrace the dark side and all the souls residing therein."

"Step forward to greet your master and the master of all

who dwells on this plane."

Lawrence tried to still the tremor of fear racing forward in his mind. Telling himself he must stand firm and show the one coming he deserved this gift.

A great howling erupted into the quiet, and as the piercing sound filled the air, everyone bowed their head.

His mind screamed in panic as he watched a shadowy figure move towards him.

"You will show no fear, Lawrence," Rafael told him. "This night, you will look into the face of darkness and receive the power of the master!"

Lawrence tried not to flinch, but his body began to twitch and then convulse in spasms.

Rafael jerked him upright. "Stop it, Lawrence!" Rafael hissed close to his face. "Do you want to be known as weak in front of all our people? You are the son of Jonathan Hindel! You will stand upright and show no fear!"

"Come forward," the vaporous shadow commanded, holding out his hand.

Lawrence could not make his body respond. He could hear himself moaning and weeping, but he could not seem to stop.

"LAWRENCE!" his name exploded inside his mind seeming to release him from the paralyzing terror holding him in its grip.

The shadowed figure stood watching him, his hand extended, waiting for Lawrence to acknowledge him.

At last, Lawrence held out his hand. He felt himself being wrapped in the arms of the dark energy.

Sickening visions ripped through his mind of tortured souls withering in the throes of a burning fire, their charred and bleeding bodies convulsing as they tried in vain to escape the flames. He could hear their screams and smell the putrid stench of burning flesh. Then, without warning, the vision changed to one of quiet calm and souls dressed in white walking beside a shimmering lake of turquoise blue water. Their faces held a tranquil serenity, and they laughed and sang as they walked towards a figure surrounded by a blinding white light.

Lawrence saw himself standing in a rich green meadow and felt his mind settle as the light moved towards him. He felt all his fear and terror drift away as an overpowering feeling of love surrounded him. He began to walk forward when someone stepped in front of him.

The dark figure blocked the shining light and all else from Lawrence's view.

Lawrence blinked, unable to believe his eyes as he saw his father standing before him.

"This night, you will make a choice of where you wish to spend eternity, my son," Jonathan told him. "But know this, if you choose to follow the dark side, you will know power the likes of which your mortal mind cannot imagine. You will never have to fear the ravages of disease torturing this plane or die a painful death at someone else's hand. You will be in control of all you choose. No one will be able to harm you. You will be able to live on this plane for hundreds of years without having to die and come back to start over. All this will be yours if you choose to give your soul to the dark side."

For a moment, Lawrence tried once more to see the beautiful meadow, but Jonathan stepped closer until all the light became foreshadowed in darkness.

"You are my one son, Lawrence. I wish for you to know all the greatness this night can give you."

Although he tried not to let fear enter in again, he felt himself losing the battle as the grotesque images shot into his mind once more.

"You saw but a moment in time, Lawrence. When you become immortal, you will have centuries to enjoy this life. The Olivier's of this world will never make you cower before them again! You will walk with your head high, and it will be you who is in control of all the weaker souls of this plane."

When Lawrence opened his eyes, Jonathan had disappeared.

"What life will you choose, Lawrence?" Rafael asked him.

"I choose to walk the path of my father." Surprised at how strong and sure his voice sounded in the surrounding silence.

Rafael reached out and drew him into his arms. "The choice you have made is wise, Lawrence. I am proud of you."

A shrill scream split the silence, and Lawrence turned to see where the sound came from. In the light of flickering torches, he watched a young woman being led towards him. When she stood within his reach, the two men beside her stepped back out of the way.

"Please don't hurt me," she cried. "If you let me go, I promise not to tell anyone what has happened here."

Lawrence looked at her, noting the sheer white dress clinging to her ripe curves and her long black hair falling down her back.

He turned to Rafael. "Why has she been brought here?"

"She is here for you, Lawrence. She will be the first to feed the hunger that after this night you will never get enough of." A deep laugh rumbled from his throat as he stepped forward to rip the dress from her body. "Take her, Lawrence. Feel the power well up in your soul as you taste the sweet wine waiting for you."

Almost against his will, Lawrence felt himself move forward to take the terrified girl into his arms.

In her terror, she lashed out, slapping him hard against his face.

Her brazenness brought forth an uncontrollable rage in Lawrence. He jerked her against him and, without thinking, sank his teeth into her flesh.

Sweet, intoxicating blood gushed into his mouth. Then he felt another desire begin to overpower him.

The girl continued to fight him when he threw her to the floor of the cave. She stared up at him, unable to move as she saw him tearing at his robe.

"No," she screamed in her terror, "let me go! You filthy little creep! Don't you dare put your hands on me!"

All the shame he had endured from others wielding their

control over his life exploded in a frenzy of outrage as Lawrence yanked her legs wide to ram himself into her. He could feel her body buck upward as she tried to rid herself of this unwanted intrusion. Her futile struggles but fueled his need. When he, at last, felt the hot juices pour from his loins, he stretched his body out straight.

The power he enjoyed as he lifted his head to stare down at her felt overwhelming. He leaned forward to lick the blood from her wounds. The more he licked, the more he craved.

The girl kicked out one foot catching Lawrence in the groin, making him roll off her body. Instead of withering on the floor in agony, he found he enjoyed the pain she had unleashed on his body. With a low growl, he straddled her and, bending forward, began to enjoy her blood and body in earnest.

Rafael watched Lawrence gorging himself on the girl's flesh, and he smiled, sure in his mind that at long last, Lawrence had now become the man Jonathan would want him to be.

The smell of blood and raw flesh whipped those in attendance into a frenzy. As they came forward to take part in the feeding, they found themselves turned away.

"You will wait to be asked before you enjoy the fruits of this night! It is for Lawrence to say who will join him in his feasting!" Rafael told them.

At last, Lawrence stood, his mouth covered in blood, to look around at the faces watching him. He held out his hand in invitation for them to come forward. "You are welcome to satisfy your hunger."

Rafael pulled his grandson against his chest. "You have made me proud this night, Lawrence."

Lawrence drew in his breath as his body began to throb with excruciating pain. "Grandfather, what is happening to me?" he screamed out his words.

"To live, Lawrence, you must first be willing to die. You are being reborn. Your body is changing into what you traded your soul to inherit. You are becoming one of us, Lawrence."

CHAPTER EIGHTEEN

Two pictures in plain wooden frames sat on a small table covered in white linen. One picture showed a striking young girl, the other, a handsome young man. A single white rose lay atop each picture. Symbolic of youthful innocence.

Seated between Jack and Donavan, Christina Crawford forced herself to look at the pictures, and her heart cried out in anguish. She covered her mouth to stop the screams from spilling out into the silence.

As the pastor walked to the altar, Donavan and Jack reached out to take her hand.

"Today, we are gathered here to say goodbye to two young people who will be sorely missed by their family and friends."

At his words, every eye in the church turned to gaze at the pictures.

"Since they spent the last moments on this earth together," Pastor Donaldson continued, "Ms. Crawford thought it appropriate they share in this memorial. It is hard to imagine the passing of Tina Crawford and Paul Statler being any sadder than it is on this day." He paused to look out over the faces of the congregation. "However, when I learned what else their death has cheated them of, I wept. In less than forty-eight hours Tina and Paul planned to join their friends, on their special night, to receive the diploma they have worked so hard to achieve. Earning their right to step into the adult world and see what the next chapter in their lives held for them. Now, that will not happen."

From the podium, he picked up two scrolls, each tied with a gold ribbon. "Parish High School has elected to give these deserving young adults what they have earned."

The congregation rose to their feet as Donaldson walked to the small table to place a scroll before each picture.

To the utter shock of everyone there, an obese man leaped to his feet to stride up the aisle. When even with the table, he reached out, slapping the white rose and scroll to the floor.

Overwhelmed at the man's blatant disrespect, the pastor took hold of his arm. "You are in the house of the Lord. What are you doing?"

The man stopped. "You will remove your hands from me this instant!" He jerked his arm away. "I am Reverend Statler, and this," he held up the picture for all to see, "is my son, Paul!"

"Reverend Statler," the pastor's hand dropped to his side, "I realize you are in mourning, but this is no way to behave at your son's memorial."

"My son's memorial?" The angry words spewed from his throat. "No one gave permission for this church to hold a memorial for my son!"

At the very moment Donavan and Jack eased from their pew, Seelah heard a deep voice whisper within her mind.

"Look at the man your God has placed before the people to teach his word."

She turned in her seat to see a stranger standing at the back of the church. As she continued to stare at him, he bowed in her direction. Seelah breathed a deep breath in an attempt to calm herself and then faced forward to focus on the goings on around her.

By now, Donavan and Jack stood at the altar. Donavan placed a hand on Statler's arm. "Reverend Statler," Donavan eased in close, "don't make this any harder than it has to be. I realize you are upset, but you are making a complete fool of yourself. And, you are interrupting Tina Crawford's memorial."

"Do you think I care about her?" he yelled, turning to stare at the stunned faces watching him.

The grimace on Statler's face had Donavan looking to Jack for his help in removing the man from the church.

"She pulled my son down into the darkness and allowed the devil to take his soul!"

"Come on, Reverend Statler, Detective Olivier' and I are going to help you get away from here. All you have to do is turn around and walk down this aisle."

They had taken but a few steps when Statler's gaze fell on Christina. He stopped, pointing an accusing finger in her direction. "Fornicator of demons, I will see you burn in hell for what you have stolen from me!"

"Oh, for Christ's sake, will you give it a rest?" Jack's voice exploded into the silence, spurring Donavan to quicken his steps in removing Statler from the church.

In the midst of all the drama, no one noticed a tall man dressed in black leave his pew to move up the aisle to seat himself beside Christina. "I will see he is made to suffer, for all the hell he has put you through." He took her small hand in his.

Christina turned to gaze at him. "Thank you. He is a man without mercy."

"By the time I am through with him, he will beg for mercy."

Seelah grabbed Jenny's hand and, motioning Barbara to follow them, scurried from their pew. Leaving Christina in the hands of the most charismatic man she had ever met.

Outside the church, Donavan and Jack released Statler's arms. "Reverend Statler, I think you should go on home and think about all that's just happened here," Donavan told him. "You don't want your congregation to think less of you."

"The people who fill my church know better than to disrespect me! I am their leader. I stand between them and the Lord God Jehovah."

"In other words," Jack spoke up, "if they want to talk to God, they need to go through you. Is that it?"

"They know I sit at the right hand of God!" The smug look on Statler's face dared him to disagree

"Funny," Jack looked over at Donavan as he shook his head, "I may not be up on all the Bible verses, but I coulda swore it's Jesus who sits at the right hand of God!"

In spite of himself, Donavan had to laugh. "I thought so too, Jack."

"You dare to blaspheme me!" Statler took a step forward. "I am the one who says what will happen to the souls of this parish!" His heavy jowls shook with anger. "Without me, they are all doomed to burn in the fires of an everlasting hell!"

"What do you think?" Jack's voice took on a serious tone. "Paramedics? Or us?"

"Neither, although he's for sure a candidate for the psyche ward."

"Good Christ! Do ya think?"

"I would advise you to go on home, now," Donavan said, turning his attention back to Statler. "Jack and I are going back to be with Christina Crawford at her daughter's memorial. If you come back, we're going to have to arrest you."

With an angry glare, Statler turned away.

"Thank God that fiasco's over," Jack said as he reached for the door to have it flung open as Seelah, Barbara and Jenny ran headlong into him.

"Jack," Seelah cried, rushing into his arms, "you and Donavan need to come back inside!"

"What's goin' on?" Jack drew back to look at her.

"A man is sitting with Christina. I think there's something wrong with him. He spoke to me in my mind about Statler. For him to be able to do that, he has to know I am psychic."

In unison, the two men looked at each other. "Rafael Hindel!"

"You three go back inside and sit down in the back of the church," Donavan told them. "We'll handle this."

Once inside, Donavan walked up one side of the aisle while Jack walked up the other. When they got to the front pew, they saw Christina sitting alone.

"Where's the man who sat with you, Christina?" Donavan

whispered.

"He left."

"He must have gone out the side door," Jack said. "We might still be able to catch him."

In haste, they made their way outside to find the grounds empty.

"Sick son of a bitch!" Jack breathed. "I never gave it a thought he would show up here."

"Me neither, although we should have. The killer almost always shows up at the funeral."

"Yeah, they do. As much as I hate to say it, I guess we better get back inside with Christina, 'case any more lunatics crawl outta the cracks!"

"Before we leave today, I want to ask Christina what Hindel said to her. We both know he didn't come here to hold her hand."

"Not that sick prick! If anything, he came to offer his services on getting revenge on Statler."

"First thing tomorrow, guess where we'll be going?"

"The one place I would give your left nut not to go?"

"Yep!" Donavan told him as they made their way back to the church.

CHAPTER NINETEEN

Growing up in a world interlaced with the other side, Seelah had faced many chilling trials in her young life, but the one confronting her now had to be her most terrifying.

She remembered talking with Chandra once about all the times Jonathan had crept into her mind to wreak havoc on her life. Now Rafael Hindel was seeking her out.

Seelah picked up the phone to dial Barbara's number. As she waited for the call to go through, she tried to stop shaking. At last, she heard a voice on the other line.

"Barbara, I'm so glad you're home."

"Seelah, what's wrong? Is it the baby?" Her voice became anxious.

"No, the baby's fine. I just needed to hear a kind voice is all." Without warning, she felt as though a dam had burst inside her, and she began to cry nonstop.

"Seelah, go sit down and put your feet up. I'm on my way."

Seelah made her way to the couch to lie down, but she couldn't stop crying. "Oh, god, I'm so scared," she moaned. "I don't want this evil around our baby."

She heard the front door open then felt Barbara's loving arms surrounding her. "I'm so glad you're here!" She tried to sit up, but she shook so hard she couldn't.

"You're all right, now, Seelah. I won't leave you." Barbara

pushed her hair away from her tear-stained face. "Try and tell me what's wrong."

"I started thinking about Rafael Hindel knowing I'm psychic, and I just lost all control!"

"Well, of course, you would. He's a terrible man. For him to do what he did to you is unforgivable."

"What am I going to do?" She sat up on the couch, then leaned into the loving arms still surrounding her. "He can get into my mind anytime he wants to!"

"First of all, I want you to try and calm down. Use some of those relaxing exercises you taught me."

"Yes, I do need to calm myself." She began to breathe deep breaths. "Being this upset isn't good for the baby."

"That's right, it isn't, and he's the one we need to think about right now.

"I can't stand the thought of that monster being around him." She began crying all over again.

"Seelah, listen to me." She turned the other woman to face her. "Jack and Donavan are going to see to it that he never comes close to any of us. Do you hear me?" Her own voice shook at the thought of what Hindel could do to them.

Seelah heard the tremble. "You know they can't protect us. Don't you?"

"I know that as long as the Hindels of this world are left to roam free, we're all in danger." She turned, reached for the phone.

"Who are you calling?"

"I want to make sure Jenny is all right. I left her a note telling her where I would be." She punched in the number. "I'm going to tell her to come here."

Without warning, Seelah felt her stomach tighten in fear. She worked on calming her jumbled thoughts enough to concentrate. The picture floating into her mind had her jumping to her feet. "Jenny's in danger!"

"What kind of danger?" Barbara dropped the receiver back in the cradle.

"A man I've never seen before is standing at your door. I can see Jenny coming downstairs to answer the doorbell. We've got to hurry!"

Within moments the women sped to Barbara's home a short distance away. As Barbara turned into the driveway, they could see a man standing on the front porch step talking with Jenny.

"Who the hell are you, and what do you want with my daughter?" Barbara slammed the car door to stride across the lawn.

Horrified, Jenny stepped between her mother and the man still standing on the step. "Mom, this is Mr. Lybbert! He's a teacher at my school!"

"Yeah, right!" Barbara said, never breaking her stride, pleased to see the man step away from Jenny. "I know all the teachers at your school, and he isn't one of them!"

"That's because he just started," Jenny hastened to explain. "Oh god, I can't believe this is happening."

Barbara looked into the dark blue eyes staring at her, and she stood still. "Are you a teacher?"

He brushed a hand back over his short red hair and smiled. "Yes, I am. I guess I should have called before coming over. I wanted to drop off some papers Jenny forgot when she left today."

Seelah watched the man smiling at Barbara and saw his hand tremble as he drew it down his well-groomed beard.

"I'm so sorry. I behaved like a shrew." Barbara reached out her hand to him.

"No need to apologize." He took her small hand in his. "A person can't be too careful these days. Our children must be protected."

"Have you always lived here, Mr. Lybbert?" Seelah spoke up.

"I'm from New Orleans." His attention swung to include her. "I had been teaching in the same school for almost fifteen years, and when I heard about the vacancy here in the parish,

I thought I would look into it." He moved to hold out his hand then thought better of it. "Guess luck surrounded me because they hired me right away."

"Do you have a family?" Barbara entered the conversation.

"No, not yet." The grin he turned on her had her laughing.

"We'll have to see what we can do to remedy that."

"Mom!" Jenny looked at her, horrified. "I'm sure Mr. Lybbert doesn't like talking about his personal life with a complete stranger!"

"Don't let it bother you, Jenny." His eyes lit up. "Your mom is a typical woman. She can't stand to see a man running around loose and enjoying his life."

Seelah watched the interaction between the three, and her stomach knotted without mercy. She tried to relax, but the tension grew worse until she had to speak up. "Are you aquatinted with the Hindel family, Mr. Lybbert?

"I'm afraid I'm not familiar with anyone by that name."

Seelah saw a quick flicker of fear shoot across his blue eyes before he smiled.

"As I said, I'm from New Orleans."

"Yes, that's why I asked if you are aquatinted with the Hindel family. They are a very old name in New Orleans."

He looked into her eyes. "In that case, they are also very wealthy, and since I am a teacher, earning a teacher's salary, that would explain why the name is not familiar to me."

"Does that answer your question, Seelah?" Barbara gave her a pointed look.

"For now," Seelah told her.

"Would you like to come inside, Mr. Lybbert?" Barbara asked. "I could give you a glass of cold lemonade."

"Thanks, but I better be going. I have a lot of papers to grade tonight." He looked over at Jenny. "I hope I won't have to come back with any complaints."

"Jenny giggled. "Don't worry, you won't. My parents are strict when it comes to homework."

"I've enjoyed meeting you, Mrs. Hays." He gave her hand

a gentle squeeze. "Perhaps we can talk again. Under calmer circumstances."

"I'm sure we'll be seeing a lot of you now that you're Jenny's teacher."

He nodded a brief nod at Seelah before walking to his car.

"He's a very nice man, Jenny. I think you're lucky to have him as a teacher." She watched him walk away. "Don't you agree, Seelah?"

The sick fear twisting her insides warned her not to trust him. "I'll wait to make my judgment until I know more about him."

"Aunt Seelah, don't you like him?" Jenny took hold of her cold hand. "He's the most sought after teacher in school. All the girls think he's cute." She got a dreamy look in her eyes. "I like him."

"Aunt Seelah just has eyes for your Uncle Jack, Jenny." She tried to make light of the conversation.

Jenny replied as they made their way inside, "Of course she does! My Uncle Jack is the best looking man in the world. Other than Dad!" she hastened to add.

"Have a seat, Seelah, and I'll get us something cold to drink." Barbara walked to the refrigerator.

"Jenny, could I see the papers your teacher brought over?"

"Of course." Jenny handed them to her. "You won't find them interesting, though. They're just about some project Mr. Lybbert wants us to do."

Barbara turned from filling the glasses with ice. "Getting some insight on school projects, Seelah?" She caught her breath as she saw Seelah run her fingers over the pages. "Jenny, why don't you go get your school clothes changed? Your dad will be home pretty soon, and we're going out to dinner." She filled the glasses with lemonade.

"Are Aunt Seelah and Uncle Jack going too?"

"Of course," Barbara replied, grinning as she saw a bright smile spread over Jenny's face.

"Okay." She took off to change.

"Why did you want to see the papers?" She set the glasses down on the table, plopped herself into the chair nearest to Seelah. "And why are you running your fingers over them?"

"This man is not who he seems to be, Barbara." Her eyes popped open.

"What are you talking about? Of course, he is. He wouldn't make up a story about being a teacher if he couldn't prove it. It's too easy to check." She gave a nervous laugh.

"I don't know all the answers of why he would pretend to be something that he isn't, but I'm telling you right now, he's a fraud."

"Seelah, if you're sure about what you're saying, then we need to tell Jack and Donavan about this right away." She lowered her voice as she heard Jenny coming down the stairs. "In the meantime, you need to call Jack and let him know where you are and that we're all going out to dinner tonight."

"All right, but before I do, there's something you still need to know." She inhaled a deep breath in an attempt to calm her warring nerves.

"I'm anxious to hear it, but I don't want Jenny knowing about all this."

"You don't want me knowing about what?" Jenny asked, coming into the room.

"Adult conversation, Jenny." Barbara pulled her close.

"Enough said, Mom." She gathered up the papers to put them in her backpack.

When Seelah left the room to make her phone call, Barbara reached out to pull Jenny into her arms. "Jenny, I know you like Mr. Lybbert, but I want you to do me a favor, all right?"

"Sure, Mom. You know I always listen to you and Dad."

"I don't ever want you to be alone with this man. He's new, and we don't know anything about him."

"Mom," she squealed, pulling away, "he's a nice man, and he's very nice to me. Any time he needs something done in the classroom, he asks me to do it."

Barbara felt uncomfortable, and she tried not to let her

unease show as she asked, "Does he ever ask you to stay after class to help him?"

"Yes, but just for a few minutes. He knows I have to catch my bus."

"All right, that sounds harmless enough. But, if he ever asks you to stay longer, you are to tell him no. Is that understood, Jenny?"

"Yes, Mom. Jeez, I'm not a baby, you know."

"You'll always be my baby, Jenny." Barbara kissed her on the top of her head. "That is one thing that will never change."

Seelah stood watching this tender scene and tried to remain calm. However, the fear pushing its way into her mind refused to be ignored. Someone had placed Jenny in danger and the sooner her parents knew about it, the better prepared they would be to protect her.

CHAPTER TWENTY

Donavan rapped on the door to the mansion, then waited. "I wonder how long it will take him to give up and answer the door?"

"They might not even be home. The doors on the garage are closed, and with no window, I can't look in to see. Although I doubt they would leave the gate unlocked."

They both turned as the door crept open. "Well, well, to what do we owe this little surprise?" Lawrence stood in the doorway, glaring at them.

"Where's Rafael, Lawrence? We need to talk to him," Donavan told him.

"My grandfather is out at the moment. If you would like to leave a message for him, I'll be glad to give it to him when he returns." He braced his feet wide apart to block their entrance. "I would ask you to come in, but I am busy at the moment and don't wish to be disturbed."

"Jack, I got nothing important to do. How about you?"

"Nope. My time is your time. Guess we'll just wait 'til he shows up."

"You know you could call before driving all the way out here," Lawrence told them, the anger in his voice apparent.

"Yeah, we could, but then we would lose the element of surprise. See, we're detectives, and we thrive on catching people unawares." Donavan smiled into the hostile face of the man staring at him.

"What is it you need to talk with my grandfather about that can't wait?" He left the door ajar to step outside.

"We wondered why he thought it would be in his best interest to go to Tina Crawford's and Paul Statler's memorial yesterday afternoon," Donavan said. "In most cases, when you don't know the people the memorial is for, you have no interest in going. Memorials are very sad and not someplace you make a point of being. Unless, of course, you're one of those people who get off on other people's grief."

Lawrence thought for a moment, then replied, "I'm sure a lot of people attended who didn't know the children being memorialized. They came to show their respect. My grandfather and I are very well-known in this parish. It's almost like we had to go."

"In that case," Jack spoke up, "what's your excuse for not goin'?"

"As I told you, I have things to do. Since my father is no longer here to see to the properties, the duty falls to my grandfather."

"I gotta hand it to you, Lawrence. You're quick on your feet. And you're right, now that your daddy ain't here to carry the Hindel torch, it's pretty much left up to old grandpa to carry on the tradition." Jack stepped closer and took pleasure in watching the other man back up a few steps.

"Jack, do you remember one of the first things we learned about investigating a murder?" Donavan entered the conversation.

Jack glanced at him, a confused look on his face. "I remember a lotta things. Which one are you referrin' to?"

"I'm thinking about the laws of average in the killer making an appearance at the funeral or memorial of their victims."

"Oh yeah!" Jack nodded, knowing where Donavan was going on this one. "Nine times outta ten, the killer or killers will always show up for one last hurrah. And, if the service is "open casket," that just makes their day! That way, they can look into the face of their victim and know their hand is the hand that put them in that nice, satin-lined box. I'm surprised you didn't make a showin', Lawrence. You must love your granddaddy a lot to let him enjoy all that excitement by himself."

"How dare you cast aspersions on my grandfather! He went there to honor the dead! As monarch of the Hindel name, it is his right to do so!" Lawrence lashed out at them. "Before my father's death, it was he who held that title. No one gave more to the people than he did!"

"I agree with all my heart, Lawrence." Jack laughed. "Your daddy had to be the most givin' and most takin' man in this whole damn parish. When it served his purpose, he gave to every charity the people of our little parish could come up with. When it served his greed, he took advantage of every trustin' soul he could feed upon!" He leered into the hostile eyes staring back at him. "Don't bother to pardon the pun!"

"Someday, Jack, you will go too far. I hope I am here to see it. My grandfather is not someone you want to anger. Trust me on that one, Jack.

"Listen, you little prick!" Jack reached out, snatching him forward. "You don't threaten me! You don't, and your grandpa don't! You got that straight, you little puke?"

"You don't scare me, Jack. You can beat me until I am black and blue, and I still will not fear you." He refused to drop his gaze.

"Oh, now what? You gonna tell your grandpa on me? You slimy little bitch!" Jack threw him back away from him.

Donavan stood watching this show of bravery and felt surprise. "I see you're getting some backbone of late, Lawrence. Mind telling us why?"

"I don't have to tell you anything, Detective Hays. You are standing on my property. How I behave in the privacy of my own home is my business."

"You have a valid point, Lawrence. This is your home, and you are entitled to say what you want. Just try not to get too comfortable with your newfound power. If you do, it could land you in a lot of trouble. Remember, the Hindel name is not what it used to be. For sure after we learned about your daddy being a werewolf."

"You would do well to remember the real Jonathan Hindel! The greatest man this town had the privilege to know." Lawrence looked beyond the two men standing before him.

"You've just proven our point, Lawrence," Jack told him. "The people of this parish never knew the real Jonathan Hindel. They just saw what he wanted them to see. You forget Detective Hays and I had the privilege of seeing the face behind the mask, so to speak. When we did, we destroyed him. You might want to remember that!"

Lawrence gazed up at him, and his light eyes took on a look of venom. "And if I were you, I would be thinking about all I have to lose. You both have families you love. I warn you now, keep them very close and never trust their well-being to anyone other than yourselves. You never know who might wish to do them harm."

"You worthless piece of piss!" Jack grabbed him by the neck. "If you or any of your kind even comes close to one of our loved ones, I swear to Christ, right here and now, I'll cut your filthy heart out and stuff it down your fuckin' throat! You got that, you evil son of a bitch!"

"Jack, turn him loose." Donavan came forward to loosen his hold on Lawrence's neck. "We came here to talk with Rafael, and we can see now he isn't here. Let's go."

For a long moment, Jack stood with his hand on the butt of his gun, glaring at the man who had him shaking with anger. "Stay outta my way, or I swear one of these days, I'll blow you straight into hell!"

Donavan slammed the door on his side of the car and started the engine. "Let's get the hell out of here, Jack. I hope I'm wrong, but I think Junior has joined the ranks of the undead." He drove around the circular driveway, then down the lane, and through the open gate.

"What makes you say that?" Jack turned in his seat, giving

Donavan his complete attention.

"He has no fear of us anymore. You know yourself that before if anyone even came close to threatening him, he would cower down like a whipped animal! He don't do that now! Something has happened to take away his fear!"

"I'm worried, Donavan. He was too open in his threats towards our families. He don't care we know he's out to destroy us."

"Why do you think that is? Think god-damn-it! Rafael has made him into the same evil scum he is!"

"All right. I'm not arguing with you." His voice shook, and he did nothing to stop it. "We can't let Barbara and Jenny know what the hell's goin' on. They would be scared shitless. And I don't even wanna think about what this kinda stress could do to Seelah."

"I know you want to protect her by keeping all this quiet, but right now, her safety is more important. Starting tonight, you and Seelah *are* moving in with us. And before you start, it ain't open for discussion!" He gave him a sideways glance.

"You're not gonna get any argument from me. I just want what's best for her. Right now, there's safety in numbers."

"I don't know how I'm going to tell Barbara either, but between the two of us, we'll come up with something. I just hope they believe us."

"Why the hell wouldn't they? They both know about Jonathan bein' a werewolf. Stands to reason his kin could be too. Seelah's pretty good 'bout listenin' when I tell her it's important. 'Sides, she can tune in and see for herself if we're tellin' her the truth."

"If you don't think it would put too much pressure on her, I'd like her to do just that." Donavan looked over at him. "Then we would know for sure if we're just imagining all this or if Lawrence is a threat."

"I can ask her. Sometimes I get so worried about her I feel like grabbin' her and movin' the hell outta this whole god damn state!"

"Funny you should say that because I've been thinking along those lines myself. I thought when we got rid of Jonathan, the evil was done for. Now, here we are again facing the same exact problem."

"They're like a god damn nest of vipers!" Jack watched as Donavan pulled a cigarette from the pack sticking out of his shirt pocket. "Too bad we can't get them all inside the mansion at the same time, then lock the door and blow the whole fuckin' place right off its foundation!"

"Would solve a lot of problems." He lit the cigarette, went to put the pack back in his pocket.

"Hand me one of those. And don't give me any shit 'bout it." He eyed Donavan waiting for him to argue. When he tossed the cigarette across the seat, Jack snagged it in mid-air. "Thanks. My nerves are on overload." He put the cigarette between his lips, lit it and drew the nicotine into his lungs. "Seelah's just gonna have to understand that right now, I need all the help I can get. I'll go outside to smoke. That should be enough to satisfy her."

"You can always use the old 'it's better than chasin' women' argument. That works for some men." Donavan chuckled as he watched Jack turning over his advice in his mind. "It was a joke, Jack. Don't even go there."

"Speakin' of chasin' other women, not that I ever would, I wonder what Chandra thinks 'bout all this shit? We already know she's still at the mansion."

"Good question. But since she's just a spirit now, I don't know how much she can do about all the goings on out there."

"You know, it still boggles my mind to be sittin' here discussin' werewolves, ghosts and psychics. Two years ago, we would have laughed about all this."

"Two years ago, we would have been welding nets!"

"Thanks, Donavan." He slapped him on the shoulder. "I don't know if it's havin' a smoke or what, but it feels good to be able to laugh."

"It does, but we still have the problem of what to tell the girls about all this." He stubbed out the cigarette in the ashtray.

"I hate like hell to bring all this fear back into our lives. And now with Seelah `bout to give birth, it just don't seem fair."

"Life's not fair, Jack. Just when you think you got everything under control, something comes along to let you know you ain't even close."

"Are we gonna tell them right off or wait 'til later on this evenin'?"

"No sense in putting it off. You and Seelah will need to pick up what you're going to need. Might just as well get on it."

"Hit it head on, right? I was just hopin' we could wait at least until after the baby is born." He reached into Donavan's pocket and took out a cigarette.

I gotta feelin' we're in for a long night."

"Yep, and once again, it's all thanks to the Hindels."

"Makes you wonder why God doesn't send down his angels and wipe them off the face of the earth."

"Maybe someday he will. In the meantime, all we can do is depend on each other."

"Here we go again, partner."

CHAPTER TWENTY-ONE

The Gentlemen's Elite Club was one of the few places in the parish that called for a membership card to step foot inside the prestigious club's heavy oak doors. The club catered to male members. The females allowed inside the posh establishment worked there. Although rumor had it the girls did more than serve drinks and strip, no one could prove the rumor. Although many wives in the small parish tried.

Seated at a private table near the back, a tall, middle-aged man sipped from a glass of white wine while he waited for the reason he was there to emerge. She was all he could think about.

He looked around the dimly lit room, his gaze taking in the plush, blood-red carpet and the dark oak-wood paneling. His steel-gray eyes moved over the girls moving about the room to interact with the men waving them forward. Their scanty outfits leaving little to the imagination. His steady gaze fell on a tall girl with raven black hair. Almost as though she could feel him looking at her, she turned and with an inviting smile broadening her lush red mouth, she walked over to his table.

"Is there something I can offer you?" Her voice was soft and pleasant to the senses. Dark brown eyes crinkled with knowing as she watched his gaze linger on the full breasts spilling over her low-cut dress.

"What is your price?" he whispered, his eyes snapping upward.

"Ain't we curt and to the point?" She smiled as her long red nails skimmed down the side of his face.

His hand shot out to curl around her slim wrist. "Your price."

For a moment, their eyes locked, then she purred low in her throat. "You like it rough, don't you, baby? That's fine, but I have a few rules." She waited to see his reaction.

He continued to stare at her.

"You are allowed to leave bruises where they won't show. My face and body are my living. Do you understand what I am telling you?"

Her answer was a curt nod.

"Good." She leaned forward to nip his ear with her pearly white teeth. "I will meet you upstairs." She nodded towards a wide staircase. "The room number is 223. I'll be ready for you in ten minutes." She bit down hard on the lobe of his ear. "Don't be late," she warned him. "I don't like to be kept waiting."

He could feel warm blood trickle down his neck, but he made no move to wipe it away.

She had already walked away when she stopped, turned and then delivered, "My price is one I am quite sure you will be willing to pay. I have never had a complaint about my services."

He motioned one of the girls to refill his glass as she continued on her way up the stairs. When the glass was again filled with sweet wine, he lifted the glass to his lips. No, she was not the one he wanted to be with this evening, but she would have to do, he told himself. The thin cheroot he held between his fingers complimented the taste of the wine, and he leaned back in his chair to relax and wait out the minutes.

The room went dark, and he looked around, trying to see in the dim light of a single candle sitting on his table. He could hear loud snickers and guffaws filtering throughout the room, then loud applause as a bright light clicked on to illuminate a large stage

She stood in the spotlight, a tall statuesque beauty. A long, low-cut black dress clung to every inch of her firm, curvaceous body, and she knew without a doubt she held the eye of every man in the room.

He heard his breath catch as he allowed his eyes to feast on her beauty. He leaned forward in his chair, not wanting to miss a moment of her performance.

The music played soft and provocative, and she moved to its seductive beat. Every move had a purpose, from the shy unzipping of the dress to the teasing smile she bestowed on her admirers.

He could feel the heat of his arousal spread throughout his body. He could not take his eyes off her as she began to disrobe.

The music flowed through her veins like molten lava, and she allowed its magic to consume her. To shut out everything else around her until the beat is all that remained. In an instant, her eyes moved to the back of the room. Although she couldn't see him, she could feel his eyes caressing her, sliding over her like a lover's touch, and at that moment, she danced for him alone.

His hands ached to touch the long, silken mane of dark auburn hair cascading down her back, and he pushed back his chair to get to his feet. Like someone in a trance, he made his way towards the stage when he felt someone yank on his arm.

"You think you can make a fool of me? That I will wait until you are ready to come to me?"

He turned to look down on the dark-haired woman scowling at him.

"I do not wait for anyone!" Her dark green eyes came alive with fire. "You will come with me now or pay me for the time I've wasted on you!"

Her screeching voice grated on his already taut nerves, and her body blocked his view of the one his eyes longed to see. "Leave me," he told her.

"How dare you speak to me in that tone!" she screamed at him, drawing the attention of the other men nearby.

He stared into her eyes and, in a voice that she alone could hear, replied. "You will go to your room and wait for my arrival. Now!" His leashed anger warned her not to argue.

Without a word, she turned towards the stairs. When she glanced back, she saw him staring at the stage and knew she was already a forgotten thought. Anger, for the one who had replaced her, burned without letup inside her mind, and she vowed her revenge.

For a brief moment, Christina stood in the spotlight in all her natural glory then disappeared into the darkness. The lights came up on an empty stage.

Rafael felt his breath explode from his chest. He had to find her and hold her in his arms. But first, he had something to do. He turned towards the stairs. Each step he took seemed to soothe the anger churning through his mind. He walked up to room 223 and taped on the door.

She pulled open the door, a slow smile etching her full mouth. "I knew you could not stay away." She stepped back to allow him to enter the room. "I will prove to you who is the better woman for you." She unbuttoned his shirt, all the while rubbing herself against him. "All the men think she is so hot because she shows off her body. But that is all she will do." She raked her long, red nails over his bared chest. "Christina will get their juices flowing, then walk away. She is just a tease. I," she ran a pink tongue over his hardened nipples, "will finish what she has started and when I am through, you will keep coming back for more."

Her spiteful words soothed his tortured soul. Already he could not allow himself to think of his beautiful Christina being with any man except him.

She stood back, allowing the skimpy robe to fall from her luscious body. She watched lust leap to his dark eyes and laughed deep in her throat. When he reached for her, she came to him. "In a few moments, I promise you, she will be but a memory."

Rafael yanked her against him. Telling himself to take it slow and bide his time with her. She would serve his purpose for the moment, and when the time proved right, the one who would be a memory would not be the woman who filled his heart, but the one, right at that moment, dowsing the fires his Christina had ignited.

CHAPTER TWENTY-TWO

All through dinner, Donavan tried to correlate his thoughts on how to tell Barbara about what they might be up against with the Hindels.

"My, you two have been quiet this evening." She glanced around the table. "In fact, everyone, except me, has been very quiet this evening."

"I'm sorry, hon. Guess I got a lot on my mind." Donavan picked up his fork to continue eating.

"Would you like to share with us?" She looked over at Seelah. "We're pretty good listeners, you know."

"Maybe later." He looked to Jenny, then back at his plate.

"That's fine because Seelah and I have something we want to discuss with the two of you later this evening."

"'Bout what?" Jack watched as Seelah squirmed in her chair.

"We'll discuss it later. Let's just enjoy our dinner."

"Aunt Seelah thinks I have a bad teacher," Jenny piped up. "All because he isn't from around here, she thinks he's dangerous."

"Where's he from?" Jack talked around his mouthful of chicken.

"New Orleans," Jenny told him, then jumped from her chair as Jack spit food across the table. "Good grief, Uncle Jack. What's wrong with you?"

"Sorry, Jenny," he apologized, wiping his mouth on a linen napkin. "Guess I shoulda taken smaller bites."

"Well, duh!" She wiped the food from the front of her dress.

"Myself, I think Jenny's new teacher is very nice," Barbara spoke up on the man's behalf.

"I think we should order dessert. Looks like everyone is finished with their meal," Donavan said, not wanting to discuss anything heavy right at the moment.

"Sounds good to me," Barbara motioned the waiter to their table. "I'm going to have a large slice of your German Chocolate cake with a large scoop of chocolate ice cream, and I want you to smother it all in whip cream. What about you, Donavan?"

"A slice of cherry cheesecake will be fine." He tried to quiet his fear, but Jenny's words kept repeating themselves in his mind.

The waiter looked to the others seated at the table.

"Yummy, cherry cheesecake sounds good to me, too," Jenny declared, rubbing her hands together.

"Jack," Seelah nudged him, "is that what you want?"

"Whatever you're havin' will be fine," he told her, his mind whirling with the latest bit of news.

Seelah looked up at the waiter. "We'll both have the cherry cheesecake," she told him, then leaned in close to whisper to Jack, "What is going on with you? You've been miles away all evening. Is it something I've said?"

Her words snapped him from his stupor. "No, hon. I guess, like Donavan, I'm still on the job. I'll tell you all about it later. Although there is something you need to know now." He lifted a bottle of beer to his mouth.

"We're going to be staying with Donavan and Barbara tonight?"

"That about sums it up." He finished the beer, set the empty bottle down on the table. "No surprisin' you, is there?"

"Nope." She leaned her head on his shoulder, smiled when he dropped a quick kiss on her dark head.

"Holy snake shit," Donavan breathed, unable to believe his eyes.

"What?" Jack asked, then drew in his breath at what he saw.

"Donavan, what's the matter?" Barbara turned to follow his line of vision. "Who are you staring at?"

Across the room, a tall, dark-haired man seated a beautiful redheaded woman at their table. His hand lingered for a brief moment on her shoulder before he drew away to seat himself in a chair across from her.

"I don't believe what I'm seein'." Jack pushed back his chair to get to his feet.

"No, Jack, don't interfere." Donavan motioned him back to his chair with a wave of his hand, then moved back out of the way as the waiter set the small plate of cheesecake down on the table in front of him. "She has a right to go out to dinner with someone. Even if that someone is Rafael Hindel."

"Oh no." Barbara whirled back around. "That's the man who frightened you at the church the day of the memorial, Seelah. He's evil!"

Seelah sat very still as she watched the couple lift their glasses of wine in a toast.

"Who's everyone looking at?" Jenny asked, forking a bite of the rich dessert into her mouth. When her eyes fell on the couple in question, she replied, "Oh, him. He's a friend of my new teacher. Mr. Lybbert introduced him to me when I helped him carry in the fish tanks he brought for our room. He's a very nice man."

The thought of Jenny being so close to a man the likes of Rafael Hindel sent a shiver of fear down Donavan's spine. "Jenny, I want you to stay away from this man. He is not a good person."

"Oh, Daddy, don't be a boob. Of course, he's a nice person. If not, he wouldn't have bought fish tanks for the entire sixth grade."

"Jenny, if your father says you are to stay away from someone, then you will stay away from them," Barbara spoke up.

"Being a well-trained detective, he's in the best position to know good people from bad."

"Does Hindel come to your school often?"

"No, Daddy." She gave him an impatient glance. "I just think you're making too big a deal of all this. Mr. Lybbert is a nice teacher, and I like him. He likes me, too. He told me I'm his favorite student."

"Is that right?" Jack said, his voice taking on a biting tone. "What else has he told you, Jenny?"

"Just that. But I can tell he likes me better than the other kids, 'cause any time he needs help after class, he always picks me."

"That's what Barbara and I wanted to talk with you and Donavan about," she whispered, leaning her face into the crook of his neck, so Jack alone could hear what she said. "Her teacher came to drop off some papers at their house earlier. "I'm telling you, Jack, he's evil."

"I'm not arguing with you, baby. If he's connected to Hindel, that's already a given."

"I think we should end this conversation and enjoy our dessert." Barbara gave Jack and Seelah a pointed look. "Remember, this is supposed to be a fun evening out?"

"It started out that way, but it sure as hell ain't anymore," Jack told her, looking across the room as soft music drifted through the room. "Would you look at that arrogant fu...fool?" He amended as Jenny snickered.

"Uncle Jack, you don't need to watch your language around me. I hear that all the time."

"That may be so, Jenny, but Uncle Jack does need to watch his language around you and every other female." Donavan shot Jack an angry scowl.

"Sorry." He chanced a quick glance at Seelah, who smiled at him.

"I don't know about the rest of you, but I'm ready to get out of here. I don't think I can watch Rafael Hindel play the swain on a full stomach." Donavan pushed back his chair.

As they prepared to leave their table, Christina called out to them in her soft voice. "Detective Hays, how nice to see you and your family enjoying the evening." She held out her hand to him.

"Christina, it's good to see you." Donavan took her hand to give it a quick squeeze. "I'm surprised to see you here."

"You mean you're surprised to see me out having dinner and dancing with a friend so soon after my daughter's murder." Her voice lost its softness, and she stepped back, welcoming the gentle yet firm hands gripping her shoulders. "Rafael took pity on me enough to invite me to have a bite with him."

"I'd be careful, Ms. Crawford." Jack stepped in front of her. "I hear a bite from a Hindel can be a death sentence." He looked into Rafael's eyes.

"Jack, what a lovely wife you have. And I see you both are to be congratulated." His gray eyes skimmed over Seelah's swollen stomach. "It must be so worrisome for you, Ms. Olivier', what with your husband having such a dangerous job and all. I would imagine there are nights you worry about his safety."

"Naw." Jack pulled Seelah close to his side. "She knows as long as I got my gun loaded with them silver bullets, I'm as protected as if I wore a suit of armor."

"Have a safe evening, Christina," Donavan said as he ushered Barbara and Jenny ahead of him. "Let's go, Jack," he called back over his shoulder.

"You behave yourself tonight, grandpa. And try not to stay out too late. Remember, you have five people who can attest to your bein' out with Ms. Crawford this evenin'."

"You can rest assured I will take very good care of our Christina, Jack." Rafael snuggled her close, smiled as he watched anger spread across Jack's face.

"Rafael has been a complete gentleman all evening, Detective Olivier'," Christina purred, running a slender hand down the side of Rafael's face.

"Evenin' ain't over yet," he told her, keeping his gaze fixed on Rafael.

"Jack," Seelah pulled on his arm, "I'm ready to go. Have a good evening. And please," she touched Christina's arm, "take care of yourself."

"Goodness." She watched them walk to the door. "The way everyone is behaving, a body would think I'm spending the evening with a mass murderer."

"Put your mind at ease, my beautiful Christina." He pulled her around to face him. "No one will ever do you harm as long as I am with you." He dropped a gentle kiss on her forehead. "Now that I've found you, I'll never allow you to be far away."

CHAPTER TWENTY-THREE

Chandra walked through the rooms of Jack and Seelah's home and tried not to let her fear of what she knew overpower her. Instead, she cried out to the Holy Ones to do something.

"You can stop this. I know you can! Why do you allow evil to keep feeding on people who have done no wrong? I destroyed Jonathan Hindel and thought that would be the end of it! Except it isn't! Why did you allow me to waste my very soul? I committed the unforgivable sin! I took my own life to destroy a dark spirit, and now I will have to answer for that act. And in the end, I did nothing to stop the evil!"

Chandra dropped to her knees, waiting for someone to come to her. When she looked up, she found she remained alone. No one stepped from the light to comfort her.

"You have abandoned me in my darkest hour. Because I dared to do the unforgivable, you leave me alone on this dark plane to fend for myself."

"Where is your mercy? I know I have offended you, and for this, I am so very sorry. You know I turned my face from the dark side before I destroyed my body. I always believed Holy Mother and Holy Father God would not abandon me if I repented. Now, I find that is not so."

She got to her feet to stand gazing around the room. *"There is so much love in this house, so much goodness. Nevertheless, it will all be shattered because I dared to destroy the all-powerful Jonathan Hindel!"*

"No! No! No!" she screamed out her anger. *"If you have*

abandoned me, then I have nothing to lose in my vengeance against the horror coming down on this family!"

As fast as her anger spewed to the top, it cooled, bringing with it a cold calmness, as the face of the man she still loved floated into her mind.

In her old, familiar way, she wrapped her arms around her chest to give herself comfort. *"He will try and destroy you, my darling. I cannot and will not allow that to happen."*

"Chandra." She heard her name spoken in a clear deep voice, and she looked up to see who called to her.

"We have not abandoned you, Chandra. Nor do we condemn you for taking your own life. You did what had to be done to rid this plane of one of its most evil entities."

A tall man garbed in a long white robe stood before her. His long hair and beard were as white as his robe. His dark blue eyes sparkled with an inner glow.

Guilt at not trusting in the love of the Holy Ones and in their protection filled her until she could no longer look at him. *"I have failed you once again. I did not trust with my soul but with my human heart."*

"You have not crossed over to be cleansed by the loving light of Mother and Father God. Until you have done this, you will continue to straddle both worlds."

"Jonathan Hindel did not reign alone in his evil. Those of his blood have now come to wreak vengeance on those they hold responsible for his destruction. What can I do to protect those I love from their evil?"

"This is a time of testing, Chandra. One of those you love will be tempted to turn their face from the light to embrace the darkness. We are all given the freedom of choice on this plane. We spirits of the light cannot intercede in their right to choose."

"This can't be so. No one I know would choose darkness over light. These people are all fine believers of God. Their souls are surrounded with the white light of the Holy Spirit!"

"Yes, they embrace the light, and for now, that protection will keep them in good stead. But, as time passes, one will be introduced to the wiles of an entity so dark, this person will need all the love and

protection you and all in the Holy Light can bring forth."

"*Who is this person you speak of?"*

"*The laws of spirit do not allow me to share that information with you, Chandra. That way, it will be their choice whether they will allow their soul to be touched by darkness."*

"*Then I can't help them,"* she whispered.

"*Their soul is not in your hands. Their soul must have the chance, good or bad, to travel its own path. If you wish to help, keep yourself attuned, but always remember, it must be their choice, not yours, to walk away from the dark side."*

"*Wait,"* she called out as he began to fade, "*if I don't know who it is I am protecting, how will I know who to stay attuned to?"*

"*You will know, Chandra,"* he told her before disappearing from her sight.

Chandra turned as she heard a key turning in the lock, then watched as Jack and Seelah walked through the door.

"Jack, I don't think we should hang around here for long. I have a bad feeling."

"We'll just be here long enough to grab a few clothes and whatever else we'll need." He moved down the hall to the bedroom. "I'm not psychic, and I have the same feeling."

Seelah pulled clothes from hangers to put them into the opened luggage laid out on the bed. "I'm so worried about Jenny. She's such a trusting girl."

"I pity the son of a bitch who tries to put his hands on her!" He pulled open drawers to remove his underwear and socks. "Donavan's the most level-headed person I know, but if he even thinks Jenny's in danger, he'll blow the head off the one posin' the danger!"

"This Lybbert person is not what he pretends to be, Jack. Now that we know he's involved with the Hindels, I'm even more sure he's evil."

"*Jenny!"* Chandra whispered as she watched the couple pack what they would need. "*Now I know who to watch out for."*

"I think this will do it, Seelah. We got enough for at least a week."

"I'll go get our toothbrushes and everything from the bath." She walked out of the room, leaving Jack to finish.

Chandra moved forward. "*You are not wrong about being in danger here, my darling.*" She ran a gentle hand through his thick dark hair.

Jack stood up and looked around. "I know you're here. I can feel your touch."

"Who are you talking to, Jack?" Seelah walked back into the room.

"Someone is here. I can feel their touch. I think you're psychic abilities are startin' to rub off on me, sweetheart."

"Hello, Chandra." Seelah came forward.

"*I have come to warn you about the danger you are both in, but I see I was worrying without cause. You are getting very strong in your psychic abilities, Seelah.*"

"I have to be on top of things." The smile disappeared from her face. "It seems like this plane gets darker and more dangerous every day."

"*Yes, and now that Rafael has returned to the parish, it is even more so.*"

"What do you mean, Rafael has returned? Are you saying this isn't the first time he has been here?"

Jack stood listening to Seelah converse with the spirit of Chandra, and he could feel himself getting more and more on edge.

"*Rafael came to the parish many years ago when Jonathan was married to Angelia. He did his best to destroy their relationship. But Jonathan would have none of his interference. He loved Angelia with all his heart.*"

"From what I understand, she was the first and last woman he ever gave his heart to."

"*Yes.*" Chandra looked away, remembering those long-ago days. "*Jonathan behaved like a different man then. While Angelia dwelled in his life, he seemed almost happy. But after her death, he became a man inconsolable in his grief. Angelia was the good part of Jonathan. Her death brought out the rest of the monster.*"

"Earlier, you said you came to tell us of the dangers concerning Rafael. Will you share your concerns with me?" Her heart beat faster as she waited for Chandra's reply.

"I have to be very careful here, Seelah. You see, there are laws on the other side that tie my hands. They are called the laws of spirit, and I must abide by them."

"But you haven't crossed over yet. How can you be bound by the laws of spirit if you have chosen to remain earthbound?"

"I have not crossed over, but the ones who protect me and help me to help others have. They are my Holy Ones." Her full mouth widened in a broad smile as she talked about the ones so close to her heart.

"How long have they been with you?" Seelah patted a place on the bed beside her, then reached out to take Jack's hand as he joined her.

"The Holy Ones are very old, and they have been with me throughout all my lifetimes on this plane."

"I never heard you mention them before."

"I don't tell others about them because they are so special. I like to think they belong to me alone, but they don't."

"Have I ever heard of them?" She gave her a puzzled look.

"Yes, Seelah, you have. But you know them as The Circle of Elders."

Her breath caught on a loud gasp. "Oh my god! You work with The Circle of Elders? They are as old as time itself!"

She nodded. *"I thought, when I continued to be so involved with Jonathan's evilness, they would turn their face from me, but they never did."*

"How can that be? I mean, they are so holy. Why would they be around evil?"

"We all go through a testing of the soul. During this testing, the Holy Ones stand back and allow us our freedom of choice. Even though it took a lot of years on this plane for me to turn my face from evil, they never turned their face from me."

"It's my understanding they never turn their face from anyone."

"That is true, except they know a white soul can never turn all the way to the dark side. They already knew that in time I would come back to them. And Mother and Father God in their infinite goodness would be there to welcome me with all their love."

"You must be a very advanced soul, Chandra. I know this is the worst planet in the universe, and souls that are brave enough to come here to be tested can advance their souls faster, but even so, I had no idea a soul could go all the way to the darkness and be welcomed back."

Jack remained sitting beside Seelah on the bed, and although he heard but half of the conversation, he heard enough to tell him they discussed a topic he himself had always wondered about.

Seelah turned. "I know you must have a million questions right at this moment, Jack, but perhaps we should be on our way."

"You're right. We need to get going."

"Yes, the danger that threatens all of you must be dealt with in a very careful way. And, Seelah?"

Seelah turned back at the fear in Chandra's voice. "What is it?"

"Keep the young daughter of Donavan Hays protected at all times. She is in great danger and will need all the love and protection each of you can give her."

"Oh my god!" Seelah went to her. "I knew it! Her new teacher is a friend of Rafael Hindel. Chandra, what can we do to help her?"

"I must go now. I cannot answer all your questions. Please keep her close and never allow her to be alone with her teacher or any of the Hindels."

"You mean Rafael or Lawrence?"

"No, Seelah, she must be protected from all the Hindels."

"But...." she began, then stopped as Chandra disappeared from her sight.

"I don't understand her last warning." She looked at Jack as he hefted their luggage to his shoulder.

"Why, what did she say?"

"That we need to protect Jenny from all the Hindels. I thought just Rafael and Lawrence live in the parish."

The mess they had come upon when he and Donavan checked out the cave flew into his mind. "I think Chandra just gave us some very important insight into what we are dealing with, Seelah. I wish I had known about this before she left because I would like to thank her."

"I think you're at long last seeing the real Chandra."

"Yeah, and I'm startin' to feel like a heel for the way I treated her."

"You know what they say, love," she kissed the side of his face, "it's never too late to learn."

CHAPTER TWENTY-FOUR

When Jack pulled into the driveway, he saw Donavan walk out the front door. "Wonder where he's bound for?" He turned off the engine, stepped out of the truck. "Where you goin' in such an all-fired hurry?"

"You need to start paying more attention to your cell phone," Donavan called out as he walked towards him. "I been trying to call you for almost 45 minutes. I was coming to get you."

"Why? Somebody robbin' the parish bank?" Jack met him halfway.

"No, it seems one of the girls, who works at the Gentleman's Elite Club, got worked over pretty bad. She's at Saint Anthony General in I.C.U."

"Can she identify her attacker?"

"She's unconscious. I guess one of the customers had a date to meet her and when he knocked on her door she didn't answer. He went to the manager, and together they went up to her room and found her all beat to shit."

"Give me a minute to carry in our luggage and let Seelah know what's goin' on, and I'll go with you."

"You need to make it fast. I should have already been at the hospital. They said she may not make it."

"All right, let me get done here, and we'll be on our way." He hurried back to the truck and to Seelah. "We got a call, babe. Soon as I get our stuff inside, I gotta go."

Seelah slid her feet to the ground. "What's going on?"

"A girl got beaten up out at the Gentleman's Elite Club."

Barbara met them at the door. "Let me take that for you, Jack. I know you need to get going." She took the luggage, moved out of the way for Seelah to come in.

Jack dropped a quick kiss on her mouth then turned to leave.

"Jack, wait a moment." She reached out, halting him. "The woman was with Rafael Hindel. He's the one who beat her."

"You sure 'bout that?" He spun around.

"Yes, Jack, I can see it. He beat her until she doesn't even look human."

"Why? Can you see what set him off?"

"Men like Hindel don't need a reason. He beat her just to hurt her. He's evil!"

"I gotta go. Keep the doors locked while we're gone. And look into your crystal ball before opening it!"

"Stop worrying, Jack. We know what to do."

"Just makin' sure. The son of a bitch knows you'll be able to tell us who did this, so he'll be thinkin' 'bout comin' for you."

"Jack, just go on." She shooed him away. "Don't you think if I felt any danger, I wouldn't let you out of my sight?"

"You gotta point. We'll be back as soon as we can." He waved to her over his shoulder.

"Jack, when I say we need to go, I mean we need to go now, not an hour from now."

"If you're through bitchin', I got some info for you." He slid into the seat, pulled the door closed as Donavan backed out of the driveway.

"What's that?"

"Seelah said, the one we're after for the attack on the girl's none other than our ole friend, Rafael Hindel." He lit a cigarette, waited for Donavan to begin thanking him for solving the case. When he remained silent, Jack turned in his seat to look at him. "Ain't the least bit surprised at this?"

"No, Jack, I'm not. We saw Hindel at the restaurant with

Christina Crawford, which means he went to the club, which means he had access to the girl we're on our way to see."

"Right."

"Granted, he had no way of knowing we'd all run into each other tonight, but the fact remains, we got him being at the scene."

"How so? For all we know, he coulda picked her up at her place."

"It's easy enough to check." He grabbed his cell phone from the dash, hit the button to scan the names on the list.

"I hope to hell you ain't callin' Christina Crawford. If you are, all you're gonna do is tip Hindel that we're on to him. You know he's at her place."

"He won't be there. Too soon into the game. He'll want to come off as the complete gentleman before he makes his move."

"If I didn't know better, I'd think you've used this little ploy yourself."

"Maybe I have." He chuckled as he saw the look of surprise crossing Jack's face. "I haven't always been a family man."

"You never cease to amaze me."

"Hello, Christina. I hope I'm not disturbing you. This is Detective Hays calling." He listened to her reply then laughed. "No, I'm not calling to apologize for Detective Olivier's remarks, although I am sure I should. Yes, I agree. He does tend to say just what's on his mind." He glanced at Jack.

"Ask her how lover boy's holdin' up. If he can even get it up."

"What was that, Christina? I had a little interference on my end." He pushed the phone against his chest. "Will you shut the hell up?"

Jack flipped the third finger at him, grinned as Donavan glowered back.

"The reason I'm calling is I need to ask you a question. I know you spent the evening with Rafael Hindel. No, I know that's none of my business. Who you spend your time with is of no concern of mine. Yes, I agree with you. But...if you will give me just a moment, I'll explain why I'm calling."

"Little on the defensive, ain't she?"

"I need to know if Mr. Hindel picked you up at the club." He held the phone away from his ear while she screamed her anger. "I'm sorry. Yes, I agree that was a poor choice of words. However, if you will calm down and let me begin again, I'll get to the point. That's better. What I meant to say is, did Mr. Hindel meet you at the club before taking you out to dinner?"

"Hell, I coulda done better'n that!" Jack didn't bother to halt the laughter in his voice.

"I have a reason for asking you this question, Christina. I am not interfering in your business. I thought you and I have become friends. Friends don't speak to each other like that. Now, take a deep breath and answer my question. Thank you, that's all I needed to know. Have a good evening, Christina and again, I'm sorry for having to bother you." He turned off the phone, tossed it back on the dash.

"So, did he pick her up at the club?"

"Yep. We can place him at the scene." Donavan pulled into a parking space.

"Christina didn't seem too hot on answering your questions." He reached for the door. "Gramps must be one hell of a wooer. I don't know why a woman who looks like she does would want anything to do with his decrepit old ass in the first place."

"That decrepit old ass is loaded. Christina Crawford earns her living by stripping for a room full of those decrepit old asses! Need I say more?"

"I can't see anyone bein' that hungry."

"You're not earning your living by taking off your clothes, Jack."

"No," he snickered. "but I bet I could!"

"You wouldn't have the balls, and you know it, you crazy bastard!" Donavan stepped from the jeep.

"Detective Hays, hold up there," a voice called out.

Donavan turned as a uniformed officer walked towards

him.

"We just got word the woman brought in from that strip club expired about fifteen minutes ago."

"Was she able to ID her attacker?"

The officer shook his head, looked away.

"God damn it!" Donavan breathed. "Have they moved her to the morgue yet?"

"They'd just finished gettin' her ready as I left. So I'd say they already have."

Donavan smacked a hand against his shirt pocket to make sure he had his small camera. "Come on, Jack. I want to get there before they get started on her."

"Thanks, Roberts." Jack nodded to the officer.

"It's started. By this time next week, we could be looking at three or four more bodies."

"This don't make sense. Why would Hindel put himself at the scene? Hell, he has to know we're gonna check on him."

"After we get through here, I want to go to the club and see what we can turn up. Yeah, I agree with you. Putting himself at a murder scene doesn't make any sense. Even though he's a wily bastard, I'm anxious to know how he plans to slip out of this one."

"Simple, he's gonna go with 'prove I did it.' Rafael thinks he's invincible. The laws don't apply to him." Jack could already feel his stomach tighten as they stepped from the elevator.

Donavan growled, "That's what Jonathan thought, right up until his ass got fried. It's just a matter of time until we get Rafael, too."

"I hope he don't stack up the whole parish before that happens." Jack wiped a shaky hand across his forehead.

"You still haven't gotten used to coming here, have you?"

"I doubt if that will ever happen. God damn place gives me the creeps!"

"Remember to breathe through the mouth and step out if you feel yourself getting faint." Donavan pushed on the swinging door.

"Yeah, I know the routine, Donavan. Remember?"

"Perkins," Donavan held out a hand to the man tying a leather apron around his waist. "I see you're already hard at work."

Perkins finished tying the apron, reached out his hand. "Somebody worked her over pretty good." He nodded to a covered body lying on a stainless steel table. "Without a doubt, you got a rage-killing with this one." He whipped off the sheet to uncover a well-proportioned female.

When he saw the extent of damage done to her face, Jack stepped back from the table. "Good Christ!" He covered his mouth. "He hit her so hard the entire left side of her face is caved in."

"Took a strong person to do this much damage. When I first saw her, I thought she'd been hit by a truck."

Donavan stepped up to the table and, with complete calmness, snapped off some close-up pictures.

"I know it has to be done, but god damn, do you have to be so nonchalant about it?" Jack gave him a sour look.

Perkins moved back out of the way to allow Donavan room to work.

"This doesn't bother me at all, Jack and I'll tell you why." He continued to snap off pictures as he moved around the table. "I'm going to make a copy of every picture I take here, then, when the timing is right, you and I are going to pay Christina Crawford a little visit."

"If you want my opinion on that idea, I vote we hold off until we know for sure what we're dealin' with."

"Ain't she a stripper at The Gentleman's Elite Club?" Perkins spoke up.

"Yeah, this woman was one of her co-workers," Donavan told him.

"No shit?" Perkins stared at him. "I always thought that was a pretty upscale place. Is that where she got attacked?"

"That's where she got attacked and murdered," Jack said.

"This is going to sound heartless, but you can bet your

ass when this hits the papers, every wife in the parish is going to be dancing a jig in the streets." Perkins unwrapped a package of different instruments to line them up one by one on the small Mayo table. "They've been trying to get that place closed for years!"

"When this hits the papers, it's gonna rile more than just wives. It's gonna get a lotta people thinkin'!"

"About what?" Perkins reached for a pair of long-handled tweezers.

"About who did this," Donavan told him.

"I don't know why that should cause a ruckus. Murder isn't all that foreign to the parish. When you mix booze and naked broads, you have to expect something like this." Perkins tweezed a short dark hair from the woman's navel to place it in one of the many jars arranged on the table. "I don't know how true it is, but I've heard the girls do a lot more for the gentlemen than take off their clothes."

"Oh," Jack threw up his hands, "there's a fuckin' bulletin."

"Just trying to be of help." Perkins scribbled on a small label, placed it across the jar and then capped it. "The way you two are acting, you'd think we have another Hindel massacre on our hands." When they remained silent, he looked up. "You aren't serious?" He waited for a smile that didn't come

"We are, but you know enough to keep that to yourself. It seems Rafael Hindel showed up at the club last night. Now, all we have to do is tie him to the girl." Donavan placed the camera back inside the case.

"Wait a minute," he gave them his full attention, "are you telling me Rafael Hindel murdered this girl? What the hell are you basing that on?"

"We got our reasons," Jack spoke up.

"That's obvious. Look, just because Lawrence is a nut and his dad was a nut doesn't mean Rafael Hindel's a nut, for Christ's sake."

"Perkins, you and I have known each other for a lot of years. Right?"

"Of course. But that don't..."

"I think you know I would never jump to conclusions in a case."

"That's right, I do, but..."

"If you'd shut the fuck up and let Donavan say what he wants to say, you *could* find out what you want to know."

"Thank you, Jack." Donavan grinned over at him. "Now, as I said, unless I got more than theory going here, I'm not going to zero in on one person."

This time Perkins waited to hear him out.

"We've been investigating the Hindels for some months now. Starting with the disappearance of the two teens."

"That's right, the estate is the last place anyone saw them. I forgot about that. Even so, this is a whole different ball game here. This girl's been beaten to death."

"Can I finish?" Donavan asked.

Perkins spread his hands. "Go ahead."

"After the two teens came up missing, we started keeping a closer eye on the Hindels. What we found is they got a lot more going on out there than people know about."

"Such as?" Perkins pulled a stool over close to the table.

"For one thing, people are living in the cave, again. That and some evidence we took from the estate involving the kids came up missing from a locked evidence room."

"Can you prove the Hindels did it?" His tone held both surprise and fear.

"We're working on it. The night the evidence came up missing, we got Rafael and Lawrence on video at the station. In addition, the outside video showed a man entering the department at the same time. Does that sound like a mere coincidence? I don't think so. Now, we have Rafael present at a murder scene. Do you still think we're jumping to conclusions?"

"Sounds like you got a lot of circumstantial evidence to me."

"What the hell do you want, Perkins," Jack stepped forward, "Hindel caught on camera beatin' her brains out?"

"That would sure tie up any loose ends. All I'm saying is with Hindel's money, you're gonna need a lot more than theory."

"I think you've been inhalin' too much formaldehyde," Jack told him, his eyes scanning the body on the table. "What the fuck...," his breath caught, and he stepped back, "am I seein' things or is that there?"

Perkins got to his feet to get a better view. "What are you seeing?"

"Jesus Christ! What do you mean, what is he seeing? Are you blind?" Donavan stepped closer to the table, pointed at the woman's groin.

"How the hell did I miss that?" He grabbed a pair of magnifying glasses off the table. "Who would shave a pentagram in their pubic hair?"

"Someone who wanted to be sure it got seen." Donavan cast a quick glance at Jack. "You can bet your ass it wasn't her! Still think it's all circumstantial, Perkins?" Donavan pulled the camera back out of his pocket to snap off a close-up picture of the shaved pentagram.

Perkins' head shot up. "Are you implying the killer did this?"

"I'm not implying anything, god damn it! I'm telling you," he punctuated each word with a jab of his finger, "this...is... Rafael...Hindel's...calling-card!"

"Now, just hold on a second." He laughed outright. "You're trying to make me believe that whoever killed this woman took the time to shave a pentagram on her crotch?"

"Perkins, you ignorant fuck! He might as well have signed his name."

"In all my years of practicing forensics, I got to tell you, I've never seen anything like this!"

"You're seeing it now," Donavan told him. "Rafael Hindel's obsessed with letting us know it's him. What does the mark of a pentagram mean to you?"

"Hell, I don't know." He thought for a moment. "Oh yeah," he slapped a hand to his forehead, "all those Lon Chaney movies. Means someone's going to be attacked by a werewolf."

"That's right." Jack gazed at him.

"Jack, I thought you got off the sauce." A wide grin spread across his face. "If you're going to stand here, with a straight face and try to convince me Rafael Hindel's a werewolf, you better start going to those meetings again. Because it's a sure fact, you ain't cured!"

"What's your excuse for my thinking the same thing?" Donavan asked. "Didn't you learn anything from the Jonathan Hindel nightmare?"

"I guess I'm dense because I have no clue what the hell you're even talking about, Hays."

"I'm talking about Jonathan Hindel being a real-life, card-carrying, in-your-face, werewolf! That," he poked a finger in Perkins' chest, "is what the hell I'm talking about!"

"You've got to be kidding!" He backed away out of Donavan's reach. "Hays, there is no such thing as a real-life werewolf."

"Cajuns call it a Rougarou," Jack spoke up. "Just a little bayou folk-lore."

"I don't give a rat's ass what it's called. There's no such thing as a human-wolf. I swear to Christ, you two are over the edge!"

"You know anything you're told, or hear, about an ongoing case is confidential. I want to make that clear." Donavan continued to hold his gaze. "If I hear you've been talking outside this room about anything said here today, I will be filing a grievance against you."

"For what? Werewolf gossiping?" Perkins bent to look at the shaved pentagram again.

"Nope!" Jack got right in his face. "Hinderin' a murder investigation."

"Jack's telling it to you straight, Perkins. You and I been friends a long time. We both know how strict the department is about leaks. For your own protection, keep this to yourself."

"All right." Perkins turned away. "Is there anything else I

should be looking for, Detective Hays?"

Donavan ignored the sarcasm. "No, just the usual. Rape kit, fingernail scrapings, fibers and toxicology findings."

"No animal hairs to be searched for?"

"Not this time. He was still in human form when he did this one."

CHAPTER TWENTY-FIVE

Rafael poured himself a glass of white wine, placed the stopper back in the bottle. Lifting the glass, he walked to the living room to seat himself in a chair before the fireplace. The glowing embers reached out, inviting him to settle back to enjoy its relaxing warmth.

The taste of sweet wine and the changing hues of the flames reminded him of Christina. He breathed in the wine's aroma and brought her forward into his thoughts.

She was everything he had ever wanted in a woman. Beauty of face and body, the softness of voice and an innocence of life's cruelties. For the first time in his life, he wanted to protect someone. He resolved to have Christina Crawford for his very own.

"You aren't like the others, my beautiful Christina," he spoke his words aloud into the quiet. "Someday soon, you will do me the honor of becoming mine alone."

"*Perhaps now you are getting an inkling of what Jonathan felt for his Angelia.*"

Rafael looked up to see Chandra standing beside his chair.

"*You would do well not to intrude upon my private moments this evening, Chandra.*"

"*Why? So you can daydream about a woman who can never belong to you?*"

"*You do not know that. Christina found me very charming.*" He took a sip of the wine, allowed its warmth to flow throughout his body. *"She is a very special woman. One I could be content to spend my days with."*

"And your nights, Rafael?" She sat in the chair next to his. *"Would she welcome you into her bed with the reek of rotted flesh still clinging to you?"*

"Enough!" He sat forward in his chair. *"You will leave me! Now! Or I will send for Lawrence!"*

"If that is your wish. I will not cower before you, Rafael. I know the time will come when you will tell Lawrence I am his mother."

"When I am finished telling him about all the things you have done, he will loathe the very sound of your name."

"This plane is a testing ground for the soul, Rafael. Before I destroyed Jonathan and my body, I would have begged you to keep my secret from Lawrence. Now, I see you will do what you will do, and I will have to accept."

"I don't believe you. Lawrence finding out everything you entered into of your own free will, not just with his father, but everyone he brought to you, will destroy you."

"No, Rafael, it will not. For that was then. I no longer wallow in the filth of the dark side. I have turned my face to my Mother and Father, and they have opened their arms and welcomed me back."

"You are a liar, Chandra! A poor pathetic liar!" He was on his feet now, shaking a fist into the air. *"You cannot return to the light after your soul has dwelled in the darkness my son led you into!"*

"Can a dark spirit call on the spirits of light to come to them? Can a dark spirit ask for the evil you sent to harm Jack, to be bound and sent back to the dark side? You are not thinking, Rafael." She held out her hand to him. *"You can still call on Mother and Father to cleanse your soul."*

"Your naiveté' never ceases to amaze me, Chandra." He sat back down in the chair, picked up his glass of wine. *"You think because you have turned your face to the light that every evil you have committed against your fellow man will be wiped away?"*

"No, that is not true. I know when I return to the other side, I will need to answer for all the pain I have caused on this plane."

"*And that doesn't bother you.*" He swirled the wine in the glass. "*You gave up all the power, all the respect of being a voodoo priestess, to embrace the light. Even knowing that when you step through that tunnel, everything you've ever done in the name of darkness will have to be made right before you will be accepted into the light.*"

"*I will be accepted the moment I step foot on the other side. Our Holy Mother and Holy Father God will be there to meet me with their arms thrown open. It will be my choice to erase the stain on my soul.*"

"*That is the most absurd thinking I have ever heard. You have a free pass to enter into the Kingdom of Heaven, and instead of accepting that pass, you choose to work for it.*" He left his chair to walk to the small portable bar. "*Since I seem to be lacking in white-spirit etiquette, perhaps you will enlighten me on why you would want to go to all this trouble?*"

"*To perfect my soul, Rafael.*" When he continued to stare at her in confusion, she tried once more to explain. "*When a soul comes to this plane, each one is given the gift of free choice.*"

"*I already know about free choice, Chandra.*" He poured his glass full of wine, turned to walk back to his chair. "*What I am waiting to hear about is why, if the choice is yours, you would wish to work for something you already have. You used your free choice to live on the dark side. Therefore, you have already made your choice. When a body dies, unless they decide to remain earthbound, their soul either goes to the light side or the dark side, or what people call heaven or hell! What I am trying to figure out is if you are able to convince those in the light your soul is not bad enough to go to the darkness but pure enough to stroll through the gates of the other side, what are you worrying about? You are home free! Shut up and consider yourself lucky you are able to fool them of your goodness!*"

"*You cannot fool Mother and Father God, Rafael. If* **They** *do not think your soul is worthy, then* **you** *will not think it is worthy.*"

"*Oh, I beg to differ, Chandra.*" A smile lit up the gray eyes as he gazed over at her. "*I think my soul is worthy of anything I wish to do. Now, or in the future, including when I leave this plane.*"

"*That is because, when you leave this plane, your soul will go to the dark side. On the dark side, there will be no one to judge you.*"

"*Wrong again, Chandra.*" He lifted his glass high into the air in a toast. "*I will not just be judged. I will be revered for all I have accomplished on this plane!*"

"*Rafael, when Jonathan offered me the gift of immortality, he was bound by the laws of spirit to show me what I would endure if I chose to give my soul to the dark side.*"

"*I know that. And although you saw what waited, somewhere down the line, you still chose the darkness. What is your point, Chandra?*"

"*Just that you know what awaits you. Don't you ever think about all the agony you are going to have to go through? I know I did.*"

"*No, Chandra, I don't. And I'll tell you why.*" He brought the glass of wine to his lips, sipped. "*The ones who will feel the agony are the ones who stay there. I intend to return to this plane right away.*"

"*How do you intend to do that?*" She felt uneasy, and she could not figure out why.

"*I will be reborn. Soon after my death, an innocent young woman will find she is pregnant, and her joy will consume her until I start to grow up and she sees what she has given life to.*"

Choosing to ignore his words, she replied, "*I wonder if Jonathan has returned to begin his life of destruction all over again.*"

"*If I care to venture a guess, I would say he is waiting until the time is right. One doesn't want to be in utero too soon. That would be boring. I think he will wait until the woman is about to give birth before he makes his entrance.*"

"*How terrible. My heart goes out to any mother who would have such an evil thing happen. And the poor baby. He or she would be doomed from the very start.*"

Rafael looked at her, and in his eyes, she saw something that made her jump to her feet. "*Who's child is Jonathan planning on entering?*"

Rafael laughed, enjoying her terror of the moment. "*A soul is a terrible thing to waste, Chandra. This way, Jonathan returns to start living his life, and the vendetta against Jack Olivier' and Donavan Hays will be complete. A life for a life.*" He watched as horror mounted in her eyes. "*Sometimes, no matter how much we wish to protect a loved one, we find our hands are tied. It is unfortunate that this is one of those times!"*

Chandra knew the warning had to come from her. First thing tomorrow, she would go to Seelah and tell her of Jonathan's plans to destroy her son.

CHAPTER TWENTY-SIX

Donavan and Jack stood outside the gate of the Hindel Mansion, waiting for someone to answer on the intercom. They could hear the deep-throated grunts of gators out in the swamp as they left the water in search of unsuspecting prey.

"God, I hate that sound." Jack scanned the area around him. "I'm always wonderin' if one of them big fuckers is crawlin' up on me."

"Looks like we're leaving anyway." Donavan turned to walk back to the jeep.

"I'm not surprised they don't want company. If I'd committed a murder, I'd be hidin' behind locked doors, too. He knows we'll be comin' for him."

Donavan reached to open the door to the jeep when a voice comes back to him over the intercom. He moved back to the gate.

"Yeah, Hindel, it's Lieutenant Hays and Detective Olivier' out here. We need to come in and talk to you."

"Is it important? It is getting quite late."

Jack punched the button. "Open the fuckin' gate, Hindel! You know why we're here!"

"Always the professional, Jack!" Donavan glared at him. "Thanks to you, we'll be doing good if we see him a week from now."

To their surprise, the gate slid back to allow them entrance onto the grounds.

"See," Jack grinned as they hurried back to the jeep, "you just gotta show him who's boss!"

Donavan drove forward in the darkness. "I think we should have brought backup. We already know we're dealing with a psychopath."

"That's true, but I've yet to see a psychopath who can stop a bullet."

Donavan braked outside the front steps of the mansion, shut off the engine. "First, we're going to go in here and see what he has to say for himself. I know you think we can handle this son of a bitch alone, but I'm not so sure."

"Hindel's voice sounded human on the intercom." He was already stepping from the jeep. "Yoo hoo, Rafael!" Jack cupped his hands to his mouth.

"God damn it, Jack!" Donavan hastened around the jeep. "Do you have a death wish? The bastard already hates us!"

"Oh, calm down, Donavan. I'm just havin' a little fun. I want him to know I ain't afraid of him!"

"Yeah, well, maybe you should be. Remember, he's not out to get just us. He wants to destroy our entire family!"

"Lieutenant Hays, Jack," Rafael greeted them as he walked out onto the porch. "I'm surprised to see you back so soon. I hope nothing has happened in the parish to throw suspicion on Lawrence and me, again."

"Why would you think that, Rafael? Maybe we just want to shoot the shit for a little while." Jack walked up the steps.

"As appealing as that might be, Jack, I already said the hour is late. Lawrence has already retired for the evening, and I am about to do likewise. So, if that's all you came for, I'll let you see yourselves out." He turned to go back inside.

"Hold up there, Mr. Hindel." Donavan came forward. "We have a few questions we need to ask you. We'll try to be brief."

Without a word, Rafael waved them forward.

When they sat at the kitchen table, Hindel relaxed back in his chair to stare over at them.

"What?" Jack drew back his head, spread his hands wide. "You're not even gonna offer us a glass of wine? You're not much of a host."

"According to Lieutenant Hays, this isn't a social call, Jack. I guess we will have to make do without the social amenities this evening."

"Okay. Why'd you kill the hooker at the Gentleman's Elite Club?"

The expression on Hindel's face never changed. "I have no idea what you are talking about, Jack. I have not killed anyone."

"You're a lyin' puke!" Jack bent forward in his chair. "Case you don't know it, we got a witness who places you at the scene of the murder."

"I still have no idea what you are talking about. Maybe if you tell me who this unfortunate person is, I could better understand what their demise has to do with me."

"One of the girls at the Gentleman's Elite Club got herself beaten to death." Donavan entered into the conversation.

"How sad. Although the club being what it is, I am not surprised. I understand it has a very bad reputation. As you can see," he held out his hands for the detectives to look at, "there are no cuts or bruises on either of my hands. If you say the girl died from being beaten to death, whoever did the killing would have to have marks on his hands."

"Yes, that's true he would if he beat her with his fists." Donavan tried not to let surprise show on his face at Hindel's unmarked hands. "We're not sure about that yet. Have you ever been to the Gentlemen's Elite Club, Mr. Hindel?"

"Why are you asking me a question Jack has already answered?"

"When did you go there?"

"I went to the club earlier this evening. I saw you and your lovely family at the restaurant. If you recall, I sat at a table with Ms. Crawford. I am sure she has already apprised you of this information."

"That's right, she has. Although she shared this knowledge

with me after I asked her how she came to be with you."

"What'd you do, Rafael, sample the goods 'til you could be with the eye-poppin' Christina? I think you're gonna have to wait a while for that luscious little tidbit to spread her legs! A woman that fine can have her pick of men!"

The sick feeling in Donavan's stomach sharpened as he waited for Hindel to react to Jack's callous disrespect towards Christina Crawford.

"The thing I don't understand is why she would be with you when she can lay down for a good-lookin' man and still get paid for her time. I mean, come on, we all know what goes on at that club! It's nothin' more'n an upper-class whorehouse!"

Rafael contained his anger as Jack worked on baiting him into saying something incriminating.

"Mr. Hindel, if you got close to one of the girls and she made you lose your temper enough to strike out at her, we can understand how that could happen."

"Yeah, like snickerin' when you couldn't get it up!" Jack laughed outright. "Although I've never had that problem, I can sure understand how it could happen to you. And I can see where it could be a real fuse blower!"

"If you gentlemen are through throwing out aspersions against Ms. Crawford, I think our time here is finished." He rose to his feet. "I will be sure to let her know how you feel about her."

"Who the hell else would shave a pentagram in a woman's crotch, other than you, Rafael?" Jack jumped to his feet to stand toe to toe with the man glaring at him. "A pentagram left on someone's person means that person is gonna be killed by a werewolf!"

"That is very true. It does. As we can see, that prediction came to fruition since you are here investigating a murder."

"So you admit it!" Jack balled his fists, ready to fight. "What the hell did you kill that girl for, Hindel?"

"I never said I did. I agreed with you about the symbolism."

"How do you know about this symbolism? I mean, we know about Jonathan and what he turned out to be, but that don't mean everyone in the bayous knows `bout him. I think you got some explainin' to do."

Rafael's deep laugh filled the silence. "If you are going to accuse everyone who has ever watched a horror movie of being a werewolf, then I think you had better rethink your theory."

Undeterred, Jack plopped back down in the chair. "Let me ask you something. Just how the hell does someone get turned into a monster like that?"

"The answer is simple." Rafael seated himself once more in the chair next to Jack, gazed into his anxious eyes. "To become a werewolf, a person must first be bitten by a werewolf; or and this is very important, Jack, he must be willing to give his soul to the dark side."

Jack felt his mind recoil. "Which one did you choose?" He leaned forward to reach for the gun secreted in his belt.

"There is no reason to reach for your gun," Rafael told him without dropping his gaze. "We are discussing how one would go about becoming a werewolf if one should so choose."

"All right." Jack left his hand where it was. "Then let's discuss Jonathan."

For a flicker of an instant, white-hot anger shone in the steel-gray eyes, then disappeared. "Each soul on this plane is given the gift of free choice. My son chose his path many years ago."

"You're sittin' here tellin' us that of his own free will he chose to become a monster? I thought at the very least someone had to force it on him." Jack scratched his head as he tried to understand what he was being told. "That don't make no fuckin' sense!"

"Why?"

"Why? Because no one in their right mind would choose to become somethin' that enjoys killin' people! Jesus Christ! You need help."

"Calm down, Jack. You asked Mr. Hindel a question, and he's trying to answer that question. I think we should hear him out." Donavan leaned in close as Rafael continued to expound on the dark side.

"Do you believe in immortality, Jack?" Rafael continued to gaze at him.

"I think the closest a person can come to havin' immortality is when he dies and goes home to the other side."

"Which side are you referring to, Jack? There are two, you know."

"Yeah, the light side and the dark side." Jack gazed at him, a smug smile tugging at his mouth. "I'm pretty well up on what happens after we die."

"Ah yes, your wife is psychic. I am sure she has taken the time to explain all of this to you."

"How the hell do you know 'bout my wife? I never told you she's psychic."

"Chandra was kind enough to enlighten me." He waited to see what this latest information would have on the man sitting at his table.

"Let's leave my wife out of this conversation. You had been fillin' us in on how your son came to be a werewolf. Remember?"

"I remember very well. You said you believe a person can achieve immortality when their soul passes to the other side. In a way, that is true. But, what you don't know, is a person can also achieve immortality without ever leaving this plane."

"Bull shit!" Jack scooted back in his chair. "There's no way in hell a person can live forever!"

The conversation going back and forth between the two men made Donavan feel all the more anxious. He knew they had not yet arrived at where they needed to be in questioning Hindel about the murder, and he forced himself to remain seated.

"Up to a point, what you are saying is true." Rafael continued to enlighten Jack. "However, when a person has given his soul to the dark side, he can reside on this plane much longer than the average mortal without having to die and come back."

"How many years are we talkin' 'bout here, Rafael? I mean, this is a big trade-off!" Jack glanced at Donavan to see if he, too, found the conversation puzzling. When Donavan continued to focus his gaze on Rafael, Jack replied, "I sure wouldn't do it for a few extra years."

"Would you do it for a few centuries, Jack?" Rafael took great pleasure in the shocked faces staring back at him.

"Now I know you're outta your fuckin' mind, Rafael! No one can live for centuries! The human body wasn't designed to withstand that length of time!"

Donavan had had enough. "I think I've heard about all I care to about the ins and outs of the dark side, Mr. Hindel. Although it's very interesting, as most fairy tales are, we need to get back to the subject at hand." He laid his notepad down on the table. "What time did you arrive at the club?"

Instead of becoming angry at having his words thrown back in his face, he replied with a quiet calmness, "I can but guess at the time."

"Best ballpark figure." Donavan watched him, the pen poised and ready.

"I would have to say before 5:30 p.m."

"Did you make a date to see one of the girls later on? I'm sure you know all this can be checked out at the club."

"As a matter of fact, I did make a date to see one of the ladies for later on that evening. However, I changed my mind."

"Why?" Jack spoke up. "Did you get a better offer?"

"Let's say I had something more interesting to occupy my time." A look of yearning moved across his face, and he dismissed it, knowing the importance of staying focused.

"The girl you made the date with, can you describe her?" Donavan looked at him.

Rafael glanced up and to the side as though trying to bring the girl's image into his mind. "As close as I can recall, I will say, tall, very attractive in a cheap and vulgar sort of way, and she had long black hair. Oh yes," he gave a derisive little laugh, "she had a very loud, screeching tone in her voice when angry."

Donavan's brows lifted. "Did she get angry with you, Rafael?"

"She got very angry." A wry smile shot across his face

as he recalled the moment. "When I neglected to keep our appointment, she let everyone within hearing distance know how much I had inconvenienced her. I am sure you will have no problem verifying all of this with members of the club."

"All right, you say you broke the appointment, and she became irate in front of others at the club that night. Is this right?"

"Yes."

Knowing he and Jack to be alone on the estate with a man who could turn their lives into an unspeakable nightmare, Donavan weighed his options on how far he could push the man to get at the truth. The pathetic sight of a young woman, her face beaten beyond recognition and lying on a cold slab, drifted through his mind. Swallowing against the sickening image, he pulled the notepad closer. "Mr. Hindel, with your approval, I'd like to throw out some theories about what may have happened."

"Of course, Lieutenant Hays." He sat up straight in his chair placed both hands on the table. "You are doing your job."

"Thank you. Now, let's say you had second thoughts about this girl's availability and decided to keep your appointment with her."

"No, I will not say that."

"Why not?" Donavan tried to read the man's body language, but Rafael remained so calm he showed none of the telltale signs.

"I have already answered this question. However, since you seemed to have missed that part of our discussion, I will answer it again. I did not wish to see the girl as I already had something more interesting to occupy my mind."

"Would you mind sharing with us what this interesting sight might have been?"

"Christina Crawford," he spoke her name on a mere whisper as he brought her image into his mind.

Jack caught the signal Donavan aimed at him and responded by glancing over at Rafael. What he saw was both telling and frightening. The man seemed oblivious to his surroundings.

Donavan cleared his throat, glad to see Rafael respond. "I think we lost you there for a moment, Mr. Hindel."

"I am sorry. I guess my mind wandered to someone else for a moment."

"Yes…well…getting back to our discussion, let's just say you did decide to see this girl, and in the course of your frolicking, she made you angry. In fact, she made you angry enough to strike out at her. We can understand how these things happen." He waited to see how Rafael was processing this line of reasoning, and seeing no response, he continued with his theorizing. "If you hit her in a fit of passion, you could be looking at a charge of manslaughter. Manslaughter carries a lesser degree of culpability than…let's say…murder."

Jack tried to stay calm, as Rafael remained silent and unmoving. The urge to reach for his gun felt almost overpowering. In what seemed like hours, he, at last, heard Rafael's sharp intake of breath.

"Yes, sometimes the human mind can lose control and lash out."

"That's right!" Donavan tried not to become too excited. "This can happen in, say, a fit of passion. There have been documented cases of a person, while in the throes of out-of-control anger, blacking out with no memory of what he did. Is that what happened, Mr. Hindel?"

Rafael smiled then looked into Donavan's eyes. "I am sure the human psyche can snap and leave no recall of what has transpired. However, since, as I have already stated, I did not keep my appointment with this unfortunate individual, I can but surmise that the person who did this terrible thing has a dire anger problem."

Since he now knew Rafael had been toying with him, Donavan tried to hold onto his anger. "Then you're saying you had nothing at all to do with this girl's murder?"

"Believe me, Lieutenant, if I could make it any plainer for you, I would. No, I did not have anything to do with her murder."

"Then, when you walked away from her, you left her

healthy and alive," Jack said.

"Yes. Or more to the point, she walked away from me healthy and alive. The last I saw of her is when she walked up the stairs."

"I guess we got all the information we came for." Donavan put the notepad and pen back in his pocket. "At least for now. I have to advise you, Mr. Hindel, you are not to leave town, and you are to make yourself available in case we have any more questions for you."

"Are Lieutenant Hays' instructions clear to you, Rafael?"

"Yes, Jack. If there is anything I can do to help you solve your case, I want you both to feel free to call on me." He pushed back his chair to get to his feet. "Now, I will see you out."

"We'll be back, Rafael. You can count on it." Jack sidestepped the hand Rafael held out to him. "Let's get the hell outta here, Donavan before I forget I'm a cop."

Donavan slammed the car door, pulled the seatbelt snug across his chest. "We might not have gotten all the information we came for about the murder, but one thing is for damn sure, we now know Hindel *is* into the dark side."

"He did enjoy letting us know that, didn't he?"

"Yeah," Donavan turned the key in the ignition, "now the question is, why?"

CHAPTER TWENTY-SEVEN

"You look like a kid let loose in a toyshop," Donavan snickered as Jack looked around the club.

"I sure don't feel like a kid." He tried not to stare as he spied a well-stacked redhead walking their way. "Them outfits get any skimpier they're gonna have to start sprucin' the bush."

"Wipe your mouth. You're starting to drool."

"Can I help you, gentlemen?" Her green eyes slid over Jack like a shark in blood-infested waters.

Donavan flipped open his badge. "We're here to talk with the manager."

In an instant, her demeanor changed to one of cold indifference. "Take a seat at one of the tables. I'll go get him."

"A little paranoid, are we?" Jack watched her walk away.

"I don't know why. She has to know why we're here."

"A guilty conscience can make people think they're bein' targeted."

They sat down at one of the tables to wait.

A short, stocky man, seated at the end of the bar, glared at them as the enticing redhead nodded in their direction.

"He looks like somebody just squeezed off a sneaker."

Jack laughed. "Yeah, him, when he heard we wanna talk to him."

"Would you gentlemen like to order a drink?" an older woman asked in a bored voice. "The first one is always on the house."

"Yeah, we'll both have whatever is on tap," Donavan glanced up at her.

As she moved away, the man who had been glaring at them walked up to the table.

"I'm Jerry Stalls." His tone echoed his feelings as he pulled a chair away from the table. "I understand you'd like to talk to me."

"That's right. I'm Detective Lieutenant Donavan Hays, and this is my partner, Detective Jack Olivier'."

After a brief handshake, the man seated himself at the table. "What is it this time, detectives?"

"We're here to talk about the murder of one of your girls," Jack said.

A relieved smile flittered across Stalls' face as he moved forward in his chair. "If that's what you're here to talk about, then hell, I'll be glad to help any way I can."

"What did you think we came here for?" Donavan moved his hands off the table as the waitress passed around their beers.

"I don't know." He pulled a pack of cigarettes from his shirt pocket, shook one loose. "Seems like every few months somebody from vice is in here tryin' to catch us doin' somethin' illegal."

"Like maybe, the girls working the rooms upstairs?" Jack flicked his lighter before Stalls could reach for his.

Stalls' face blanched. "Just rumors, started by all the old hens in the parish." He dismissed Jack's words with a flick of his hand.

Jack edged closer in his chair. "Look, pal, we're not vice. Nor are we here lookin' to bust you for pussy-traffickin'. We just wanna talk 'bout the murder."

Now that they were on safer ground, he relaxed. "Far as I could tell, Rolonda seemed like an all right girl. I didn't get many if any, complaints about her. She did her job and tended to her own business."

"Did she ever get out of line with any of the customers?"

Stalls shot Donavan a quick glance, then looked away. "She had a problem with gettin' a little rough. Most of the men didn't mind, but the ones who did would get pissed and try and get their money back."

"Did she get a little rough with one of the men the night of the murder?" Donavan asked.

"She mouthed off to one of them for keeping her waitin'." He tapped the cigarette on the rim of the ashtray. "I was sittin' at the bar and saw the whole thing. Didn't amount to much."

"Can you describe the man she was upset with?"

"Yeah, a tall man dressed in black. I'd guess in his middle to late fifties, dark-complexion, black hair with gray at the temples." Stalls motioned to their waitress. "Bring me my usual, honey," he told her before turning his attention back to Donavan.

"He ever been in here before that night?"

"No. If he had, believe me, I would have noticed."

"Why do you say that?"

"He had a strange air about him. Almost like he was..."

"Lord of the manor and his farts sweetened the air?" Jack finished his sentence for him.

"Yeah, that and almost like he didn't even belong in this era. All and all, he just struck me as a weird son-of-a-bitch!"

"Did you happen to get his name? I mean, this being a private club, and all aren't the customers supposed to be members and sign in?"

"I didn't hear anyone call him by name. He could have come in as a guest. But, even then, he would need to sign in. First time is on the house, but after that, they have to become a member. We got over three hundred men who come here on a regular basis, so you might have a hard time finding him."

"If you can have one of the girls bring over the ledger, I'll know who he is. We already have a pretty good idea who we're looking for."

"I'll go get the book for you myself." He gave Donavan a crooked grin. "No need for anyone else to know that sometimes we're forced to disclose the names of our members and guests."

As the waitress set down the manager's drink, she ran a deliberate hand across Donavan's shoulder. Before he could comment on her brazen behavior, she had already moved away.

"Looks like you still got it, partner." Jack snickered as he saw a pleased grin slide across Donavan's face.

"Here you go, Detective." Stalls laid a heavy book down on the table. "I ear-marked the night of the murder so it would be easier for you to turn to."

"Thanks." Donavan opened the book to the bookmark, ran a finger over the names.

Jack reached across the table to lift a long slender case from his pocket. "You might need these."

Donavan shot him a sour look then opened the case to lift out his glasses. "Thanks." He began to check the list in earnest.

"Do your members *have* to sign in and out, Mr. Stalls?" Jack asked.

"Oh yeah. That's one of the rules. If a member forgets to sign out twice in a row, he gets the boot. No excuses."

"Even if he was to say...pay a hefty fine for the privilege of startin' over?"

"Well, there are always those who will be the exception." He grinned, then turned as he heard the air whistle through Donavan's lungs.

"Here we go." He turned the book for Jack to see.

Jack scanned the names, making a mental note on what time Rafael Hindel signed in and out.

"Do you mind if I ask who it is you're talkin' 'bout?" Stalls tried to see the name Jack had zeroed in on.

Donavan pulled his camera from the case to snap off some pictures. "It would be better if you don't know the name of the person in question, Mr. Stalls. After all, we could be talking about a cold-blooded killer here. I think for your own safety, the less you know, the better."

"Since you put it that way, I guess I can do without knowin' who you're after. Although, if I wanted to know, it wouldn't be hard. He's got to be the one person who hasn't been here before."

"Mr. Stalls, as I said, for your own protection, you're better off not knowing who this person is. That way, you won't be tempted to say anything to him when he shows up here again."

"What the hell do you mean when he shows up here again?" Stalls stared in wide-eyed disbelief. "You just said he could be the one who did the killin'! Now you're tellin' me he could come strollin' through the door?"

"Calm down. We're already investigating this person. We'll be picking him up as soon as we have enough evidence to take him in."

"And in the meantime, he can walk in here and beat the hell out of another girl! This ain't right, man!" He slammed a hand down hard on the table.

Donavan grabbed the glasses of beer to keep them from tipping over. "I doubt he will be stupid enough to harm another girl since he knows we're on to him."

"I hope to hell you're right. These girls might be hook..." he broke off his words, turned away.

"These girls might be what, Mr. Stalls?" Jack couldn't stop the smile forming on his mouth.

"What I meant to say is these girls might be lackin' in morals, but they still got feelin's."

"Thanks for all your help." Donavan got to his feet, held out his hand.

"You've helped more than you know." Jack grasped the other man's hand in a strong grip.

"The evidence is mountin', Donavan." Jack pulled the car door closed. "He had ample time to do this killin'."

"Stalls has a point about Hindel maybe getting to another girl. But without more evidence, we can't do anything to stop him right now."

Donavan reached into his shirt pocket for his cigarettes and was surprised to find a folded piece of paper. "What the hell is this?" He pulled the paper from his pocket, straightened it out.

"What is it a to-do list?" Jack shook a cigarette from the pack Donavan had laid on the seat.

"No. Now I know why that waitress ran her hand over my chest. She was dropping this sheet of paper into my pocket."

"What did she write?" Jack reached for the slip of paper.

"She says she overheard something the night of the murder that we would be interested in hearing." He let the paper drop from his fingers into Jack's.

"This is a brave woman to sign her name and give us her number." Jack looked over at Donavan. "She says to call her after midnight."

"I hope she not only heard something but saw Hindel coming or going."

"That feelin' I had about him stackin' up bodies?"

"Yeah?"

"It just got stronger."

***

When they pulled up in front of the small diner around the corner from the Gentleman's Elite Club, Donavan looked around. "I hope they keep their health insurance up. It looks like a person could get botulism in here real easy."

"Then we better stick with coffee."

They walked through the door, tried to see into the semi-darkness.

"If she's here, I sure can't see her. It's so damn dark in here I don't know how people can see what the hell they're eating."

That's the idea," Jack laughed.

"Okay, she's in the back. Donavan walked down the aisle until he stood beside the booth. "Hazel?"

The plump woman with bleached hair, who had waited on them at the club earlier, looked up and nodded.

Donavan and Jack slipped into the booth across from her.

"Detective Hays and Olivier'," Donavan told her.

Jack reached out to take the hand she held out to them. "You're a very brave woman to do what you're doin'."

"Don't drop any bows. I have an ulterior motive." She picked at the sweet roll setting in front of her.

"All right, and what might that be?" Donavan asked.

"For what I'm about to tell you, I want enough money to get the hell outta here." She grew silent as a waitress walked up to the table.

"Okay, what'll it be?" The young woman glanced at the two men.

"I don't know. What's safe?" Jack winked at her.

The young woman laughed, emitting loud snorts. "I'd stick to the coffee. Made it myself, so I know *it* ain't fucked up."

"Bring two cups, please. Black." Donavan glanced at her, waiting for her to leave.

A sour look crossed her face as she walked away.

"All right, Hazel, you were saying."

"I said I need money to get outta here. I can tell you who killed Rolonda, but if I have to stick around here, I can end up just like her." Her hand trembled as she picked up her cup of coffee. "I ain't willin' to take that chance unless I can be sure I will be long gone before he knows I fingered him."

"How much do you need?" Donavan asked.

"I think I can make it on $500.00."

"All right. If what you have to tell me will help us identify her killer, then I'll give you the money. Fair enough?"

"When will I get the money? There's a bus leavin' out of here tonight. I want to be on it."

"You give us the man we're lookin' for, Hazel, and you have our word, we'll not only give you the money, but we'll also drive you to the bus station," Jack told her.

She gave him a brief nod as the waitress set two cups of coffee on the table.

"Let's hear what you got, Hazel," Donavan said, placing a small cassette recorder in front of her. "Verify you give this statement freely, give your name and the location where you saw what happened."

"My name is Hazel Hopkins, and what I am about to say is given of my own free will.

"Now, let's hear what you saw, Hazel."

"It had to be close to seven pm, May 8, 2010, when I was

cleanin' one of the rooms upstairs in the Gentleman's Elite Club. I stopped cleanin' 'cause I heard a noise comin' from the room next door. At first, I didn't pay it no mind, 'cause I know Rolonda has that room, and she's into a lotta rough stuff with her customers." She shot a quick look to Donavan. "Maybe we can delete that part `bout her havin' customers."

"It's fine the way it is, Hazel. We already know what goes on in the club."

After a moment, she continued. "I really started listenin' when I heard a dull thud, then Rolanda screams for someone to help her. I thought about runnin' downstairs to get someone, but then I thought if I go out of the room, he might hear and come after me. I shoulda gone to get help. Poor Rolanda. I saw her when the paramedics came to take her to the hospital. It was just awful what he did to her, Detectives. I mean, she didn't even look human."

"We know. We saw her at the morgue. Then what happened?"

"Nothin' happened. I guess he left because I heard the door open and close, and I was prayin' to God he didn't come after me."

"Then all you got to offer is what you heard during the murder?"

"Ain't that enough?" She gazed at him through her tears.

"I don't mean to make light of your testimony, but I was in hopes you saw who killed her." Donavan reached for the recorder to shut it off.

"But, I did see who killed her."

"You already told us you never left the room. If you never left the room, how could you see who did the killin'?" Jack's voice held the frustration he felt at being led to a dead end.

Donavan laid a twenty-dollar bill on the table. "Thanks for your help, Hazel." He started to pick up the recorder, but she reached out, pushing his hand away.

"I didn't want to tell you about it, but I did see who did the killin'."

Donavan left the recorder on the table. "Then let's hear it."

"I want you both to know I don't make a habit of doin' this." She pulled some napkins from the holder, blew her nose. "The room I was cleanin' is the voyeur room."

"The what?" Jack spoke up.

"Voyeur room," Donavan told him, the tone of his voice warning Jack to stop asking questions.

"Behind one of the pictures, in the room, is a one-way mirror. It's for the men who like to watch what's goin' on in the next room. You can see what's goin' on, but the people in the room can't see you. I removed the picture, and that's when I saw him."

"You did see who killed her!" Jack was excited now. "Can you describe him?"

"Oh yes. A tall man, in his early to late fifties," she tapped her fingers against her temples, "dark hair with gray right here. Oh, and he had on all dark clothing."

"Well, Hazel, I think you have given us one hell of a statement. I'm sorry about doubting you earlier," Donavan told her.

"Yeah, me too. And I can understand why you wouldn't want to stand up in court and face him. Although it would sure strengthen our case against him if you did. But bein' the evil son of a bitch that he is, I can understand your not wanting him to know who you are."

"He already knows who I am. That's why I want to get far away from here."

"What do you mean he knows who you are? I thought the people being viewed couldn't see who watched them," Donavan spoke up.

"I thought so, too. But when I was watchin'? He turned and looked straight at me."

"He coulda just had a feelin' somebody watched him." Jack tried to allay her fears.

"No, he knew I watched him, 'cause when he looked at me, he laughed, as though he enjoyed the fact I saw what he did."

Donavan laid four one-hundred-dollar bills and four twenties on the table in front of her. "Thank you, Hazel. I wish I could give you more because you sure as hell earned it."

"You get me to the bus station, and I'll be satisfied. I know you both have to think me a real coward for wanting to run like this, but I can't help it. The look in his eyes, when he turned to stare at me, is somethin' I know I will be seein' in my dreams for a long time to come."

"You're wrong, Hazel. We don't think you're a coward. In fact, now that you told us he knows who you are, if you hadn't decided it would be in your best interest to leave, I would have suggested it."

"After what he did to Rolanda, you wouldn't have to do much talkin'. He's a real monster."

"Hazel," Jack turned to her, "you don't know how right you are."

Chapter Twenty-Eight

Seelah lay down on the sofa and tried to relax. She felt restless and didn't know why. It felt like something foreboding waited.

"Do you feel like some lunch?" Barbara asked, coming into the room.

"Not really."

"What's wrong? You been acting moody all morning."

"I don't know, Barb. I know something is about to happen, but I can't see it."

"Is it something bad?" Barbara sat down on the hassock in front of the couch.

"I think it is. If I could just zero in on it! I don't understand why I can't."

"I have an idea. Why don't we go out and sit on the patio? I'll bring out the hassock so you can put your feet up. Maybe a little fresh air will make you feel better."

"You could be right."

Seated in one of the patio chairs with her feet propped up, she had to admit she did feel a little more fit. A little, but not much. The feeling she had that something waited to happen still lingered.

"Now that I have you all settled, I'll go get us some cold lemonade."

Seelah closed her eyes, relishing the slight breeze blowing

across her face.

"Seelah."

She opened her eyes to see Chandra seated in one of the chairs. "Chandra, what a pleasant surprise." When Chandra did not return her smile, her unease grew stronger. "Tell me what is going on, Chandra. All morning I have felt something bad is about to happen, but so far, I've been unable to see what it is."

"I thought it best to be here with you before you realize what is going on."

"Oh my god, something is going to happen to Jack. You have to stop it, Chandra! You have to!" Her breath came in sharp gasps.

"Calm down, Seelah. This isn't good for Jack's son!"

Seelah refused to be coddled. "I trusted you to protect him."

"It isn't Jack!" Chandra raised her voice to be heard over Seelah's hysterics. *"Seelah, it isn't Jack."*

Seelah wiped her face on the hem of her smock. "Then who?" Her voice still held her frustration.

"Seelah, what in the world is going on out here? I could hear you yelling all the way inside." Barbara looked around to be sure no one lurked around the patio. "Who are you upset with?"

As though she had not spoken, Seelah continued to focus her attention on Chandra. "I asked you a question, Chandra. Who is it that is in danger?"

"Danger? Oh my god." Barbara went to Seelah and pulled her into her arms.

Seelah jerked away. "Please, leave me alone right now, Barbara. I need to know who Chandra says is in danger."

Stunned, Barbara released her, moving away.

"Jonathan Hindel is returning to this plane," Chandra said the words in a straightforward voice.

"Why is Jonathan returning to this plane?"

"Oh, for goodness sake!" Barbara laughed a nervous laugh. "You had me scared for a moment, Seelah. Jonathan is in hell. We don't need to worry about him anymore."

"Please be quiet, Barbara. Jonathan Hindel is still a formidable enemy. Chandra," she turned to look at her, "I would appreciate your answering my question. Who is in danger from Jonathan?

"Rafael Hindel informed me Jonathan is returning to this plane to be reborn."

"All right, and how does he plan to do this? In order to be reborn, he must first choose an infant whose soul he will trade for his own." Seelah's feet hit the floor. "What are you saying, Chandra? Whose child has he chosen to replace?"

"Your child, Seelah."

The scream started low in her belly, gaining strength as it pushed its way out into the silence.

"What is going on? I don't understand any of this!" Barbara whirled. "God damn it, Chandra, what did you tell her?"

"She said Jonathan is going to exchange my son's soul with his!" Seelah fell into a fit of weeping.

"Oh, bullshit, he can't do that, Seelah."

Silently Seelah shook her head up and down, unable to form the words.

"That does it! I'm going to go call Donavan and Jack. If you keep behaving like this, you're going to give birth to this baby right here!"

Chandra stood, then walked behind Seelah. She spread a white light intermingled with green all around her. *"You must calm down, Seelah."* Her voice flowed over the woman still in the grips of her terror.

"Donavan and Jack are on their way," Barbara said, coming back to stand beside her. "In the meantime, you need to try and relax.

Under Chandra's healing hands, Seelah felt a calmness travel upward throughout her body to pull the fear deep inside. "Thank you, Chandra. I feel better now. Barb," she glanced over at the woman standing beside her, "what did Jack say when you talked to him?"

"I didn't talk to Jack. I talked to Donavan. I told him he

and Jack needed to get home right now. I hung up before they could ask any questions."

"*Jack needs to know about the evil coming for his son,*" Chandra whispered.

"Yes, I will tell Jack what is going on." Her voice sounded very calm and sleepy, and her words sounded a bit slurred.

"I still don't understand all this. If Jonathan Hindel is dead, why are we worrying about him? He can't hurt you." Barbara paced back and forth as she watched for Donavan and Jack.

"Barb, will you put my legs back up on the hassock, please? I can't seem to do it myself."

"I swear, if I didn't know better, I'd say, from the sound of your voice, you're blitzed. Did you hypnotize yourself?"

"Chandra has placed me in a slight trance. She knows I need to stay calm for the baby."

"And she's right." Barbara turned as she heard the breaks on the jeep screech to a stop in the driveway. "Thank god!"

As soon as Donavan turned off the engine, Jack bolted from the jeep to race across the lawn. "What is it, Baby? Are you in labor?" He dropped to his knees in front of her to gather her into his arms.

Seelah fought her way free of his constricting embrace.

"I'm not in labor, Jack," her voice held a slight slur as she answered him.

"What the hell?" He drew back to stare at her. "Have you been drinkin'! You know better than to drink when you're pregnant!"

"She hasn't been drinking, Jack," Barbara told him as Donavan slipped his arm around her waist. "Chandra put her in a trance to calm her."

Jack stood up. "What in the hell is goin' on here? We busted our asses to get here, not to mention takin' off early from work, thinkin' you'd gone into labor. Now all I'm hearin' is Chandra put you in a trance?"

"If you'd been here a few moments ago, you would have seen *why* she needed to be in a trance. Chandra had her so upset

I thought Seelah might give birth right here."

"Chandra is not to blame for my being upset. She had to tell me what Jonathan Hindel is planning."

"What the hell does Jonathan Hindel have to do with any of this?"

"I think you better sit down, Jack," Seelah told him. "What I am about to tell you is going to upset you very much."

"Seelah, I don't need to sit down. Just tell me!"

"Chandra told me that Jonathan Hindel is planning on coming back to this plane. In order for him to do this, he will first have to be reborn into a new body."

"So what's the problem? He'll come back, get born and have to grow up again." He chuckled, feeling some of the fear slide from his shoulders. "Sounds to me like we gotta lotta years 'fore he can stir up any real shit."

"You're wrong, Jack." Seelah rubbed the hem of her smock across her eyes.

"Run in the house and grab her some tissues," Donavan whispered to Barbara.

"Okay, and just how am I wrong, Seelah?"

"In order for Jonathan to be reborn, he first has to find a woman who is about to give birth."

Jack felt the fear slip back over him. "And then what?"

"Then he will replace his soul with the soul of the child she is carrying." Despite her trance-like state, Seelah dropped her face in her hands.

"Are you tellin' me Jonathan Hindel plans to exchange our son's soul with his own?" When Seelah nodded, he felt his surroundings tilt, and he slid to his knees.

Donavan watched them try to hold onto their world, and he felt his anger explode. "That evil piece of piss! Why can't he stay in hell where he belongs?"

Barbara hurried out of the house with the box of tissues just as Donavan let loose on his anger. "Donavan, I think we should handle this inside. The neighbors have had enough of a show for one morning." She nodded across the street.

Donavan looked around to see an elderly woman, hosing off her driveway and gazing their way. "The show's over, for now, Ms. Phelps. You can go on about your business." He waved to her.

In a huff, she whirled to stomp back up the driveway.

"Donavan," Barbara chastised him, "she's the biggest gossip in the neighborhood."

"Screw her!" Donavan walked over to Jack and, placing his hand beneath his arm, lifted him to his feet. "I think we need to get out of the line of nosey neighbors. I'll bring Seelah." Donavan leaned down and, with no problem, hefted the small woman into his arms.

Barbara ran ahead of him. "Put her down on the couch."

"I will be fine. It's just that I am so woozy I don't want to try and stand," Seelah said as Barbara placed one of the couch pillows beneath her head.

Donavan walked into the kitchen to find Jack twisting the lid from a fresh bottle of brandy. "Since you're pouring, pour one for Barb and me, too."

"What the hell are we gonna do 'bout this, Donavan?" Jack dumped a hefty portion of liquor into each glass.

"Right now, I don't have the foggiest. Hopefully, Chandra will come up with some answers. Because I'll tell you, right at the moment, she's all we got."

"Donavan, we don't even know if something like this is possible." He took a swallow of his drink, waited for his throat to stop burning. "I mean, how the hell can one soul push out another soul and just move in?"

"I don't know." Donavan swirled the liquor around in his glass, thinking about their problem. "It would explain a theory I've had for a long time, though."

"What theory is that?" He swallowed the last of his drink reached for the bottle of brandy.

Donavan took the bottle from his hand, screwed down the cap, placed the bottle back in the cupboard. "I'm not trying to be a poor host, but right now, we both need to keep a clear head. If you want another drink, there's beer in the fridge."

"Naw, you're right. We need to keep our shit together." He took both their glasses to the sink to rinse them. "You were gonna tell me about your theory?"

"I've always wondered about the belief some people hold of a person being born without a conscience. I just never could wrap my mind around that."

"I don't know why not." Jack tore off a paper towel, wiped the glasses dry, put them back in the cupboard. "We've dealt with some pretty coldhearted sons-ah-bitches!"

Seelah's asleep." Barbara walked into the kitchen and picked up the glass of brandy Jack had poured for her. "Chandra has her so zonked she can't hold her eyes open."

"Good, she needs to relax," Donavan said.

"You should have seen her earlier. I thought for sure she would go into labor."

"That's the last thing she needs to do right now. If any of what Chandra says *is* true, Seelah needs to hold off giving birth to this baby as long as possible."

"I don't know how to fight this." Jack peeked around the corner to check on Seelah." We can't shoot the bastard. We can't even beat the shit outta him."

Chandra stood watching as Jack paced around the room, and her heart went out to him. "*I will do all in my power to protect your son and all you hold dear, my darling. You must stay strong and trust that I will help you. The one coming back into your life must not win this battle.*"

CHAPTER TWENTY-NINE

Jack picked up the remote, clicked off the TV. As he laid the control back down on the end table, he chanced a quick glance at Seelah. "I didn't think you were any more interested in that show than I was." When she remained staring at the blank screen, he spoke up, "Seelah, we need to talk. Ignorin' what's happenin' ain't gonna get anything resolved."

"I don't know what to do," she whispered, her gaze still focused across the room. "For the first time in my life, I am unable to relax my mind enough to think." She rubbed her hands back and forth across her swollen stomach. "I'm his mother. I should be able to protect him from all this."

"How do you think I feel? You're my family, and as the man of the house, it's my place to protect the both of you." He pulled her against him. "What about your guides? Ain't they able to step in and do somethin' here?"

"I would think they could help. After all, it would be good energy combating bad."

"That's how I see it. Ever since you told me about our guides and how they can help us out of a tight spot, I've sure trusted in mine."

Seelah looked at him, and despite her fear, she smiled. "I have always trusted in my guides, too, Jack. Up until Chandra told us about what Jonathan had planned, I never doubted their ability to protect me."

"Are you tellin' me that's changed?" He drew back to stare at her. "If that's so, then we might as well hang it up." He moved away.

"It isn't that I don't trust them. It's that I don't know how much they will be able to do."

"You know, there's somethin' that has always bothered me."

"What's that?"

"Freedom of choice." Caught up in his thoughts, Jack left the couch to pace the floor. "We keep hearin' 'bout freedom of choice for the Hindel's freedom of choice for all the killers and pedophiles and all the other assholes who want a price for their soul. What about the baby's choice? When the hell does he get a say in what's goin' on?"

"That is a very good question, Jack." Seelah scooted down, rested her head against the arm of the couch.

"Yeah, I think so. And all the talk you hear 'bout women's rights. What 'bout the poor little baby's rights? Maybe he don't wanna be killed in the womb. Maybe he wants a chance to grow up and have a life. And, if she didn't wanna take a chance on startin' a new life, then she should'a kept her legs crossed."

"I have heard it said, we make a decision to come to this plane while we are still on the other side. That it is our choice to come here. If that is true, then how can someone or something go against that choice?"

"Exactly," he nodded in agreement. "Shouldn't there be spirit-laws in place to keep the abortionist and the dark spirits from intervenin' with that choice?"

"I certainly think there should be."

"Too bad Chandra ain't here right now. I bet she'd know the answers to these questions." He walked back over to the couch, plopped down beside her. "You got any way to send for her?"

"I could try. I am sure, after what she found out about Jonathan, she is keeping herself attuned to my energy." Seelah looked at Jack, waiting for him to move over and give her room to stretch her body out straight. As he scooted to the far side of the couch, she laid back, closed her eyes and, taking several deep breaths, tried to relax her body.

Without warning, a scene inside the home of Donavan and Barbara Hays slammed into her mind. As she watched, she saw Barbara pull the vacuum cleaner from the hall closet and, pushing it ahead of her, stoop to plug it into the wall fixture. As the cleaner roared to life, she maneuvered it over the floor of the living room, unaware of someone moving up behind her. Feeling a tug on her arm, she whirled to see Donavan, one hand clutched to his chest.

Seelah sat up, her breathing harsh and labored. "We need to get over to Donavan and Barb's house right away." She swung her legs to the floor.

"Why, what the hell's goin' on?"

"I saw Donavan clutching his chest. I think he might be having a heart attack."

"Ah, Christ no!" Jack was on his feet and moving towards the door as Seelah shoved her feet into her shoes. As soon as he could, he helped her out the door and down the walk to the truck. Not waiting for her to try and get into the vehicle on her own, he pulled open the door, lifted her into the seat of the pickup.

***

"Donavan!" Barbara screamed as Donavan slipped to the floor, dragging her down with him. She lifted his head into her arms, rocking him back and forth. "What's wrong? Donavan, talk to me and tell me what's wrong." She shook him, trying to get a response, then bent forward, raining kisses over his face.

"You need to move outta the way, Barb. I already called the paramedics." Jack hauled her to her feet before dropping to his knees. "They'll be here shortly."

As though in a daze, Barbara turned to see Seelah holding out her arms. "Oh, Seelah, what is wrong with him?"

"I don't know, sweetheart. The ambulance will be here soon, and then they will get him to the hospital where he can get help. Right now, we need to back out of the way and let Jack do what he can for him."

Placing fingers to the side of Donavan's neck, Jack breathed a sigh of relief as he felt a faint pulse. "Don't you die on me! Do you hear me, Donavan? I said don't you die on me!" Positioning Donavan's head up and back, he gave two sharp, quick breaths into his mouth. Seeing no results, he placed one hand over the other to press down hard on Donavan's chest. "You know what the hell we got goin' on here!" he grunted, breathed two more sharp breathes, watched as Donavan's chest rose and fell. "You know you can't leave me to handle this all alone!"

Donavan stared up at him, his eyes glazed with pain.

"Come on, we'll take over now." A man pulled him to his feet, then threw up his hands as Jack whirled, his fists balled and ready.

"Don't swing on me, man," a husky paramedic told him, dropping his hands and yanking open a large first-aid chest, "your partner needs me too much right now for you to bust me up."

Jack stumbled out the front door and onto the porch. Uncaring of the tears rolling down his face or the thick mucus dripping from his nose, he cried out to the unseen. "I ain't a prayin' man, but I'm beggin' with everything in me, don't let him die. I ain't strong enough to pass this test, that's comin', all by myself. `You got enough do-gooders. All I'm askin' is for one. I'll do anything you ask, just...don't...let...him...die." Jack wiped his face on his arm.

"Jack," Seelah put her arm around his waist, "they're going to be taking Donavan to the hospital now. I know how much you need to be with him. So why don't you go on ahead to the hospital. Barb is going to ride in the ambulance with Donavan."

"Ain't you comin'?"

"I told Barb I would stay here to be with Jenny when she gets home from school. I'll be all right, "she told him as a look of uncertainty skittered across his face. "Jenny's already on her bus, so as soon as she gets here, I will drive us both to the hospital. You can drive Donavan's jeep. I'm sure he won't mind."

"Yeah, I can do that. I left the keys in the truck."

"Jack, I can't tell you what you want to hear." She swiped the tips of her fingers beneath his eyes. "Donavan is in a very bad way right now. He might not make it. If you have ever prayed in your life, now would be a good time to offer up the best you have."

"That's all I been doin' since I found him on the floor. But, Seelah, I don't think I'm bein' heard." He pulled her against his chest for a moment. "Looks like they're loadin' him up, so I'll follow behind the ambulance."

Seelah watched as the paramedics lifted the stretcher into the ambulance, and her breath shot from her lungs. A dark shadow hovered just above Donavan's head. As she watched, the shadow turned, allowing her to see its face.

Chandra stood watching in horror as Jonathan Hindel held her gaze, his energy every bit as evil as it was before she destroyed their bodies.

Jonathan grimaced, then swooped down in front of her. *"You can do nothing to stop what is planned for this mortal, Chandra."*

"Are you saying it was you who caused this pain Donavan Hays is suffering?" She saw his smile of admission. *"Why? I am the one who destroyed you. Why aren't you turning your wrath on me?"*

"Your time will come, Chandra. Of this, I can promise you. Because of you, the vengeance of the dark side is set to fall on every man, woman and child in this parish."

"Do not think to lay the blame for your evil on me, Jonathan. I had no choice but to destroy you."

Diabolical laughter chilled her. *"You only destroyed a part of me, Chandra. The Hindel legacy lives on. Now, you and this parish will reap what you have so thoughtlessly, sown."*

"Since I am the one who ended your days on this plane, Jonathan, why don't you simply take your revenge against me and leave everyone else alone?"

"You know, and I know, right now, I am unable to touch you. However, something is coming that no one will be able to stop."

"Jonathan, just as you disallowed Lawrence in seeing what

awaited him in the White Light, you have been misled in what you can and can't do to a white spirit."

"Lawrence was not kept from seeing what his life would be like if he chose the White Side. Freedom of choice. Remember?"

"I was there, Jonathan. I saw Lawrence gazing past the vale and trying to better see into the Light when you deliberately stepped in front of him. You wanted to make sure he chose the path you had chosen for him, not the path he would choose for himself."

"The choice has been made, Chandra. Lawrence is where he belongs."

"If I have to, I will call on every White Spirit in God's legion. This evil must be stopped."

"Chandra, you can call on anyone you choose. It still will not stop what is already set in motion. This parish and all its people are doomed to suffer what you, in your ignorance, brought down on their souls."

"I do not believe you, Jonathan," she cried out. *"You are not that strong."*

Hearing fear creep into her voice, his resolve to weld the upper hand climbed higher. *"What you say is true, but with the one I serve walking beside me, my strength grows to new heights."*

Seelah jumped as the siren on the ambulance cut through the silence, momentarily calling her attention away from the unbelievable scene going on across the way.

Chandra moved across the yard. *"Seelah, I know what you are seeing has to be very upsetting to you, but you need to trust me when I tell you, Jonathan's power is limited."*

"He is going to destroy us all." She started to shake.

"Seelah, Jonathan forgets the strength of the White Side. He wants us to believe the Power of Darkness rules this plane. He doesn't."

Seelah could feel Chandra spreading relaxing warmth all around her, and she welcomed its healing glow.

"You must stay calm so the child, growing within your body, will remain safe."

Jonathan moved over beside them. *"Your child will soon be shoved into limbo to stagnate with all the other lost souls who are not needed."*

In her relaxed state, Seelah forgot her fear. "If you harm my child, I will hunt you down and destroy you even if I have to go to hell to do it!"

"Your child is but a small part of what is planned. This world, especially this country, at long last, stands at the threshold of ruination."

"If what you say is true and this plane is about to be destroyed, why would you bother to trade your soul with that of another?"

He grinned down at her. *"Always the thinker, Chandra. To answer your question, I did not say this plane is about to be destroyed. I said this world, especially this country, stands at the **threshold** of ruination. Just as a human body can be kept alive by machines, a world can continue to exist even when there is no reason for its existence. When people blindly follow someone who means to utterly destroy them, there is no chance for their survival."*

"This country will not continue on the downhill spiral it has been on."

"How do you plan to change it? We have all but had your God erased from the teachings of this world. We have stopped prayers in the schools. We have been able to stop their allegiance to this country's flag. Children all over the world are forbidden to even speak the name of God." He enjoyed delivering his message. *"They are no longer allowed to hear of your God's love for them."*

"I think you underestimate the love our Mother and Father have for their children, Jonathan. They will not turn their backs on us and allow you and your kind to destroy this world."

"We shall see, Chandra. It is the dark side who wields the greater power now. We wait and watch as the morals of this planet continue to decay. Your teachers can no longer teach your children what is right and wrong. Instead, they teach how it is all right for men to fornicate with other men and for women to lust after other women. Is it any wonder this plane is being swept away by the dark side?"

She turned away, wanting to disagree with Jonathan's ugly truths, but she couldn't. As long as people chose to follow the dark side, all those in the Light could do is stand by and hope someone decent, who put the betterment of the world ahead of their own greed, would come forth to end the evil.

CHAPTER THIRTY

Jack stared down at the man lying in the bed, and his heart plunged. "Donavan," he hesitantly touched his hand, "can you hear me?"

Donavan remained silent and unmoving.

A nurse walked into the room and, without a word to the man brushing a hand across his face, pumped the rubber bulb attached to the blood-pressure cuff wrapped around Donavan's arm.

"Is he gonna make it?"

The nurse watched the numbers come up in the small window then picked up the medical chart to pencil in the read-out. As she placed the chart back on the small table, she turned to look at him. Recognizing him, a smile slid across her face. "Jack, I'm sorry. I was so intent on my patient I didn't realize it was you standing there."

Jack tried to recall her name. Then, as his eyes dropped to the small tag pinned to her lab coat, he replied, "How ya been, Nurse Lyons? It's been a long time."

"Yes, it has." Her eyes swung to the plain gold band on Jack's left hand then to the man in the hospital bed. "Isn't this man your partner?" She picked up the medical chart. "Yes, Donavan Hays."

"Yeah, my partner." Jack wiped his eyes. "Is he gonna make it?"

She looked at him and, seeing the complete devastation on his face, motioned him towards the door. As they stepped out into the hall, she pulled the door to behind them. "We never know how much a person, who is unconscious, can hear, so we try not to say anything that could upset them. Detective Hays has suffered a heart attack. It wasn't massive, but the doctor will want to run tests to try and pinpoint what brought it on."

"So you're sayin' he will probably be all right then." The sheer relief sounded in his voice."

"We can certainly hope that will be the case. See, the thing is, once a person has had one heart attack, in most cases another attack follows."

"But, can't you give him somethin' to stop another attack?"

"He'll be on medication, and in the meantime, we'll be watching to see what the tests show."

"I'm gonna go on back inside with him. It was nice seein' you, again." He smiled down at her.

She turned the gold band on his finger, gave him a slight wink.

"It happens to the best of us. Now that I know whose takin' care of him, I'm a little less worried 'bout him bein' here."

"Jack, have you found out anything yet?"

Jack turned to see Seelah and Jenny coming towards him. "Not a whole lot. Only what we already know." He reached out, pulled Jenny against his chest.

"I'm so scared, Uncle Jack." She wrapped both arms around his waist.

"I'm not gonna pull any punches with you, little one. I'm scared, too."

"Where is Barbara, inside with Donavan?"

"No, she's down talkin' with Donavan's doctor. She should be back any moment. Let's go back inside. I don't like leavin' him alone."

Jenny hesitated just inside the room, leaned back against Jack. "I'm afraid of what he's gonna look like."

"Don't be afraid, sweetheart." Jack squeezed her hand.

"He ain't hooked up to a lotta tubes. Come on, Aunt Seelah, and I will stay close to you."

Jenny walked up to the bed. "He's sleepin'," she whispered. "That should make him feel better. You need to get well, Daddy." Tears ran down her face to fall on Donavan's hand that she held against her mouth. "We need you too much for you to leave us."

Barbara walked up to stand beside Jenny. "I just talked with your dad's doctor. He feels he's going to be all right." She sniffed as hot tears ran unchecked down her face.

Jack pulled her into his arms as Seelah reached out, pulling tissues from the box on the stand beside the bed.

Barbara wiped her face then blew her nose. "The doctor said he did have a heart attack, brought on by stress and high blood pressure. He feels that with some bed rest and *no excitement,* he should be just fine."

"How long did he say Donavan'd be out?" Jack picked up Donavan's other hand, caught his breath as he felt Donavan's fingers move. "Donavan! Can you hear me?" He leaned in close.

"Are we both dead?" Donavan's eyes fluttered open. "Or just me?"

"Neither one of us is dead, partner!" Jack gave him a brief hug, then backed out of the way as Barbara and Jenny rushed forward.

"Oh, Donavan, you scared us to death," she laughed, raining kisses over his face.

Without a word, Jenny stretched out on the bed beside her dad, laid her head on his chest.

"I'm okay, baby girl." Donavan drew a hand over her hair. "You don't need to worry."

Jenny nodded, snuggled in closer.

"Somebody going to tell me what happened?" Eyes wary, he gazed up at the three people standing beside the bed.

"You had a heart attack, darling," Barbara told him. "Your doctor feels that with some bed rest and no excitement, you should be up and around in no time."

"Did he say what caused it?"

"High blood pressure and stress. He's making a list of things to help bring down your blood pressure, like stopping smoking and taking a little vacation away from the department to cut your stress." She drew a gentle hand across his forehead.

Donavan glanced up at the ceiling then over at Barbara. "There's no way I can be away from the department right now, and stopping smoking is out of the question. If I stop smoking, cold turkey, all I can look forward to is another heart attack or a stroke."

"I hear ya." Jack grinned down at him, then became serious, as both Seelah and Barbara gave him a sour look.

"Jack," Seelah touched his arm, "I think we should go and let Donavan be alone with his family."

"Yeah, you're right." Jack leaned over, gave Donavan's hand a tight squeeze. "Try and get some rest. We'll see ya in the mornin'."

Donavan nodded, returned the kiss Seelah blew his way.

Out in the hall, Seelah smiled as she watched Chandra slip through the closed door to Donavan's room. She leaned her head against Jack's shoulder. "We can rest easy. Donavan's in good hands."

CHAPTER THIRTY-ONE

Rafael looked out over the throng of people filling up space in the main chamber of the cave. He smiled, knowing how many of those, taking their place within the growing circle, made up the parish's entitled. Doctors, teachers, lawyers and politicians. Upstanding citizens all. Who, of their own free will, chose to straddle two worlds.

"I take it the people have not been told who will be joining us this evening?" Lawrence pulled the cape up higher on his shoulders as he walked beside Rafael. "I am sure they will be as enthralled as I when they hear the news."

Rafael nodded, his gaze caressing a tall, winsome young woman whose long thick mane caught and held the reflecting fire from the torches. "Jonathan was an important part of their lives for many years. His return will strengthen their trust in the powers of darkness. However," his attention swung back to Lawrence, "to answer your question, I thought it best to keep his appearance a surprise. This night he will announce his upcoming return to this plane. Our people will join him in celebration, for they know how important it is for the dark side to remain in power."

"The time is fast approaching when this parish will know our wrath."

Two men walked through the crowd. One carried a young girl slung over his shoulder. The child did not cry out when the man sat her on her feet. She merely looked around. As her eyes lit on a man she recognized, she cried out, "Mr. Lybbert."

The man with red hair and bright blue eyes turned as he heard his name being called. When he spied the young girl, standing now before the altar, he walked, with deliberate ease, towards her.

"Melinda, how nice to see you here this evening." One hand slid over her soft cheek.

"Why am I here, Mr. Lybbert? I don't want to be here. I want to go home." Tears slid down her face to be wiped gently, away by the man who stood before her.

"But you can't go home, my dear." He placed a light hand over her mouth as she drew in her breath. "You are here for an important reason. You know you have always been one of my favorite students. You and Jenny Hays." The daughter of Donavan Hays slipped into his mind. With regret, he pushed her image away.

"I don't understand why I am here. Please tell the men who brought me here to let me go. They will listen to you. I know they will."

"Melinda, my beautiful child." He pulled her against him for a moment. "You don't want to leave and miss all the festivities."

"Yes. Yes, I do want to leave here! My mom and dad will be worried about me. They always come into my room before they go to bed, to kiss me goodnight."

"Melinda." His touch was no longer gentle as he gripped her arm. "I have told you, you cannot leave. Now, be a good girl and settle down."

The young girl cowered away from him. The man standing before her had always been so gentle with her and the other students. She started to shake and, as she spied the others in the room staring at her, began to cry.

"I see our offering to my father has arrived." Lawrence gazed across the way as he saw a young girl talking with one of the members. "Innocent blood always tastes the sweetest."

"Yes," Rafael nodded, his need to partake of this delicacy, almost out of control, "she will feed the terrible hunger clawing at each of us. It has been too long since we have allowed ourselves to feast."

"There is danger with this child. Because of who she is, she will bring police crawling over the grounds in search of her. You know Hays and Olivier' will come here first."

"They will search, but they will not find. This night is too important to settle for the blood of *any* mortal. This night our hunger demands the blood of the innocent."

As they watched, a goblet was brought forth to be handed to the child. When she shook her head in refusal, Rolan Lybbert placed the goblet into her hand.

"This was made special for you, Melinda. It would be rude to refuse to drink it."

"I don't want anything to drink," she cried out, slapping at the silver goblet. "I just want to go home."

The men who had delivered Melinda to the cave grabbed both her arms behind her back. As they held her, Rolan forced the girl's mouth open to pour the liquid down her throat.

Coughing and sputtering, she tried to move her head, but the strong hands holding her in their grip made refusal impossible.

Within moments, Melinda felt herself becoming very weak. As strong hands lifted her onto the altar, she no longer cared what was being done with her body.

Rafael's deep, strong voice rumbled out over the waiting crowd, and all eyes turned to acknowledge him.

"This night, we are gathered together to welcome the return of a much-cherished Monarch of the Hindel family. His absence in our lives has caused a strong and bitter rift. The strength of the dark side and our all-powerful Master of Darkness has seen fit to return our fallen brother to this plane."

A shadow took shape in the form of a man. A man they all recognized. Praise for their returned leader rang out, filling the cave with jubilation.

At last, Jonathan raised his hands for silence. "This night begins a new era. An era our family has waited a long time to embrace. When my body was destroyed, it was feared I would never return to this plane. The strength of the dark side would not allow that. And in this refusal, we have all been taught an important lesson. We are not our body. Our essence is in our soul, and our soul is what continues to live on. Soon I will return in a new body. Through the years, my body will grow into that of a man, enabling me to walk, once more beside my family and to take my rightful place as ruler over this parish."

He watched as, one by one, they bowed down to their leader. His eyes strayed to the child laid out on the altar. He moved forward until his hands rested upon Melinda's thin shoulders. Unable to partake of the sweet nectar laid out before him, he motioned his son to come forward to usher in the feast.

Lawrence walked to the altar and, without hesitation, gave into his all-consuming need. Sinking his teeth deep into the neck of Melinda, he welcomed the warm rush of sweet red blood. A great howling erupted within the cave as he lifted his head. His body shook as the sweet taste he so craved filled him with a satisfaction too long denied him. When his soul and body had been sated, he raised his mouth and, with arms held high, invited the others to join him in his feast.

In the early dawn, an innocent child whose blood and body fed the hunger of those celebrating the return of their darkest leader was but a forgotten memory.

CHAPTER THIRTY-TWO

The jingle of the phone had Jack barking into the receiver on the first ring. "What? Hello!" When he heard the voice on the other line, he thanked God it wasn't the hospital calling.

"Oh hey, Jamison, what's up?" He shook a cigarette out of the pack on the nightstand. "Ah, shit! What's her name?" He sat up, flipped the sheet off to the side to slide his feet to the floor. As he felt Seelah stirring beside him, he motioned her to grab a pen and paper.

"Okay, go ahead. Melinda S.a.y.e.r.s? Age? Yeah, I'll get down there soon as I can." He dropped the receiver into the cradle.

"What's going on?" She fanned away the smoke and, breathing a deep breath, tried to quiet her queasy stomach.

"We got a missin' kid." He ran a hand over the slight stubble covering his face. "She's the same age as Jenny. Which means they probably know each other."

"Do you want me to see what I can find out about what happened to her?" She snapped her robe closed, slipped her feet into a pair of fuzzy slippers.

"No, I don't. I want you to stay calm and relaxed. You go delvin' into the spirit world, you're just gonna get yourself all upset."

"I don't think it would hurt me to help you. If I feel myself getting upset, I'll simply back off."

"I don't want you involved in this, Seelah." His unease at what may have happened to another child sharpened his tone. Glimpsing her frustration, he gathered her into his arms. "I'm sorry, babe. I don't mean to be harsh with you. I guess I'm a little leery of what's goin' on. With Donavan in the hospital, I don't relish workin' with another detective."

"Speaking of Donavan, I sure don't envy his nurses if he gets wind of this. They'll have to tie him to the bed to keep him there!"

"He's gonna know about it, 'cause I'm gonna tell him," he declared over his shoulder, as she trailed after him down the hall. "He sure as hell ain't gonna hear somethin' this important on the news."

"In that case, you better bypass the station and head right to the hospital. When this gets out, it'll spread through the parish like wildfire."

"That's what I got planned." He spit, then rinsed his mouth, dropping the toothbrush back in the holder. "Try and keep Jenny away from the TV as much as possible. Today bein' Saturday, I know she'll want to watch her programs." As his robe fell to the floor, he stepped into the shower.

"I'll go turn on the coffee."

***

Jack stood for a moment outside Donavan's room, then, pasting a smile on his face, tapped on the open door. "Looks like I made it in time for breakfast."

Donavan looked up, a wide grin spreading across his face. "Jack! Am I glad to see you!"

"I figured you'd be bored and in need of some company.

"Bored ain't the word for it." The grin left his face to be replaced with a look of utter misery. "I want a cigarette so damn bad I'm about to jump out of my skin. They've stopped the smoking in the rooms. Hell, they've made it where you can't even smoke in the waiting rooms."

"Think they'd let you go outside if I was to go with you?" Jack sandwiched some leftover bacon and scrambled eggs into a piece of toast.

"I don't give a shit if they let me or not, throw me that robe, and we're outta here." He snagged the robe in midair, pushed his feet into a pair of slippers lined up beside the bed.

"Donavan, they're not gonna let you just stroll outta here. Let me go get a wheelchair. Sit back down on the bed `til I get back."

"Hurry up and get the damn thing then, `cause I'm about to light up."

Out in the hallway, he saw an empty chair, and since no one seemed to be in need of it at the moment, he turned it in the direction of Donavan's room. As he walked back down the hall, he caught the face of a young girl on a TV. He stopped for a moment outside the patient's room, then hastened back to Donavan. Walking through the door, he heard the anchorman describing the disappearance.

"Fuck!"

"Did you know about this?" Donavan gestured to the TV.

"Yeah. I was gonna tell you about it. I was just waitin' for the right time." He swung the chair around and put on the break. "Plant your ass in here, and we'll go talk about it over a cigarette."

***

"I got the call about an hour ago." Jack stretched his legs out straight, his feet resting on the wooden bench across from him. "I wanted to be the one to tell you, so you didn't get all upset."

"Missed that one, didn't you?" Donavan flicked his lighter.

"Don't get pissed at me! Ain't my fault the reporters are ahead of the fuckin' sheriff's department!" He pulled the lighter towards him.

"So what do we know?"

"Another kid's missin'. That's all I know. Well, that and her name and age."

"She looked a little familiar."

"Melinda Sayers. She's the same age as Jenny. I've been

afraid the girls might know each other." He took a deep drag on the cigarette.

"They do. Melinda Sayers is Jenny's best friend. They started kindergarten together. They need to get a better picture of her to circulate. I didn't recognize her."

"Ah, shit! I'm sorry to hear that. The poor kid already has enough going wrong in her life. And now her friend bein' missin'…" He blew out a long breath, shook his head in frustration.

"Soon as we finish here, we're going back upstairs so I can get ready to get the hell out of here."

"Whoa…hold on there." Jack stubbed out his cigarette in the large ashtray. You ain't goin' nowhere!"

"Don't put any god damn money on it." He dropped the cigarette butt on the cement, ground it beneath his slipper. "I feel fine, and I got a job to do. I'm not about to lie in bed while a young girl, who is like a part of our family, is missing."

"Donavan, god damn it! You just had a fuckin' heart attack! If you don't care 'bout yourself, at least humor the rest of us, who do!"

"If I lay in bed while you run around looking for this little girl, I am going to go nuts!" He unlocked the brake, turned the chair in the direction of the hospital entrance. "Come on! We got a job to do!"

***

Jack slammed the door, snapped the seatbelt into place. "You better hope you don't have another attack. That doctor wasn't kiddin' when he told you, by checkin' yourself outta here, your insurance ain't gonna cover you."

"Fuck him."

"If you die on me, Donavan, I swear to Christ, I'll knock your head so far up your dead ass, you'll need a closed casket!"

"Drive!"

CHAPTER THIRTY-THREE

Seelah stepped from the shower being careful to hold onto the bar Jack had installed for her safety. As her feet touched the floor, she caught her reflection in the long mirror. She ran gentle hands over her swollen stomach, smiling when she felt the child, growing in her womb, move as though reaching out to her.

"You are safe, my darling, and I am going to do all in my power to keep you that way."

She finished drying off, then slipped on a robe to walk into the bedroom.

"Seelah."

She stopped just inside the door as she saw her visitor. "Ron." Surprise flittered across her face at the sight of her deceased husband. "Why are you here?"

"Have you forgotten my promise? I told you, if you ever need me, I'll be here for you. I'm keeping my word."

"But, I didn't call you to come to me." Feeling her strength ebbing, she sat down on the bed.

"No, you didn't. However, that still doesn't mean you don't need me."

"Now, you are scaring me, Ron. If I wasn't in danger, you would not be here."

"You are about to bring a new life onto this plane, Seelah." He ran a tender hand down the side of her face. "This should be a happy and special time in your life and in the life of your son and husband."

"You are worried about the threat Jonathan Hindel has made about the safety of our child."

"I fear not only for your child, Seelah. I fear for all children on this plane."

Seelah's heart fluttered in fear as she recalled Jonathan Hindel telling her, her child is but a small part of the plan. "What do the children on this plane have to do with a threat against my child?"

"Jonathan Hindel is not the only dark entity on this earth, Seelah. He is but one of many."

"What are you trying to say, Ron?" Her small hand covered her mouth.

"The dark side is gathering to wreak havoc on this plane. Their strength grows stronger each day."

"No, you will never make me believe the dark side is stronger than the light." For the first time since they met, Seelah wished Ron would go away. His words made her feel uneasy.

A light tap on her door drew her attention. "Come in," she called out.

"Seelah, I thought I heard you talking to someone," Barbara said. "Is everything all right?"

"Everything is fine. I have a visitor is all."

"Oh, okay." She looked around. Not seeing anyone, she backed out of the room. "I'll come back later."

"No, Barbara, you don't have to go." She turned towards Ron. "He must leave now."

Ron took Seelah's hand in his. "I didn't mean to frighten you. I know how important it is for you to remain calm at this time. But, I want you to know, I will never be far away from you until this matter is settled." With that said, he turned and was gone.

"Seelah, what is going on? Who were you talking to?"

"Ron." She sat down on the bed. "He came to warn me about all the chaos the dark side has planned for this plane."

Barbara walked over to sit beside her. "It never ends, does

it?"

"For the first time, I am worried about this world. A battle is coming that will leave us all in peril. But I will tell you right now, no matter what happens, my faith in the Holy Ones and the Light of the Holy Spirit will never waver."

Needing to get off the subject of evil, she replied, "I see Jack got an early start on the day. Did he say if he would be stopping by the hospital to see Donavan?"

"Jack received a call earlier this morning, from the sheriff's department, about a missing girl."

"Oh no! Not another one. Did he say who the girl is?"

"Yes. Her name is Melinda Sayers…" her voice drew to a halt at the sick look crossing Barbara's face.

"Oh my god, no!" Barbara leapt to her feet. "Melinda Sayers is Jenny's best friend!"

"Jack was afraid the girls would be aquatinted due to the closeness in ages." Seelah grasped Barbara's hand. "He suggested we keep Jenny away from the TV today, in case they run the girl's picture on a news break.

A shrill scream from the living room had both women moving to the bedroom door.

"Mama!" Jenny screamed. "Come quick!"

"Jenny, what in the world is wrong?" Barbara ran into the room.

"A news bulletin just broke in on my show to say a girl in the parish is missing, and they showed a picture of a girl who looks like Melinda!"

"We know," Barbara said. "We thought it best to keep it from you until we can find out more about what's going on, but I guess that's not going to happen now."

"Then the girl who's missing is Melinda?" Jenny sobbed.

Barbara nodded, pulling Jenny against her chest.

"Let me get a local news channel. See if we can learn anything more." Seelah grabbed the remote control off the end table. "Yes, it looks like they are getting ready to have a news conference.

"Oh my god! I don't believe it!" Barbara cried as Donavan stepped up to the podium, Jack right beside him.

"When did they let Daddy out of the hospital?" Jenny turned, staring at the TV. "And why didn't he come here so we can take care of him?"

"I seriously doubt anyone *let* your dad leave the hospital. It would be my guess he left on his own accord!" Barbara told her, then grew silent so as to listen to what Donavan had to say.

"Good morning. I'm Lieutenant Donavan Hays of the Saint Anthony Parish Sheriff's Department. Earlier this morning, our department received a call from the father of Melinda Sayers, saying she has disappeared from the family home. According to Mr. Sayers, Melinda was not in her bed when he and Mrs. Sayers went to check on her earlier this morning. Their frantic calls to family have not turned up any leads on where Melinda could be. As soon as we are through here, Detective Olivier'," he nodded towards Jack, "myself and deputies will be conducting a thorough search of the Sayers' property in hopes of finding a lead that can tell us what has happened to their daughter. In the meantime, if anyone has any information on this disappearance, please call the Saint Anthony Parish Sheriff's Department at 555-0431." Donavan put up his hands as cameras clicked and microphones were shoved forward. "No questions at this time. Thank you."

Seelah clicked off the TV, then reached to answer the phone. "Hello."

"Hi, sweetheart, I only have a moment, but I wanted to tell you that Donavan checked himself outta the hospital and just finished giving a news conference on the Sayers girl. You need to be sure and keep Jenny away from the TV." Jack said. "We'll talk when we get home tonight."

"You're too late with your warning, darling. We all three just finished watching the news conference.

"Ah, shit! We figured since it's still so early, she wouldn't be up yet. Is Jenny all right?"

"She's pretty upset. But then that is to be expected." Seelah stretched the phone cord around the corner so as to talk without being heard. "Do either of you have any idea what has happened to the girl yet?"

"No, not yet."

"Why did the family wait until this morning to report the child missing? I would think they would have been screaming for help the moment they discovered her gone."

"I guess, according to the police report, the parents had an older friend staying with Melinda while they were out partying with friends. When they came home, after going to breakfast, they found the friend asleep on the couch and Melinda missing. Listen, Babe, I gotta go. I'll see you this evening."

***

Jack pulled up to the address on the notepad and switched off the motor. "Do you know these people personally?"

"Yeah. The girls being best friends and all, we've had barbecues and get-togethers." He rubbed a hand across his eyes.

"Donavan, are you sure you're up to this? These people are friends of yours, and we don't have any idea what the hell we're gonna find."

"I'm hoping against hope, Hindel isn't involved in this disappearance, but I have to tell you, I got a strong feeling he is."

"Seelah wanted to see what she could find out, but I told her to not even think about it.

"She wouldn't try if she thought it was going to hurt her."

"I can't take that chance..." He clipped his words, snatched the ringing cell phone from off the seat. "Yeah, what?" He listened to the voice on the other line then blew out his breath. "Okay, Jamison. We're on our way."

"Why the hell did you tell him that? We're about to go talk with the Sayers."

Jack continued to sit behind the wheel, the phone clutched in his hand.

"What the hell's wrong with you?" Donavan smacked him, smartly, on the arm.

"Seems Melinda Sayers ain't the only child missin',

Donavan." Jack turned to look at him. "Jamison said the station's bein' flooded with calls on missin' kids."

"Oh my god." Donavan's stomach rolled into a hard knot of fear. "Let's get the hell outta here. If that sick son-of-a-bitch is hell-bent on destroying kids, you can bet your ass my daughter is going to be at the top of his list."

***

Rolan Lybbert pushed the doorbell on the Hays' front door, then stood back to wait. As the minutes slid by, he pushed the doorbell again. Turning to leave, he saw a truck slide to a stop in the driveway.

Jack slammed the door before making his way up the walk.

Donavan slid from the pickup. "Who is it you're looking for?"

Deciding on the lesser of the two least volatile, the man held out his hand to Donavan. "We haven't met. My name is Rolan Lybbert. I'm Jenny's teacher."

Jack swung, his fist catching Lybbert in the side of his jaw, dropping the man to the ground. Before he could react, Jack yanked him to his feet, his fist connecting once more with the man's already bleeding face. "You just made your last pretense of bein' a teacher, motherfucker!"

Lybbert gained his footing to stand, staring at the man who had just laid him low. "I think you have this all wrong." He wiped the blood from his nose on the sleeve of his shirt. "I am Jenny's teacher. Jenny herself introduced me to her mother."

"Your bullshit ain't acceptable here, asshole! We already know you're related to Hindel!"

Donavan got right in Lybbert's face. "If you come creeping around here again, I *will* shoot you. And you can tell the other evil sons-ah-bitches the same goes for them!"

Lybbert stumbled backwards away from the man who never dropped his gaze.

"Now, get the fuck out of here, or I won't wait."

Lybbert took off across the lawn, got into his truck.

"They're already lookin' for Jenny." Donavan watched the

man pull in behind Jack's truck then back up to drive away. "We can't let anyone in our family out of our sight until all this is over," Donavan quickened his steps as they moved towards the truck.

"It won't take them long to figure out if Jenny ain't at your house, she'll be at mine." Jack aimed the truck down the street.

"I wanted to shoot that son-of-a-bitch so bad." Donavan rubbed the back of his neck. "Hell, I don't even have my gun with me."

Jack pulled in behind Seelah's green, Mustang convertible. "At least everyone's still here." He switched off the truck but remained seated. "I don't have the foggiest notion how we're gonna swing keepin' everyone together and still do our job."

"I don't either, Jack. We're already expected at the Sayers' house and the station." Donavan laid his head against the back of the seat.

"Why don't you go on inside? I'll go to the station. Maybe you could give the Sayers' family a call and explain what we're up against. That way, at least one of us can be here with the family."

"Are you sure you don't mind?" Donavan breathed the words in a long breath. "I am feeling a little tired."

"Naw, I'll handle it. You go on inside and let everyone make over you. It'll take their minds off of what's goin' on. `Specially Jenny." When Donavan remained where he was, Jack tried not to become anxious. "Do you think maybe I should run you back up to the hospital?"

"Hell no!" He popped the belt from across his chest, opened the door. "At least here I can have a smoke."

Jack pulled his gun from the back of his belt, "You better take this. I'll grab yours from the station. Now ain't a good time to be unarmed."

Donavan palmed the 38, then laughed. "I'll bet you all the bills in my wallet, Barb has *her* loaded-38 in her purse." He stepped from the truck, shut the door. "Be careful, Jack. This whole damn parish is in the eye of a hurricane right now."

"Jack walked into the station and almost retraced his

steps. The place crawled with people sobbing and moaning and all trying to be heard at once.

"Jack," Jamison yelled, his face lighting up at the sight of the detective, "you need to get over here! Jack!" He jumped up on a chair, trying to wave Jack forward. "I need you over here!"

Jack ignored him to continue walking towards Donavan's office. Once inside, he pulled open a desk drawer to remove a manila envelope, and a loaded 44 Magnum Donavan always kept secreted in his desk. With both in tow, he walked back out of the office to almost collide with a pale Jamison standing right outside the door.

"Jack, I need help over here! These people are out of control! I can't even hear myself think! You need to do something! Please! Help me!"

The deafening sounds of gunshots, along with chunks of plaster falling on their heads, had everyone in a frozen state of shock. "Okay, now that you have their attention, tell them to file their concerns in an orderly fashion if they want you to help them," Jack told him.

All Jamison and the other deputies could do is look from Jack to the gaping holes the Magnum had left in the ceiling.

"Oh yeah, don't forget to fill out an incident report on Donavan's gun accidentally, goin' off," he advised over his shoulder as he continued on his way out of the station.

***

A disheveled Christina Crawford made her way down the hall to answer the persistent ringing of the doorbell. When she opened the front door, her anger, at being disturbed, only intensified when she saw who stood on her front step.

"Detective Olivier'', what in the world are you doing here this morning?" She pulled her robe into place stepped forward to block the entrance.

"We need to talk." He brushed past her into the house. "But first, you need to go get some clothes on because as soon as we're through talkin', you and I are gonna take a little ride."

"I am not going anywhere except back to bed." She turned

away, walked down the hall. "You can let yourself out."

Before she could close the bedroom door, Jack pushed it all the way open. Without a word, he grabbed her hand to lead her out into the living room. "Why don't you make us some coffee while I fill you in on why I'm here."

Christina walked into the kitchen, flipped the button on the coffee pot. Crossing her arms across her chest, she waited for him to enlighten her.

"Let's come over here to the table. I have some pictures I need to spread out for you."

She backed up, one hand going to her throat. "I thought you said there weren't any crime-scene pictures of Tina and Paul's murder."

For a moment, he glanced up at her, then returned his attention to the pictures he had already pulled from the envelope. "These ain't pictures of Tina and Paul, Christina. These are from another crime scene." He finished laying them out, then turned to look at her. "I would never spring something like that without letting you know, first, what I had planned."

Without taking her eyes from his, she moved over to the table, then looked down. "Oh my god!" she screamed. "These are pictures of Rolonda!" Her gaze sprung upward. "Why in God's name would you want to show me these? I knew this woman."

"I want you to take a close look at this one." Jack tapped a finger on one of the pictures. "Do you know what a pentagram is, Christina?"

"Yes." Her voice was low and fearful.

"A pentagram, on someone's person, means that person is gonna be the next one to be attacked by a werewolf. Whoever killed Rolonda and shaved this pentagram onto her privates might just as well signed his name to the murder."

"But...I still don't see why you are showing this to me." Her stomach recoiled at the gruesome sight in front of her.

"We know who did this murder, Christina."

"Who?"

"Rafael Hindel."

For a long moment, the expression on her face remained one of sick fear then changed to one of out and out anger. "Are you out of your mind? Why in the world would you want to blame something this sickening on a fine man like Rafael?"

"I take it then, your relationship with Hindel has evolved into something more than hand holding?" The repulsive frown on his face voiced his feelings.

"Not that it's any of your business," her green eyes flashed her anger, "but yes, Rafael and I are lovers!"

"You better sit down for this next shocker." He yanked a chair out from the table, shoved her into it. "I didn't come here to tell you everything I know 'bout the Hindel's, but now that you've dropped this little surprise, I see I'm gonna have to."

Christina jumped up from her chair. "I think I have heard all I need to hear from you, Detective Olivier'. I want you out of my house! Now!"

"Not yet. You're gonna hear why when I leave here, you're gonna be with me."

"I'm not going anywhere. And I certainly am not going anywhere with you."

"Christina, we have every reason to believe Rafael Hindel is responsible for the deaths of Tina and Paul Statler."

"Now I know you've lost your mind." Her words no longer carried the heat of anger but fear of the man standing over her. "What makes you think this, Detective?"

"Because of the fact his son was a werewolf."

The blood drained from her face as she inched from her chair. "I think I'll get us that coffee now."

"You don't need to be afraid," he placed a hand on her shoulder, "I'm not the one out to do you harm. The one you need to fear is the man you've been takin' to your bed."

"I don't believe this is happening." Her eyes welled up to spill over. "I love this man. I don't know what I would have done without Rafael in my life right now. I trust him. Now, you're standing here telling me he is the one responsible for the death of my own baby and…and Paul?"

"Christina, Rafael Hindel's an evil man. His son Jonathan Hindel *was* a werewolf. This is not hearsay. This is a fact. Detective Hays and I actually saw the monster he would change into."

"I don't understand why you are saying this! Werewolves don't exist!"

"That is exactly what Donavan and I thought until we were confronted with the proof. I can even tell you *why* Rafael Hindel is out to destroy Donavan, me and our families." He tore off a paper towel, handed it to her. "We're the ones who destroyed his son."

Christina dabbed at her eyes. "Are you telling me that Rafael is a werewolf?"

"I believe he is. I believe his family, who has come here from New Orleans, may also be werewolves. Christina," he tipped her face up, making her look at him, "children are disappearing from all over this parish. No one is safe right now. Because of this, you're comin' with me." He placed a finger over her full mouth as she made ready to argue. "I ain't takin' no for an answer, so you best get your things together. You'll be stayin' with Seelah and me at our house. It's gonna be a little cramped, 'cause Donavan and his family are bunkin' with us, too." He gathered up the pictures, stuck them back inside the envelope.

"I still can't accept all of this, but if it's going to make you settle down, then I'll get dressed and come with you." She got to her feet. "Donavan Hays and his wife have been very nice and helpful to me. For that reason, I'll come with you."

"I wish I could say you're right and all this is just a nightmare we're all gonna wake up from, but I can't. Everyone in Saint Anthony Parish is in danger right now."

"I won't be long," she whispered as she turned to walk out of the kitchen.

"Christina," he waited until she looked at him, "I hope you ain't gonna put all our lives in danger by calling Hindel and telling him where you're gonna be."

Without dropping her gaze, she replied, "I won't. If things are really as bad as you say, then I will wait and give you a chance to prove all you've accused Rafael of."

"That's all I ask," he told her, hoping against hope he wasn't wrong in entrusting their well-being into the hands of yet another of Hindel's victims.

CHAPTER THIRTY-FOUR

Seelah lay down on the bed, tried to relax her body enough to bring Chandra forward. But all she could see was the black nothingness of a cluttered mind, and Chandra refused to answer her call.

She opened her eyes but stayed still. The child inside her body moved slightly as though reminding her of the importance of staying calm, thus allowing him to stay safe.

The face of a man, handsome, with steel-gray eyes that seemed to look into her soul, crept into her mind. Seelah shrank back as his image sharpened. With real fear, she sat up, looking around.

In a corner of the room, she could discern a dark shadow. Its pulsating blackness covered the wall as it began to take shape.

Immediately Seelah called out to her guides, who rushed to her side. But they were not alone. Chandra hovered beside her on the bed.

"What is going on, Chandra?" Her voice quivered as the shadow materialized into the body of a tall, middle-aged man.

"I want you to stay calm, Seelah. Your guides and I are here to protect you. You know evil cannot touch you when you are surrounded by the White Light of the Holy Spirit."

"You should not be interfering in what does not concern you, Chandra."

"You do not frighten me, Jonathan. I destroyed you once. I can

do it again."

"I am ready to be reborn onto this plane. This woman will house my soul, raising me from a helpless child to the man who will once again lead the dark souls of this earth."

"You will not touch this child growing within her body. He is protected by the light and all that is holy. Go back to the darkness where you belong, Jonathan."

Seelah tried to remain strong, but the battle going on in the room filled her with such terror it all but consumed her. As she saw the figure move, she cried out to her guides in a voice strangled with fear to stop the evil from moving towards her.

In an instant, Jonathan found himself being driven back; a bright light emanating from the guides blotted out Jonathan's dark energy.

"They are binding him in chains. Where are they taking him, Chandra?"

"They are taking him over to the dark side where he will remain until he asks to be allowed to enter the light." Chandra's voice was filled with pure exhilaration at seeing Jonathan, at long last, being forcefully removed from her sight.

Instantly Seelah dropped her feet to the floor. "Then if he is trapped on the dark side, that means he can't pose a threat to my son." Tears of relief streamed down her face.

"That is true, Seelah. He cannot do you or your son any harm ever again."

"But why now, Chandra? Why could Jonathan Hindel be stopped now and not before? I begged them to do something to stop Jonathan from destroying my son. But they did nothing. Now, not only did they stop him, they took his spirit to the dark side?"

*"Jonathan was not just **threatening** the life of your son, Seelah. This time he was actually going to follow through. When you called on the guides, just now, to stop him, you untied their hands to do whatever was needed. Spirit laws forbid them to destroy another soul. Even a dark soul. We are all God's children, and we are all given the choice to return to God."*

Seelah felt a great weight lift from her shoulders, and she could not wait to tell Jack their son was now safe from Jonathan Hindel's evil.

CHAPTER THIRTY-FIVE

Reverend Statler sat alone at a small table, his huge bulk overflowing both sides of the chair. Every few moments, he would turn to look towards the stairs. He jumped as someone walked up to the table.

"Reverend Statler, how good to see you here this evening." A pretty, skimpily-dressed waitress smiled down at him. "Will you be having your usual tonight?"

"Yes…yes, that will be fine, Miss." His lascivious gaze slid over her, and he licked his lips. "I'll also have the steak dinner."

"I'll put your order in with the chef and be right back with your drink." She started to walk away but stopped as he placed a fat hand on her arm. "Was there something else you wanted?"

"Is Christina gonna be dancin' tonight?" His voice was low and personal.

"I'm sorry, Reverend, but Christina is gonna be away for a while."

"She ain't sick, is she?" He hastened to ask.

"I don't really know why she won't be in the club for a few days. We're not privy to that information," she told him, patting his hand and pulling away.

"It's very nice of you to ask about our Christina."

Statler looked up to see a tall man dressed in black standing by his table. "Do I know you?"

"Not at this moment, no." The man reached out his hand.

"Allow me to introduce myself. I am Rafael Hindel."

Statler turned away, ignoring the outstretched hand.

Refusing to be set aside, Hindel pulled a chair away from the table and sat down.

"I don't mean to be rude, but I prefer to be alone this evening."

"I disagree." Rafael shot a look of knowing across the table. "You and I came here for the same reason. We both want a woman."

Statler's head snapped up. "I will have you know. I am a man of God!"

Hindel laughed deep in his throat.

Statler glared at him. "I am the Reverend Statler. It is my duty, as caretaker of this parish, to see to the fallen and bring them back to God's bosom."

"Is that why you were inquiring after Christina Crawford?"

"Ms. Crawford and I have known each other for a long while. I have ministered to her many times."

"I find that odd, given that Christina has told me about your, shall we say, fixation on her?" Hindel pierced him with his steely gaze.

For the first time since the man had made his presence known, Statler felt uneasy. "I have tried to help Ms. Crawford see the life she is leading is not one she should continue to embrace. But, she refuses to heed my warnings. However, as a speaker for the Lord God Jehovah, I cannot allow her refusal to be brought around, to silence His voice."

The waitress sat a plate of food in front of Statler, followed by his drink. "Will this do you for the moment, Reverend?"

He nodded, stuffing a linen napkin into the collar of his shirt.

"And what can I bring you, Sir?" she asked, looking at the man staring at her.

"You may bring me a glass of your finest white wine. In fact, you may bring me a bottle. Reverend Statler can enjoy a few glasses with his meal."

"I'll bring it to you right away." She smiled down at him.

To an astonished Statler, Rafael caught one of her hands and, holding her gaze, skimmed his lips, lightly, across the palm.

As the young girl walked away, a knowing smile pulling at her full mouth, Statler talked around the forkful of steak he was enjoying. "She could have slapped your face for that."

"But she didn't, did she?" he laughed, then grew silent as he watched blood, from the rare steak, run down Statler's chin to drip onto the white linen napkin.

"She's probably like the rest of the harlots here," he growled, his hand continuing to rise and fall, shoving vast amounts of food into his mouth. "They prostitute the bodies that house their souls. The souls that Jehovah has entrusted them with. Now, it's up to me to save them." He picked up his glass, threw the liquor down his throat and banged his empty glass on the table.

"Would you like to save a soul this night?"

Statler finished his food, pulled the napkin loose from his collar to wipe his mouth. "Are we talking about your soul, Mr. Hindel?"

"No, not my soul, Reverend. My soul is just fine right where it is."

"Then whose soul are you referring to?"

"After we have finished our wine, we will buy the pleasures of two young women who are in need of your help. I am sure Jehovah will not hold it against you for testing the depths of a lost sinner."

As they walked from the club, a shaken Jerry Stalls stepped quickly back into his office to watch them leave.

***

Rafael led Statler and two young females through the torch-lit cave. Loud sighs could be heard from the girls as they tried to remain calm in the eerie surroundings.

Up ahead, they could see a large, four-poster bed complete with a white-gauze canapé.

Without being told, the girls disrobed then turned to help

the men do the same. Rafael brushed their hands away, directing them instead to the good Reverend, who welcomed their eager hands as they pulled and tugged the clothes from his body. Rising to his feet, his slurred and pompous voice filled the cave. "Harlots of Satan, you will kneel at the feet of God's messenger!"

Instantly they obeyed. Giggling as they did so.

In his drunken stupor, he did not question the whip he suddenly found in his upraised hand. "You have blasphemed the gifts bestowed upon you by our Lord God, and for this, you must suffer the pain you have caused Him in your self-serving wantonness!"

The girls screamed as Statler brought the whip down on their nakedness time and time again. When at last he threw the bloodied whip to the side, he leaned down to pull the sobbing girls to their feet. "You will each kiss the hand of the one who has meted out your penance and saved your souls from everlasting damnation."

In turn, each girl bent forward to kiss the hand of the man who had abused them.

"Now, you will enter into the perverted acts your putrid flesh has addicted you to." As the three rutted on the bed, Rafael stood back, watching, until a movement caught his eye. Without taking his eyes from the perversion being played out before him, he motioned the one standing nearby to come forward.

"I see you have brought entertainment for this night's festivities," Lawrence Hindel said.

"This will be a special night of rejoicing. The man giving into temptation is the Reverend Statler."

"The same Reverend Statler who has treated your Christina so disrespectfully?" Lawrence glanced at Rafael then away. "This night will not end well for him."

As one of the girls rolled her body from Statler's enormous girth, they watched as the other girl was dragged atop him to satisfy his voracious appetite.

"I see the people are beginning to arrive. I think it is time to enlighten the good Reverend on what all is about to transpire in his honor."

At the sound of his name being called, Statler sat up in the bed, swung his feet over the side. Surprise crossed his face as he saw all the people staring at him. "What are all these people doing here? How dare you bring them here to spy on me!"

"Oh my dear Reverend Statler, these are not just any people. Look closely. Don't you recognize them? Many of them are from your own congregation." Rafael threw back his head, his deep rumbling laugh filling the cave.

Statler tried to pull his clothes over his body, but his hands were too shaky. "You are never to speak of this! Do you hear me? I am a messenger from the Lord God Jehovah! He has given me power over these fallen women. You know it is not a sin to fornicate with a woman whose soul has been touched by Satan!"

To his horror, the people laughed at him. He shrank back, pulling the sheet over to cover his nakedness. "This ain't really happenin'. It can't be happenin'! I'll wake up soon, and all this'll be a terrible nightmare!"

Rafael walked forward. "Your nightmare has yet to begin, Reverend Statler."

"Follower of Satan!" Statler pointed an accusatory finger in his direction. "You brought me here to shame me in front of my congregation! You plied me with the fruit of the devil's vineyard to steal my mind!" He got to his feet and, snatching his clothes from the floor of the cave, dressed himself. "I am leaving here right now. And if you're smart, you won't try and stop me."

"You are too important to this evening's festivities to be allowed to leave. You see, you and these lovely young ladies," he gestured to the frightened girls sitting on the side of the bed, "are here for a feast."

"I don't want your food. I am leaving! You and the gutter trash you have thought to shame me with will remove yourselves from my sight!"

"Reverend Statler, is that any way to talk to me after I went out of my way to give your son Paul and Christina's daughter, Tina, such a ceremonial send-off on their last night on this earth?"

Statler could feel the blood drain from his face. "What are you talkin' 'bout?" he whispered.

"I'm talking about the last moments your son drew breath. It was right here on the grounds of the Hindel Mansion. Paul and Tina fed our hunger and stilled our insatiable thirst for blood."

Statler screamed. "Oh my god! Who are you?"

"As one who has been called upon to lead His people, you should know who we are." Rafael's words came forth, soft and low. "We are the dark souls put upon this plane to destroy those who refuse to come over to the dark side. I will give you a choice, Reverend Statler. You can die right here right now for what you profess to believe in. Or…you can join us and have life eternal. The choice is yours."

"What do I have to do?" Statler gazed at him then out over the crowd.

"I will tell you what you will garner if you renounce your God and give your soul to the dark side. But first, I will show you what you will keep if you choose to die for your God."

Statler waved away his words. "Show me what I can expect if I choose to follow the dark side."

Rafael nodded knowingly, and draping an arm over the massive man's shoulders filled his mind with every perversion known to man. When he had finished, Statler licked his lips, his arousal apparent in his glazed eyes as he stared over at the trembling girls still sitting on the bed.

"I choose to live the rest of my life singing the praises of the one who rewards those who pay him homage." He declared, smiling as he saw the welcoming looks from the people milling before him.

"I applaud you, Reverend Statler. As one who has spent his life trying to bring souls to Jehovah and being rebuffed for your efforts, I am glad you see the wisdom in accepting the one who rewards such loyalty."

A woman, who bore a striking resemblance to Christina Crawford, walked from the crowd. Smiling, she took Statler's hand to press it against her breast. Statler leered down at her, his breath rushing from his lungs. He pulled her roughly against his chest then screamed as blood ran down his chest. She gazed up at him, her mouth covered in his blood. "I admire a man who is secure enough in his manhood he can speak his heart without fear of reprisal."

He moaned deep in his throat to hear such praise from a woman of such beauty. "I have never heard such words from a woman who looks like you." He tried to ignore the blood covering her full mouth as she rubbed her lush body against him.

"The one you serve now will see to your needs and reward you for the fruits of your labor. Soon you will be reborn into a child of the dark side, James."

"Yes, he agreed." For a fleeting moment, he thought of Paul and what Rafael had told him about his last moments on this earth. Then quickly put the thought from his mind. He was where he belonged. With people who understood the need for dominance over the weak. He did not allow himself to think about all he was giving up for this acceptance. For the first time in his life, he was being shown the respect he deserved. And all he had to trade for this respect was his eternal soul.

CHAPTER THIRTY-SIX

When Jack arrived back at the house accompanied by Christina Crawford, Seelah immediately felt a strong warning of danger around the woman. Not wanting to be rude, she greeted their guest and welcomed her into their home.

"I thought it would be safer for Christina to come and be with us until all the mess going on in the parish is over. I knew you wouldn't mind, hon." He gave her a little boy look before drawing her forward for a quick kiss.

"Of course, I don't mind. We can put the roll-away bed in Donavan and Barb's room for Jenny, and you will take the other guest room," she told Christina.

"I'm so sorry to be such a burden to you, Seelah," Christina said, her beautiful face flushed with embarrassment as she nodded to Donavan and his family.

"Don't worry about it. Besides, I doubt you had anything to say about coming here. Jack thinks you will be safer here, and I tend to agree with him."

"Alone is not where you need to be right now, Christina. This town is black with evil, and the only way to be safe is for everyone to stick together," Donavan spoke up, trying to put her at ease, then reached to answer his cell phone.

"Jack, I do need a moment of your time, though," Seelah beamed up at him. "I have some news I think will make you happy." She took his hand to lead him down the hall.

Closing the door behind them, he followed Seelah over to sit down on the bed. "All I ask is, please don't tell me we are going to have one more guest in the house."

"Seelah became serious as she looked over at him. "We already had a guest today, Jack. Jonathan Hindel decided this was the day he was going to replace our son's soul with his."

Jack jumped to his feet as extreme anger shot through his body. "Did that son of a bitch harm you?"

"He tried, Jack. But he didn't factor in the strength of my guides. When I screamed for their help, they bound Jonathan in chains and took him to the dark side. We don't have to worry about Jonathan Hindel doing any harm to our son, Jack," she laughed as tears of joy streamed down her face.

Afraid to speak, he gathered her into his arms while thanking her guides over and over in his mind.

***

Christina watched the two women sitting on the couch across the room and tried not to feel like an imposter. She could see the closeness between the two and scolded herself for being envious.

Seelah looked over in time to catch the look of sadness on Christina's face. "Christina, why don't you come over here and sit with us? Or, better yet, why don't the three of us go in the kitchen and dish up something to ruin our figures?" She stood up, laughing, as she stuck out her swollen stomach. "I think it's already too late for me."

"No need to feel bad, Seelah. We've all been where you are now," Barbara chimed in on the conversation.

"When I was ready to give birth to Tina, I was so ashamed of my body I couldn't pass a mirror without cringing." The admission caught her off guard, and she covered her mouth.

"I know what you mean," Barbara laughed, taking Christina's hand and pulling her to her feet. "I was so huge at the end, poor Donavan had to tie my shoes in the morning. If he had to go into work early, I just made do with slippers."

For the first time in her life, it seemed, Christina felt herself being accepted by other women instead of being the brunt of their petty jealousy and envy, and she liked the feeling it gave her.

Seelah stood with her hand on the freezer door and peered inside.

"What are you coming up with that can turn us into three blobs with no hope of returning to our beautiful selves?" Barbara pulled a chair out from the table.

"Vanilla ice cream?" She pulled the door forward to hide her face.

"That's it?" Barbara shared a wrinkled nose look with Christina. "I have better to offer at my house, and I'm not even pregnant."

Christina spoke up with a giggle. "I have an entire Chocolate Cream Pie sitting in my refrigerator at home. I can't stand the thought of it going to waste."

Both heads turned in her direction. "Are you serious?" Barbara asked, already licking her lips.

"Yes, I'm serious. I bought it from that little Greek bakery on the corner."

"Makers of Magic and Chocolate Dreams?" Seelah flipped the freezer door closed. "Oh my god! I love their baked goods and cream pies. They are a fat girl's dream come true!"

The two women laughed as they watched Seelah waddle over to the table, one hand tapping her big belly. "I vote we all jump in the car and run over to your place, Christina. The guys and Jenny are in the bedroom watching a movie. If we hurry, they will never even know we're gone."

"I don't know," Barbara tapped a long fingernail against her front teeth, something she did when she was nervous, "Donavan said we're supposed to stay in the house together."

"Oh, for goodness sake, Barbara." Seelah pulled her sweater from the peg on the coat rack. "Just grab your purse. I know you keep a loaded 38 in there!"

"Well, if we hurry and don't go anywhere else, I guess it will be all right. What do you think, Christina?"

"I think we'll be all right. It shouldn't take us longer than fifteen minutes there and back. Ten if you keep the motor running while I run in and grab the pie."

"Then let's go. The sooner we get there, the sooner we can get back." Barbara ran into the living room to pick up her purse.

"I'm right behind you. The sooner we get back, the sooner we can dive into that chocolate dream!" Christina chuckled, following Barbara out the door as Seelah pulled the door to behind them.

***

Jack leaned into the fridge to pull out a beer for him, a coke for Jenny and lemonade for Donavan. "Hey, while I'm pullin' out drinks for everyone, is there anything you girls want?" He called out. Hearing no reply, he grabbed the bottles, pushed the door shut with his hip to walk into the living room. Finding the room empty, he continued on his way down the hall. As he passed the dark bathroom and guestrooms, he walked back up the hall to the master bedroom. "Guess the girls must be outside on the patio," he said, handing over the bottles. "I'll go out and see if they need anything while the commercial's on."

"Hold up," Donavan said, sliding his feet into a pair of slippers, "I might as well go have a cigarette while you're playing host." He turned towards Jenny. "Pay attention to what we miss so you can fill us in when we get back."

"I'll think about it," she gave him a scolding look. "You know the doctor said you need to quit smoking, Dad."

"I will, but right now, I got too much on my mind to quit." He ruffled her hair. "We'll be right back." He grinned, jabbing a finger in the direction of the TV.

"Come on, Donavan." Jack pulled the glass door closed behind him.

Donavan picked up on the tenseness in Jack's voice. "What's goin' on?"

"The women are gone. I checked out front, and Barb's car is gone too. Guess they thought they could run out for a minute and not bother telling us since we were engrossed in the movie and wouldn't know they were gone."

"That was a very stupid move on their part. Barb sure as hell should know better than to leave when she knows all that is coming down in this town right now." Donavan pulled the glass door open and listened. Hearing the TV still going, he closed the door. "I waited until I could talk with you alone about something I learned earlier when you went to talk with Seelah."

"What's that?"

"I got a call from Jerry Stalls. He said Rafael Hindel showed up at the club tonight and sat at a table with none other than our old friend Reverend Statler."

"He didn't harm another girl, did he?"

"Not at the club, but Stalls said when he left he was with Statler and two women who work the club."

"It keeps gettin' worse." He punched in some numbers on the cell phone. "Where in the hell are the three of you?"

***

"Here, Seelah," Barbara handed over the phone, "it's for you."

"Hi, Babe, I know we shouldn't have left but, there was something Christina wanted to pick up at her house. As soon as she comes back outside, we'll be on our way home."

"You got ten minutes to get your asses back here!" he told her before ending their conversation.

"I think he's upset," Barbara grinned at her as Seelah handed her back the phone.

"Jack is a worrier, especially now with the baby about to be born."

"I wonder what in the world is keeping Christina? She should have been back out by now."

***

Christina jumped as someone called out her name. She had not bothered to turn on a light thinking to grab the pie from the fridge and leave. Slamming the door to the refrigerator, she bolted for the door only to find herself being spun around by unseen hands.

"Christina, I have been waiting for you," he told her.

"Rafael, you scared the life outta me." Christina fell into his arms.

"I have been here waiting for your return." One hand caressed her long hair as she continued to allow him to hold her. "All day, I have been waiting."

"I've been visiting with friends." She kept her face hidden against his neck.

"Would it be encroaching on your privacy for me to inquire as to who these friends are?"

Christina pushed herself out of his arms. "Let's go into the living room, Rafael. I have people waiting for me, and if I turn on a light, they will see I'm not alone."

Christina seated herself on the couch and switched on a small lamp.

"I am waiting for you to tell me who you have chosen over me to spend the day with, Christina. You and I had made plans to be together today." His deep voice remained calm.

"Detective Olivier' came to see me this morning. He seems to think I am in danger being here by myself."

"Do you feel you are in danger?"

"I don't know. He had some pretty frightening things to tell me. Things about you." She forced herself to look at him.

Rafael sat forward in the chair. "Please, enlighten me on what he had to say." He could feel his anger fighting to be released, but he held it at bay.

"Both Detectives feel you were the one responsible for the deaths of Tina and Paul Statler."

"And you, Christina? Do you feel I could have done such a terrible thing to your own daughter?"

Suddenly all the love she felt for this man came rushing forward, and she left the couch to go to him. "No, Rafael, I don't."

Holding her close against him, he whispered, "Who are the people waiting for you outside?"

"Seelah Olivier' and Barbara Hays."

"Wives of the detectives."

"Yes. The Olivier's want me to stay with them in their

home. They feel I am not safe here alone. They didn't want you to know where I was," she cried softly as he pulled her tighter against his shoulder.

"Would you rather return with them, or would you rather come stay with me at the Hindel Mansion?" He steeled himself to hear her answer.

All the stories she had grown up hearing about the old house shot into her mind, but she pushed them away. "Oh, Rafael, of course, I would rather be with you. But what am I going to tell them?"

"You won't need to tell them anything, my sweet Christina. We will go out the back door and leave in my car parked a ways up the street."

"Yes, Rafael, whatever you say," she murmured as he pulled her to her feet. But...what about clothes? I took most of my clothes with me when I left here."

"Let me worry about that. Right now, we need to go."

She placed her hand in his and felt a warm calmness envelope her.

"I promised no one would ever hurt you as long as you are with me. I mean to keep my promise. Soon you will know the very depths of my love for you, Christina. And those who tried to steal you away from me will know the very depths of my wrath."

***

Barbara ducked down behind the thick hedge bordering Christina's yard as she saw two figures going out the back gate. As they walked beneath the street light, she could see them both clearly. Wasting no time, she ran back to the car. "We got problems, Seelah. I just saw Christina leaving through the back gate with a man I would bet my life is Rafael Hindel."

"Is she out of her mind? He's a cold-blooded killer!" Seelah turned in her seat.

"Jack and Donavan tried to warn her about him. If she chooses to ignore the truth, then all we can do is get back to the house and tell them what has happened."

"We can bet they aren't going to be happy. And the ironic

thing about all this?"

Barbara sat still, hoping she wasn't going to give her any more bad news. "What?"

"We never even got the damn pie!"

CHAPTER THIRTY-SEVEN

Christina was lost as soon as they walked through the front door. It had always been her dream to live in a beautiful house like this. When she had married Tina's father, he promised to fulfill that dream, but the closest they ever came was at one of the luxury hotels in Vegas, where he got her a weeklong stint, stripping at the hotel's showroom.

"I hope the mansion is to your liking, Christina."

"Are you kidding?" She spun around, trying to look everywhere at once. "It's absolutely beautiful. I have always wanted to live in a house like this."

Rafael turned her to look at him. "It has always been my dream to find a beautiful woman to love and cherish. If you will consent to remain here, we will both have fulfilled our dream."

Christina's eyes widened in complete amazement. "Oh my god! Are you serious? I mean…are you actually asking me to marry you, Rafael?"

Instantly, he dropped to one knee and, taking her hand in his, whispered, "Will you consent to be my wife, my beautiful Christina?"

"Yes! Oh my god! Yes!"

Getting to his feet, he picked her up in his arms. "Then tomorrow, we must go into town and find you the biggest diamond engagement ring this town has to offer."

Lawrence cleared his throat as he walked into the room.

"Lawrence, come and join us." Rafael waved him forward. "We have wonderful news. Christina has agreed to become Mrs. Rafael Hindel."

Lawrence tried to hide his shock as the beautiful woman with the bright green eyes reached out to embrace him.

"I will go to the wine cellar and bring up a bottle of our best wine. This is a night to celebrate."

"I have heard some very nice things about you, Christina. My grandfather speaks quite highly of you." Lawrence hoped his voice did not betray his utter disbelief at what was happening. The entire parish was in utter chaos, and Rafael was behaving like it was just another normal day.

"Rafael is an exceptional man. He makes me very happy." Her eyes shone with excitement. "I have never met a man who can satisfy my every need like Rafael," she exclaimed, then blushed as she realized what she had just admitted to a complete stranger.

Lawrence turned away, glad to see Rafael coming towards them, a bottle of wine in each hand.

"I hope Lawrence has kept you entertained in my absence." He bent forward to drop a light kiss on her brow.

"Lawrence is a complete gentleman. I love him. In fact, tonight, I love the entire world!" She twirled around happier than she had been in months.

"Let's get this wine open and toast our coming life together, and you can tell me how big of a wedding you want to have." Rafael laughed as she put her arm around his waist to follow him out of the room.

Lawrence hung back, hoping they would not notice.

"Lawrence," Rafael called back over his shoulder, "I expect you to join us in a toast."

Seated in the living room, Lawrence watched the couple from across the room. He had never seen his grandfather behave in such a carefree way before. It was almost laughable. However, now was not the time for laughter. He had to think of a way to stop these ridiculous plans. If this marriage took place, it could well be the ruination of the entire Hindel family. Somehow he had to reach the spirit of his father, the only one who could stop Rafael's madness before it was too late.

Lawrence got to his feet. "I am going to leave the two of you alone. I have some things I need to finish."

"I will bid you a good evening then. We will see you in the morning."

"Good night, Lawrence. I am so glad we have finally had the chance to meet."

Lawrence nodded, not trusting himself to say anything more. As soon as he was out of the room, he quickly descended the stairs to the basement. Moving through the cave, he called out into the quiet then waited.

Rolan Lybbert walked towards him. "I see we have company this evening." He took a seat on the couch, stretched out his legs.

"Yes." Lawrence joined him, rubbing an agitated hand across his brow. "I have just received some very disturbing news."

Rolan looked at him. "Then this is a day for unsettling news. I, too, have learned of something I am, as yet, unable to fathom."

Only half-listening to the man, Lawrence spoke aloud his fears. "My grandfather has chosen to put all our lives in danger with his immature desires. He has advised me of his impending marriage to Christina Crawford."

"Rafael is leaving the estate? This cannot be." Lawrence had his complete attention now.

"No," Lawrence turned to gaze at him, "from the way my grandfather is showing off my home, I would say he plans on making it their home."

"But...this would put all of us in danger of being found out. We have to be able to move about the estate freely. Allowing an outsider to live on the property, right now, is out of the question."

Lawrence held up a hand. "I am trying to stay calm. I am

sure when my father learns of these ridiculous plans, he will put a stop to them."

"That cannot happen now, Lawrence."

At the stark resignation on Rolan's face, Lawrence leaned forward. "Why do you say this?"

"This day was to be the onset of your father's rebirth. However, as Jonathan made ready to replace the soul of the fetus with that of his own, the mother's guides answered her pleas for help. They bound Jonathan and took him to the dark side, where he will remain until he chooses to turn his life back to God.

"Tell me this is not true, Rolan." Lawrence leaped to his feet. "How did you learn of this?"

"I am the one your father chose to remain close to him while he lived out his years waiting to become a man. When his spirit left to begin the transfer of souls, I kept my energy attuned to his."

"We must tell my grandfather of this without delay." He hastened his steps towards the cave entrance, his effeminate voice sounding breathless in his fear. "He will have no choice, but to send this woman away, now. The family must be together. We cannot have an outsider knowing how many people live on this estate. Especially since the police are now aware of the disappearance of so many of the parish's children."

"It is almost as though those already in the Light are coming forward to blanket our wrath."

"When my grandfather learns what new injustice has befallen his son? This parish will learn the children are only the beginning."

When Lawrence and Rolan walked into the living room, they were surprised to find the room empty.

"Now, what do we do?" Rolan asked.

"We will have to interrupt his dalliance with his lady of the manor," Lawrence told him over his shoulder as he climbed his way up the wide staircase. "This cannot wait until morning."

"Rafael will be very angry if he is interrupted. I will go with you. Perhaps, between the two of us, we can stay his rage."

"Believe me, he will be even angrier if we don't tell him what has happened."

Lawrence tapped on Rafael's bedroom door. When there came no reply, he tapped again. Stronger this time.

An angry Rafael yanked open the door to step out into the hall. "This had better be important, Lawrence. You know better than to bother me after I have retired for the evening. And, especially, now that Christina is here."

"I apologize for our intrusion, Grandfather, but this concerns my father."

"Give me a moment." He went back inside his room. When he reappeared, he wore a robe and slippers and the anger was now gone from his voice. "Let's go downstairs, and you can tell me what is going on."

"Can there be any doubt about what you have told me?" Rafael poured them each a large amount of Brandy.

"None," Rolan spoke up. "I witnessed it all in my mind's eye."

"And you did not send for the legions of darkness to intercede on Jonathan's behalf?" Rafael's voice rose in his anger.

"You must temper your anger, Rafael. We are not alone tonight. The Legions of Darkness are not strong enough to go up against the Legions of Light. You know this." His tone was bitter at being forced to speak the truth.

Rafael threw the liquor down his throat and reached for the bottle of Brandy to replenish his thirst.

Rolan pulled the bottle from his hand to put it back on the bar. "You cannot allow your senses to be dulled, Rafael."

Rolan braced himself for a confrontation. "I always believed you would never allow a woman to come between you and the family. What has happened with Jonathan is unforgivable and must not be allowed to go unpunished."

The coldness in Rafael's eyes simply fueled Rolan's anger.

"Christina is not just any woman. She is the woman I have given my heart to, and she is the woman who will be my wife."

"Then you intend to make her one of us? For we both

know she cannot be a part of this family unless she is. She would put all our lives in danger."

"I will take care of my affairs without any help from you, Rolan. Until our enemies are made to suffer for what they have done to my son, no one will escape my wrath." Rafael's anger flared at being refused what he desired, then relaxed as Lawrence poured him a glass of white wine. "I will tell Christina tomorrow. She must return to her own house for now. Our people must come first."

"I knew you would see the wisdom of keeping the family together, Grandfather," Lawrence breathed, thankful to have some of the stress removed for the time being.

CHAPTER THIRTY-EIGHT

"Donavan, are you sure you're gonna be safe while I'm gone?"

"Jack, one of us has to get back to the job." Donavan relaxed back amongst the couch pillows, propped his slippered feet up on the footstool. "Besides, you're the one who's going to be where the action is."

"You gotta point. I just hate leavin' all of you here without some backup."

"I know you do, Jack, but right now, with all the shit coming down in the parish, everyone is needed on the job." He pulled the afghan from the back of the couch to spread it over his legs. "Remember, I had a heart attack, not a stroke. My shooting hand is just fine." He laid the .44 Magnum in front of him on the coffee table. "I could say it's because of my recent heart attack that I've come back home, but that would be a lie. I'm not leaving my family for anyone right now. I appreciate you and Seelah putting up with us when I left the hospital, but there is just nothing like being in your own home surrounded with your own things to make you feel better. I know you can handle anything that needs taken care of. So while you're out saving the world, I'll stay here and look after our families."

"Fine with me. I'll feel better knowin' you're here. The fact my son's safe has gone a long way to relieve a lot of my fear.

"I bet it has. It sure relieved a lot of the tension in this family. I'm glad that evil son of a bitch is in hell. God might think he's worthy of another chance to do good, but I sure as hell don't. I can't help but feel bad about not being able to protect Christina, though. For all we know, Rafael Hindel may have put her in some kind of trance."

"I doubt that was the case, Donavan. She told me herself she's very much in love with our hairy friend."

"Yeah…well…she seemed to be all right with being here. I just feel bad for her."

"I don't. I told her flat out Hindel's under suspicion of killin' her own daughter and Paul Statler. You'd think that alone would keep her from wantin' to jump into the sack with him."

"You don't think he took her to the mansion, do you? The same place where he killed her daughter?" Donavan kicked a foot outward to straighten the afghan. "My god. That's a creepy thought."

"If he did, we'll know. The mansion's on our list of places to check out today. Gonna be strange not havin' you there."

"Let's hope that's the only strangeness you have to deal with. And try and keep in mind, if you do run into Christina? You can't strong arm her into leaving with you. She's an adult and can pick and choose where she wants to be. She's been warned. That's all we can do."

He stubbed out his cigarette, dropped a full pack into his shirt pocket. "I gotta get outta here. Do me a favor while I'm gone, though?"

"Yeah, what do you need?"

"Try and get Seelah to stay off her feet as much as possible. She's due to deliver any day now, and I want her to get as much rest as she can. I hear first labors are always long and hard."

"I'll try, but I can't be too forceful with her. Right now, she welds the upper hand."

Standing on the porch, Seelah raised her hand as Jack backed out of the driveway. As she closed the front door, she shot a look at Donavan.

"He'll be all right. He knows the mansion is nothing to

play with."

"He's going to go to the Hindel Mansion today? Hmmmmmm," she turned away, "I didn't pick up on it, and he didn't say anything to me about it."

"Shit." Donavan chided himself under his breath. "Aw, don't worry, he's tough. Besides, I'm sure Chandra will keep an eye out for him."

"Yes, I'm sure she will." Seelah brightened at the thought of having someone with Jack.

"Jack asked me to do something for him today while he's gone. I thought maybe you could help me to see that it gets done?"

"Oh, Donavan, you know all you need to do is ask." She perched herself on one side of the footstool.

"He asked me to see that you stay off your feet. He wants you to be as rested as possible before you go in to have the baby. He has a point. This being your first, you do need to get a lot of rest."

"Jack is such a fretter," she told him, unable to keep the happiness from spilling over into a giggle. "I don't know how he will ever get through being in the labor room with me."

"We'll make him leave his gun with me."

Jenny walked into the room and plopped down beside Donavan. "I was hoping you weren't going to go to the department with Uncle Jack, Dad."

"Oh, you were, were you? And why is that?" He snuggled her close.

"I want you here where I can keep an eye on you. Make sure you don't smoke more than two or three cigarettes a day."

Donavan caught the smug smile flowing between Jenny and Seelah. "I feel like I'm being ganged up on." His tone held a slight edge of irritation.

"You are, but it's only because we love you. There isn't anything I wouldn't do to keep you safe, Dad."

"There isn't anything I wouldn't do to keep you save either, Jenny." He snuggled her closer, then drew in his breath at a picture forming in his mind. A picture of Jenny, lying on an altar, dressed in a long white dress, her arms down by her sides. As he watched, a figure stepped from the shadows to stand beside the altar. The figure was cloaked in a long robe with a cowl. As though aware he was being watched, he reached up to slowly push the hood back from his head. Donavan recognized him as the man claiming to be Jenny's teacher that he and Jack had encountered the day before. The picture disappeared as quickly as it had entered his mind.

"Donavan, are you all right?" Seelah reached out a hand to him. "Your face has grown very pale."

"I could use a glass of water."

"You stay still, Daddy," Jenny jumped off the couch. "I'll get you a glass of water."

As soon as she was out of the room, Donavan turned to Seelah. "I just had the damnedest thing happen." He rubbed a shaky hand across his brow.

"What?" Seelah moved to sit beside him on the couch.

"I just saw a picture in my mind of Jenny lying on an altar, and the man who says he's her teacher was there with her. I think the altar was in the cave at the Hindel Mansion." He clipped his words as Jenny hurried back into the room carrying a glass of water.

"Here, Daddy, drink this. It will make you feel better."

"Thank you, sweetheart." Donavan tipped the glass up, relishing the coolness on his parched throat.

Jenny reached out, taking the empty glass from his hand. "Do you want me to go get Mom for you?" She was already moving away.

"If you would, yes. Try not to scare her, though, Jenny. Tell her I need her to come here for a moment."

"We'll be right back." Jenny patted his arm.

As Jenny left the room, Seelah turned back to Donavan. "Yes, I know who you mean. He *is* her teacher, but remember, he's also related to the Hindel's. What I don't understand is why you would see something like that. That is what is called a psychic picture. You aren't psychic. Unless…" her voice dropped to a whisper, "sometimes when a person has had a near-death experience, they can become psychic. I'm not getting that, though. There could be another possibility at play here."

"Donavan, Jenny said you aren't feeling well." Barbara wrapped him in her arms. "Is it your heart, Darling?"

"No, no. I just felt a little funny for a moment. I'm all right now."

"We aren't going to take any chances. I'm going to go call the doctor."

"I'll go with you, Barbara." Seelah left the couch. "Come in the kitchen, and I'll fill you in on what's going on," she whispered. "I feel safe in saying I don't think it's medical."

Jenny placed a pillow beneath Donavan's head, then pulled his legs out straight on the couch. "You just relax now, Daddy, and everything will be okay."

"You don't need to worry your head about me, Baby Girl. I'm all right. I do need to talk with your mom and Seelah for a moment, though. Do you think you could go and watch TV in your room for a little while? I'm sure Brandy will be glad to keep you company." The big German shepherd raised her head at the mention of her name.

"Are you sure you feel all right? You're not hidin' anything, just because you think I'm still a kid?"

"No. I'm feeling better. I need to have an adult conversation with your mom and Seelah for a few moments. Mom will come get you when we're through."

With some reluctance, she got to her feet, but before she walked away, she bent forward to drop a kiss on his cheek. Like before, the same picture flew into his mind with such clarity he pulled a surprised Jenny into his arms. "I love you so much, Jenny. Don't ever doubt that!"

"I love you, too, Daddy," she told him, an uneasy feeling creeping over her at the raw emotion sounding in his voice.

Alone now, they discussed what could be going on.

"Donavan, have you ever had this happen before you had your heart attack?" Seelah asked him.

"Not like this, no. But I was having trouble sleeping for a while. And, I was having some really strange dreams."

"Like what?"

"One night, I dreamed I had sex with Chandra, and she was all burned, and…god, it was awful." He drew a shaky hand across his eyes. "I could actually smell her charred flesh."

Barbara ran a soothing hand over his arm.

"Was that the only bad dream you had like that?"

"No, they kept coming until I was afraid to go to sleep."

"Donavan, you never told me that." Barbara drew back to stare at him.

"I didn't want to worry you."

"Donavan, if you will trust me, I think I can help find out what is going on with you."

"I trust you completely, Seelah. You know that."

"What I'm going to do then is put you in a light trance. You will be aware of everything going on around you. The trance will simply relax you to where you can be comfortable talking about your dreams."

Within a few moments, she could see Donavan's respiration deepen, and she knew he was ready to begin.

"When you had your dreams, were they in sequence or all mixed up?"

"They were very vivid. And they were still clear in my mind after I woke."

"How many of these vivid dreams have you had?"

"Too many to count. I didn't mention them, because like I said, I didn't want to alarm Barb."

"Do you recall if the dreams had a certain theme each time?"

"Yes." His voice lowered, became less distinct.

"Don't be embarrassed. Just tell me about them."

"They were always filled with sex and perversion."

"Don't feel guilty about what you felt during the dreams, Donavan. You were feeling exactly what you were meant to feel."

"I don't understand. Are you saying someone is

deliberately making me have these dreams? That doesn't make any sense."

"It would if you were more learned on how the dark side uses the powers of darkness. If you recall when Jonathan was still alive, he could put thoughts and dreams into a person's mind. For instance, the deputy he turned into a werewolf. Then, when we were at Tina and Paul's memorial? Remember how Rafael Hindel transferred his thoughts to me?"

"You're right."

Seelah heard the alarm in Donavan's voice and hastened to bring him out of the trance. "Maybe tomorrow we can learn why you were having these dreams, Donavan. Right now, I want you to put all this out of your mind. You are safe, and you know Jenny is safe."

Jenny drew back, icy chills running down her back. She had never deliberately gone against her parent's wishes to eavesdrop on an adult conversation. However, this time it was as though their very lives depended on what was going on around them and that included her. Why would someone want to hurt her dad? It seemed as though her very world was spinning out of control, and she had no way to stop the spin. For the first time in her life, she had no one to call on. Without warning, the face of her favorite teacher, Mr. Lybbert, drifted into her mind. Her parents and her Uncle Jack and Aunt Seelah believed he was bad, but that didn't make it so. He had always made a point of telling her if she ever needed a friend to talk to, she could come to him. Since she didn't have Melinda anymore, she had no one else to call on. Her mind made up she walked down the hall and to the phone in her parent's bedroom.

CHAPTER THIRTY-NINE

Jack and another man stood outside the locked gate. "I've said it before, and I'll say it again, I hate this fuckin' place." He tried to slow his breathing. "Negativity is so thick you can feel it."

"I know what you mean. If you remember right, I was still a deputy when we learned about Jonathan Hindel being a werewolf. This goddamn place gives everyone the creeps," Detective Jerome Carpenter said.

"I could have done without that reminder, Carpenter." Jack gave him a sour look before punching the button on the intercom. "You got company out here, Hindel."

"Which Mr. Hindel did you wish to speak to, Jack?" Rafael came back to him, his tone complacent.

"Whichever one's pawless at the moment and can open the fuckin' gate!"

"Do you have a warrant, Jack? Otherwise, we will have to schedule your visit for another time as both Lawrence, and I are really quite busy today."

"Yeah, I got a warrant, Hindel. And a squad of deputies and a full K9 Unit. So, unless you're ready to rebuild this goddamn gate, I suggest you stop playin' games to impress your girlfriend and let us in."

The gate swung outward, allowing them to drive onto the property. As the cars came to a stop in front of the mansion, Jack tried to still the images flashing into his mind.

"I got a feelin' you're havin' the same problem I am."

With brows lifted, Jack turned in his seat.

"Tryin' to quell the flashbacks creepin' into your mind?" Jerry removed his cap, rubbed a shaky hand over his blond head. "Hell, I still wake up in the middle of the night with nightmares!" He replaced his cap, pulled up on the door handle. "Ready?"

"Not really, but it ain't gonna get any easier sittin' here."

Blain walked towards them, Magnum close by his side. "Where do we start this time, Jack?" He nodded to Carpenter, who rubbed a gentle hand over the dog's head. "I got a real sick feelin' 'bout bein' here."

"You ain't alone." Jack flicked the chamber closed on his .38. "This whole goddamn estate reeks of death."

"Not surprising with all the kids we got missing," Jerry spoke up.

"My goodness, Jack, do you really feel you need this much protection?"

Rafael stood on the porch, his arm placed securely around the trim waist of Christina Crawford.

"I see you've chosen to ignore our warnings, Christina." Jack remained standing by his rig.

"Your warnings were unfounded, Jack." She leaned her head on Rafael's broad shoulder. "Rafael means me no harm."

"I will never allow anyone to harm you, my darling Christina, not even me."

"Remember that next time the moon's full and you're lopin' `cross the lawn on all fours."

Jack refused to drop his gaze as bitter hatred glittered in the gray eyes returning his stare.

"I don't find your humor amusing, Detective Olivier'. In fact," she smiled up at Rafael, "I think you owe my fiancé an apology."

Jack's breath caught in his throat, but he quickly regained his composure. "Then all those tears and moments of sadness over the death of your daughter and her friend were just a pretense on your part, Ms. Crawford? Otherwise, you wouldn't be speakin' up on behalf of the number one suspect in their murder."

Rafael felt Christina's body stiffen, and he tightened his hold. "My Christina knows I would never do anything to bring her pain. What happened to the children had to be an unfortunate accident. There were drugs and alcohol being used that night. I would guess they decided to go for a swim and were attacked by alligators. After all, if you remember right, the clothes *were* found by the water's edge."

"You mean the clothes Lawrence washed, then spread amongst the reeds?"

Christina stepped away from Rafael's tight embrace. "Why would you accuse Lawrence of washing the clothes, Jack?"

Rafael's anger rose up, knowing his control of the situation to be ebbing away. "Do you have any proof this is what happened? Didn't Detective Hays say the clothes came up missing from your evidence room?"

"That's right. They came up missin' the night you and Lawrence and the other goon you dragged along showed up at the department in the middle of the night. Tell me, Christina," his gaze moved to include her, "do you use name-brand wash detergent and softener? I know for damn sure, Mrs. Statler doesn't, and yet the clothes all smelled the same. If you want to know what they smelled like, you can find the detergent in the Hindel basement."

"You never said anything about any of this when I came into the station. You said you couldn't show us the clothes because they were being tested by a medical examiner."

"That's true, I did. Donavan and I thought it best to keep it from you and Statler about the clothes bein' missin'."

"And all that time, I thought the reason you didn't want to show me the clothes is because they were covered in blood." She sidestepped Hindel as he tried to pull her back against his side.

"If I had to guess, I'd say they were covered with blood, and that's why Lawrence, in his ignorance, washed them. If you'd like, I can take you to where we found the clothes. There won't be any blood to see, but you can still get a good idea of where your daughter and her friend spent their last moments on this earth. Since you're plannin' on livin' out your life here on the estate," he spread his hands, looked around, "you can go visit their murder-site every day."

A long, soul-wrenching wail fought its way up and out of Christina's throat.

Rafael took a menacing step forward then stopped as Jack shoved the loaded .38 Magnum against his chest. "Come ahead, mother-fucker, you're not in your monkey suit now."

"Jack," Christina whispered, "I want to leave here."

Rafael felt pain he had never experienced slice through his heart. "You can't mean that, Christina. You have promised to be my wife."

"I can't stay here. I can't be where my baby breathed her last breath...where she..." Jack's arm shot out to pull her against him.

Rafael snarled, then lunged, slapping Christina to the ground.

Her scream of pain brought all six shots from the .38 slamming into Rafael's chest.

At the sound of shots being fired, Lawrence came running out of the mansion. "Oh my god! What have you done?"

"Your grandfather attacked Ms. Crawford. I had no choice," Jack told him.

"My grandfather would not attack Christina. He is in love with her." Lawrence dropped to the ground to pull Rafael's head into his lap. "You did not have to use such drastic measures."

"I disagree," Carpenter came forward, "this gun fell to the ground just as he was shot. Must have been shoved down in the back of his belt."

Jack's head snapped up as the gun went flying out of Carpenter's hand to land with a ping onto the cobblestone driveway. "Oh shit, I can't seem to hold onto anything anymore. But I can attest that's the same sound I heard when the gun fell out of Hindel's belt and hit the driveway."

Jack turned to the nearest deputy. "Check and see if he's got a pulse," he nodded to Hindel, "if he does, call an ambulance. If he don't, call the coroner." Then, before Lawrence knew what was happening, Jack jerked him to his feet to slap the cuffs on him.

"What are you doing? I must see to my grandfather."

"As a convicted felon and one who has been in a mental hospital, I have to make sure *you* ain't gonna try and attack us, too."

"You know that gun does not belong to anyone living in this house!" Lawrence screamed his anger.

"Detective Carpenter saw it fall from Rafael's clothing. Can't argue with a witness carryin' a badge."

As everyone stood around, entranced with what was going on with Jack and Lawrence, no one noticed Carpenter stoop down, rub a handkerchief over the pistol, then, deliberately, press the fingers of Rafael's hand against different parts of the gun. Getting to his feet, he motioned to a nearby deputy. "I need an evidence bag."

The officer took off in the direction of his car.

"Is Hindel breathin'?" Carpenter murmured.

Jack shook his head, leaving no doubt Hindel no longer posed a threat.

"I thought a werewolf had to be burned or shot with a silver bullet." The grin spreading across his face dictated his feelings.

"Guess when they're in human form, and the shots are fired right into the heart, there ain't much chance for recovery. Even a werewolf can't live without a heart."

"What the hell we planning on doing with that little puke?" Jerry nodded towards Lawrence. "We know he's still carryin' a heart, and since he's too much of a chicken-shit to attack, there's nothing we can do to stop it."

"I'm gonna have him taken to the station and put in a padded cell. If he starts changin' into a werewolf, all the officers on duty can do is pump him full of bullets and hope for the best!"

"Well, hell! With Hindel dead and Lawrence in jail, this should be a pretty easy investigation from here on out."

"Don't place your last buck on it. I gotta sick feelin', this whole damn estate's crawlin' with these furry fuckers! Only two places I know they could be hidin'. Quigley's old cottage or in the cave. My money's on the cave."

"What would you say to our getting our hands on some dynamite?"

"You serious?"

"We don't know what the hell's waiting for us inside. I think we would be within our rights to make sure we're gonna be safe."

Jack's lips drew back. "I swear to Christ, Carpenter, you and I could be twins as much as we think alike."

"I swore the last time we were threatened with these sons of bitches that I would do all in my power to destroy each and every fucking one of them."

"We gotta pretty good start. If you know who to call with your dynamite idea, by all means, get them to bring all they can lay their hands on. I always said I'd like to blow this goddamn place off its foundation. Looks like now, I just might get my wish."

With Rafael taking a ride to the morgue and Lawrence safely secured and on his way to the station, Jack took time to call Donavan on what all just went down at the mansion.

Donavan sat straight up on the couch. "Jack, this better be a goddamn joke! Tell me you did not shoot and kill Rafael Hindel!"

"No can do, partner. He attacked Christina, and I shot him. He's deader'n hell!"

"The whole goddamn estate is surrounded by cops, and you shoot the son of a bitch full of holes! I knew better than to leave you alone."

"The bastard left me no choice, Donavan!" Jack could feel his anger rising. "What the hell would you have done?"

"I sure wouldn't have shot the asshole!" He tried to calm

down, knowing his risk factor for high excitement. "If this parish survives what is going on, you can bet your ass the heads of the department are going to have a fuckin' field day with this."

"He was armed, Donavan."

"Are you serious? You have the gun that was in his possession?"

"I do."

"Did that gun belong to Hindel, Jack?" Donavan's voice lowered as he spoke.

"Carpenter swears he saw it fall to the driveway from where he thinks Hindel had it jammed in the back of his belt."

"Will Carpenter swear to that fact in court?"

"I'm sure he will."

"Then I won't ask you anymore about it. What was Lawrence's reaction to all this?"

"He went snake-shit! Insistin' the gun was not Rafael's. I handcuffed him and sent him to the station to be put in a padded cell. I told the deputy who transported him to tell whoever's on duty to keep an eye on the son-of-a-bitch and if he comes tearin' through the bars in full werewolf regalia, open fire and don't stop till he's no longer twitchin'. Right now, we're gettin' ready to get the dogs started on the grounds, then start on the cave."

"Be careful. We know that cave ain't empty."

"No shit! In fact, Carpenter just put in a call to a friend of his for some dynamite."

There was complete silence on the other end of the line.

"Donavan? Are you still there?"

"Yeah, Jack, I'm still here."

"Thought I'd lost you there for a moment."

"Tell me you are not planning on using dynamite."

"The only way we'd use dynamite's if we find the damn cave full of werewolves. You know as well as I do, Donavan, once those fuckers start changin', we're gonna be walkin' targets."

"Jack, do us both a favor? Just sit tight. I'm on my way."

As soon as he finished talking with Jack, he hung up the phone.

"Did I hear you right, Donavan? You are going to go and meet Jack? Do you think that's wise, given the fact you should be taking it easy?"

"If I want to keep the job that pays our bills, I do."

"Has Jack done something to anger you, Donavan?" Seelah moved up to stand beside Barbara.

"As a matter of fact, yes."

For a moment, she tried to tune into Jack's energy then gave up. "What is it he's done?"

"Killed Rafael Hindel."

Both women drew in their breath to stare at him. Barbara regained her composure first. "Oh my god. I know none of us have any liking for the man, but this could cause Jack all kinds of problems with the department."

Not trusting himself with a response, he merely kept walking down the hall to their bedroom. When he opened the door, he was surprised to find Brandy lying across the foot of the bed.

"What are you doing in here, girl?" He ran an affectionate hand over the dog's head. "I thought you were keeping Jenny company in her room."

"So did I." Barbara walked out into the hall. "She must have decided to take a nap. She tried to still the fear creeping into her stomach as she pushed open Jenny's bedroom door. "Oh my god, Donavan, she's not in here!"

"Don't start panicking. She could be out on the patio." He raced down the hallway.

"What's going on?" Seelah got up from the couch.

"Jenny's not in her room." Donavan slammed the patio door behind him. "She must be in the backyard." He raced out the kitchen door in search of her. "Jenny! Jenny, are you out here?"

Fear slammed into his gut when he didn't catch sight of her.

"Donavan, is she out there?" Barbara called out to him and bent over, clutching her stomach when he came back to the door alone. "I am going to go call Mrs. Jennings. Maybe she went to visit with her."

"No! Don't touch the phone! I can hit the redial and see if she called anyone!" He ran past her into the bedroom. With a shaking hand, he pressed the button for redial. As he heard the number continue to ring, he was about the hang up when he heard the voicemail come on. His heart jumped into his throat as he heard the voice of Roland Lybbert. "That sick bastard!" He wrote the number down quickly.

"Since we can't call, I'll just run over next door and see if she's with Mrs. Jennings." Seelah was already walking out the front door.

Donavan tried to blot out the pictures he had been seeing earlier of Jenny lying on an altar in the Hindel cave. "Seelah!"

Seelah turned back at the sheer panic sounding in Donavan's voice. "What?"

"Never mind. She's not over there. I want to know about the pictures I was seeing earlier about Jenny. You said they were psychic pictures!"

"Yes, Donavan, I believe they were. And now I think I know who sent them for you to see!"

"Who?"

"Chandra." Seelah breathed deeply against her fear. When at last she felt a small amount of calmness creep over her, she tuned into Chandra's energy. Within moments, Chandra stood before her. "What is happening here, Chandra? Is Jenny in danger?"

"*Jenny is in extreme danger, Seelah. She has gone to meet Rolan Lybbert.*"

"Oh my god!" She threw up her hands.

"What is it, Seelah? What are you seeing?" Barbara moaned the words.

"Chandra is here, and she says that Jenny has gone to meet Rolan Lybbert!"

"That goddamn evil piece of piss! If he puts his filthy hands on her, I'll rip his fucking heart out!"

"Donavan, you need to calm down! You and Seelah both

need to calm down!" Barbara told them while at the same time feeling her own fragile grip on reality slipping out of her hands.

Seelah ran a comforting hand over Barbara's back. "Call Jack," Seelah told him. "The pictures you saw of Jenny were in the cave. Tell him what is going on."

"The hell with that! Come on. We're going to find Jenny!"

***

Jerry held up his cell phone. "Jack, this is my call back on the dynamite. Are you sure this is what you want to do?"

"Hell yes, I'm sure! Tell him to bring it on!"

As Carpenter turned away to speak into the phone, Jack saw one of the deputies shake his head. "What's the matter, Hendrickson? You think we're makin' a wrong call here?"

"No, just tryin' to wrap my mind around the idea's all." Hendrickson grinned over at him. "I do think it'd be a good idea to pass the hat to all the deputies, who are already here, so the dynamite man can get paid for his merchandise. It's for damn sure the department ain't gonna spring for the bill!"

"Damn good idea, Johnny." Jack laughed. "And you're right about the department not springin' for the bill. When they hear about this latest escapade I'm involved in, I'll be lucky if they don't kick me to the curb. Again."

"Guess while we're waitin' for the demolition man to show, I might as well take some of the men and the dogs and get started on checkin' out the house."

"Might just as well. Donavan should be showin' up any minute, so we better look like we been doin' the job." He handed over a crisp twenty.

Pocketing the money, Hendrickson motioned Blain and some of the other deputies forward as he and Jack walked up on the front porch of the mansion.

"Jerry."

Carpenter pressed the phone against his chest, gave Jack his full attention.

"We're gonna be checkin' out the house, so when you're finished with your call, join us inside." He saw Carpenter nod and walked on into the house.

"There's something I want to do while we're here." Blain walked across the room.

"What's that?" Jack joined him inside the library door.

"I've noticed that every time we checked out the house, Magnum always zeroed in on this heavy oak bookcase." He ran his hands up and down the sides. "I didn't pay it much heed at the time, but later I started thinking about the possibility of a hidden panel."

"This goddamn house is known for hidden rooms and passages." Jack felt beneath the shelves and the top of the bookcase. "Bingo!"

"I was right."

"Jack!" Donavan called out, coming into the house.

"In here, Donavan," he yelled into the quiet. "We'll come back to this." He turned as Donavan walked into the room, closely followed by Barbara and Seelah. "Donavan, do you think it was a good idea to bring the girls with you?"

Seelah hastened across the room to wrap her arms around Jack's waist.

"He's got Jenny, Jack!" Donavan said, his voice filled with both anger and fear.

"Who's got, Jenny?" Jack's breath shot forward from his lungs.

"Rolan Lybbert, one of the assholes who lives in this goddamn house!"

"How the hell do you know this?" Fear wound its way into his mind.

She called him from the house. I hit the redial, and it was his voice mail that came back to me." Donavan reached for a breath that wasn't there.

Quickly, Chandra came forward. "*You will breathe deep breaths. You will let go of the fear in your mind and heart. You will put your trust in the Holy Ones, Donavan Hays.*"

"Are you all right?" Barbara ran both her hands down the sides of Donavan's face."

"Yeah, I'm all right, now. Had a little trouble catching my breath for a moment."

Seelah glanced over at Chandra as she stood by Donavan's side. "Thank you," she whispered.

"Jack, my friend just showed up, if you want to come outside." Jerry motioned him forward.

"That the man with the dynamite?" Donavan walked towards the door. "Tell him we'll take every goddamn stick he's got!"

"You heard the man," Jack told him. Then turned his attention to Blain. "Since we know there's a secret panel in the living room, I want you to take the dogs around every part of this house. That son-of-a-bitch has Jenny, so she could be anywhere."

"Are you sure he'd bring her here?" Blain followed behind Magnum. "He's got to know by now we're on the grounds."

"He probably hasn't put it together yet 'bout Rafael joinin' the spirit world and Lawrence coolin' his heels in the county lockup. So, my guess would be he has her hidden behind one of the panels."

"Jack," Seelah touched his arm, "I am going to see what I can find out about Jenny."

"Are you sure you're up to it? I don't want to have to worry about you, too, babe."

"I'll be all right." She kissed the tips of her fingers touched her fingers to his cheek. "Chandra is here. She'll help me. Just as she helped Donavan a few moments ago."

"Does she know where Lybbert's hidin' Jenny?"

Seelah turned, her gaze moving across the room. "Chandra, do you know where Jenny is being held?"

"*No, Seelah, I do not.*" She looked away, unable to meet the other woman's eyes.

"What is it you are not telling me, Chandra?"

"*I am being blocked from seeing where Jenny is.*" Her voice was filled with fear.

"How can that be? No one is stronger than you."

"*There is a very dark entity pitting his strength with mine.*"

"Oh my god, Chandra! Who is it?"

"*Rafael Hindel.*"

"How can that be?"

"What?" Jack turned her around.

"Chandra said the one who is blocking her from seeing where Jenny is being hidden is Rafael Hindel."

"I'm gonna have to disagree with her this time. I sent that son-of-a-bitch to hell!"

"*Rafael's spirit is still here. And his evil is even stronger than when he was in body. As with most dark entities, who know what awaits them on the other side, they refuse to leave this plane,*" Chandra told her.

"Call on your guides to transport him over to the dark side, like you did before."

"They cannot do anything about Hindel until he tries to do one of us harm."

Seelah breathed deeply against a sudden wave of pain starting low in her belly.

"*You must leave here, Seelah and go to the hospital. Your son is ready to make his entrance onto this plane.*"

Seelah responded with a slight shake of her head. Unwilling to admit Chandra was right, she turned her attention back to Jack.

"Then I guess we'll start checkin' for hidden panels with the K9s."

"What hidden panels are you talking about, Jack?" Donavan asked, trying to keep his fear of what might be happening to Jenny, shoved to the back of his mind.

"Blain said every time he's been in this house, Magnum keeps hittin' on this heavy oak bookcase. We checked it and found a control button on the top. If there's one panel, there's got to be more."

"Then let's get on it." Donavan walked over to the bookcase, ran his hand over the top until he found the button. Pulling his .44 from its holster, he pushed the button to send the sheet of wood paneling swinging around to uncover a hidden room.

"Empty!" Jack said.

Donavan ripped the button from the bookcase, leaving the room open for all to see. "That's one secret brought into the light."

"I think we need to get down to the cave. That's where all the action in this shithole seems to take place!"

"Bring your buddy with the dynamite in here," Donavan called out to Carpenter.

"He's right here, Lieutenant." Carpenter came forward closely followed by a man carrying a wooden crate.

"I figured this should be enough to do the trick," the man carrying the crate told them.

Donavan wiped a hand across an end table, sending a lamp and a vase filled with water and fresh flowers flying onto the floor to make room for the crate. "Let's see what we got here." He lifted off the top, dropped it beside the end-table. "I'd say this should do the job right smartly." His hand shot outward. "I'm Donavan Hays."

"Glad to know ya, Hays. I'm Rick Stalls. You met my brother, Jerry, awhile back at The Gentlemen's Elite Club? He says you two are a couple of all right cops." When Donavan nodded, Rick added, "Carpenter tells me you think these assholes grabbed your little girl."

"Yeah," Donavan pulled Barbara into his arms.

"I wanna tell you somethin'. If we come up against anything that you cops ain't allowed to do, just let me know." He clasped a hand on Donavan's shoulder. "There ain't nothin' I'm afraid to do. And very little I can't get done."

"Thanks, Stalls, I appreciate that. And, I'll let you in on a little secret. Yesterday I would have told you that ain't the way we do things here. Today? Anyone gets in my way, they might as well kiss their ass goodbye."

"Hays, Olivier'," Hendrickson called out, coming into the room, "the dogs are hittin' all over this house. I'd say we got hidden rooms everywhere."

"Then let's get started on bringin' them out in the open." Jack moved forward, then stopped. "Before any of you open a panel, be sure you have your guns drawn. If you find anyone, shoot to kill."

"And don't stop shooting until you're sure they're dead," Donavan added.

CHAPTER FORTY

Jenny tried not to show any fear as Rolan Lybbert led her across the floor of the cave.

"You don't need to be afraid, Jenny." He ran a hand down the side of her face. "You know I would never harm you."

"I don't understand what we're doin' here. This is a very bad place."

"You shouldn't listen to rumor, Jenny." He sat down in one of the chairs, motioned for her to seat herself in the chair closest to his.

"My dad and Uncle Jack say this is a place of darkest evil." She was beginning to feel sick to her stomach. "I think I've changed my mind about talking to you about my problems, Mr. Lybbert. I'm not feeling well, and I think I better have you take me back home."

"Nonsense, Jenny. You just got here." He left the chair to walk across the floor. On a tray, someone had placed a decanter of water and some ice. Returning to her, he handed her a glass filled with cold water. "Drink this. It will settle your stomach."

"You still haven't said why we're here." She sipped from the glass.

"You told me you are very worried about your father. About his health. I have brought you here to talk with someone who can help your father."

"A doctor lives here?" Jenny looked at him: Her young

face showing her doubt.

"He isn't your typical doctor, no. He is what people call a healer." Lybbert watched her trying to gauge how much he could push her into believing him.

Jenny sat up straight in her chair. Her fear of their surroundings easing as she waited to hear more.

Someone walked from the shadows. "Is this the child whose father is in danger of losing his life?" a tall thin man asked in a clear voice.

Jenny sat back further on the couch as the man walked over to seat himself beside her.

"Yes," Lybbert answered him. "This is Jenny Hays. Her father is in dire danger of dying soon if he isn't healed."

"Then we must do all we can to see that does not happen." The man reached for Jenny's hand. "I have it in my power to heal your father, Jenny."

"Yes, please. I love my daddy so much, and I can't think about being without him." She had begun to cry, her worry over her father silencing her fear.

"Let me show you what your life will be like if your father is taken from you."

Jenny wiped a shaking hand beneath her nose as the strange man rose to his feet.

A bright whirling light appeared in front of her. She watched as different colors blended together, seeming to merge into one soft yellow orb. For some reason, as she continued to watch, she felt herself feeling very relaxed and somewhat sleepy. She felt someone pick her up then lay her down on a soft couch.

"Jenny, can you hear me?" she heard the voice of Roland Lybbert asking.

"Yes, I hear you," she answered him, her voice sounding as though it came from a long way off.

"Good, now I want you to watch as you are shown what will be your life if your father is taken from you."

As though a movie played out before her eyes, she saw her mother and herself sitting on the couch in the living room, holding onto each other as the two of them shared their pain.

"I can't believe your father will never walk through that door again, Jenny. But, he was in so much pain, I am almost glad he is gone and no longer suffering."

"I can't stand it! No, he can't be dead! He just can't. He was getting better. You said yourself he was getting better."

"He was getting better, Jenny. Only, when you left the house to go and meet your teacher, Mr. Lybbert, your father was so frightened for you that it brought on another heart attack. It's all your fault your father is dead, Jenny. You are to blame for his suffering. I don't think I will ever be able to forgive you, Jenny. You destroyed the man who would have given his life for us."

"But, I didn't mean to hurt Daddy. I love my Daddy. You know I love my Daddy."

Jenny heard herself repeating over and over how sorry she was.

"This doesn't have to be, Jenny. You can change everything that you just witnessed."

"How?" she whispered.

"You can change everything with only a promise."

CHAPTER FORTY-ONE

Donavan stood alone in one of the rooms trying to get a hold of his emotions. He had used the pretense of having to use the bathroom. He knew how terrified Barbara was right now over the abduction of Jenny. She was feeling the same gut-wrenching fear he was. But he was a man and therefore had to stand strong for her.

"I don't know if I can be strong," he spoke his thoughts aloud into the quiet. "I'm so scared right now I feel like I'm going to throw up." Tears dripped down his face, and he didn't bother to wipe them away. "If I lose Jenny, I don't know what I'll do."

"You don't have to lose Jenny, Donavan. You can save your daughter anytime you want to."

Donavan looked up to see who was speaking to him and what he saw made his heart pound in his chest. "Who the hell are you?" The words came out of his mouth hushed and fearful.

"Don't you recognize me, Detective Hays? You should. I have been dead but a short while."

Donavan backed up, trying to tell himself what he was seeing couldn't be real. "Get the hell away from me, you evil son of a bitch. Jack killed you."

The eyes staring out at him were focused, and the diabolical laugh was deep and filled with fury. "How much do you love your daughter, Detective Hays? How much? How far are you willing to go to save her before it is too late?"

"What the fuck are you talking about too late? You dirty piece of filth, if you dare to put your hands on her, I will send you straight to hell where you belong."

"You can do nothing to me. Your bullets are useless, and your threats hold no fire. It is the dark side who is in control now. We are destroying your children one by one until there will be no one left to repopulate this plane."

"You and the rest of the evil mother-fuckers on this estate have no power on the planet. You are only a few pieces of shit! Don't give yourself more power than you have."

"We in this parish are but a few, but our kind walk this plane by the millions. The one we worship has the power to destroy this entire universe!"

"Go back to hell where you are welcome. We don't need you here." He started to walk away when the next words he heard stopped him in mid-stride.

"Jenny belongs to us now, Detective Hays. You have lost her."

Donavan fired all six shots from the .38 directly into the ugliness taunting him. The spirit vanished.

Jack and some of the other deputies ran into the room closely followed by Barbara and Seelah. "What the hell are you shootin' at, Donavan?" Jack stood looking around the room. Donavan's .38 held tightly in his grasp.

"Taking out the trash."

"What trash? What the hell are you talking about?"

"Rafael Hindel is who I'm talking about. He said Jenny has joined them of her own free will."

"Oh my god, no!" Barbara screamed.

"Come on!" Jack whirled. "If he's sayin' that, then she has to be on this goddamn estate. I don't think we need to beat our brains tryin' to figure out where that would be."

"She's in the cave!" Seelah cried.

They all ran for the kitchen and the stairs at the same time.

With only a door to separate the cave from the basement, Jack jerked it open. "Jenny! Jenny!" he screamed her name.

Everyone stopped to stare straight ahead. There, on a marble slab that looked like an altar, they could see Jenny.

Jack moved to the back of the people standing still and gazing at the horror ahead of them. Being very quiet, he fished inside his pocket to bring out his bullets. One by one, he filled the cylinder of his .38. Its familiar feel giving him some much needed confidence.

Seelah could see two dark spirits hovering on each side of the altar. She shuddered as she saw the small body of Jenny laid out in a long white dress.

"You can stop right there, Lybbert." Donavan stepped forward, his Magnum aimed and ready for any sudden move the man might choose to make.

"You are all too late to save this child. She has already given her soul to the dark side." Rolan Lybbert looked at the people standing in the cave.

"She is only a child." Donavan's hand trembled on the gun. "Come here to Daddy, Jenny." He walked forward.

Instantly, Rolan raised a dagger he held in his hand high over the body of the child. "If you move, I will kill her. It will not matter. Since she is one of us, she will waken to take her place beside the rest of the family on the next full moon."

Donavan felt a cold hand clutch his heart. "Before I would allow my baby to become the evil piece of piss you are, I will rip her heart out myself."

"What do you think of our power now?" They all looked to the dark spirit standing beside the altar. "When we are finished, there will be no children left in this parish. When we are finished, all that will be left will be the dark side."

Chandra materialized, walking towards the man who stood watching them. *"Rafael, you have no power here. Your soul is marked for the dark side. Now you will reap what you knew awaited you if you did not turn your face back to God."*

"Leave here, Chandra. You are not wanted. The child you are trying to protect is already promised to the one who rules this plane. Do you dare to go up against his strength?"

Chandra laughed, her lilting voice bringing a snarl from the dark entities who stood waiting to do their evil. *"You and I both know your ruler is no match for the light side."*

"Satan is ruler of the universe! He is the one who will drink the blood of all your God's children." He looked at Rolan Lybbert and gave a slight nod.

Rolan raised the dagger above his head, then fell back as Donavan and Jack both emptied their guns into Lybbert's chest. As his body slipped to the floor of the cave, Donavan and Barbara ran forward to embrace their child.

"Jenny, oh my god, Jenny." Barbara cried as she rocked her daughter in her arms.

Jenny did not stir.

"Donavan, why isn't she waking up? What have they done to her?"

"I would guess they have her sedated." He pulled his keys from his pants pocket, flipped on the small flashlight he kept attached to the key ring. Lifting each eyelid, he flicked the light quickly over each eye." He checked her pulse and was happy to feel the even rhythm. "Jack, you have your cell phone, don't you? I left in such a hurry I forgot mine. Get an ambulance out here."

"And tell them to hurry, darling. Your son is tired of waiting to enter this world." Seelah tried to laugh but doubled over instead.

"Ah, shit!" Quickly Jack punched in the numbers. "Get an ambulance out to the Hindel Estate right now for transport of two white females! One of them is about to have my baby!" He ended the call slipping the phone inside his pocket. "Come on," he picked up Seelah in his arms at the same time Donavan lifted Jenny into his, "Let's get the hell outta this shithouse and breathe some fresh air."

As soon as they walked out of the mansion, Donavon could see color flooding back into Jenny's face.

"I'll lay down the seat, and you can lay her inside." Barbara hastened to the vehicle.

Donavan sat down on the tailgate of the jeep, unable to let

Jenny leave his arms. "You're going to be all right, Baby Girl. I trust in God to bring you through this safely." He rubbed his face in Jenny's hair.

Daddy?"

"Jenny! Oh my god, Jenny!"

Barbara pulled Jenny's hand to her mouth, raining kisses over the palm. "You're going to be just fine, darling. I know you are."

"Where am I?" She tried to sit up, but Donavan pulled her tight against his chest. "You're with your mama and your daddy, Jenny! That's where you are."

"I had the strangest dream," she whispered.

"You are safe now. You just put all that out of your mind."

The wail of the ambulance sliced through the air, and Donavan set Jenny down beside him. "You are going to take a ride in the ambulance, Jenny. They will want to check you out and make sure you're all right."

"Why wouldn't I be all right? I feel fine." She said, then looked around and drew in her breath. "Oh my god! It wasn't a dream. I am really here at the Hindel Mansion."

"Do you remember coming here?" Barbara asked.

"Yes." She hung her head. "I called Mr. Lybbert and told him I wanted to talk to him, and he told me to walk to the next block, and he would come to pick me up. I'm so ashamed."

Donavan pulled her against him. "It's all over now. You're safe, and that's all that matters."

"There was a man in the cave who said he was a healer, and if I promised to give my soul to the dark side, he would heal you, Daddy."

"I know. That's how dark entities work, Jenny. They are liars. They play with your mind and make you believe things that aren't so just to get you to trust them."

"Jenny," Seelah came over to the jeep. "All the things that you saw while in the cave were put in your mind to control you. They weren't real. So don't be afraid anymore, sweetheart. No one can hurt you." She told her, then doubled over as another contraction gripped her body.

"What's wrong, Aunt Seelah? Did they try to hurt you too?" Jenny edged her way from the tailgate.

"Your Aunt Seelah is getting ready to bring our baby boy into the world, Jenny, my love." Jack pulled Jenny into his arms for a big hug.

"Oh!" Jenny hugged his neck then stood back, clapping her hands. "He will be here today!"

Donavan laughed, glancing at Seelah. "I think we can pretty well bet on it."

The ambulance is here, sweetheart. I think you better come lay down and let them check you out." Jack said, scooping her into his arms.

She remained silent, waiting for the pain to subside before answering. "Yes, thank you, darling."

As Jack and Seelah left to go to the ambulance, Donavan threw one arm around Jenny's shoulders. "You need to let the paramedics check you out too, Jenny. When we got to the cave, you were out cold."

"oh, Daddy, I was only sleeping." She reached up to drop a quick kiss on her dad's cheek.

"Still, I will feel better if you go with your mother and Aunt Seelah and Uncle Jack to the hospital. You can do that for me, can't you?"

"I don't want to leave you, Daddy." She threw her arms around his neck as hot tears streamed down her face.

"Jenny, sweetheart, your mom will be with you, and you can be sure your Uncle Jack won't let anything happen to you."

"I know, but I want to be with you. I know no one can hurt me if I'm with you."

The memory of walking into his bedroom to find Jenny gone flashed into his mind. "I can't be with you right now, Jenny. I still have a job to do." Guilt at having to send her off while he attended to other matters weighed heavy on his mind, but he knew he was doing the right thing. "I have to make sure this Parish is safe for everyone." Donavan hugged her tight. "Uncle

Jack will keep you safe."

"You better believe your Uncle Jack will keep you safe." Jack walked up to pull Jenny into a bear hug. Besides, I want you and your mom to be in the birthing room when your little cousin breaths his first breath."

"Jack, I don't think they will let Jenny be in the birthing room. She's too young."

"Of course they will, Donavan. I gotta gun." He grinned as he picked Jenny up in his arms. "We need to get over to the ambulance, sweetheart. They are ready to take off."

Donavan answered Jenny's wave then turned away as Detective Carpenter walked up to him.

"I know that had to be a difficult decision to make."

Donavan glanced at him. "We still have a job to finish here. You and I both know there are still some of Hindel's family lurking around this estate. We just need to flush them out."

"The K9s have been hittin' all over the mansion. Wood panels down the basement, and they really went nuts in the cottage."

"Come on. I want to find Sills and Blain and have them come with us down to the cottage. I want to see how many cockroaches we can get to come crawlin' out of the woodwork."

"We won't have to do much looking. They're standing on the porch with Deputy Hendrickson."

"I was going to get the coroner out here, but I thought I better check with you first, Donavan," Blain said, coming forward.

"He can wait; the Hindel's aren't going anywhere."

Carpenter shook his head, a wide grin covering his handsome face. "Two less we need to concern ourselves with."

"Sills," Donavan turned to the rugged man standing on the porch, "I need you to grab about three sticks of dynamite, and you and John meet us at that little cottage over yonder." He pointed down the path to the entrance.

"`Bout damn time we get to put some of those bad boys to work." Sills started to walk off.

"It's not for sure we're going to blow anything up, but if

we run across any Hindel's hiding in there, we might as well get rid of them all at once instead of wasting our bullets."

"Jack's sure going to be sorry he missed this. He's been wanting to blow this place off its foundation for a long time." Carpenter laughed, falling in beside Donavan and Blain as they made their way down the driveway.

"He'll bitch and bellyache for a while, but he's where he wants to be at the moment. His son is about to be born, and he won't want to miss that." Donavan halted the two men just outside the cottage. "Blain, what I want you to do is take Magnum over every inch of this house. If he gets over three hits, we can be pretty sure there are people inside."

"Donavan, if Magnum says someone is inside, you can bet your ass they're there."

"All the same, I want to make sure we get enough hits so when we blow the son-of-a-bitches to hell, we know we had no choice."

With guns drawn, they made their way inside the cottage.

Donavan followed behind as Magnum walked through the house, sniffing and moving on until he came to a large paneled wall. He sniffed the wall then laid down in front of it.

Blain held up a hand then placed a finger against his lips, cautioning them to silence.

Donavan jabbed a finger in the direction of the wall, at which point Blain nodded in the affirmative.

"Well," Hendrickson said loudly, "looks like we can mark the cottage off our list of places to check for someone being here."

"Sure looks like it. We been over every inch and nothing," Carpenter said, running a hand over the groves within the paneling. Then gave a thumbs up to Hendrickson as his fingers touched on the tiny button. "Guess we can get back to the mansion and start looking there."

Donavan directed everyone out the door with a jab of his thumb.

When he felt they were far enough away from the cottage that they could talk, Blain spoke up. "Someone's in there,

Donavan. There's a hidden room behind that panel."

"You are absolutely sure of this." Donavan gazed at him.

"There's people in there. The button to open the panel is in the groves. I almost missed it. It's so small," Carpenter spoke up.

"They're there," Blain said. "Magnum never lays down unless he has a sure hit."

"Sills, how many sticks do we need? I want to go back in, find the mechanism to open the pane, throw in the lit dynamite and close the panel back up."

"Then run like hell before the whole fuckin' place goes up in smoke!" Sills laughed. "Do you want the cottage in ashes or just kill those inside?"

"I want it gone!" Donavan said, heading back to the cottage. "Blain, Hendrickson, I'm going to leave you out here with Magnum, `case any of them come running out from another part of the cottage. If they do, shoot to kill. Carpenter, you get ready to push the button after Sills lights the fuses and as soon as he throws in the dynamite, push the button to close the panel and then run like hell."

They were almost to the cottage when Donavan held up a hand for them to stop. Pulling his cell phone from his pocket, he punched in some numbers.

Jack answered on the first ring. "Yeah!"

"Jack, it's Donavan. I thought you might like to be in on what we're about to do here at the mansion."

"What the hell you gonna do, blow the place off its foundation?" He laughed, dropping a light kiss on Seelah's damp cheek.

"No, not the mansion, just Quigley's cottage. Magnum says there are people hiding behind some wood paneling, so we're about to see if he's right."

"Any other time, I would be foamin' at the mouth to be with you, but right now, I got more important things to take care of."

"Everything going all right on your end?"

"The doctor hasn't shown up yet, but they got Seelah in

bed and all ready to bring our son into the world." The happiness in his voice could not be hidden.

"Well, good luck to all of you. Give Seelah and my tribe a big hug and a kiss for me. I'll keep you on the line so you can at least hear the explosion."

Jack couldn't help himself. "Blow that mother-fucker to hell, partner!"

Donavan jabbed a finger towards the cottage, and Carpenter and Sills walked through the door. Within moments they came running back outside and away from the cottage, to where Donavan and the other three waited and watched.

A loud explosion ripped through the silence, closely followed by billowing smoke as the small cottage disappeared into a heap of ashes.

"Did you hear that, Jack? There is nothing but ashes left of Quigley's shack."

"Sounds like you got the job done. What now?"

"We're going to keep looking for more vermin."

"Be sure and call me if you decide to blow the mansion away. I sure as hell want to hear that one."

"Will do, partner." Donavan dropped the phone in his pocket. "Okay, let's go see what the hell else we can blow up." He motioned them forward to the mansion.

Raphael Hindel stood watching the destruction of the cottage, and his anger spun out of control. *"You will pay a high price for what you have wrought this day."*

Donavan and the men walked into the mansion and went to work. Each time Magnum hit on a secret room, the panel was opened, and a lit stick of dynamite was thrown inside. Large gaping holes showed in the mansion's interior. Screams cut the silence following the explosion as those left alive ran out of the room in search of safety but instead found themselves being stopped by a hail of gunfire.

When at last the rooms that had been a sanctuary for many of the Hindel family were completely destroyed, the men made their way down the basement stairs and into the cave.

"This is the place I want to blow to hell." Donavan breathed, his eyes glued to the marble altar where only an hour earlier, his own daughter had been in danger of losing her life or worse.

"We got more than enough to do the job, Donavan," Sills told him, setting the crate of dynamite down on the altar.

"What I want to do is blow up the basement. I feel pretty certain there aren't any Hindels alive on this estate."

"A person can actually feel the evil in this place." Hendrickson shuttered, looking around.

"It's no wonder you can feel it a lot of evil has been done in this place."

"I think we can rest assured that right here in this fuckin' basement is where those missing kids lost their lives," Blain spoke up.

"Yeah, I would have to agree. With all that we already know about this place, that would have to be a given. Right here is where they hold their rituals. This is why I think this filthy place needs to be taken down."

"Okay, since we ain't findin' anyone in here, I suggest you let me start situating sticks around the walls and all the way back to the water entrance. Then we can light about four sticks, throw them into the cave and run out. The lit ones should be enough to ignite the rest."

"Are you sure the dynamite won't destroy the upstairs too?" Donavan asked.

"I'm not makin' any promises." He gave them all a sheepish grin. "Truth be told, this is the first time I have tried anything of this magnitude."

"I swear to Christ I feel like I am standing here with Olivier'."

"Now that's one hell of a compliment. Jack's a man that gets it done." Sills chuckled as he laid out sticks of dynamite on the basement floor.

For a long moment, Donavan watched him, then shook his head in resignation of the fact that after today the Hindel

Mansion would no longer exist. "What's it gonna be, Donavan?" Stalls asked.

"Lawrence is going to be pissed if he finds out his house is gone. Although I think he's already joined the ranks of the undead anyway."

"Too bad we couldn't get his ass back here before we blow the place." Carpenter grinned. "You know what they say, if you leave one cockroach alive, then you know you're going to be infested again."

He saw once more the image of Jenny lying on the marble slab, and his mind was made up. "Lay enough powder to blow this place to hell, Stalls."

"Which end are you planning on setting the main blast?" Hendrickson asked.

"What I'd like to do is mark a long enough fuse to be able to get out of the cave by the back entrance. I'm a good swimmer, but I don't have any idea how far it is to shore." Stalls stopped what he was doing to think about his escape.

"What we need is a boat that can be anchored far enough away from the entrance to the cave so the concussion won't cause a tidal wave." Donavan laughed.

"Do you think Hindel has a boat around here someplace? He should since they've been known to get in and out of the cave from the lake," Hendrickson said.

"Carpenter, you and Hendrickson go check out the garage. If you find a boat, let me know, then one of you can anchor it offshore a good hundred yards for Stalls to get back to us."

"Come on, Jerry, " Hendrickson said, "let's go figure out which one of us gets to take a swim today."

Alone in the cave, Donavan and Stalls stood waiting to hear what they were going to do about the destruction of the mansion.

"Do you think there's a chance Lawrence Hindel might leave the parish and go elsewhere to do his dirty work?"

Donavan rubbed a hand over his chin. "I wish. No, when he finds his house has been reduced to ashes, he'll be out for revenge. With any luck, he'll try something in front of me, and I can end his suffering." He pulled the ringing phone from his pocket. "Yeah.

"We found us a boat in the garage. So one of us will anchor it about a hundred yards out from shore. Stalls will be able to see it when he comes up for air. Tell him we said, good luck."

"Will do. I'll catch up with you in a few minutes."

"I take it they found a boat."

"Yep, they're going to anchor it about a hundred yards offshore. You won't have any problem seeing it. Now is there anything I can do to help you get this show on the road?"

"Nope, it won't take me but a few minutes. You best get your ass movin' away from here, 'cause when this is ready, I ain't stickin' around."

"Good luck, Stalls." Donavan shook the other man's hand. "See you onshore."

"You got it. Now get your ass movin'."

Donavan was almost to the basement stairs when he heard Stalls call out.

"Race you to shore, Hays!"

Donavan made his way down the drive towards the lake. When he was almost there, he turned back to stare at the mansion. "I don't like to feel smug, but I'm looking at over two hundred years of evil, and I'm involved in taking it down." He reached for his cell and punched in Jack's number.

"We 'bout ready to make a boom?" Jack laughed into the phone.

"We sure as hell are, partner. I told him to take that evil son of a bitch down."

"You're actually gonna destroy the Hindel Mansion? Ah shit. This is too good to be true."

"Wish you were here, Jack. I know you'd enjoy seeing this sight."

"I would, but the doctor finally made a showin', and he said Seelah could give birth at any time now."

"As soon as I see this piece of shit tumble, I'll be on my

way to the hospital. Tell Seelah to hold off a few minutes 'til I get there."

"I'll relay the message. Don't be surprised if, for the first time in her life, she tells someone to get fucked, though!"

"There it goes, Jack! Oh my god, he did it! Burn in hell any of you son of a bitches who are still hanging around!"

"I gotta go, Donavan. Things are startin' to get serious here."

"I'm on my way, Jack," Donavan said as he saw Stalls climbing into the anchored boat.

***

Chandra stood watching as Seelah labored to bring her son into the world.

"How easy it would be to crawl into that little body and begin my life all over again."

She didn't need to turn to see who spoke. *"Then why don't you try and do that, Rafael? I don't think you are strong enough."* She quickly threw up a block to keep their conversation private as she saw Seelah looking their way.

"Your destruction of me will not be that easy, Chandra. I have too much to do before I leave this plane. My grandson has nowhere to go now. Now that his home has been destroyed."

"I will say the same thing about the Hindel Mansion I said about Jonathan. It is time for the evil to be over." She moved out into the hall, knowing he would follow.

"It is time for your God's children to know who the real leader of this plane is."

"Rafael, how many of your family do we, who are surrounded by the Holy Light, need to destroy before you give up and leave this parish?" She took some small comfort in seeing anger spread over his face. *"The mansion has been laid to ashes. Your son has been taken to the dark side, where he will remain. You are no longer in body. Why don't you simply leave and acknowledge you and your kind have been bested by those in the right?"*

"That will never happen, Chandra. This plane must be made ready for the one who is returning soon."

"Rafael, don't you know that before Our Holy Father would allow Satan to destroy this plane, He would come here personally with his legion of Angles and stand between His children and Satan's wrath? You think your Satan is strong enough to destroy God's children? He isn't. Take the rest of your kind and leave here. Or they will all suffer the same fate you have suffered."

"I cannot leave my grandson to fight this fight alone. He needs me now more than ever."

"No one needs you, Rafael. Least of all, Lawrence."

"Lawrence is the last of the Hindels. All of our family came here to band together in the destruction of the parish children. They were destroyed along with the Hindel Mansion," There was genuine sadness in his voice as he spoke his thoughts.

"You are saying that Lawrence is the last of the Hindel name?" Chandra watched him looking for any deception. *"The Hindel Family has been living here in Louisiana and abroad for some two hundred years."*

"Yes, we are much revered. It was a dark day when Jonathan was taken from us." Anger replaced sadness in his eyes and his voice.

"And even though I am the one to see to his demise, you and your family sought a vendetta against Jack and Donavan Hays."

"Yes." Although his voice was a mere whisper, the fire in that one word carried all the hatred his black soul was feeling.

"Why have you been so lax in trying to destroy me, Rafael? Were it not for me, your son would still be walking by your side." She watched the anger boiling up, and she pushed him to further its heat. *"You say you need to stay on this plane even though you are no longer in body to aide and protect Lawrence?"*

"I must. He is all we have now. He must carry on the Hindel bloodline."

"But you know how weak and feminine Lawrence is. Perhaps he will not want to build the Hindel bloodline." She disliked talking about her son in such an ugly manner.

"This is why I must stay here instead of finding a fetus to house my soul. I must see to it that Lawrence impregnates as many females

as he can. I will not allow our family to be wiped from this plane! I will not allow it!"

Chandra watched as his anger spun out of control, and she knew the time had come to bring an end to Rafael Hindel. *"Rafael, I am going to tell you something that will release you from your obligation to Lawrence and allow you to go from this parish."*

"There is nothing you can say that can release me from my obligation to my grandson, Chandra. You are but a filthy sow my son rutted with to bring my grandson to this plane. The only reason I did not destroy you when Jonathan found you and kept you as his whore is I knew my son would impregnate you and bring forth another soul into the Hindel fold. The bloodline is all-important. I will not allow it to die out."

"It already has, Rafael."

"What are you talking about? Nothing has happened to Lawrence, or I would have known it." He cast her a smug smile and waited for her to enlighten him.

"The only way Lawrence can carry on the Hindel bloodline is if he is your grandson."

"And since he is my grandson, then our conversation here is a waste of time. Make your point, Chandra."

"Rafael, Lawrence is not your grandson. The one, I refuse to use the term man, who fathered Lawrence is none other than our old friend and caretaker, Mr. Quigly."

"You lying slut! I will destroy you for trying to make me believe my son is not Lawrence's sire!" He took a menacing step in Chandra's direction, his hatred of her completely out of control now. *"I will destroy you!"*

At the same moment, two white spirits stepped forth to bind Rafael in chains. A baby's cry cut through the silence.

"Take him to the dark side and cast him in. He has brought too much evil to this plane." As the white spirits with Rafael in tow disappeared, Chandra walked into the room to greet Jack's son.

"You have a strong and healthy son, Mrs. Olivier'. Congratulations to you both," the doctor said, laying the mewling baby on Seelah's stomach.

A slight tap sounded on the door as Donavan pushed his way inside.

"You're just in time, partner. Donavan Matthew Olivier' just popped into the world." Jack said, uncaring of the tears of joy streaming down his face.

Without a word, Donavan pulled Jack into his arms for a big congratulatory hug.

With Barbara and Jenny wrapped safely in his big arms, he watched as Jack and Seelah marveled at their new son.

Seelah felt a touch on her arm and looked up to see Chandra standing beside her. Uncaring of who might be listening, she smiled up at the woman who had helped her so much. "Isn't he beautiful, Chandra?"

"*That he is, Seelah.*" She ran a hand over the baby's dark head. "*And now, with all the Hindels safely out of the way, he can lead a normal and safe life.*"

"Thank you for all your help, Chandra," Jack spoke into the quiet.

Chandra moved over beside Jack and, with deliberate ease, pulled his face forward to place a loving kiss on his cheek. "*You are ever so welcome, my darling.*"

As everyone gazed at the newborn son of Jack and Seelah, Chandra turned and walked happily into the White Light waiting for her.

ABOUT THE AUTHOR

Judith Ann McDowell is a novelist with four finished books. When not working on a manuscript, Judith, along with her husband, like to travel to different cities such as New Orleans to talk with people about voodoo and to talk with those who have experienced firsthand true hauntings. Judith is the mother of four grown sons Guy and David and Rhett and Nick, and lives in the Pacific Northwest with her husband Darrell and their two Pekingese Chi and Tai and three cats Isis and Lacy and Keefer. Judith is at present working on her next novel.